Praise for April Smith's

JUDAS HORSE

"Wonderfully tense and vivid. . . . [Smith] piles on the twists as the novel concludes." —*The Oregonian*

"Why does the FBI still seem so sexy? Part of the reason is murder mysteries like April Smith's *Judas Horse*. . . . It's creepy, chest-thumping stuff, with snitches and loyalty tests and the good guys and villains constantly in flux." —*Los Angeles* magazine

"A thoroughly American-style thriller."
—*The Boston Globe*

"Smith's superb third thriller to feature Ana Grey. . . . Ana's nuanced and coolly observational narrative voice perfectly complements the well-paced action, which builds to a satisfying conclusion that leaves open the next chapter of Ana's story."
—*Publishers Weekly* (starred review)

"[With a] heart-pounding narrative and explosive nonstop action. . . . [*Judas Horse*] incorporates domestic terrorist cells, runaway teenagers and a band of wild horses into a mix that twists Ana Grey—and the reader—into tight knots."
—*Sacramento News and Review*

April Smith

JUDAS HORSE

April Smith, the author of *North of Montana, Be the One, Good Morning, Killer,* and *Judas Horse,* is also an Emmy-nominated television writer and producer. She lives in Los Angeles.

www.aprilsmith.net

JUDAS HORSE

APRIL SMITH

JUDAS HORSE

An Ana Grey Mystery

VINTAGE CRIME/BLACK LIZARD

VINTAGE BOOKS

A DIVISION OF RANDOM HOUSE, INC.

NEW YORK

FIRST VINTAGE CRIME/BLACK LIZARD EDITION, FEBRUARY 2009

Copyright © 2008 by April Smith

The Library of Congress had cataloged the Knopf edition as follows:
Smith, April.
Judas horse : an FBI special agent Ana Grey mystery / by April Smith.—1st ed.
1. United States. Federal Bureau of Investigation—Officials and employees—
Fiction. 2. Undercover operations—Fiction. 3. Animal rights activists—Fiction.
4. Anarchists—Fiction.
PS3569.M467J84 2008
813'.54—dc22

Vintage ISBN: 978-0-307-39064-6

Book design by Anthea Lingeman

www.vintagebooks.com

Printed in the United States of America
10 9 8 7 6 5 4 3 2

For FBI Supervisory
Special Agent
Pam Graham,
and for
David Freeman

In order to be a good warrior, one has to feel
this sad and tender heart. If a
person does not feel alone and sad, he cannot
be a warrior at all.

—Chögyam Trungpa

PART ONE

One

I am standing in the middle of nowhere, eating an oatmeal cookie, when the word comes down the hallway like an ill wind that SAC Robert Galloway wants to see everyone in his office. I glance at the TV monitors—no airplane crashes—and figure this would be Galloway announcing with his usual gloomy hysteria that some honcho is coming from FBI headquarters, or maybe, because of budget cuts, we all have to bring our own copy paper.

The boss is waiting behind his desk, eyes downcast, fingertips tapping the blotter, and he does not speak or look up until the office is jammed with agents in shirtsleeves and wide-eyed administrative assistants. Cautious silence settles in.

"Another blow," he says, because there are all kinds of blows, all day long.

The silence twists tighter.

"Special Agent Steve Crawford is dead."

A collective gasp of shock. Some of us clutch, as if kicked in the gut.

"We have a positive ID on his remains."

"How?" someone finally asks.

Galloway clears his throat. Everybody knows Steve Crawford was his golden boy and heir apparent.

"A hiker found a piece of jaw with a couple of teeth in a stream close to where Steve disappeared." He takes a breath. "The forensic dentist matched the root furcation on the X-rays."

"Cause of death?"

Galloway rubs his forehead. "He was an experienced hiker. A fall? Hypothermia? We don't know. He was hiking alone. It's a remote location. You have big animals, little animals; they're dragging pieces hither and yon. The coroner says the manner of death is a very difficult call, based on the evidence and the length of time Steve was out there."

It is like losing Steve all over again. Like those stomach-churning hours thrashing through the soaking undergrowth up in Oregon just days after I'd come back from administrative leave. I get sick just thinking about the empty yelping of those dogs.

When Steve had failed to call his wife, Tina, from a solo hiking vacation in the Cascades, his abandoned SUV was discovered at a trailhead. Four hundred volunteers scoured the national park, casting a net of inquiry from Eugene to Bend. Everyone from the Los Angeles field office went up on their own time to knock on doors. Worse, indescribably worse, were the visits to Steve and Tina's house down here in Gardena—a dining table of foil-covered casseroles, two dazed grandmas from out of town, a couple of sisters, the scent of baby powder from the children's room.

Standing now in Galloway's superheated office, I do not want to hear the aren't-I-smart questions. What does it matter if the molars have fillings or not? After weeks of uncertainty, there is no doubt. Steve is dead; at least his family has something to bury.

Seven months before, a crazed detective on a suicide mission tried to drag me into his car, and I shot him.

When you are involved in a shooting incident, they take away your weapon and credentials. You are no longer identified as a federal agent, no different from any bozo who cannot get past the metal detectors. There is an investigation by the Office of Professional Responsibility and what we call "critical incident training," psychoanalyzing with other agents who have been through a life-changing trauma. When they decide you are ready to come back, the tradition is that another agent waits downstairs to "walk you in."

Steve Crawford was waiting in the lobby of the federal building when I returned after seven insomnia-racked months on administrative leave. In the FBI family, Steve and I were closer than most, having graduated in the same class at the Academy in Quantico, Virginia. Those who go through new agent training together are eternally bonded in young blood. We had shared many defining moments, but that image of Steve in the lobby is especially vivid, not only because of his kindness to me on that first awful day back but also because later, when he disappeared, I struggled to enhance every memory of him in the days before, in search of a detail that might explain why.

A tall drink of water with ash-blond hair, thirty-eight at the time, he was leaning on a counter with a distracted look, wearing a nylon strap around his neck with a clip on the end for ID tags and keys. We each have one, personalized with goofy stuff. His was red, white, and blue, studded with pins from police departments around the country and two teddy bears—representing many cases, years of work, and becoming a new dad. The lobby was crowded with civil servants and foreign nationals, but in the light streaming down through the atrium, all I saw was that strap, glinting with honor, and I was hungry for it.

"Everything all right?" he asked, touching my shoulder.

We were in the elevator. I stared at the floors ticking by.

"Why am I nervous? It feels like the first day of school."

"You have plenty of friends on the playground," Steve assured me.

After he got a law degree, and before he joined the Bureau, Steve played outfield during two seasons of minor-league baseball. He was the real thing. He knew all about disappointment and bone-wearying hard work. Sometimes I'd ask, "How many times in your life do you think you've swung a bat?" and he'd deadpan, "Not nearly enough." No question he had the talent. If he'd wanted to make the majors and cash out, he would have. It was just that Steve Crawford cared more about helping people than he did about himself.

The elevator doors had opened and we stepped into a hall. Steve swiped his card. I followed through the secure door, fighting an embarrassing impulse to hold on to his hand. He got me through those first brutal hours; got my old handcuffs back, the weapon in its clip, the case in black dress leather that holds credential and badge. There was a drawer full of clean new key straps. I chose red, white, and blue.

"Take a breath," he said. "You'll be great."

Just as I was getting my feet back on the ground, Steve Crawford was on his way to infinity.

The U.S. Federal Office Building on Wilshire Boulevard, isolated in a flat grass tract behind a queue of concrete bunkers, is a soulless tower meant to keep excitement out. If you had business here this morning, you might wonder at the numbers of dark-suited judges, cops, and politicians gathered beneath the breezy portico, and the white chairs set in rows. You might notice the Marine honor guard, and the guy in the kilt with the bagpipes, and figure out this is to be the annual FBI memorial service.

You could not know that SWAT is patrolling the perimeter, or, from the chatter, that emotions are tender, because in this year's program book there appears a handsome new face, that of Special Agent Steve Crawford, beside the tough-guy G-men who died in the thirties, and the earnest boys wearing skinny ties, forever frozen in the fifties.

It is by now just a few weeks past the official identification of his remains. Tina is seated with their children in the front row, wearing the same black silk dress and shiny black straw hat she wore to the funeral, as if she has never taken off her widow's weeds.

It would be nice, before stepping into the merciless sunshine, to rest for a moment in a circle of colleagues and let the feelings flow. I notice my former best friend, Barbara Sullivan, the bank robbery coordinator, commiserating with a couple of gals on her squad. They are whispering about Tina, and how she has still not been able to clean out Steve's closets, trading stories about going through your childhood stuff and selling the house when your last surviving parent has died.

As I approach, they stop talking.

"Tough morning," I say.

"Very sad."

Nobody says anything.

"Steve loved the mountains," I remark. "I hope they talk about that."

"You knew him," Barbara replies accusingly, as if it is my fault he went to the mountains and met with a fatal accident.

"Yes," I say. "I miss his smile," and I walk away in a backwash of silence.

When you are involved in a shooting incident, the Office of Professional Responsibility talks to all your friends. During my investigation, rocks were overturned concerning Barbara Sullivan's handling of bank robbery witnesses who had been waiting to be polygraphed. Instead of placing the witnesses in a secure area, she had allowed them to wait in the hall. It was a meaningless oversight that had nothing to do with my case, but with typical Bureau anality, they could not let it go, and Barbara Sullivan, a working mom who puts in twice as much as everyone else, received a reprimand. Not my fault, but that kind of thing accumulates nasty gossip, like a snowball in dirt.

Even though OPR found my case to be a righteous shooting—that the detective was a disturbed individual and the choice was either his life or mine, with a good chance he might have taken out a couple of civilians, as well—I had become tainted meat and nobody much wanted me around. Behind my back, Barbara called me "a cowgirl," and it stuck. The word was I had tried to be a hero and lost all judgment. Who wants to partner up with that?

Don't be stupid; this isn't high school. But at the memorial service, I sit well away from Barbara and her friends in their identical black trouser suits, white shirts, and flat rubber-soled shoes.

If this isn't high school, why do they all have to be blond?

Over the roar of the nearby 405 freeway, I listen to the Bureau chaplain honor our dead: "True heroes live a life of goodness, and enter the battle between good and evil to make the world a better place. These are not just names on a piece of paper. These are people just like us, who put themselves in harm's way, knowing each day could be their last, whose loved ones were sometimes afraid to kiss them good-bye in the morning . . . until the day they made the supreme sacrifice. They gave the last measure of devotion to defending freedom."

The roll call procession has begun. A bell tolls for every name that is read, and a photograph of each fallen agent is carried by an honoree who also bears a yellow rose. There had been a spat about who should carry Steve's memorial, but it went to Jason Ripley, because he is the newest agent.

I am battling for control. My facial muscles are twitching and hot tears threaten to break. This is the task: *Never let it show.* Rows of graven faces reveal nothing but discipline.

I have noticed that as you get older, you do not regret the affairs you've had, but the ones you didn't have. What nobody here knows is that Steve and I were not just buddies who met as kids in our twenties at the Academy and went through new agent training together. We did exactly what new agents are not supposed to do: We fell in love. And despite the prohibitions of the time, we were going to get married. The painful circumstances that tore us apart hit me all over again as Jason Ripley passes, bearing a large color photo of Steve's earnest all-American face—a testament, in so many ways, for so many people, to what might have been.

Jason, a twenty-eight-year-old skinny farmer's son from Illinois, is doing a credible job of appearing not to be terrified. It must scare the heck out of him, standing in for a dead man; called upon to demonstrate the egalitarian nature of death, along with other agents and support staff (each carrying a photo and one yellow rose), hauled out of the faceless building and exposed in full daylight, made to walk in a single line at the same funereal pace—the alert, the self-conscious, the burdened, the humble, the casual, the aggressive, the broken.

For months after the shooting incident, I had headaches and malaise. I was on every type of med but still couldn't make it through the night without sweating through at least one pair of pajamas. I'd get up and read in the living room—one light burning, a desert wind rattling the empty garbage cans, a storm of tiny flowers driven off the pittosporum trees—and like the homeowner who has iced an intruder, or a soldier who destroys a tank, I gained the special knowledge only righteous shooters share: Even the most selfless action, *even the defense of your country*, doesn't mean a happy ending. They save the worst for the so-called hero.

I killed somebody.

Who am I?

Two

Galloway calls me into his office again. This time, it is just the two of us. I find him tilted all the way back in his chair, as if he is going to take a nap. His hands are clasped over his chest and his eyes are looking somewhere through the wall. He seems almost peaceful, snuggled up in his customary black turtleneck.

"Steve Crawford was murdered," he says.

"No. How?"

"He was pretty much blown to bits."

"In the *woods*?"

Galloway agrees it sounds improbable. "Figure the odds."

When the molar in the jaw fragment married up to that of a missing federal agent, a crack team of investigators from the Portland police department and Oregon state police immediately returned to the site. SAC Galloway was there, along with the ASAC from the FBI's Portland division. Galloway brought his green tactical parka and heavy boots; the locals wore windbreakers and jeans. As they tromped up the trail, two forensic anthropologists were arguing about whether or not the best way to clean bones is to boil them. You'd think science would have come up with the answer to that one by now.

The team had been formed in order to search for more remains. Cause of death was still unknown. It was a clear, cold day and the woods were dazzling under three inches of new snow. Conditions were judged to be good because the sun was out and the ground was already bare in spots. Might be a long shot, but you could get lucky. If you delayed until spring, the remains would migrate even farther. Besides, emotionally, nobody could wait.

When they reached the spot in the stream where the hiker had found the human jaw, they stopped and caught their breath. The thermos bottles and PowerBars came out. There were a lot of organized people trying to organize one another, so Galloway wandered off alone, climbed an outcrop, got up high, and wrapped an arm around a tree to steady himself on the slippery granite. He stared at the ice-colored water riding through the gorge.

His feet were cold and his thoughts morose. He was back in his childhood home in Brooklyn, New York. Cold linoleum, cold sheets, even the wall against his bed felt frigid. Seven years old, watching a blizzard whipping and wailing through the bars of the window guard, he was certain it would blow the brick apartment building away.

The sun was in his eyes now, reflecting off the placid snow that quilted the forest. Snow was different in the country. To his parents, "in the country" meant Westchester. He recalled a wooded place like this on a wintry day—*Was it a Sunday? A botanical garden?*—and him sledding on a found piece of cardboard. His parents had moved off behind a barren tree. There he saw his father open his mother's coat, lift her sweater, and put his hand over her breast.

Galloway was lost in reverie about this particular image and why it was making him queasy, while a different part of his brain was seeking information about a depression it had noticed in the newly fallen snow: a space that resolved with more and more urgency as it began to melt away; a small, clearly defined circle in a cluster of young saplings; a sparkling white crater.

Galloway pauses at his desk to chew an unlit cigar and muse on the oddity of perceiving such an important piece of evidence at the same time he was experiencing disturbing memories of his father's hand on his mother's large and conical breast. I do not remark on the oddity of him telling me. Galloway is a New Yorker. He has no boundaries.

The impression in the earth was the seat of an explosion.

"You did a postblast crime scene?"

"No, we all went out for sushi."

I cannot believe it. A force that powerful in the middle of nowhere? Animals or no animals, you'd need fifty pounds of explosives to blast a human body into the pieces that remained of Steve. And why isn't everybody talking about it?

Galloway puts the cigar away and swings the chair upright. "We pulled the bomb techs from the Portland division. Nobody knows about it down here."

There had to have been fifteen or twenty people involved. You had photographers, guys with shifting screens and shovels, teams marching the quadrants shoulder-to-shoulder, someone with a global-positioning system mapping the site to within a tenth of a millimeter of an inch. You had, in other words, a lot of jokers all dolled up in Tyvek suits—big rubber body condoms—walking around a national forest.

And nobody knows?

"In the crater we found pieces of the box that held the components. The lab has identified the explosive. . . . There were traces in the clothes."

"Clothes?"

Galloway makes a sign with thumb and forefinger: this big.

I am without words. My sight falls, unseeing, on Galloway's collection of New York City police department souvenirs. Only he could get away with the alleged scalp of a drug dealer, and the Empire State Building wearing a brassiere.

"The debris field was extensive, but we did okay. Parts of a battery, parts of a cell phone detonator. Alligator clips, a leg wire, toggle switch. Steve must have walked right into it."

I may appear rational, but the world is falling away from under my feet, like being lifted straight up in a helicopter.

"I know he was a friend of yours," says Galloway.

I murmur something about Steve having been a great guy.

"Steve Crawford should have had this chair. He would have, one day." He kicks the chair away and unlocks a credenza.

"So what do we think?" I begin in a professional manner. "He was hiking alone in the woods when he encountered a booby trap, some psychopathic piece of shit—"

"We think it's domestic terrorism."

Galloway drops four heavy documents on the desk. The impact rattles the bones in my neck. They are three inches thick, government-printed, with red covers—the result of a years-long investigation of a well-known radical group called FAN.

Galloway closes the door. The silence throbs in my ears.

"Steve was working undercover," Galloway says.

Like everyone else, I believed Steve was on vacation. That's the way it is with undercover work.

"This is classified. How Steve died"—he waves a hand, erasing everything he has just told me—"we still don't know. And we'll never know."

"Understood."

"He was working a FAN cell. The explosive that killed him is a water-based gel called Tovex—the same type of explosive used in the O'Conner Pharmaceuticals bombings two years ago."

FAN is an invisible group of anarchists that operates behind the façade of Free Animals Now—bland enough to attract the liberals and provide a front for the hard-core element. Interchangeable in tactics with ecoterrorists like ALF and ELF, the level of violence in their attacks is on the rise. They used to glue locks and liberate research animals; now it's firebombing. There are dozens of unsolved cases in the Northwest attributed to FAN—which some investigators argue does not exist at all, but is a cover for a mixed bag of disenfranchised extremists.

"FAN is on the short list for Steve Crawford's murder," Galloway says. "We're going back in. It took some arm twisting, but headquarters finally approved. You fit the profile to take Steve's place."

"Why?"

"Right age. Right background."

"Because I'm mixed race?"

Galloway seems surprised that I would bring that up.

"*I* know you're half Latina, but the way you present is ethnically ambiguous. You could be white, or something more exotic."

"And that's supposedly good?"

"Might be an asset."

I have always found my heritage a puzzle. I was raised in whiteness by my grandfather "Poppy" Everett Morgan Grey a relentless racist, who tried to bury the El Salvadoran side of me. He did such a thorough job of biasing me against my own tradition that whenever I manage to dig it out, I find something tarnished by his scorn.

"Actually," says Galloway, "I was talking about your skills as a profiler and background in crisis negotiation. It's a deep-cover operation, six months to a year. Interested?"

Shocked. It is like going up in a helicopter and being handed the controls.

I say, "Yes."

There is a pause.

"Anything that would keep you in Los Angeles?" he asks.

"Nothing but regret." I smile poorly.

Galloway holds my gaze. "How are you around the incident?"

He means the shooting incident.

"It doesn't get easier."

It is coming on again, the sour tightening of the throat.

He is watching me.

"I've been approved for duty. Or I wouldn't be here. But you know that."

"Undercover is different. It's about developing relationships and then betraying them."

"Which makes me perfect for the job?"

"I know it's been hard, but the way you've come back from the incident makes me think you have the personality type that would be resilient to the stress of working undercover."

"What's the real reason?" I joke. "You want me out of L.A.?"

"On a personal level, I think it would be very good for you to get out of L.A."

Supervisors don't often admit to thinking about you on a personal level, or having your best interests at heart. I blush with gratitude.

"The director has formed a multiagency task force that will function here and in Portland, Oregon." Galloway nods sagely. "A major undertaking. We're calling it 'Operation Wildcat.' What do you think?"

"It sells."

"All you have to do is go through undercover school at the Academy and get certified."

All I have to do is swim to Alcatraz and back.

"It's the toughest training in the Bureau, am I right?"

"Brutal." Galloway smiles. "Two weeks, twenty-four/seven, designed to stress you out emotionally and physically and put you in intensive role-play operations to simulate realism. Remember the 'agony tree'?"

The agony tree is a big old pine at the start of the running course at the Academy. Over the years, folks have covered it with signs like SUCK IT IN; HURT; LOVE IT; PAIN; 110%.

"In undercover school maybe one in five makes the cut," he informs me. "The rest are still hanging from the tree."

Galloway opens the door and the world of the FBI comes back— the talk, the hustle of important work, sunshine falling across the bright maroon-and-navy furniture that has recently sprung up around the office.

"Thank you for this," I tell him.

"Don't thank me. There are grander themes to respond to."

I grin, amused by Galloway's quirky philosophizing. "What are the grander themes?"

"I want the idiots who killed Steve Crawford to cry on the stand," my boss says softly. "I want them to roll on the floor like pill bugs."

I stop grinning. "What if I don't pass undercover school?"

"It won't affect your job, or the operation. Someone else will qualify. And you'll come back and go on being Ana."

He pats my arm reassuringly, as if that would be perfectly okay.

Three

The road to undercover school cuts a straight line through a hundred square miles of dense Virginia forest. The raw-faced young Marines who stand in the rain, M16s over their shoulders, have zero tolerance for speeding, so I keep the rental car to thirty-five miles per hour—although my heartbeat is racing with the same giddy excitement as the first time I made this drive, when I arrived for training as a new agent, twelve years before.

This is everything I've ever wanted! That's how I was thinking way back then, until the road went on and on at the same monotonous crawl, and a deep apprehension grew. *What am I doing? Why did I leave home?* The force of life is greedy here. Oak and hickory crowd the macadam, and the tall, wet grass is heavy with ticks. Drawing closer to the FBI Academy at the heart of the base, you come to the uneasy realization there is nothing else around you—no houses, no gas stations, no options—just deep fields with rifle targets and Quonset huts set far away in the smoky mist. It seems as if you are in danger of being swallowed up by your own dream.

I met Steve Crawford on the same driver-training course I am now passing, where they taught us how to stop a felon. We drove safety cars with popped-out wheels. All the guys love this part, but Steve was an ace. In the Board Room cafeteria, a bunch of us rookies sat around drinking beer, and Steve said if he did become an FBI agent, he'd have to sell his 1978 Mustang GT. Not likely he'd be drag racing anymore. He'd just painted it a "raspberry and gold dust color," which sounded kind of luscious. This was before I had bought my '71 Barracuda, but I piped up about loving muscle cars. He told how he'd hang out in a parking lot in San Bernardino, listening to the old guys talk hot rods; how he'd raced the Bonneville salt flats. By midnight, we were back at the driver-training course, testing out the fast track.

We were two Southern California kids crazy for cars and baseball, high every day on the adrenaline of being at the Academy, working our butts off, entwined in a heroic vision of serving a better world. Made for each other, it seemed.

A sudden coldness hits the rental car and I put on the heat. As I pass the final Marine checkpoint, a thunderstorm that has been on my tail since the D.C. airport breaks with almost comic intensity. Rain plays on the windshield like a cuckoo Caribbean band of tin pots and garbage cans. Cold fog curls up close and puts its lips on the window glass. When lightning forks across the lurid purple sky, again and again, I laugh out loud, for the spirit of J. Edgar Hoover must surely be upon me.

The old man has been dead for decades, but down in Quantico it's still "Get off Hoover's grass," as if he owns our souls in perpetuity. All that stuff about him running around in a woman's red dress and heels, that's nonsense, although Hoover did make a fetish out of "cleanliness"—of body and mind, supposedly—fashioned after his own psychosexual obsessions. What a way to run a company.

Hoover liked white shirts, but he did not like homosexuals (although he almost certainly was one). Secretaries could make the coffee, but it was indecorous to be seen carrying a naked coffee cup across the office, so they would place the steaming mugs inside those wooden boxes made for index cards, pretending it was not coffee they were delivering to their white-shirted, not-gay bosses.

Laugh about it now (we don't), but how far is a mad secret coffee ritual from compliance in a cover-up of dirty tricks? Or a bollixed siege? Hoover's drive to avoid any sort of personal or bureaucratic shame created a culture of repression and fear that haunts us still. As I pull into the austere brick complex stained dark by the rain, I hear the grim, omniscient voice of the director, years ago embedded in my head: "Never embarrass the Bureau."

The groundhog! I just remembered! He used to live in a grass quadrangle outside the administration building. Steve and I would set out crackers while pretending to study and he'd taunt me about shooting it on sight, detailing the effect of different-caliber bullets. It was considered good luck if you happened to spot the little guy from one of the glass passageways that connect the towers. We called them "gerbil cages," scurrying to our classes through the glass tunnels like scores of frantic mice. For fourteen weeks, we lived inside a sealed environment with no fresh air and people always getting sick. That is why we went gaga over the groundhog: He was our brother, and he was free.

Now as I enter the lobby, water tracking from my soaking shoes, something clicks inside my chest, as if Steve is saying, as he always said, *You'll be great,* and I have answered, *This is for you, buddy.*

The rooms in the dorm are spartan and smaller than I remember—still no recreation areas, one TV to a floor. An hour after checking in, I am back in training uniform—stiff cargo pants, boots, short-sleeved polo shirt with the FBI seal, and a thick belt made of saddle leather better suited for a horse—falling in with identically dressed crowds of muscular men and women powering through the gerbil cages like rush hour in the Tokyo subway.

All sizes and ethnicities, we are the law-enforcement elite—plucked from the Bureau or police departments around the world for advanced courses like undercover school, wearing the same rictus smiles and carrying backpacks like aging college students, snobbishly throwing them in piles on the floor. There is plenty of eye contact, at once smug and scared. We have been invited to the rush—but will we make the fraternity?

When they cut you, they do it fast, anytime, anyplace, even the last night of training. By dinnertime, everyone has heard about the "adios speech," in which a counselor dressed in black takes you aside and basically says, "Thanks for coming and trying out. Just because you didn't make it doesn't mean you're not still an agent, and being an agent is the greatest thing in the world. Have a good trip home."

*Have a good time in the trash heap of failure the rest of your life.
Just go on being Ana.*

My roommate's name is Gail Washburn. We are in a class of seventeen. She is maybe thirty-five, from the Chicago field office, African-
American, with sly, narrow eyes like an egret and short hair twisted
and pinned into two tiny pigtails. I discover her unpacking a bag of
mini doughnuts, and like her immediately. She is an upbeat lady, married to another agent, funny about "my black ass," which could mean
her deepest sense of self or athletic rump; teases me about being a
"venti cappuccino ass" when I say I am half Salvadoran—"with
whole milk, baby"—referring to my pure white skin. It is a promising
friendship, but way too brief, as I will end up knowing Gail Washburn
less than twelve hours.

By 9:00 p.m. on the same day as my arrival from Los Angeles, we
are deeply into a "7-Eleven scenario" in Hogan's Alley, a phony Main
Street, like a movie set, with false storefronts, apartment buildings, a
bank and café. We are to assume an undercover identity, enter the
convenience store, and purchase a loaf of bread. That's it. We are
armed with paint-ball guns and wear protective gear. We do not know
that the counselors, playing customers and clerks, will turn the scene
into a violent hostage situation when the owner of the store is held at
gunpoint by a shopper.

One by one, we enter the store and play it out. Some of us are shot
by the bad guy, some—*oops!*—kill the victim, some blow their cover
and yell, "Freeze! FBI!" but most take correct action, which is to *do
nothing and be a good witness.* We are not told the results, just
shunted out the back and warned that we have thirty minutes to file a
report.

Gail has already gone through the test when I dash back to our
room and find her staring at the computer in bewilderment.

"The system went down."

I pound the keys. The screen is frozen with green hieroglyphics.
Gail hands me the bag of doughnuts and we share a moment of sugary
dread.

"I'll bet this is part of their damn game," she whispers.

"They shut the system down on purpose? Even for the Bureau,
that's perverse."

"Real life, girl. What do you do in a hostage situation when Rapid Start crashes?"

"Sister, I don't know what's real." I am starting to feel flushed and panicky. "But we have fifteen minutes to get our shit over there."

We start scribbling by hand in spiral notebooks and ripping out the pages. *Pounding at the door!* We both jump. It is spooky all right: Standing in the hallway is a training counselor wearing black—even a black hood—with a knife at the belt. He has a trimmed white beard and compact wrestler's body, and is not smiling. He looks like the Agent of Death.

"Agent Washburn?" he says. "Talk to me."

Gail and I look at each other. *Is this some code? Another scenario entirely?* She thrusts her report at me.

"Take it!" she says. "Run like the wind."

I run my cappuccino ass back to the command post—over a road and up a hill—in under four minutes. I am not the only one jack-rabbiting it with a flashlight. Damn if Gail wasn't right. They'd shut the damn computers down.

I deliver the reports and burst back into our room, sweating and exhilarated, to find her sitting on the bed, sobbing.

"I'm going home," she gasps. "They cut me."

"*Why?*"

"He wouldn't say. I don't understand. I have never failed anything in my life! Oh sweet Lord, my husband's not gonna believe *this.*"

Even as a kid, Gail was always a standout—basketball, track, National Merit scholar. A poster girl for the FBI, she's already been promoted to supervisor. Why wouldn't they say how she messed up? Are we back to Hoover-era punishment?

"They're wrong," I say helplessly.

Fifteen minutes later, she is packed up and gone.

Next morning, 7:00 a.m. Sixteen of us now. We take our assigned seats in a lecture hall that smells like a chemistry class. Coffee is still steaming from paper cups and people are talking in shocked whispers about what happened to Gail, when Ring Diestal, LL.D., Ph.D., a broad-shouldered hulk in a tweed coat and tie, with luxurious gray hair and eyebrows thick as scrubbing brushes, mounts the podium and starts sprinting through the attorney general's guidelines for FBI undercover work.

Backpacks unzip and notebooks open in a flurry. Three pages of text have flashed across the screen and there is no going back. Dr. Diestal is going at breakneck speed through the situations in which an undercover agent is justified to participate in illegal activity, like smoking weed and buying guns—important stuff on how not to get your case thrown out in court—but I am so burned-out from jet lag and freaked by the way my roommate vanished in the night, I can only stare in a haze at the empty chair that still bears the name Gail Washburn.

They keep it empty, and keep her name tag on it.

Remembering her wounded indignation—"I have never failed anything in my life!"—I am still fighting a sense of outrage that blocks my mind like the condensation on the windows as a cold fog settles over the campus.

"Nothing in the guidelines stops you from taking reasonable measures in self-defense," Dr. Diestal explains. "But there is a tipping point. How quickly does self-preservation kick in? How smoothly can you shift your sense of what's right in order to do what is required to complete the mission?"

My head jerks. *Did I actually fall asleep? Did he see?* But Dr. Diestal is already on to "authorization for purchase of contraband goods"—meaning when is it okay for an undercover to purchase drugs from a suspect? I sit up straight and reach for the coffee.

I'll catch up later.

But there is no catching up. Just before dinner, they come for me.

I am on my way to the library when a counselor calls my name. I think twice before answering—yes, I am still Ana Grey.

"Sir?"

He gestures with his chin that I should follow.

"You are going into an undercover role-play," he says.

"Now?"

Okay, that's obvious.

We are winding quickly through the gerbil cages, in the opposite direction from the Board Room cafeteria, where I had been looking forward to the roast beef and mashed potato dinner I'd seen on the chalkboard that morning. There had been no break for lunch.

"May I ask what the operation is, sir?"

"It's a counterfeiting case. The bad guys are printing U.S. currency using a high-tech copy machine. No inks, no plates, and therefore no evidence of what the machine is being used for. Your job is to catch them in the act."

"Isn't counterfeiting a crime that comes under the Secret Service?"

"Very good, Agent Grey."

Right answer. Still alive.

"For the purpose of the exercise, let's say it's a joint undercover operation with the Secret Service. All you need to know is that you'll be confronting someone who will be asking questions about you in your undercover role, and you will be observed for signs of deceit that suggest you're not who you say you are."

We get off the elevator at a subbasement. I follow the counselor down cinder-block corridors—near the indoor range, heavy with the smell of cordite—still trying to figure out what in hell he's just said. We pass trolleys of laundered towels and stop at a pair of metal doors framed by girders of steel. The rivets are as big as saucers.

It is an old bomb shelter, the counselor tells me, built in the fifties to save our nation's politicians. In case of nuclear attack, they were all supposed to get in their cars and drive down I-95.

I am too afraid to laugh.

The vault smells like a thrift store, like acres of musty crinoline, packed with racks of clothing for men and women. There are even a couple of dressing tables with mirrors framed in bulbs.

"Have a ball," he says. "Create a person you're not. I'll be back in twenty minutes."

"And then what?"

"You will be challenged to demonstrate a lesson learned."

And he leaves.

What is the "lesson learned"? I have been up almost thirty-six hours, am ravenously hungry, and tired of being hazed. Can't we all be grown-ups? What is the point of not even telling us the rules? I stare at the racks. I am at a loss. The amber light is faint. Suits, dresses, handbags, hats—each piece of clothing holds a thousand identities.

And that, I realize finally, is the point. During the 7-Eleven scenario, the undercover identity Gail Washburn had cooked up for herself was "Ramona," a working-class ghetto mom. She was tested on her hold over that identity, and she failed. When she walked out the door, they called, "Hey, Gail?" "Yes, sir?" "Good job." And they cut her. The mistake was answering to "Gail." She should have responded to "Ramona," no matter what. She thought the gig was over, but that was not for her to judge. Believing it is over can get you killed. That is the lesson of the empty chair and the internal warning that caused me to think before answering to my own name. Gail's mistake was a result of arrogance; an error made by a person who has always been a superstar and believes that she controls the game.

But uc work is different. It is the kind of game that possesses its own spontaneous intelligence. That is why they cannot tell you the rules. You make a move; the schematic changes. You change it. It changes with you. No past to revise, no future to predict, everything takes place in present time. Fluid. Treacherous. Addictive.

Hanging on a rack is a beat-up leather jacket from the sixties. Originally, it was a designer piece—creamy yellow, square pockets and a belt—but now it looks like Jackie Kennedy on the skids. Who would wear this jacket? From a single clue, I have seven minutes to invent another persona—someone criminal, the shadow side of me. *Okay.* She bought the jacket in a thrift shop. She doesn't give a damn about the rules. Hates authority. Steals. She's a soft touch for animals because she is a stray herself.

And more. She grew up in one of the older tracts in Long Beach, California (not far from Ana Grey)—cheap housing built in the forties for oil refinery workers, now a mixed ghetto of the unemployed. Her name is Darcy DeGuzman. Darcy because it is innocent and bouncy, although she is driven by the ruthlessness of a starving child. That's the DeGuzman part. Ethnically ambiguous. (Filipina? Spanish?) Deserted by her parents, a pair of depressive alcoholics. Growing up, it was necessary to perform favors for boys. She learned how to use people. She's streetwise and impulsive, lonely, young and foolish, and somewhere in a violent past, in a crumbling neighborhood where the working class has become obsolete, she killed somebody.

I slip my arms through the cool satin lining of the sleeves.

But I know it fits before I even have it on.

They put me in a van with blacked-in windows. We leave the Marine base and follow curving roads until we are at an outdoor mall. They give me forty dollars, a phone number, and an empty pistol secured with a plastic tie so it can be drawn but not fired.

I walk past a drugstore and a food mart. Normal citizens are wheeling carts filled with groceries, little kids in tow. It is 8:35 p.m. I intercept a pair of girls on their way into a fried chicken restaurant.

"I'm all turned around. How far is D.C.?"

"Oh," says one, giving the stained-up jacket a stare, "you're an hour and a half from D.C. If you exit here and go right, you'll be on I-95."

I have my bearings. I've been deposited about thirty miles south of Quantico. *Beautiful.*

I sit outside a Dairy Queen and devour a milk shake and a double cheeseburger. A sign claims this franchise sells the most ice-cream cakes in Virginia.

I am having a wonderful time.

Two hours later, the mist has settled in but good, and I am shivering in a stupid tank top and miniskirt torn at the hem, which I chose to wear under the thin leather jacket. I cannot see anyone observing me, but the parking lot has been busy. Now it is deserted and everything has shut down except a twenty-four-hour gym. I walk over there and sit on a bench. I go in and use the restroom. I sit on the bench some more.

A woman trainer comes out of the gym. I noticed her when I ducked inside; she was working out with a man with a shaved head. The trainer is wearing a pink sweatsuit and carrying a workout bag. Black ponytail, military posture. An alarm goes off: She's fit. She's alert. She's an agent.

"You haven't seen a white truck circling around, have you?" she asks with a nasal twang.

"Haven't seen one."

"My husband's supposed to pick me up."

I nod. "I think I'm supposed to meet you."

"Meet me for what?"

I don't answer right away. We walk together.

"What's your name and where are you from?" she asks.

I say it out loud for the first time: "Darcy, from California."

"California?" Her voice drops. "What are you doing *here*?"

"Staying ahead of the cops." I am making this up as I go along.

She seems to know it. "Crap," she says.

"Why?"

She looks around nervously. I follow her gaze. A minivan of off-duty Marines has pulled into the entrance of the Days Inn motel. My grandfather stayed there when I graduated from Quantico as a new agent. As far as I knew, it didn't have hookers cruising the parking lot then.

"You've come all the way from the West Coast? Where's your car?"

Car!

"I got a bunch of different rides."

She lowers the bag between her feet, starts redoing her ponytail. A signal? I glance at the parking lot, but there is no movement.

"I know you're not for real," she hisses. "And life's too short, honey."

It scares me. I feel Darcy falling away.

"There's my husband," she says, and now comes the white truck.

"We can do business." I step along eagerly. "We're here to do business, right?"

"Give me a break," she says contemptuously, and calls, "Lloyd!" as the truck noses up to the curb. "We can go now."

Game over?

Be cut? Never find the trash that killed Steve Crawford?

Not until they tell me to have a good trip home.

"Hey, bitch," I call.

And Darcy DeGuzman, my new undercover identity, is born.

The woman turns on a dime, feet planted like a fuzzy pink ninja.

"Excuse me?"

"Get over here."

"*What?*"

A shaved head sticks out of the truck. "Jennifer? We got a problem?"

Right on cue. They're wearing hidden microphones.

"Tell your old man to chill." I swagger up to where she stands in the fluorescent wash of the drugstore window. "This is what I'm talking about."

I flash a twenty from the money I have been given, pretending it is counterfeit.

"So, *Jennifer*?" I say. "You got copies good as this? I know a buyer."

I feel ridiculous, acting out a role in the middle of real America. But she takes the bill and examines it closely. Maybe she is giving me a chance to be creative. Or, hell, maybe it really *is* counterfeit.

"Jennifer!" calls the guy in the truck.

The woman in pink raises her eyes and searches mine.

"I don't know," she says warily.

Great acting.

"I need a million dollars." My confidence is building. "Top-quality."

Jennifer nods slowly. "I have a friend."

I press the advantage. "One condition. I have to see the operation."

"No way. Are you nuts?"

I shrug. "That's what my boss wants. He said to check out the source, make sure the bills aren't traceable."

"They're not traceable."

"I can't take your word."

I give her apologetic. She understands. We are both in the same fix: men.

She shakes her head. "They'd never agree to something like that."

"Ask. Nicely."

She hesitates. "Wait here."

She confabs with the guy in the truck and comes back and tells me the "friend" wants $100,000 in cash, for the million in fakes.

We are inching toward a deal, but where to get the money? There is one more clue, waiting in my pocket.

I say I have to make a call.

She accompanies me to a pay phone, where I dial the number I was given in the van. A voice I do not recognize says, *"Yeah?"* I do not break character as I tell my "contact" to bring a hundred grand in cash to the mall. Twenty-five minutes later, a low-rider Chevrolet, driven by a black man I have never seen, pulls up and parks away from the lighted rim of stores. A hip-hop bass seems to fill the empty space of the parking lot.

"Be right back," I tell Jennifer, aware that I am approaching an unknown individual alone.

The window is down. He watches with glittering eyes, fingers flicking the wheel. He is thirty, taut, wearing a do-rag and chewing gum. When I get close, I see his nose is running, and his hand trembles as he draws it across chapped lips.

"You it?" he says.

"Guess so."

"You *guess*? Who sent you?"

He is out of the car. So we were to play another scene for Jennifer and her husband?

"Hey, motherfucker," I muster. "What's your problem?"

He is wired and I am slow. He slams my chest against the door and cracks my neck in a reverse chokehold.

"No disrespect," I gasp.

"Don't make me nervous."

"It's cool, it's cool."

I am feeling nauseous, seeing sheets of light.

His cell phone goes off. He glances at the number. *"Fuck!"*

He lets me go, spins back inside the car, and hands a gold-embossed Gucci briefcase through the window.

"You best not be fucking with us."

"No way, bro."

My throat aches from where he brutally compressed the trachea. When I get back to the Academy, I am going to find out who this asshole is.

"It better be righteous blow, or I'm coming to get your kids."

Blow? Wait a minute. The deal is counterfeit money, not cocaine. Wrong scenario. Right?

I stare at him.

"I know where you live."

Then he is gone.

So are Jennifer, the white truck, and the man with the shaved head.

I stand in the middle of the deserted shopping center, gripping the Gucci briefcase the brother thrust at me, which is allegedly stuffed with cash. I'm hatching a brand-new plan: I will hop a ride down the highway and disappear into the Blue Ridge Mountains, marry a coal miner with large spadelike hands, and live in a hollow with a clan of hill people, who distrust and despise the U.S. government almost as much as I do.

My head is swimming with fatigue. What is the "lesson learned"? Did I learn it yet? From deep in the gnarly undergrowth surrounding the now-dead shopping center comes the croaking of toads. No counselors have stepped out of the shadows to bring me in. The game is on. Pick up the thread. Find Jennifer. Connect with the counterfeiters.

I go back to the pay phone, but nobody answers the number I just dialed.

Someone taps my shoulder. "Darcy?"

I take my time responding because I have to run a mental check and the gears are running slowly. Yes, I am Darcy. Darcy from California. *A criminal—remember that.*

I turn to face Jennifer. "Where the fuck were *you?*"

"I wasn't a hundred percent about your nigger friend," she replies.

You redneck jerk! But, no. She's pushing my multiracial buttons. Fight it.

"That fool is down." I pat the Gucci case. "It's all here."

Then we are in the cab of the truck, with me between the two of them.

"Open it," suggests the man with the shaved head. (Forty, weathered—Special Ops?) Jennifer has trained him well; his shoulders and biceps are huge, neck tattoo, and he must be local, because all he has on in the misty cold is a "wife beater" undershirt.

I flip the catch. The case appears to be filled with packets of real hundred-dollar bills. I smile complacently, but my heart is pumping. A narrow miss. I should have checked it right away; we could be looking at Monopoly money.

We pick up an access road that parallels the highway, then turn off, heading east through a maze of country lanes. The windows are tinted, but we seem to pass a development of modest homes separated by swatches of black woods before the truck pulls into the graveled driveway of a house with a sign that says NOTARY PUBLIC. Mr. Bodybuilder gets out fast.

"Make it quick."

In the blur, I notice a magnetic picture stuck on the dashboard: a shot of Jennifer and three young children. "I'm coming to get your kids," the black man said. Was he a real drug dealer who had gotten our phony identities mixed up?

Before I can ask about those kids, I am taken around the back and hustled down some steps to a basement where a counterfeit-printing operation is in full display.

They have a sweet high-definition laser color printer turning out leaves of counterfeit checks. There are shrink-wrapped packages of birth certificates and marriage licenses, piles of magazines in brown paper. For a moment, I am genuinely elated, as if we have actually busted a big interstate operation.

The guy who allegedly runs the show looks like a nerdy bean counter; he is wearing horn-rimmed glasses and a saggy red cardigan sweater. Balding. Potbelly. Sallow face moist with sweat.

Jennifer says, "This is Darcy, from California."

He scans my getup, says in a taunting voice, "You look like shit from California."

A couple of lowlifes working the copier snicker.

"How about the bogus?" I ask impatiently.

Nobody answers. I notice Jennifer becoming agitated. She is stamping her foot and redoing the ponytail.

"We're out of here," says the man with the shaved head.

"Relax."

"Sure."

He exchanges a look with Jennifer.

Something has changed. Some note of tension has started to wail.

Addressing her, I say, "What's the deal?"

But the guy with the shaved head answers. "Jennifer has to get home to the kids."

"Past their bedtime," I agree. It is 3:00 a.m. "Can we cut to the chase?"

The accountant indicates plastic bins lined up against the wall. A million bucks takes up a lot of room. I can tell just by looking they are down by half.

"You're a little short there, dude."

"When we finish this job, we'll print more," he assures me. "That's the beauty of it. Sit down. This is pure Colombian. Free samples, limited time only."

The plastic bag is out. He cuts some lines on the cover of a pornographic magazine.

"Oh man." I laugh. "I just did some."

"More is better."

"Go for it," I say. "I'm done."

"Bullshit," he replies. "You're a cop."

"Get a life."

"Then what's the problem?"

I stare at the lines of coke. *What is the parameter for—*"Just because I politely decline your hospitality doesn't mean I'm a cop. I hate cops."

Jennifer says, "Just do it, honey."

—illegal activity?

"See," I vamp, "we just met. So how do I know it's not rat poison?"

The accountant snorts a line and offers up the rest.

If I do it, will I be breaking the law?

"My boyfriend said I gotta keep my head clear—"

Will that invalidate—what did Diestal say about authorizing—

The accountant whips a .38 automatic from an ankle holster and holds it to my head.

"Fuck you. I've never seen a cop do dope. You're a cop."

The hammer pulls back with a sound like rolling thunder. The steel barrel presses against my brain stem and at that moment I stop trying to figure out who is who, and what is true, and why I am falling through this cruel labyrinth.

Enlightenment at gunpoint.

"Jesus Christ," pleads Jennifer.

"I'm doing it, okay?"

Cocaine—real cocaine—burns the lining of my nose and drips down my throat, and shortly my mind begins to hum a distracted tune while my heartbeat soars into the red zone: dreaming in bed and sprinting to the finish line at the same time.

Things have shifted again. Is it the drug, or is everyone else melting down also? I see a briefcase open on top of the copier. It is empty. But it is not the briefcase I brought. I hear the guy with the shaved head trying to explain.

"Look, we have a problem. There's been a mistake, but don't blame Jennifer," he says.

"I never said I knew her!" Jennifer is shouting.

"She ripped us off." The husband shrugs.

The accountant scratches his ear. I notice he is still holding the gun.

"So what happened?"

"We picked up the wrong person," says Jennifer. "I had a bad feeling about it when that ghetto car drove up—"

"No way." I swim toward the briefcase. "There was a hundred grand."

Well, there isn't now.

"That's not my briefcase. That's not the one I came in with," I blurt. This one is cheap plastic. "I had a Gucci."

It echoes strangely. *Gucci?* Is that a real word?

"What are you trying to say?" asks the accountant calmly.

I catch Jennifer's panicked look and switch direction as best I can.

"I don't know," I say, "but something's . . . messed up."

He fires the gun at close range into the chest of the man with the shaved head, who lifts up off the floor and flies backward, blood splattering the wood-paneled walls. Jennifer screams, "No, please God, no, no, no—" and he shoots her, too, and she jerks over a chair and sprawls on the floor, the pink sweatsuit staining red. The lackeys start dragging cartons containing freshly minted contraband away from a spreading pool of blood.

The accountant is breathing hard. "I don't like that kind of shit," he says.

Undercover operative may be authorized pursuant to section four—

I have to save my own life.

"They switched the briefcases," I tell him. "They double-crossed us. You and me."

"You and me?"

"You and me," I insist. "We have to get rid of the bodies."

"Is that what they taught you in cop school?"

He turns toward me and his eyes are tiny dots behind the glasses.

"I'm going to help you," I say. "Get some of that plastic and we'll put these losers in the truck."

"I'll tell you who's a loser."

He shoves me into a windowless bathroom and locks the door. The bathtub is stained with old brown blood. Chains are embedded in the walls, handcuffs looped around the rusty pipes. Everywhere there are bunches of human hair. I think it's called primal fear.

I am imprisoned by a backwoods mental case.

I listen to muffled voices. Someone curses and rattles the lock, but then the banging stops. It stops for a long time.

Soon there is daylight under the door. I turn the knob and it opens. The room is deserted, the printer quiet, the bogus gone, blood splatters still on the walls.

I crawl out of that basement into the dawn, like the lone survivor of a nuclear holocaust, to discover that I am on a deserted lane in a perfectly preserved little town. I am back on Main Street, in Hogan's Alley, at the FBI Academy. The misty light and cold, wet air, the fake buildings, they are at that moment no more surprising than finding myself alive.

I walk down the center of the street, past the Biograph Theater, perpetually playing *Manhattan Melodrama* with Clark Gable and Myrna Loy, and the neat brick Bank of Hogan. A family of real live deer has wandered into the dewy grass of the city square.

I cross the road that runs through the Marine base and climb the hill to the agony tree, where a counselor is waiting, dressed in a black watch cap and heavy jacket against the chill.

"You lost two informants," he says, "but otherwise you did pretty well. You never broke cover and stayed on point. It's okay," he adds softly.

"What's okay?"

"It's okay to cry."

Breakdown of the ego by sleep-deprivation, humiliation, and abuse is a well-known brainwashing technique. It renders the individual compliant, and eager to serve the cult.

"Everyone cries," says the counselor. "But nobody tells."

Four

It is Easter Sunday when I leave Los Angeles for Portland, Oregon, three weeks after being certified at undercover school. People in dark clothes holding babies are lined up in front of churches, and on the airplane, stewardesses are wearing rabbit ears. Yellow flowers grow wild between the runways. Despite the urgent beating of my heart, I have the extraordinary feeling that everything is all, all right.

It is right to be ascending on this day of holy mysteries. Somewhere in the clouds, a silent transformation will occur. When we land, Special Agent Ana Grey will be gone from the world, and a fictional person named Darcy DeGuzman will walk off the airplane in her place.

Two days before, sometime before dawn on Good Friday, animal rights terrorists smashed the windows of a butcher store in southeast Portland, spray-painting the word *Holocaust* on parked cars. Moments later, a firebomb exploded at Ernie's Meats, a wholesaler on the docks. Three employees were injured by shrapnel.

Operation Wildcat took off.

As we fly over the snow-pocked ridges of Yosemite, I go through Darcy DeGuzman's backpack, to get the feel of her personal objects, provided by the backstopping team at the Bureau's secret off-site in Los Angeles. Besides a phony driver's license, credit cards, and bank statements, there is a copy of *Animal Liberation* by Peter Singer that was run over by a car to make it look used, and keys to a rented apartment in Portland.

The off-site is concealed in the midst of a raucous Central American nation of street vendors and discount malls opposite the green ice towers of downtown. We'd practically lived there the past few weeks, concocting scenarios aimed at infiltrating Darcy DeGuzman into the FAN organization. On Good Friday morning, five weeks ahead of schedule, I climbed out of the Crown Vic and never looked back.

The gates swung closed. Cameras scanned a crowd of Spanish workers waiting for the morning bus, for whom the aging industrial building was just another unremarkable front for an indiscernible business.

I found myself before a black steel door, fumbling at the Cyber-Lock, messing up twice inputting my code. The numbers loomed like kabbalistic signs: LAST CHANCE TO STAY IN LA! BUY A CONDO! MEET A MAN! But when the green light flashed, there was liberating happiness, as when a tiresome family member finally leaves.

Ana Grey was free to go, and take her baggage with her.

For decades, the place had been a state unemployment office, and the Bureau had not done much to change it. I badged the on-duty, who buzzed me into a vestibule that smelled of old guns and wet plaster. Tired fluorescents cast a sallow patina along empty corridors that were laid forty years ago with sea green linoleum, now worn to the floorboards.

Special Supervisory Agent Mike Donnato appeared wearing a trim charcoal suit, making things look a little less like a mental institution. Donnato, my old mentor on the bank robbery squad, had been pulled off his cases to act as contact agent, or handler, for Operation Wildcat. Management knew that Donnato and I make a formidable battery, like a pitcher and catcher who work together to control the game. This was no time to be fooling around with rookie matchups.

He turned a corner and we fell into step, instantly in psychic sync. That's the way it is with partners.

"We finally got my father-in-law into rehab," he said.

"You're a good man."

Donnato looked skeptical. His father-in-law is difficult.

"The way you take care of him," I insisted. "You're responsible; you visit all the time—"

"He had a catheter," said Donnato dryly. "So it pops out."

"The tube?"

"His penis."

Partners. No topic in the world, no place inside the other individual that you cannot reach out and touch.

"Rochelle's trying to help the nurse out," he said of his wife. "Fussing with the sheets and stuff, and suddenly it's right there."

I started to giggle. "What does she do?"

"Her eyes get real big and she says, *I just saw my father's penis!*"

I lost it. Must have been stress. Donnato shook his head with wry despair. He enjoys getting a reaction from me. "We didn't need *that,* I'll tell you."

SAC Robert Galloway joined us.

"The team is meeting downstairs. They want Ana to get her driver's license first," Galloway said. "Go see Rooney Berwick."

The brick exterior of the old unemployment office is just a shell for a top-secret laboratory in the center of the building, where Rooney Berwick and his cohorts manufacture high-quality, indisputable lies.

The Rooneys of this world are shy. They never have a date for the movies; they work the concession stand. They are collectors. They store data banks in their heads. Ask them what year Samuel Colt patented the revolver. They shop for groceries at two o'clock in the morning, are semi-intimate with a couple of oddball associates, live in a garage apartment across from Mother, who still makes dinner for them every night. They are fifty-eight years old and their pants don't fit, and they haunt comic-book conventions because they are lonely for a hero; the kind of loneliness that never bottoms out.

Rooney Berwick may have been all those things, but on home turf in the FBI lab, sporting multiple ID tags, key rings, and belt-mounted eyeglass cases, he projected a kind of arrogant underground status. He had stringy white hair and an ovoid belly that bulged out of a black button-down shirt tucked into dusty black jeans as he sat on a bench with big boots planted, threading a flex light down the barrel of a gold-plated AK-47.

He looked up. "Can I help?" he asked gravely.

I told him I was a new undercover and needed a driver's license. I asked what he was looking for inside the machine gun.

"Trying to see the rifling." He cocked an eye down the shaft. "Take a look?"

"I've seen rifling, thanks," I replied, referring to the spiral marks left by exiting bullets.

"She isn't loaded, don't worry."

"It creeps me out to see anyone looking down a gun."

"Just trying to keep busy. My mom is dying. They're not saying that, of course. She's in the hospital, but it doesn't look good."

When strangers stun you with this kind of stuff—when you're waiting on line, or in an elevator—it derails you in the headlong rush to get somewhere, forcing you to see their anguish leaking over everything, like accident victims, beyond propriety. I was touched by Rooney Berwick's confession. Why would he say this to someone he scarcely knew, except that we are all part of the Bureau family?

"I'm so sorry."

"She has cancer."

I hesitated. "That is rough."

"What they put her through. They keep doing tests, just to justify their existence."

"I hope they're making her comfortable."

"What does that mean?" he asked rhetorically.

"Well," I said, fumbling, "at least no pain."

"Uh-huh."

We abided for a time in the quiet of the lab.

Finally, he smiled crookedly and latched and unlatched the magazine. "What's the matter? You don't like my toy? That's real gold on there."

"A collector's item," I agreed. "I wish I could talk more, but I've got to get to a meeting."

"Everybody's got a meeting," Rooney said with spite.

He gave up the weapon, moving heavily, like everything in his soft, bruised body hurt.

"The uc name is Darcy DeGuzman," I told him gently.

Beyond the quickies we came up with in training, a deep-cover identity is carefully constructed, like a computer-generated creature in a special-effects studio, with input from FBI psychologists and experts in terrorist organizations. You're trying to create a three-dimensional character that will credibly blend with the target; whose believability will withstand whatever they throw at you. The identity of Darcy DeGuzman, born in a slash of light off a Rexall window in a Virginia mall, had been refined by the focus of a dozen minds to fit the profile of a drifter looking for a cause; someone ripe to be recruited by FAN.

No more blow-dried hair and prim Brooks Brothers suits. Darcy has dark wild curls and an old purple parka that looks as if it has seen many bus stations and campouts. After an abusive childhood in the ghetto tract in Long Beach, she made her way to the Northwest, "where people are real and care about the environment." Because of her politics, she's had trouble holding jobs. She was fired from a bio-tech company for hacking the system when she learned they wrote programs for cosmetic testing on rabbits. She was booked for assault on an employee of the City of Los Angeles Animal Services during a demonstration outside the shelter. It's all on phony police records for anyone to verify. With the recession going on, things haven't worked out, and right now the money's almost gone; Darcy is single, desperate, and emotionally needy.

Rooney Berwick was waiting impatiently behind the ID machine.

"It's a California license," I said helpfully. "Darcy DeGuzman just moved up to Oregon."

"Got it right here." Rooney Berwick tapped some papers. He knew his damn job. "Look at the little babies now."

Tacked to the wall was a snapshot of four pug puppies with walleyed faces scrambling to get out of a cardboard box.

"Are those your puppies?"

"Please hold still, Miss DeGuzman."

The camera strobed.

Rooney said, "Pick it up when you leave."

But I could not just leave. Searching for his eyes I said, "I'm really sorry about your mom."

He looked away and mumbled, "Have a great day" in the burned-out monotone of mid-level technical services personnel who inhabit the hidden compartments of the Bureau: doing it thirty years and never seen daylight. *Their* ideas, and *their* expertise, make other people famous. Nobody cares about the grunts.

I joined the team in a damp wood-paneled alcove in the basement. Coffee cups, water bottles, and documents marked OPERATION WILDCAT—TRUSTED AGENTS ONLY littered the table.

"The firebomb that blew up Ernie's Meats is consistent with the explosive that killed Steve Crawford," Special Supervisory Agent Angelo Gomez told us. "The bomb techs are calling it a signature device."

Angelo Gomez is a legendary undercover investigator who favors the narco look—slicked-back hair, earring, mustache, Hawaiian shirt (to cover the gun), two-ton Rolex, and chubby pink sapphire ring. One eye is smaller than the other and set at a skewed angle. A kiss from a bullet, rumor goes. Angelo is the case agent, running the show from Los Angeles. Mike Donnato will fly up to Portland as needed.

"How are the bombs the same?" my partner asked.

"Both built the same way, by someone with skills, using the explosive Tovex. Just like in Steve's case, the TPU was built with everyday materials—cell phone, digital clock, batteries—connected with alligator clips."

"The alligator clips," I remarked, "are worthy of note."

Galloway was looking through files and doing something with a calculator, but he was listening. He had taken the supervisory position on the case because Steve Crawford meant that much to him.

"What's the significance of alligator clips?"

"It means he's a lazy bomb builder," I replied. "Wants to build it fast. Confident, not a perfectionist, doesn't have to have the wire wrapped just so—just wants to get the job done."

"What's the profile?"

"Off the top of my head? He's a white heterosexual male. The way he builds his TPUs—the alligator clips and ordinary wire—says he's not high-tech, goes with the classics."

"Older?"

"Maybe. We can eliminate vandalism or experimentation as a motive. This guy is on a mission."

Galloway nodded. "Ideology. That's what our pals at FAN stand for—Free Animals Now."

"Don't let the soft and furry animal rights bullshit melt your heart," Angelo agreed. "These are criminals, bad as Timothy McVeigh. Their end goal is to change society—into what, who knows or cares—but the immediate goal is to put fear in people. Chaos and destabilization—that's their stock-in-trade."

I reached past Donnato to sneak a corner of the blueberry muffin he was delicately breaking into crusts. Automatically, he slid it toward me—one of many small, endearing moves during a long partnership in which we often found ourselves sharing the same thought: *Doesn't matter what the boneheads call themselves. They killed Steve.*

"What's on your mind?" Galloway asked, seeing my frown.

"Opening-night jitters." I shrugged.

Never let it show.

"Afraid you won't know your lines?"

"I'll figure it out. I've read every transcript of every intercept."

"Anarchists don't care about the issues," Galloway reminded us. "Don't feel you have to spout the rhetoric. The cause is never the cause."

On the laptop, Angelo had pulled up surveillance photos taken at demonstrations throughout the Northwest. They were mainstream protesters—do-gooders and tree-huggers—mostly middle-aged, plus the requisite young and hairy types. "Free the mustangs." "Milk is torture." "McDeath to McDonald's." "All meat is murder." "Dairy is rape."

What does an anarchist look like?

"Not so easy to connect the dots," observed Galloway. "FAN has no central leadership. It's structured like an international terrorist group engaged in net war."

Net—or network—war is the war of the future, an agile system of "committees" or "cells" that seem to act invisibly, strung together by the braided cables of money and belief. Armies based on infantries are about to become obsolete.

"Where do I start?"

Angelo hit the laptop. "Herbert Laumann."

Galloway: "Who is Herbert Laumann?"

"Some penny-ante bureaucrat at the Bureau of Land Management," I replied. I'd seen the files. "The idiots are really after this dude. They call him 'the face of evil.' "

A photo of Herbert Laumann filled the screen. The "face of evil" looked like the manager of an electronics store—the Joe in the tan shirt and brown tie who scurries out of the back when the wide-screen TV you ordered two months ago has disappeared off the delivery list—pouchy cheeks, line mustache, thinning hair.

"Our latest intel indicates the movement is going to target wild mustang horses," Angelo said.

The Wild Horse and Burro Program is mandated by federal law to protect the last remaining herds of free-roaming mustangs in the United States. These are the pure and graceful descendants of horses that were brought over by the Spanish explorers and then mated with hardy U.S. cavalry mounts. Along with a lot of other folks, Congress felt the mustangs are part of our unique western heritage and should be scientifically preserved in their natural habitat. The weaker ones may be put up for adoption by the public, but wild mustangs can never be sold or slaughtered.

"The herds are protected by federal law," Angelo went on, "but the goofballs don't like the way the government is doing it. Laumann is in charge of the Wild Horse and Burro Program in Oregon. He's already been harassed. We think FAN infiltrated the group."

Donnato: "Ana hits the ground. She finds a wild-horse protest. She works her way into a FAN cell."

Galloway held up a finger. "Patience," he advised. "The hardest part is waiting to see whether your uc identity is taking effect or not. It's the loneliest time."

While I was absorbed in this, Angelo had come up behind. Now he cuffed me hard across the head.

"Darcy! What are you doing up in Portland?"

Instantly, I am Darcy and he is FAN. We have these fire drills often. They make your adrenaline rock. There is no transition, isn't meant to be.

In undercover work, it is always midnight in the universe, and you are always alone.

"I got fed up with the anti-life corporate agenda," I said. "I quit my job in L.A."

"That's bullshit. We checked, and you never worked in a biotech company in L.A."

Galloway was watching this improvisation with folded arms.

"That doesn't make any sense," I protested.

"Why do you keep going down to L.A. when you don't work there?"

"Why don't you come with me one time and I'll show you? Jesus Christ." I smiled with feigned exasperation. "What's wrong with you guys? I'm starting to get paranoid."

"Darcy would not say *Jesus,*" Donnato murmured.

I muttered, "Yes, she would."

Angelo circled my chair. Leaning close, his distorted upper face was beginning to look like a malevolent Picasso mask. He yanked me to my feet by my hair. The chair tipped over.

"What's the problem, bro?"

Donnato: "She wouldn't say *bro.*"

Angelo, moving like a snake, had my arms pinned and a nasty little knife, which he had been secreting just for that moment, flat against my throat.

"We're all a little paranoid at FAN," he whispered into my burning ear. *"Spies like you know the reason why."*

Panic. I needed to pee. I wanted to yell *"Time out!"* What would Darcy say? I didn't know. I wasn't ready. I couldn't think.

Never hesitate. Get back in their face.

"I came here to save animals," I shouted. "I'm on your side."

He tightened his forearm across my neck, half-lifting me off the ground.

"If you are who you say you are, show us your driver's license."

"No problem." I groped on the table and came up with the waxed muffin wrapper. "Here it is!"

"Really?" Angelo snapped the paper, testing it, and growled, "Bull-shit!"

Then, in a normal voice, he said, "You're dead," and let me go.

I was breathless, flummoxed. "Why?"

"Never give them anything physical. Anything they can check."

"Okay, it's a muffin thing, but in real life I'll be backstopped with an untraceable ID—"

"I said *anything physical.*" He crumpled the paper for emphasis.

In undercover school, I had learned never to argue with an instructor.

"Okay."

I was sweating. They could cut me now, halfway through, anytime, just like my roommate at Quantico. I looked toward Donnato for help.

"I liked the fed-up-with-corporate-America concept," he offered.

Angelo was wired. "The false documents we give you will be as good as it gets, but backstopping is only a screen door we put between you and the truth. If you stand back, it looks solid. If you walk up close, you're going to see through the holes. *Don't let them touch the screen,* or they'll know it's a story. A story that isn't true. And then you'll be toast."

It was searing and unpleasant to stand there with head bowed while Angelo berated me with stuff I already knew.

I swallowed the humiliation.

I believe in this work.

The plane banks, revealing the snow-covered Olympian bulk of Mount Hood. I try to relax and let the power of the engines carry me, but I can feel that searing mortification even now. A vapor of jet fuel leaking up through the floor is smelling a lot like the smell of burning brake lining that swamped my senses during the shooting incident. I pop a mint as the landing gear unfolds.

Take all your greens from the crayon box and color in a patchwork of moss and olive and sage, and that is Portland. *What a tidy city,* I think as the airplane passes over neat rows of houseboats on a sparkling river, then curves, delivering a spectacular view of three or four intricately wrought iron bridges.

Despite everyone's gloomy talk of rain, it is seventy-three degrees and sunny when we land. On the ground, girls are wearing halter tops, and grandmas flowered pants, and there are hugs and chocolate bunnies for Easter Sunday.

I am not met at the airport. There can be no risk of Ana Grey/ Darcy DeGuzman being seen in the company of law enforcement. Rehearsal's over. I'm walking alone onstage, backpack over my shoulder. The glass doors swing wide. Outside, the air smells sweet as cotton candy.

I find Darcy's banged-up Civic waiting for me in the parking lot. The freeway is empty under an eggshell blue sky and everywhere there are flowering trees.

So this is what people who don't live in Los Angeles call spring.

I leave the quiet of the holiday freeway and wind through the southeast part of town, until the road becomes a two-lane blacktop fronted by clapboard duplexes and airless Victorians with weed-strewn yards. A person in transit would live in a transitional neighborhood, we figured, where radicals mix in with blue-collar families on the scrubby streets.

I park in the long light of a late northwest afternoon, pulling up in front of a small four-story brick building built a century ago. Darcy's rental apartment is on the top floor. I stare at the empty windows.

The loneliest time.

Five

The lights of downtown Portland beckon like a seaport in the mist, gently bobbing through the rain-streaked windshield as the Civic bumps along. Beside the Burnside Bridge, homeless men are scrabbling through a glistening mountain of garbage bags left over from the food and crafts market, held on weekends under the shelter of the iron span. Bent-over figures dragging bundles and wet cardboard cartons stop in front of the men's rescue mission to trade cigarettes in the rain. They look impossibly old to be foraging on the skids.

Over the course of my second day in town, the crystalline weather had given way to tiers of clouds, moving and melding, waiting and cruising. As drops of rain tapped the windows of Darcy's apartment, I watched the street and waited for nightfall. Within a block of her building, there was a mom-and-pop grocery with psychedelic flowers painted on the windows, and an Asian market where you could get live chickens. There were peeling cottages with bay windows curtained by cut lace beside postmodern town houses. There was a hip designer resale store, as well as a Laundromat and a fifties coffee shop that was now a vegan restaurant called the Cosmic Café. The sidewalks were overgrown with marigold and outlaw mint.

What did Darcy DeGuzman think, looking out the window?
I could have a life here.

The furnished apartment, with its wicker bookcases and new TV and nesting aluminum pots under the sink, smelled like the musty fake storefronts in Hogan's Alley at the FBI Academy. This, too, was a stage set—but the action was real and I was working to weave it all together in the existent world: How did Steve Crawford's last known location at a downtown dive called Omar's Roadhouse tie in with a radical group that likes to play with explosives?

I wondered if rain was falling on the bare steaming backs of wild mustangs in the high desert to the east; and if the ultimate sacrifice that Steve Crawford made would turn out to be a small and hollow loss in a larger war to defend their freedom.

The person who knew was Marvin Gladstone.

"Aw hell," said Donnato the day Galloway introduced us to Gladstone at the off-site. "Do we have to talk to Marvin?"

Special Agent Marvin Gladstone had the ill luck of having been Crawford's handler, the last person to see him alive.

He was sitting on a folding chair outside the dank little room in which we were meeting, looking like the last man on earth. He was wearing a windbreaker and visitor's tags—the former employee who was no longer part of the working world. Since his abrupt departure, he had puffed up twenty pounds. With his crew-cut gray head downcast, pink jowls lax, and hands in his lap, he was the picture of middle-aged male depression.

As a handler, you can't do worse than losing your undercover, and Marvin, no way around it, had lost Steve. Stricken with grief, he'd resigned from the Bureau the day Steve's remains were identified. In doing so, he gave up his pension.

When Galloway called out to him in the hall, Marvin straightened up and walked into the room with an attempt at Navy pride. He did not remove his windbreaker but reached into a pocket for a road map of Oregon. Poignantly, he had brought a map, as if to show us all the stations of his shame.

"I've been thinking it would make sense for the next undercover to start by picking up the trail where Steve left off."

Galloway's tone was mocking. "Good plan, Marvin. Steve was one of the finest agents to come through here. You think we're going to cock around?"

"No, sir."

Donnato and I did not like having Marvin Gladstone in the room, either. It was as if minutes before boarding our flight we had met a pilot who had been in a plane crash. Would you really want to strike up a conversation? Gladstone's breath as he leaned over the desk smelled like old library books, like what is dead and gone.

"The trail stopped at an anarchist hangout in downtown Portland called Omar's Roadhouse." Marvin pointed to the map with a stubby finger. "Crawford's last known location. The last place he called me from."

"What was your last conversation like?"

"Nothing out of the ordinary."

"What was Steve doing there?"

"Watching a basketball game. After that, no communication."

"Why Omar's Roadhouse?"

"Omar's is a marketplace for illegal goods. You have your bikers, your druggies, your interstate theft. Steve had a theory that FAN was being financed by methamphetamine labs and that the dealers went to Omar's to do business. They've got a lot of those labs in the mountains."

"Is that why he went into the national park?"

"I'm sorry," Marvin said. "I can't tell you."

"Steve deserves better," Galloway reminded him.

"I'm not making excuses, but it was not unusual for Steve to drop off the radar. I tried to rein him in, but sometimes he'd go dark for a couple of days. I should have done a better job," he added, and stood there like a prisoner with his eyes out of focus.

By that time, I had run out of what remained of my sympathy for Marvin Gladstone. Steve had been a pro—if he'd needed reining in, it was for a reason, and the old codger should have found out why.

"What's the place like?" I asked with false politeness. "Omar's Roadhouse? Because I'm going there."

Marvin woke up. *"You?"* He looked at me—five four, 112 pounds—and then he looked around the room. *"Alone?"*

"Ana is the undercover," Galloway explained.

"I'm here to tell you." Marvin's eyes were wide. "Omar's is rough trade."

Now it is night and I am driving alone, past the men's rescue mission, down a dark cobblestone lane once lined with shipping companies and foreign brokerage houses. At the turn of the last century, they called this street the "gateway to the Orient," but tonight it is another deserted business district in twenty-first-century global America— vintage stone-and-brickwork buildings overwhelmed by tall black boxes made of glass, and not a mariner in sight.

Trolley tracks, gleaming dully, curve into the diminishing light, where between two seedy parking lots a nondescript tavern of red timber, punched out with a row of small and unfriendly windows, identifies itself as one of those everlasting beacons of alcoholic wretchedness that through the ages have drawn the outcasts of the world—those who suffer, shuffle, buy or sell.

Steve Crawford's last known location.

I park in a smattering of broken glass.

Six

Like many of us, Omar's Roadhouse has two sides.

There are two separate entrances to help you choose between Omar's Café and simply the bar. Inside, the common air is infused with cigarette smoke, the division between the two just a booth with a maple-stained partition, as if to prove the boundary between criminal and not is as makeshift as a quarter-inch piece of plywood.

On the brighter side of the partition, two clean-cut African-American men in Polartec vests and corduroys are eating meatballs and spaghetti off paper plates, and there is pickled cauliflower in the salad bar. But here in this murky pool of bottom-feeders, blue light pours from an ancient cigarette machine and the brightest eyes are in the heads of the deer, elk, raccoon, bobcat, fox, and wolverine set up in rows above the redwood paneling like a mute jury. Decor is simple: a flag with a skull and crossbones, big enough for a coliseum.

I settle at an L-shaped bar, going slow with a Sierra Nevada pale ale. How did Steve Crawford, on the same assignment, play this scene? I can picture his lanky body wrapped around a bar stool. A washed-up hippie? Meth addict? Lost businessman? Sloppy drunk? I really don't know. They did not share his uc identity. Although we'd been colleagues for a decade since those days as naïve rookies, so high on the Bureau that we wanted to be married in the chapel at the Academy, I never saw the undercover side of him and he never saw the Darcy part of me.

Would he have loved me anyway?

I make an effort to look uneasy and forlorn in Omar's swamp dive, paying particular attention to the 250-pound bruiser with a full dark beard down to his waist at the other end of the bar. It took him a long time to grow that beard, I reflect, and therefore he must mean it, or whatever it stands for, which cannot be pleasant.

He is wearing an entertainer's tall black top hat and mirrored sunglasses, and rings on every finger—skulls and swastikas, it looks like from here. No shirt, just a vest showing massive biceps no doubt hardened by lifting motorcycle parts. He could carry me out of the place under one arm, like a baguette. Embroidered across the vest are the flowered words *Terminate the helmet law.*

Although his bulk dominates like Mount Hood, Mr. Terminate is not the only major bonehead on the horizon. The area where Steve Crawford was murdered is known for meth kitchens and marijuana farms. Drug wars are fought in our national forests; left-wing anarchists and redneck Klansmen trying to blow each other up, and bikers after the spoils. On the face of it, each patron at Omar's would fit one or more of those profiles. The one thing you could probably say about everybody in this bar is they all hate the United States government.

Rough trade.

Marvin Gladstone got that right.

It is 10:00 p.m. on a Monday night and this must be the crossroads of criminal activity in Washington County. Two fat truckers and two even fatter hookers are squeezed rump-to-rump, pitcher-to-pitcher at a table littered with pizza and chips, openly popping pills. Mexican gangbangers hover near a TV showing the fights, palming nickel bags of coke, muttering and complaining, flicking butts, grinding the worn heels of their western boots to jukebox Santana. The female neo-Nazis are big into black eyeliner and leather halters that show off their breasts, but I am wearing one of Darcy's yellow oxford shirts with a collar, jeans with a belt, and beat-up Timberlands. ("Bad guys don't have good boots," Angelo warned.)

The only woman at Omar's less conspicuous than I am seems to be the lady in a calf-length denim skirt with a flounce, who is standing at my left, patiently waiting for the bartender's attention. She has been there long enough, and close enough, for me to pick up her scent, like fresh almond soap, underneath the bitter stench of cigarette smoke. And then I notice the sheaves of richly colored gray-and-silver hair caught up in barrettes and falling past her shoulders, and that the woman, although twenty-some years older than I am and as many pounds heavier, radiates the sturdiness and ease in her body of someone who labors outdoors; her finely creased skin seems to hold the moist glaze of cold and foggy mornings.

The bartender darts his chin at her as he blows by. "Give me a sec, Megan."

"Sure thing."

"You've been waiting a long time," I observe.

"The waitress is busy," the woman replies without a trace of resentment, and there is an eager jolt as I recognize this person shows an inherent sympathy for the underdog—such as a lonely stranger in a new city?

Opening move: "I love your necklace."

A heavy silver pendant of interlocking triangles rests upon her pillowy chest.

"A valknot. Ever heard of it?"

I shake my head.

Megan answers with a forgiving smile. "A Nordic symbol for the three aspects of the universe."

"Now," announces the bartender, sweating from his shaved head, "what can I get for you, Megan?"

He pours white wine and mixes up a Salty Dog with fresh grapefruit juice and premium gin while Megan stares across at Mr. Terminate. And Mr. Terminate glares right back at her.

"You know that guy?" I ask.

"That's John. I think he likes you."

"No."

"Yes. He's looking right at you," she says without moving her lips.

"He's looking at *you*."

It is hard to tell what is going on underneath the top hat and mirrored sunglasses.

"He knows better than to mess with me," Megan says lightly.

Mr. Terminate has picked up an ashtray. It is a white ceramic ashtray, like the one in front of us, and it says *Coors*.

Megan says, "Uh-oh."

"What's he doing?" I ask, alarmed.

"If you're wearing a leg holster for a primary weapon, you're an idiot," Angelo always says, but for the second or third time that evening, I wish Darcy DeGuzman were carrying a .45 automatic.

I have noticed we are often burdened by our own creations.

"Look out," Megan warns.

"Why?"

Instead of answering, she starts to back away from the bar.

Mr. Terminate is examining the ashtray closely, hefting it in his hand as if it were an apple.

Then he eats it.

He chews it, and chomps it with his back teeth, and there is an extraordinary sound, like marbles grinding against one another in a soft cloth bag. A pause, then he spews a great shower of white shards and pink-flecked foam across the bar. He picks the remaining pieces out of his beard, and then, with a meaningful look at me, lifts his glass and drinks the rest of the whiskey down.

Nobody bats an eye. The bartender is there with a rag.

I turn to the woman in disbelief. "What was that?"

Megan is matter-of-fact. "That's John."

"You've got to be kidding."

Megan's answer encompasses the feminine dilemma, and seems to draw us both together in it.

"It's what we've known since seventh grade," she says. *"Boys are stupid."*

A wild laugh escapes me, while Mr. Terminate remains impassive, body language boulderlike and calm, as if he has not just eaten a glass ashtray and spit it out in our faces. He is waiting for an answer, but the question remains—*What is the question?* Is this some kind of brain-dead buffalo love, or has he made me, in the same way he might have made Steve Crawford for an undercover cop?

The bartender finally sets down the white wine and Salty Dog but waits a moment longer, keeping his hands on the drinks.

"What can I get your friend?" he asks Megan.

"We don't really know each other," I explain.

"Well, you should. Two beautiful ladies?"

I introduce myself as Darcy DeGuzman and it rolls right off my tongue. *Her* name is Megan Tewksbury, and she would like to pay her bill. But the bartender lingers, drawing things out.

"So, Darcy, another beer?"

White, built, maybe forty—he's giving me a very friendly look. Is he trying to pick me up? It's my lucky day. His black T-shirt says *Does Not Play Well with Others*. His lip is pierced, and he sports a bearded braided thing hanging off his chin.

The Darcy part likes it that some oaf is looking at me. I hope he makes a move, just to see what it would be like. This never happens in normal life, when I am Special Agent Ana Grey. Even on a weekend, even at a car wash, looking like everybody else in a tank top and shorts, my first reaction to a guy staring is, *What are* you *up to?* Not exactly a turn-on.

Megan: "What do I owe you, Rusty?"

"No worries. I'll just run a tab." To me: "What're you doing here, girlfriend?"

"I must have read the guidebook wrong," I say, flirting.

Rusty grins. "Don't fret. We get a lot of nice folks stopping in après the market. Megan has a booth there. She's a regular. Guess what *she's* sellin'?"

Megan carries the drinks away. "Nothin' *you'll* ever afford."

"She sells homemade hazelnut brittle!" Rusty shouts. "She's a nut." He winks. "Lives on a nut farm, along with some goats and about a hundred cats and dogs. Got a whole thing going where she rescues animals."

"She's an animal lover?" My head swivels back toward the woman, who is now sitting at a table with the man who ordered the Salty Dog.

"Who is she with?"

"That's the boyfriend. His name is Julius Emerson Phelps."

Broad-shouldered, six three, hard-built but with enough gut to put him over two hundred pounds. It would be difficult to pinpoint his age. Young girls would find the implication of sexual mastery in his craggy smile and wish for his attention, while men of my grandfather's generation would resent having to relinquish their grip on the world to a male who still looks young. I make him for a middle-aged farmer with a ponytail; he must be some type of an agro guy, because there's a flying ear of corn on his cap.

Above the rows of liquor bottles, in a mirrored sign for Becks, I watch Megan Tewksbury drape a possessive arm over Julius's shoulders. They are talking cheek-to-cheek without really looking at each other, eyes scanning the room. I am surprised to see myself in the mirror—looking happy. My cheeks are flushed from the heat and noise and sexual signals snap-popping off the crowd. I'm feeling all warmed up, looking for a friend. Someone local, who would be a way into the community. Megan? Approachable?

Not while they're nuzzling. I nip at the mug and observe. The beer is cold, and after a while I realize that it has been going down nicely with the wigged-out nasty metal guitar band coming from the jukebox.

The mirror shows it is Julius Emerson Phelps who has changed the music. He is holding on to both sides of the machine, bent over the glass as if in a trance. The heavy ridges of his face are colored blue by the jukebox lights, a handsome face that has gone to seed. He wears a worn-out denim shirt and blondish hair that, if unloosed, would fall below the shoulders. But here's what really dates him: an improbable pair of frayed red suspenders only old hippies can pull off.

> *I choose to steal what you choose to show*
> *And you know I will not apologize*

"Anybody know what that is?" I ask in general.

" 'Career of Evil,' " rasps Mr. Terminate, like he's still got pieces of ashtray stuck in his throat. "Blue Oyster Cult."

"Weren't they big in the seventies?"

But Mr. Terminate goes stone-cold silent.

I slide off the stool and meander to the jukebox.

"Blue Oyster Cult," I say. "Weren't they big in the seventies?"

Julius's eyes are slow coming out of the trance.

"You are way too young to know about Blue Oyster Cult."

"That's the only song of theirs I recognize." I smile truthfully.

He straightens up. There's a silver loop in one ear. I like earrings on men. I like the kind of face that knows you're looking at it.

He indicates the lighted selections. "One song left. You pick."

"Jackson Browne."

He approves. I move closer, so now we're peering over the titles together. The heat of the machine jumps up.

"I like your friend, Megan."

"Good lady."

"You come here after the market?"

"She sells her hazelnut brittle. I grow 'em, she sells 'em."

"I just moved to Portland. I haven't been to the market, but I hear it's awesome."

"You should go," Julius says.

We listen to the piano riff at the opening of "Fountain of Sorrow." The mood shifts, low-key and melancholy.

"Why do you have a flying corn on your hat?"

Reflexively, as if to be sure it's there, Julius touches the red-and-green ear of corn with wings that adorns the cap.

"DeKalb," he explains.

"What's DeKalb?"

"DeKalb, Ohio. Corn-seed capital of the world."

"What does corn seed have to do with hazelnuts?"

"I was born there," the big man tells me. "Picked corn when I was in high school, lying on my back on this very uncomfortable contraption, a mattress they put on wheels—"

Megan is on her way. She's had enough of us talking. She slips two fingers in the waistband of Julius's jeans, sliding him close.

"I was just telling this young lady about Ohio."

"Is he boring you with his life story?" she asks.

"Yes," replies Julius, glad for the intrusion.

"Your friend, Rusty, at the bar, he was saying that you rescue animals? At the hazelnut farm?"

Julius's attention snaps back. "Rusty said that?"

"Why not?" says Megan. "It's true."

"I'm a total animal person," I say, boasting. "I once got arrested for getting into a fight with a dude at a shelter who euthanized this cat I was going to adopt. Because I was *fifteen minutes* late."

"That's awful. Where are you from, Darcy?" Megan asks kindly.

"Southern California. Don't ask."

"Heat, traffic, smog?"

"And the most repressive attitude toward animal rights. We have to fight for every soul."

"Are you in the movement?" she asks.

"I show up. Done a lot of cat and dog adoptions. Can I come to the farm and see your operation, maybe help?"

Megan hesitates. "We don't encourage visitors. It upsets the animals."

"But don't you want to adopt them out?"

"Once we get 'em, we keep 'em. We're not open to the public," Julius says abruptly, and downs a beer.

Regroup.

"I've been reading in the *Oregonian* about the wild mustangs," I say barreling on. "I think it's terrible what the government is doing to them."

"Infuriating," Megan agrees.

"Ever heard of FAN?"

"Are you a member of FAN?" she whispers conspiratorially.

"Me?" I strike my heart with surprise. "No, are you?"

"No," she says slowly. "But I don't condemn what they do. Especially concerning Herbert Laumann," she adds bitterly.

My stomach goes *whoa!* Angelo's intel just paid off.

"The deputy state director of the BLM? What's he up to now?"

"Killing horses."

"They can't be killed; it's the law."

"He steals them."

"Steals them?"

"He's been stealing the horses he's supposed to protect. Since he's been deputy director, Herbert Laumann has supposedly adopted one hundred and thirty-five mustangs."

"*What?*"

"This is a guy who lives in the suburbs." Megan nods, disbelieving. "Where is he going to put a hundred and thirty-five horses?"

"The man's a scumbag," Julius says, scanning over people's heads. Waiting for someone?

"Know what he's been doing?"

I shake my head. My eyes are wide.

Megan's voice is rising. "Government employees aren't allowed to bid on the mustangs that are up for auction. So Laumann adopts them illegally under his relatives' names." Her cheeks are pink. "Then he sells them to a slaughterhouse in Illinois, where the horse meat is packed and shipped for human consumption in France."

"They eat horses, don't they?" comments Julius, not taking his eyes from the crowd.

The scam sounds too bizarre to be radical propaganda.

"Why isn't this front-page news?"

"It will be. FAN discovered the paper trail and leaked it to the press. It'll be up on their Web site."

Two or three Mexican gangbangers jump the bar. Glass shatters with earsplitting blasts as bottles fly off the wall. Omar's quiets down and roars at the same time—women freeze; men cheer the fight—as Rusty, the friendly bartender, is tossed hand to hand and then trammeled below the mahogany.

"What are they doing?" Megan gasps.

Julius restrains her. "Stay out of it."

"No! How can you stand there?"

Three on one? My blood is roaring; I'm out of my body with outrage. But this is training: I do not yell *"Freeze! FBI."* I do not speed-dial 911. I am a witness.

I see that neither Mr. Terminate nor Julius makes a move to intervene, but watch with calm and unworried expressions, as if this were a regularly scheduled TV show.

Sickening thuds. Someone's turned up the music.

"This is revolting," Megan says, breaking from her aging boyfriend and elbowing through the crowd, which has gone frenetic, standing on tables, laughing girls waving beer bottles perched on the shoulders of burly guys, like the place is about to erupt in a massive game of chicken. I scramble along with Megan as she pushes her way behind the bar.

Rusty's arms are pinned and they've got his head in the ice bin. They pull it out by his chin hair, repeatedly smash his nose against the chrome, then plunge him into the ice again. His face is a mass of bruises and splintered bone, teeth are gone, and the ice cache has become a hemoglobin cocktail.

Megan is screaming, "Leave him alone," trying to pry the Mexicans away. A small one jumps on her back and clings.

I'm saying, "Chill out, brother," but they laugh, so I get the little monkey dude in a rear chokehold and pull him off Megan and maneuver his flailing body around until I can flip him flat onto the wet wooden joists of the catwalk behind the bar. He lies there, stunned as a fish.

There's a baton Rusty keeps near the cash register. I've got it ready for counterattack, when a big warm hand grabs my wrist. Julius has put himself between them and me.

"Don't worry yourself. Rusty had it coming."

I stare at the destroyed face of the barely conscious human being slumped in Megan's lap on the floor, where she kneels in a nest of broken glass. Her shirt is soaked with his blood. The space looks like Laumann's mustang slaughterhouse—blood on the mirrors, blood in the drains. The attention of the crowd has shifted to the cash register.

"What'd he do?" I shout.

"He's a cop," Julius says, and Rusty awakens just enough to roll an eye toward me, piercing as the bloodred sun.

Seven

My grandfather Poppy taught me that everything must be earned. As a lieutenant in the Long Beach police department, he believed in progress through the ranks. But his black-and-white view of the world carried beyond the patrol car, right into our kitchen, where he would subject my young mother and me to sadistic quizzes on current events, or rate her cooking as if he were a restaurant critic.

"Dry as dust," he'd proclaim about her roast turkey. "You're stupid," he'd say, frowning when I failed to name the secretary-general of the United Nations. Give him a sweater for Father's Day and his face would go into a soft paralysis and his eyes would drift, and he'd give you a neutral "Hmmm." He literally did not know what to do with a gift.

If you did something bad, like flooding the garage with a garden hose, there would be punishment—washing your mouth out with soap, or making you stand in the scary backyard at night in your pajamas. Like Darcy, I did bad things anyway. Things that tested Poppy's love against Poppy's rules. When I was a child, a vein of longing wound through my body, like coveting those ribbons of marshmallow set in chocolate ice cream, and just because he knew I wanted it more than anything, Poppy would never let me have it—no matter how many chances I gave him to say "I was only kidding. You really are okay. Here's my love, with whipped cream on top."

Screw you, Grandpa.

The girl who used to stand in awe of you was Ana.

At Omar's Roadhouse, I was Darcy, acting out like crazy. Darcy, all Darcy.

And I liked it.

Donnato tugs his tie loose and drops into a chair. We have met at a seedy motel near the Portland airport.

"Why wasn't I told there was a Portland police detective working undercover?"

"Don't yell," he says with a sigh. "I just found out myself. They know Omar's is a nexus of criminal activity. They've had undercovers embedded for years—"

I'm pointing a finger, an aggressive habit.

"*Goddamn it,* I should have been told!"

"Look, Ana, it's the same old tune. The local cops want our assistance on a task force, and then resent the hell out of it when we show up. The cop goes down," he says tiredly. "And you throw money?"

"They smashed the cash register, so I grabbed a couple of handfuls. It was a diversion. If anyone asks, 'Who is this new girl in town named Darcy?' they'll have an answer. 'She's the one who got up on the bar and started throwing cash to the crowd.' I gave a handful to Megan for the horses."

"Don't try so hard is what I'm saying."

"That's the juice, Mike. Darcy being out there, that's the key to this new identity. Will Rusty live?"

"Yes. Was he helpful?"

"Before he almost died of internal injuries? Yes, he put me in bed with Megan Tewksbury. He knows she's an activist. That's why he made a big point of introducing us, even though I had no clue what he was doing at the time. He must have thought I was a real lamebrain fed—"

"He accomplished the mission. Calm down. I got Salvador Molly's." Donnato opens a fragrant bag of Caribbean takeout. "Have an empanada."

I do not calm down. "What's going on? You look wasted."

There are bruised dark circles beneath his eyes, sweat stains on his white shirt. We have met in a neighborhood of unreconstructed streets, dotted with bakeries and thrift stores, in a working-class part of Portland. The Econo Lodge, situated on a gritty avenue of easy-credit used-car lots, is a stucco relic of the sixties weathered to the color of a strawberry milk shake, a couple of salesmen's hatchbacks parked outside.

You always have to worry about countersurveillance, so I trudged to the top floor carrying an empty suitcase, and casually unlocked room 224. Using an old FBI maneuver, Donnato was set up two doors down in 228. That way, nobody could put us as meeting together. The average bonehead would not realize the rooms were adjoining, because the Bureau had rented all three.

The connecting doors are still open, creating a triplet of empty cubes identically stocked and sanitized, down to the crispy tissue-wrapped plastic cups. Even the daylight looks dry-cleaned.

"My father-in-law threw a blood clot and had another stroke."

"I'm really sorry, Mike. How is he?"

"Back in the hospital. It's touch and go. We've been up all night."

He draws the curtains to discourage telephoto lenses from neighboring rooftops, and turns the clock radio to NPR. Not because he likes their politics but because at this hour they provide a screen of background jabber so nobody can hear us through the walls. With the curtains closed, the place is dark as a theater. Weak pools of light drop from the table lamps like halos.

"I don't know if we've got a cult here, or what," I tell him. "The female was wearing a triangular silver necklace called a valknot."

"Asatrú," says Donnato.

"God bless you."

"Don't push it," he warns.

"*What'd I say?*"

"Asatrú is a modern-day religion based on ancient Norse beliefs." He reaches for a habanero and cheese fritter. "Its adherents practice a pagan philosophy that talks about preserving nature. The white supremacists have adapted a form of it and switched it around to justify their views."

"There were neo-Nazis at the bar."

"What were they doing?"

"One of them was eating an ashtray."

This doesn't register as anything strange.

"Barriers are coming down," Donnato muses without missing a beat. "Interesting alliances are starting to form between terrorist groups. Right there you have a potential affinity between environmentalists and right-wing thinking. It's not beyond the realm of possibility that these groups could get together. 'The enemy of my enemy is my friend.' "

"You have blood enemies at Omar's who should be tearing each other's throats out."

"It's called business."

"You can buy anything there. Hookers, dope, hazelnut brittle—"

"Hazelnut brittle? Pretty damn subversive. That's it. Now I'm hooked." He rolls his eyes.

"Shut up. Megan Tewksbury is our way in. She will lead us to FAN."

"Why?"

"She's accessible. Funny. Openhearted. I liked her."

"She is not supposed to be your mom."

"I know that."

"It's my job to remind you that in isolation the bad guys can start looking pretty good."

"That's not it. Look."

I flash him the latest issue of *Willamette Week*, a liberal throwaway I snagged at the vegan Cosmic Café. There were piles of it near the bulletin board, underneath an unpleasant chart of a side of beef. The whole front page of the newspaper is a poster in the style of the Old West: WANTED — FOR GETTING AWAY WITH MURDER, with a photo of BLM's deputy state director, Herbert Laumann.

"Megan gave me the heads-up that FAN would break the story, and here it is. Laumann has been illegally adopting mustangs under his relatives' names and selling them to a slaughterhouse in Illinois."

Donnato studies the paper.

"She rescues animals on a farm; she's hooked in. They don't like visitors, which is an excellent reason for me to get my butt out there and see what's going down."

He still doesn't like it.

"Sounds weak. We commit the resources, and your friend Megan turns out to be a housewife who likes cat calendars."

Donnato brushes his tie of crumbs. He is maddeningly fastidious about his Calvin Klein suits and fine tasseled loafers, even in a sleazoid motel. But today his meticulous mannerisms are pissing me off.

"What would be solid enough for you?"

"Give me Bill Fontana."

Bill Fontana is a leader in the movement who did two years in prison for setting fire to 250 tons of hay in an animal-husbandry building at UC Davis. Fontana is a scrawny, bright-eyed kid, still winning hearts and minds with his "fearless saboteur" shtick. The prison sentence only added to the mythology.

"Wonder Boy Fontana is speaking here at a big animal rights convention. I met with the Portland task force that has been assigned to FAN—"

"Wait a minute," I say stubbornly, interrupting him. "Can we go back to Megan? We're looking for me to make my bones. This is a legit way in. Megan is a can-do person, the type who gets things done. I'm telling you, she's good."

"She may be good, but Angelo will say she's weak."

I don't like the innuendo. *Weak* because we're talking about the two of us establishing a *female* relationship? *Weak* because she doesn't fit the prototype of the male junkie informant guys like Angelo understand?

I lift my chin. "I've identified a true believer and I'm getting close to her. That's procedure, absolutely! I need your help to find a way of getting out to that farm."

Donnato stands, thoroughly irritated.

"Tell me something, Ana. Why is it always your agenda?"

I am dumbfounded. "*My* agenda?"

"You are fixated on this woman, and I know why. Not because it's a knockout idea, but because it's *yours*. Yours against mine. You against the badass bureaucracy. It's been that way as long as I've known you."

My fastidious partner has never attacked me like this before. "What is wrong with you? I thought I was the one with the hormones. You've been touchy since I walked in the door."

Men hate it when you use the word *hormones*.

"Omar's Roadhouse was Steve Crawford's last known location," Donnato insists. "And we still don't know why he was there, and why he was not following procedure."

"Who said he wasn't?"

"Marvin Gladstone."

"You believe that? Marvin's just covering his ass."

"Why wasn't Steve checking in?"

I shrug. "He was running his own game. The old-timer couldn't keep up."

"What game?"

I snort slowly through my nose. I become aware of afternoon traffic. I wish we had some beer. Okay, I'll be the one to say it.

"Maybe he was meeting a woman."

Now Donnato is incensed. "Steve was a good father and a good man! What on earth would make you say something like that?"

"It's an idea," I protest. "I don't like the implications, either, but I throw it out for discussion, like any other case, and you go off on me. We all love Tina and Steve. Nobody's trying to stir something up. Him getting it on with someone else—it's just a theory. Why does it bug you so much?"

The two of us arguing about Steve's marriage in a sterile box in the middle of a strange city is suddenly absurd and strangely familiar. It reminds me of undercover school, and the dead-serious games they forced us to play. It is almost as if, against our wills, Donnato and I have been cast as a pair of ridiculous personages—I a naïf named Darcy, and he all buttoned up in the Bureau uniform.

Or is it *failure* of will that has ignited Donnato? Could the true source of his distress be the unbearable frisson (God knows, I'm feeling it) of a man and woman who have worked together twelve years, alone in the late afternoon, in not one but *three* empty motel rooms? No, no—of course we have a lid on it. Donnato is back with his wife after yet another separation. *Isn't he?*

If we continue to look at each other in this pleading way a minute longer, one of us will drift over the line, and that will tick off the obsession, and then we will be back in that sweet morass. We have been successful in avoiding it for years now, clean and sober despite the ache. It happened only once, and for good reason, in a wet field of strawberries, beneath the shuddering bellies of helicopters patrolling a military base—the kind of memory you can put on the wall and be happy just to look at for the rest of your life. He was going to leave his wife; then he wasn't. Finally, we had to put an end to the possibility and soldier on. It is an adjustment we have learned to make, swiftly and silently, a dozen times a day, often right under the noses of our instinctively suspicious FBI colleagues. Nobody is watching us now, which makes it imperative that I sit down in a chair as far away as possible.

"I take it back," I say, crossing my legs primly. "Steve was not meeting a woman."

Donnato accepts the move without a blink. "Steve *was* meeting someone, but he misjudged them badly and—"

His Nextel buzzes. It is Special Agent Jason Ripley, calling from L.A. Odd to look at, because his strikingly milky skin and white-blond coloring are like some kind of an albino rose, Jason remains to the bone the lanky son of a Midwest farmer who was raised to behave deferentially around his elders yet give no ground to wickedness or sin. He is, in the FBI garden of belief, a perennial.

Donnato and I are both patched in on our cells to L.A.

I start the debrief. "Julius Emerson Phelps was born in Ohio—"

Donnato: "Based on what evidence?"

"There was a flying ear of corn on his cap. I learned in uc school that when you see a flying ear of corn, ask."

"Was it red and yellow, with wings?" Jason pipes up.

"How do you know?"

"That's an old barn sign. The DeKalb Company is a big seed grower. The flying corn is the logo; it used to be on barns all over when I was growing up. But DeKalb is based in Illinois."

"No," I say patiently. "The subject plainly stated that he was born in DeKalb, Ohio, and picked corn when he was in high school. He provided a detailed description of lying on a mattress on a contraption with wheels—"

This being his first counterterrorism case, Jason is anxious to make everything right on the status report he will send to headquarters in Washington, D.C.

"Sorry, ma'am, but it doesn't track."

"Which doesn't?"

"He might have picked corn in *Ohio,* but the DeKalb Company is based in *Illinois.* They have a corn festival every year. I won the Diaper Derby when I was two years old."

Donnato and I exchange a look and say nothing.

Jason fumbles. "I know. The Diaper Derby. It's kind of embarrassing."

Another pause.

"Ana?" Donnato asks finally. "Are you sure you heard Mr. Phelps correctly?"

I glare at him.

"I heard it right."

"Run Megan Tewksbury and Julius Emerson Phelps through NCIC," Donnato instructs the kid. "Search the databases for birth certificates, Social Security numbers, driving records, military records, and arrests for Phelps in Illinois *and* Ohio."

We hang up and sit in silence in the motel room, where the once-savory remains of Caribbean takeout are starting to smell like a back street in the Yucatán.

"I need you to trust me," I say after a while. "Why do you second-guess me in front of a rookie?"

"I'm not second-guessing you."

"You are. Not only on Megan as a source but on a simple piece of intel, too. Did the subject say *Ohio* or *Illinois*?"

My voice is rising. My heart is beating fast.

"Look—" He takes off his reading glasses and rubs his forehead. "Here's the thing—"

"I know the thing. You shot a guy. A lot of people didn't share that judgment call, or the way it worked out with OPR. So you're feeling . . . scrutinized."

"But not by you?"

"Not by me," says my partner, and his eyes are soft.

Eight

Against a wash of middle-aged do-gooders perking along through the lobby of the convention hotel, with their important name tags and goodie bags of giveaways, radical leader Bill Fontana stands out like a gangsta hit man.

He has shaved his head since our most recent surveillance photos, which makes his cheekbones seem wider, and ears, with multiple earrings, stick out like a Chihuahua's. Tall and muscle-bound, he is dressed in black, with heavy work boots meant to rip the shit out of laboratory doors. Despite a throng of groupies, he looks less like a media star and more of what he really is—an ex-con. You can spot it a mile away. He's got what they call a "joint body"—the overdeveloped torso, the bullying prison strut.

I am not here alone. Undercover detectives from the Portland police department have mixed with the crowd, some posing as reporters to document the faces. You can bet if these good liberals knew they were being covertly photographed, they'd scream violation of civil rights. To protect my identity, the local cops do not know I exist; if my face surfaces in their reports, we're doing something right. Donnato, disguised by a couple of days' worth of beard, gold-rimmed glasses, and a beat-up denim jacket, is somewhere nearby.

This is not one of your great moments in espionage. All we did was walk through the door. The hotel is on a strip near the airport. You go up the escalator to the convention suite and buy a ticket for thirty bucks. If it's easy for us, it is easy for FAN, whose members, you can bet, are also working the room.

These people—excuse the expression—are sitting ducks for recruitment by terrorists. The affable retirees with big bellies and gray beards are not likely to be fashioning Molotov cocktails in their home entertainment centers during the commercial breaks, but the young guard, the lean and hungry male youth who gather around Fontana, with thin grasping fingers, and tattoos, and "I've-been-up-on-speed-for-thirty-six-hours" hair, just want to be bad—any kind of bad. Well, so does Darcy DeGuzman in her ratty purple parka.

"I'm a great admirer of yours," I tell Fontana, shaking his hand. "Going to prison, that was really brave."

"It isn't brave. It's the only choice. The earth is our only home and fighting for its constituency is a sacred war."

I give him a bedazzled smile and hold his brown eyes. "Bill, tell me how to fight and I'll do it."

"Create chaos," he advises. "On the edge of chaos, that's where change begins."

I'm glad that I am close enough to get a good look. His eyes are at once vacant and hostile.

"Radical resistance comes in lots of ways," he says. "Walk through these halls." He indicates the booths for farm sanctuaries, and organizations that save ducks from having their livers turned into foie gras. "You'll find your path."

Not surprisingly, given his glib style, Bill Fontana has a handler, a pretty Asian woman in a nice suit, who maneuvers him toward a couple of print reporters who ask about the story in *Willamette Weekly* about corruption at the BLM.

"Our wild horses are not for sale for the personal profit of government drones," Fontana says as their pens fly. "We refuse to allow free spirits of nature to become pawns in an elitist scheme to benefit the corporate ranching interests."

Donnato must be watching, because my cell vibrates.

"Fontana's on in fifteen minutes and the ballroom's packed," he reports.

"How's the crowd?"

"Tense. Something's up. I'm hearing Herbert Laumann from the BLM is going to show."

"Why?"

"He wants to debate. About the wild horses."

"That's not smart."

"Your hazelnut friends are in the food aisle," Donnato says, and we click off.

In spite of myself, the fragrance of rice soup and fried lentil crackers draws me to the food concessions. Among them is a booth for Willamette Hazelnut Farm, and sitting at the table behind golden piles of hazelnut brittle is Megan Tewksbury, stacking flyers.

"Megan! It's Darcy!"

She glances up and breaks into a smile. Then a big warm hug.

"You were awesome at Omar's the other night," she gushes. "That was thinking on your feet. You liberated over three hundred dollars."

"Hey, the cash register was open."

"The mustangs will benefit, I promise you that."

"What are you doing?"

"Organizing. Julius is too impatient for this kind of stuff."

Megan is more fluffed up than she was at the bar, wearing her business attire: a white shirt with an Indian vest embroidered with tiny mirrors, her hair loose and frizzy, lots of chunky silver jewelry.

I pick up a flyer. "Save Our Western Heritage" appears above a photograph of the most stirring animal I have ever seen, "Mesteno, legendary Kiger stallion." His ears are erect, his neck strong, and he has a fine muzzle and intelligent eyes. He is dun-colored, with darker legs, and the musculature of his body is athletic. His long flying mane and tail remind me of a children's book illustration.

"This is a mustang? He is stunningly beautiful."

"That's because he's free."

I have fallen in love with a horse. It is peculiar as hell.

"We've forgotten what freedom is," Megan goes on. "Mesteno is saying, This is the way it's supposed to be."

Something inside me melts. "It breaks your heart," I say, not quite understanding why.

"It *softens* your heart," Megan replies, correcting me. Her moist green eyes hold mine. "Will you come to our rally? We want to call attention to the deputy state director of the BLM slaughtering these animals. And *profiting* from it."

"Where?"

"At his son's school. When all the kids are getting out."

"I don't know. What about the son?"

"Nothing to do with him—nobody wants to hurt a child. We've been tracking Laumann. We know his routine and when he's there."

"Okay, I'm in. Hey, Bill Fontana's speaking. Are you going?"

"If Julius ever stops jabbering. He admires Fontana, and he wants to get over there. Just never ask him a question about the law."

The big man is holding forth with another guy his age. He is wearing a fresh pinstriped shirt and jeans, the frayed red suspenders, and a beanie over his ponytail because of the air-conditioning. His pal has asked if the school can legally force his daughter to dissect a frog. Now he's listening to Julius's answer with acute concentration, arms crossed, one hand thoughtfully pressed against his cheek. I can see why. Julius Emerson Phelps's intelligence is a breath of clarity in a sea of nutcakes.

"If your daughter is averse to cutting up a frog in biology class," Julius is saying, "I'm afraid she's on her own, Ralph."

Ralph ponders. "Can we argue it's against her religious beliefs?"

"Great thought, but there's no *legislation* in place to protect that belief when it comes to student dissection. Trust me. I have *written* model laws regarding alternatives to dissection in the classroom, but to my knowledge, no statute has ever been enacted." He checks his watch. To Megan: "We'd better head over to the ballroom. It's going to be a showdown."

"I'll close up," she says. "You get seats."

Julius, still lecturing, hurries off with his friend.

"Julius is a lawyer? I thought he was a farmer."

"He went to law school, but he doesn't practice. He helps folks out for free. Figures the advice is worth what they pay for it."

My cell phone buzzes.

"Just got a call from L.A." Donnato's voice is urgent. "Where are you?"

"At the hazelnut booth." I smile at Megan. She is locking the cash box.

"We have a situation," Donnato says. "Julius Emerson Phelps is an alias."

"That's interesting. I can't wait to talk to you about it."

"When the status report went to headquarters—bingo—the alias hit the computers. Julius Emerson Phelps was an infant who died of meningitis in DeKalb, Illinois, in 1949. This guy is an imposter who has taken on the name."

I watch the big man disappear down the hall. The last I heard, Ralph was asking for free counsel on his divorce.

"At this time we don't know who Phelps really is, or why he's living under an assumed identity. Exercise caution."

"Okay, Dad," I say cheerfully. "See you there."

I close the phone.

"That's my dad. He loves hazelnut brittle. Could I get a couple of pounds?"

Megan has already shouldered her handbag.

"You're packing up," I say apologetically, pocketing a card with the farm's phone number.

"Chocolate or regular?"

"Regular. Thank you."

She puts her bag down.

"I know we're in a rush, but—sorry—would you mind wrapping it up with some ribbon?"

"For a friend of the horses? Of course," Megan says graciously, and unrolls the cellophane.

Her fingerprints will be all over it.

Nine

A weighty mist invades the city, rain without really raining, beading up in beards and hair. The deserted streets are mirrorlike and slick. We, the protesters, are staked out for the anti-BLM rally in an artsy, mixed-race neighborhood dominated by gangs; even at 2:30 in the afternoon, the place feels edgy. A dozen of us huddle in a staging area beneath the defunct neon marquee of the Excelsior Theater, a plasterwork movie castle built in the twenties, long boarded over.

Megan is on the cell, listening to Julius track the target.

"There he goes. It's Laumann!" she reports excitedly as a burgundy government sedan sweeps by.

For a moment, we glimpse a profile of the BLM's deputy state director, a thin fortyish white male wearing a tan raincoat—like a character actor in a supporting role, cast because his unremarkable looks will not draw attention from the leading man. But, of course, all he desires is to be the leading man, which is why he squared off with Fontana at the convention. You can see it in the tense shoulders and self-important squint, like he's driving a vehicle of distinction, and, as the taillights flash in a spray off the road, in the decals that declare his support of the sheriff's office, the police and fire departments.

Herbert Laumann travels in the brotherhood of heroes.

"Where's he going?" I ask. "The school is the other way."

"He'll park in the red zone at the coffee place. He stops there every day, and every day he gets a refill of Irish vanilla," Megan replies. "Then he jumps back in the car and makes it over to the school just in time to cut a few people off and get a good spot in the car-pool line."

"You know his pattern."

"Julius taught us to do our homework."

"It was *so* easy," mocks a young man with a long neck and heavy black-framed glasses. "Laumann always gets a refill in his Bureau of Land Management nifty commuter mug."

Other protesters giggle and snort.

"To show he cares about the environment?"

"Because he's such a good guy."

I smile and nod approvingly. What a bunch of dipshits.

"What's the plan?"

"When Julius tells us, we head up the hill. St. Luke's is on the right. The kids will just be getting out."

"Is there security at the school?"

"This is Portland, Darcy."

"Okay, but what about Laumann's son?"

"Alex?" Megan says the name as if she's somehow claimed it.

"How's he going to react?" I ask eagerly.

Darcy craves action. Excitement. Blood on the walls.

"Nobody wants to hurt a child, but *hopefully* Laumann will be so humiliated in front of his son that he'll finally get the message."

Her cell again. She looks up with eager eyes. "Julius is at the school. It's a go."

A swell of anticipation sends people rushing to their cars to retrieve homemade signs and lock up watches and rings and wallets in the unlikely event of arrest.

Laumann rolls down a fogged-up window and sets the hot coffee mug in the cup holder. He makes sure to flash the BLM logo every place he gets a refill, eager to set an example of earth-friendly recycling. As deputy state director, he *is* the government—not an easy role these days.

Just this week, the psychos at FAN accused him on its Web site—

and it made the legitimate press—that he has been stealing the horses he's supposed to protect. Since then, the phone and fax lines to his office have been jammed with threats of violence against *anyone* who supports the Wild Horse and Burro Program—including secretaries, suppliers of tack and hay, even veterinarians. He thinks he kicked that poser Bill Fontana's ass pretty good at the animal rights convention, calling the story "a fabricated radical conspiracy," but in truth, Herbert Laumann needs the money. His civil service pay grade is way out of line with tuition for a private Catholic school, and Laumann and his wife want the boy to have a good education, and to be safe. Even in this transitional neighborhood, where angry white youth patrol the streets, Laumann (who grew up in a farming community) believes his son is less likely to come into harm's way than in the public schools.

St. Luke's is on a hill, protected by wrought-iron gates—a shabby plot of dull redbrick buildings and a couple of elms. The bright spots on campus are a Romanesque Church built in 1891 and the indoor tennis courts. Laumann's twelve-year-old son is a talented player, and St. Luke's has a good team, which makes it almost worth the price tag. Waiting for scrawny, long-legged Alex to come through the gates in his blue plaid uniform, toting his racket in a junior varsity bag, yakking it up with scores of red-cheeked, cheerful friends, allows Laumann to believe, for fifteen minutes in the car-pool line, that his insanely overstressed, overburdened, slightly criminal life might be worth something.

Carrying signs but silent still, we reach the entrance to the school. The gates pull back automatically, right on time, and the sidewalk becomes alive with the random energy of a couple hundred bouncing children in blue plaid uniforms. The engines in the line of waiting cars fire one by one, and Laumann sits up with anticipation. They have a new baby girl at home who isn't doing well—respiratory problems, underweight, and waking in the night. Whenever he stops moving, even for a minute, he falls into an exhausted daze. The weather is still soupy and the wipers make it worse, so Laumann hasn't turned them on. Looking through the watery glass, he never sees us coming.

At first, we mix in with the crowd—all of us with the same greasy hair, grungy denim, and attitude as the neighborhood types. Many of us are not much older than the miscreants on the corner, or the seniors at St. Luke's. Moving in clusters of three and four, we wave our banners: MURDERER! WE KNOW WHAT YOU DID LAST SUMMER!

The schoolchildren slow down.

"Save the wild horses!"

"Save our American heritage!"

Chanting in unison, we, the protesters, bulldoze through the students, whose faces have softened with confusion and fear.

My heart is beating hard. The adrenaline rush has hit both sides. Parents are getting out of cars and clogging the sidewalk. Laumann jumps into the role of deputy state director, striding through the scene with cell phone to his ear, reporting the action to 911. He has been through this before, and means to assert his authority, but then on the police recording, later, in the midst of a calm recital, you will be able to hear his naked panic: *"They're going after my son!"*

Two agitators have surrounded Alex, chanting, *"Your daddy kills horses!"*

Alex's blue eyes are wide as he stares at one angry face, then another.

"Your daddy kills horses!"

Louder, closer, not giving way. One of them, a girl with a couple of nose rings, tries to force Alex to take a stuffed horse, dripping red.

Harassing a twelve-year-old was not the game plan.

Nobody wants to hurt a child.

But Darcy is committed to the cause.

"Free the horses!" I shout.

"Fuck you, motherfucker," the boy yells, and hits the girl with the nose rings in the knees with his tennis racket and keeps on swinging.

Laumann's running through the mob, awkward in a business suit and the raincoat, face contorted with desperation, screaming at someone behind me to stop. I turn and catch sight of a streaking figure—a young man wearing a backpack and a denim jacket with neo-Nazi ornamentation. I had not seen him in the staging area under the marquee, but now he is barreling like a missile directly for Alex. *POP!* Like a firecracker, and the child staggers, eyes in shock, splattered with blood.

The small explosion triggers utter terror. Parents there to pick up their children find themselves grabbing them and rolling under cars, or dragging them away, running wildly.

I stay where I am for one slow-motion fraction of a second as Laumann gets to his son.

"Alex, are you shot? Show me where!" he cries, frantic hands all over the boy, who is breathing hard but standing on his feet.

"I'm okay, Dad—they didn't do anything."

"Didn't do anything?"

Laumann pulls Alex—he's walking—out of the crowd. The white shirt of his school uniform is streaked with crimson, which has grotesquely stained the sidewalk, along with Laumann's raincoat and Alex's pale and freckled cheeks.

"I'm o-*kay!*" He twists away from his father's anxious touch. "Leave me alone! It wasn't a gun; it's just red paint."

But where Laumann grew up, you slaughtered your own meat, and he knows the slippery consistency and sickly iron smell. It's blood—real cow's blood. Filthy, unclean putrescence, degrading innocent children.

The father's hands become fists. "They're dead," Laumann vows. "They are *dead*. Come with me; let's wipe this off."

Someone has found a water bottle, and now Laumann attempts to soak a tissue and cleanse his son's face, but his hands are shaking and the tissue dissolves.

"Dad, you have to chill," instructs his twelve-year-old soldier.

Laumann wipes his own wet eyes and whispers hoarsely, *"Where are the police?"*

Ten

Waiting by the window, I keep watch for the connect. Moonlight decants through the slats of the blinds the way I remember moonlight as a child—so steady and substantial, it seemed as if you could wash your face with it, a potion of radiance that seeped through the drowsing windows of the brick house in Long Beach, penetrating the gloom of my grandfather's world.

From Darcy's window, I can see two girl punkers with hair like crested Gila monsters locking up the Cosmic Café. Terribly young and terribly thin, one of them is pregnant. Doo-wop resounds from the African drumming center. The girls put their arms around each other, matching steps along the darkened avenue.

The war is escalating in our little world. The techs are calling the attack on twelve-year-old Alex Laumann a "blood bomb." The best evidence for this comes from analysis of the bloodstain patterns—the "spines" of the splatter pattern on the sidewalk and on the clothing of the victim, which tell you the amount of energy transfer. The smaller the droplets, the greater the force that projected them. The force of cow's blood as it spat out of the backpack was created by a small amount of gunpowder, detonated by the attacker as he approached the child.

We are back to the signature device that killed Steve Crawford, which is tied to the firebomb that blew up Ernie's Meats on the docks of Portland, and possibly other unsolved attacks over the past years credited to FAN: a fire at a genetic-engineering company that resulted in fifty thousand dollars' worth of damage; two explosive devices using Tovex that went off at 3:00 a.m. at the construction site of a new pharmaceutical facility, destroying three concrete trucks and causing the abandonment of a twenty-million-dollar project.

Megan Tewksbury had to have known about the blood bomb and the mysterious young man, which is, finally, the best argument for infiltrating her. At last, the Operation Wildcat team agrees with what I've been saying all along—until we can ID the person using the alias Julius Emerson Phelps, Megan is our best way in.

A black van pulls up and double-parks in the street below, taillights blinking. Angling sideways at the window to get a better view, I see two figures emerge and open the rear doors. This is the unit I have been waiting for. I am at the door to the apartment even before there is knocking, urgent and sharp, like the Gestapo in the night.

"*Darcy?* Are you in there? *Darcy DeGuzman!* Open the door."

I unlock the door. "People are sleeping!"

Two shaggy hipsters stand in the hall. One is a white male with silver earrings and baggy India-print pants. The other is a gregarious African-American female whose long cornrows are woven with beads. Both wear heavy rubber boots. Their faces are sweaty and streaked with mud. The stench of hay and dead things is a sharp hit to the nose.

"Are you Darcy DeGuzman?"

"Who are you?"

They show their creds. FBI, Portland field office.

"We have your ducks."

The male agent drags a plastic bin over the threshold. It contains four confused white ducks.

"I didn't think it would be *ducks*."

"Those were the orders."

"Get them out of here. I can't deal with this."

"We just stole 'em," says the female. "*No way* we're taking 'em back. I'm not crawling through bird poop again in this lifetime."

"Wait a minute. What's wrong with *him*?"

One of the ducks is lying down in the bin.

"It's sick."

"Why'd you take a sick one?"

"What's the difference? They're all gonna die." He points to green circles drawn around their necks. "That means they're marked for slaughter."

Okay, this is absurd.

"What am I supposed to do with a sick duck?"

The female yawns. "Call your supervisor."

"That is incredibly unhelpful, ma'am."

"Sorry we woke you up," she snaps. "We enjoy doing the shit work for Los Angeles."

And they're sure to slam the door.

Three ducks are wandering around the apartment. The worst part is, it was my dumb idea to use rescue animals in order to get closer to Megan. I was thinking more along the line of puppies, but I know why Angelo authorized the poultry heist—to make it look like the work of dedicated radicals.

To get foie gras, a gourmet pâté, you force-feed the birds until their livers swell. French farmwives have been stuffing ducks and geese for hundreds of years, but it's not so quaint when they're kept in electrified metal cages with tubes down their throats. Activists have long been onto it as a rallying point. Foie gras is gruesome. It's elitist. It's what keeps people like Megan Tewksbury up at night.

I call her at Willamette Hazelnut Farm, using the number on the card. It is five o'clock in the morning. The apartment already smells like the monkey house at the zoo.

"Friends of mine broke into a poultry farm last night—"

"What friends?" Megan is on it. She must get these wake-up calls often.

"Freedom fighters, let's just say. They had no place to take them, so they left them with me. What do I do with a bunch of ducks?"

"This is not an easy time," Megan says warily. "Are you on a cell phone?"

"Yes."

"We have to hang up."

"Okay, but listen—here's why I'm calling—one of the ducks is sick!"

"What's it doing?"

"Lying down. I think it's throwing up."

"Are there whole regurgitated kernels?"

"Seems like."

There are shifting sounds, as if she's getting out of bed. The phone cuts out and then comes back.

"I'm very worried about this." I can hear it in her voice. "We need to find an avian vet."

I didn't even know such people existed. "Where?"

"How soon can you get down here?"

Back in L.A., Donnato does not answer his cell. I leave a message that I am heading south with a carload of ducks.

Those patches of green I saw from the airplane turn out to be fields of rye slashed by the interstate. They claim this is the "grass-seed capital of the world," and I can feel the pollen stinging my eyes. For another hour, there is nothing but sheep and rain. The ducks, of course, immediately climbed out of the bin and are now floating around the car like unruly balloons. One of them is flapping away in the passenger seat, and I am getting strange looks from other drivers.

As we pass a massive plywood plant, the cedary scent of sawdust fills the car, and I'm starting to feel relatively optimistic about pulling this off—until catching sight of a large mocking clown face, like the head of a court jester who failed to amuse, stuck on a pole at the entrance to an RV park.

The RV park is ominously called Thrillville.

I turn off the highway onto slick blacktop—another forty miles of vineyards and pastureland, fairgrounds and farm-equipment rentals, into the hills, past lonely ranch houses and ramparts of woods, down a couple of forking unmarked dirt roads, and finally a driveway that bumps into a shabby farmstead.

The two-story house is so deeply settled into the grassy overgrowth, it appears to have absorbed groundwater up the walls and across the roof. Brown rot grows across the siding and spreads along the junction of the gabled dormers, where old shake shingles are peeling up.

I stop the car on a patch of gravel in a light mist, wary of the country quiet. I did not imagine the place would be this isolated. The immense time and distance between here and backup is almost palpable.

The house is neglected, but the farm seems functional. There are red barnlike outbuildings and a large silver greenhouse made of inflated plastic sections, a tractor, buckets, ladders, an old steel swing set, a limp American flag on a pole stuck in a bunker of crumbling concrete.

A fat white cat is ambling across the grass, so I make sure the ducks are safely in the car, careful not to close the door on their silly feet. The effort to contain them, and the long drive with zero sleep, is making me really, *really* want to hand them off to Megan.

The scent of lavender grows stronger and more alluring as I walk down the drive. There, lurking behind the house, is the hazelnut orchard, squatty trees with short trunks and thin branches, planted with mathematical precision, file upon file, clean as a mechanical drawing, every specimen eerily alike.

I see a large man in a blue jacket moving in and out of the rows, carrying something—pruning shears.

He disappears. I follow into the trees.

Julius Emerson Phelps snips a bright green sucker. He moves deliberately through the trees, parade perfect and silent. The jaws of the shears snap precisely.

Overcast days like this are flat. They narrow the perspective, as if each of us has been made in two dimensions, like that painting of the lion and the brown-breasted girl with the guitar. Heat rises from the earth and the mind hums with emptiness, like the intervals between the trees, like the leafy spaces through which the sunlight will penetrate, all the way to the ground. That is the tree farmer's job right now—to thin and sculpt—so the foliage will grow back thickly, so if you stood beneath these canopies four months from today, 100 percent of the sky would be obliterated.

Julius Emerson Phelps is the general, and the young trees are in training. They are training to widen the spread of their branches like bowls to catch the sun. As he leaves a trail of sprouts on the ground like casualties, his face recalls the trancelike look he wore at the juke-box back at Omar's, lost in the taunting sleaze of Blue Oyster Cult, until suddenly he straightens up. The crows are talking to him no doubt.

Maybe he noticed the nondescript car parked beside the house, a red 1993 Civic, one he has never seen before, with Oregon tags. The lady seems to go with the car—disheveled but clean, long, curly dark hair, a pleasing face, faintly exotic-looking, almond skin (Italian? Spanish?), average frame, or maybe smaller than average, but carrying forward with a confident stride. His eyes drop to the boots: worn. He withdraws behind another row. Observes. The pruning shears are weighty in his hands.

I step through his silent cathedral like a tourist, staring up.

He comes on me from behind.

"You're trespassing."

"Sorry! Didn't see you."

"Sure you did."

"I'm Darcy. We met at the bar. I was also at the rally at the school."

"I have no memory of meeting you anywhere."

The moment he steps from the trees, a sexual force springs off him like slow claws down your back.

"Really? I'm hurt. What kind of trees are these?"

"Ornamental filberts."

"Megan said they were hazelnuts."

"Hazelnuts *are* filberts," he says impatiently. "One and the same. We just don't use the word *filberts* anymore. People don't like the sound of it."

"Kind of like 'You're trespassing'?" I smile. "That doesn't sound very friendly."

"How do I know you're a friend?"

I give him flirty. "I can't believe you don't remember—I stole three hundred bucks from the till and gave it to the cause, when I could have gone shopping." I pretend to be entranced by the willowy branches just sprouting tiny leaves. "This is amazing. How do you do it? Every tree is the same."

His big developed shoulders shrug. His hair is in a dirty rat tail down the back. He wears a T-shirt under a grimy hooded sweatshirt, and a blue nylon jacket with a stripe down the arm. It was cold this morning. His light-colored jeans are dirt-stained at the knees.

"That's the way my mind works," he says.

I let him watch as I take in his eyes. I see a luminous intelligence. Seeking. Perching at a distance. Holding back.

"I brought the ducks."

"What ducks?"

"They were stolen from a foie gras farm last night. Megan is expecting me."

"When?"

In the muffled silence of the orchard, our voices are undistorted and strangely intimate.

"She said as soon as possible. One is sick. She was going to get a vet."

His eyes skim my unzipped windbreaker.

"I need to pat you down."

"Excuse me?"

"Security check. In case you're wearing a wire."

"A *wire*?"

Electric shock goes through me, as if I really am wearing a listening device and he can tell. I stare at the crows walking cocksure across the rows and shrug with absolute wonder.

"What am I, the bird police? Why would I wear a wire? I wouldn't even know how."

Don't make a thing out of it.

"Give me your backpack."

"Megan didn't say I'd have to go through a metal detector."

"Megan likes to think the world's a happy place." He finds a wallet. "Darcy DeGuzman?"

"Yes."

He finds my cell phone and slips it in his pocket.

"Hey! I drove down here in the frigging middle of the night!

Megan's very upset, in case you didn't know. *There's a sick bird in the car!*"

"Open your arms and legs."

I comply, but if my heart keeps going like this, it will kill me.

"May I ask what you're doing?"

"I'm just an old bandit," he says. "Just doing my thing. If I touch you inappropriately, you have permission to kick me in the balls."

"If I have permission, it won't be any fun."

His hands are expert, like I'm a perp spread-eagled on the hood of a car.

"Are you done?" I ask Julius. "Okay?"

"No."

"What do you mean, 'no'?"

"You can leave the animals and go."

"I need my cell phone back." I stamp my foot.

He replies with a sardonic smile. If I'm reading it right, the subtext is, I could have you right now in the dirt.

"Let me tell you something, darlin'. I am not the one who made me paranoid."

An instinctive part of him was watching from the moment I drove down the road. And it did not have to be his eyes.

I am not the one who made me paranoid. Then who did?

He flips my cell phone open.

A screen door slams and Megan strides angrily across the yard, followed by a tall young woman in hip-sucking jeans, with a perfect face and boyishly cut blond hair.

"Where are they?" Megan demands.

Julius's smile fades. "She says in the car."

"Why are you standing around playing games?"

"We don't have a clue who she is." He's scrolling through my cell phone.

Megan rips it from his hands and gives it back to me. "Oh please. We have an emergency."

"Watch your mouth," Julius says, his voice hard. "Before you say something we all regret."

"I could give a damn," Megan mutters, already pulling at the door of my car. "Thank you for doing this, Darcy. Sara, help me out here."

Sara, the long-legged rescuing angel, shoos the ducks out of the car as Megan lifts the bin. The sick one is too weak to raise its head.

"I am really, really afraid for this one," Megan says.

The girl strokes it. "He's not going to make it, is he?"

The screen door slams again, and a young man about seventeen, a baby neo-Nazi with a buzzed head, appears holding a shotgun.

It's the kid who streaked through the rally carrying the blood bomb.

"What the fuck?" he announces.

"Slammer!" Julius says. "Get back in the house."

Lower the gun, knucklebrain.

"Thought you needed help," he says.

"I'll tell you when I need help, pal."

In response, Slammer fires the gun into the trees. It is as if every living being on the farm is hit with the reverberation. Ducks flee in panic, dogs bark insanely, and I have the impression a herd of cows is trying to get out of the barn.

Sheared-off branches fall onto the roof, then drop to the garden in slow motion.

"He didn't mean it," Sara says, shaking visibly.

Megan puts the bin with the dying duck on her hip, an arm around the girl, and walks them both away.

Julius has taken the gun from Slammer, who surrenders it with a smirk.

"We have a visitor," he says quietly. To me: "You can leave now."

"What about the vet?"

Julius's voice is military, clipped. "Get back on the road and forget how you got here."

The inside of the car smells like a sour old pillow. Pinfeathers and droppings are everywhere. I turn on the engine and wobble off. Less than a quarter mile from the farm, I hear the chilling echo of a second shot. I could assign importance to it, or accept that I will never know.

I am still reeling with a kind of exhilaration, still dumbly clutching the cell phone, when it vibrates in my hand.

"You're not there yet, I hope," Donnato says.

"Where?"

"The farm."

"On my way back. Why?"

He curses urgently. "Headquarters did not want you to make contact at this time."

"Headquarters?" My stomach lurches. "How did I mess up now?"

My fingers tighten on the wheel in anticipation of the chastising to come. The mocking clown head on a stick is out there, a couple of miles down the road.

Thrillville.

"We have identified Julius Emerson Phelps," Donnato says. "We believe his real name is Dick Stone. And he's one of us. A former FBI agent who went bad in the seventies. If this is the guy, we have a potential problem."

Eleven

Everyone sits down in a conference room in Los Angeles. It is a discreet briefing, with shades lowered. The major players in Operation Wildcat have been assembled, including the FBI's second in command from Washington, Deputy Director Peter Abbott. All of FBIHQ reports to him. Son of a former congressman from Oregon, a decorated Vietnam veteran with a degree in international law, he's the guy who travels in an armored limousine, ready to assume authority if the director takes a bullet. From the sound of him, he can hardly wait. Beneath the crisp gray suit and red silk tie, you can almost hear the purring motor of ambition.

The deputy director seems to have a personal interest in Operation Wildcat. The Abbotts are a founding Portland family that made a fortune in railroads and diversified to construction and technology. Over the past thirty years, their real estate holdings in the Northwest have skyrocketed by developing the right-of-ways for defunct train tracks. Institutions like the Abbotts find it bad for the business climate when insurgent ecoterrorist groups blow up concrete trucks and laboratories. Almost as long as Peter Abbott has been with the Bureau, his family has pressured Washington to deal with FAN and ELF. Now that he *is* Washington, you can imagine the tone of drinks with Dad on the deck of the summer compound in the San Juan Islands.

But the younger Abbott's obligatory interest turned ravenous when we uncovered Dick Stone.

"He is a traitor. To his country. To his fellow agents," he says emphatically. "Make no mistake. He is not one of us."

"We've got a former FBI agent who's bad," Galloway agrees, "with federal warrants outstanding. He could have robbed banks and set up killings in other states. The dilemma is, when do we get Stone? Now, and blow the operation? Or do we play along with him and hope to get the bigger thing, which is FAN?"

"*I know this man,*" Peter Abbott says. "I was his supervisor out here in the seventies when we were going after the Weather Underground. Stone started out all bushy-tailed, got hooked on drugs and liberated women, and went over to the other side. Years of living with scum have made him one of *them.*"

"We were wondering why you're here, sir," Angelo interjects. He has not changed his Hawaiian shirt getup for the visitor. "There wasn't a hell of a lot of interest in FAN from headquarters when Steve Crawford was killed. L.A. had to fight for Operation Wildcat. What made you get on a plane?"

"I was deeply saddened by that agent's death," Abbott intones on key, "but enraged by the fact that a man I trained was responsible. He threw all our principles right out the window. Simply put, the identification of Dick Stone has caused us to reframe the mission. Stone is a dangerous fugitive who may have ties to international terrorism. The purpose of Operation Wildcat has shifted."

Nobody disagrees. We are all in awe of being in the same room with the adviser to the next Republican presidential candidate. Rumor is that Peter Abbott will resign from the Bureau to run the national campaign.

Charisma. Conviction. Peter Abbott has both. You wouldn't think so from the cherubic face and well-fed cheeks, the big sloping forehead and close-cut hair that starts halfway down his skull. Besides, I never trust people from Washington who wear those rimless glasses that try to make it look as if they aren't wearing glasses at all.

I have been lounging at the end of the conference table, wearing the ragged-out purple parka, dirty jeans, and work boots, insolently spinning a pen across the polished wood. For a dozen years, I have appeared in these halls perfectly put together in a pressed suit and laundered blouse, with manicured nails and polished shoes. Just off the plane from the clean air of Oregon, I haven't washed my hair since yesterday, and I find it unacceptable to listen to the politicking in this suffocating room.

There are grander themes to respond to.

The wild mustangs, for example. Mesteno, the legendary Kiger stallion—who here gives a damn about him?

Darcy DeGuzman.

"I understand the case turned on a single fingerprint off some . . . *hazelnut brittle?*" Abbott raises an ironic eyebrow. "My North Carolina grandma used to make brittle. I haven't thought of that in years."

Appreciative chuckles.

"I understand Agent Grey did some quick thinking and snagged the suspect's prints."

I sit up, surprised to find him studying me with penetrating sea blue eyes.

"Good job."

"Thank you, sir."

And not only that; he also reads verbatim of my role in identifying Dick Stone. How Megan's fingerprints on the hazelnut wrapper caused a hit off the NCIC data bank. How Megan Tewksbury turned out to be an alias and that the fingerprints of the woman using that name matched those of Laurel Williams, a young environmental scientist at UC Berkeley who disappeared in the seventies. Laurel was arrested during a protest march, and while in the custody of the Oakland police, she vanished. There was an investigation and the family sued the police department, but she never turned up. Nobody could explain how the young woman had escaped. If she'd escaped. A left-wing conspiracy theory persists that Laurel Williams was beaten to death in custody and disposed of in San Francisco Bay.

Abbott produces a surveillance photo from an environmental

protest that took place on the Columbia River Gorge in the early seventies. Against a haze of wooded cliffs, a young lady with a heartrendingly unspoiled face is engaged in an angry shouting match with a fortyish white male in a suit. I can see in her righteousness the same woman who tried to stop the fight in the bar. The confrontation here is on the edge of violence. Professor Laurel Williams has literally draped herself in an American flag, looking like an avenging Statue of Liberty—and even in black and white, the senior Abbott, sporting a curly 'fro, is red in the face. Protesters surge toward the podium, fingers stretching in the peace sign. Somewhere in the crowd is our young undercover agent Dick Stone.

"Is that the esteemed congressman from Oregon?" Angelo asks.

Abbott nods. "That's my father. Nice sideburns, Dad." He waits for the laugh. "Thanks to Ana Grey's outstanding work, we now know that Laurel Williams and former FBI agent Dick Stone are alive and well and living under assumed identities. When I was supervisor, Dick Stone was working undercover up in Berkeley to infiltrate the Weather Underground, a bunch of radicals who wanted to bring the Vietnam War home—literally blow up the government. Then he drops out of sight. There was speculation that Stone joined the subculture—"

"*Speculation?*" Angelo scoffs. "The Bureau's always made him out to be disloyal, violent hippie scum."

"We believed he might have been involved in bank robberies and bombings along with the Weathermen," Abbott says. "He was trained in munitions in the Army. But how did you tie Dick Stone to Laurel Williams?" he asks, still looking at me.

"Special Agent Dick Stone was the last one to sign out the prisoner, Laurel Williams, in order to accompany her to court in San Francisco for arraignment," I say. "Neither one showed up. At some point, he took the name Julius Emerson Phelps, who was an infant who died in DeKalb, Illinois, in 1949."

"You and I might be the only ones old enough to remember"— Galloway shamelessly ogles Abbott for attention—"but that's how the Weathermen went underground. They'd go to the graveyard, find babies who died the same year they were born, and apply for that baby's birth certificate, saying it was theirs and they'd lost it. Then they could get a driver's license and Social Security card. In those days, there was no correlation between birth and death certificates. No tracking system.

"Stone told Agent Grey that he was born in Ohio as a deliberate misdirection so that if anybody checked, they would not find Julius Emerson Phelps in that state and maybe just give up. It was another layer of deception. One more possible escape route."

Peter Abbott nods and opens a file. "Let's see what we've got here."

"It's a love story!" I announce to a dozen sets of startled eyes. "The greatest love story ever told! She's a radical professor; he's an under-cover FBI agent. They fall in love. He busts her out of jail and they join the revolution. Now they're old and gray, still together, still fighting for the cause."

Peter Abbott sends me a squinty, patient smile and drinks some water. There is a moment of silence.

"We have a former agent who flipped." Galloway waves an unlit cigar impatiently. "That's the whole deal right there."

He taps Stone's rookie ID photograph, which shows a handsome, square-jawed young man wearing a white shirt and a suit with narrow lapels and a skinny tie. He has the steely, unspoiled look of a new cadet. Invincible confidence.

It stops my mind to imagine that the same hazelnut farmer who builds bombs and gets off on Blue Oyster Cult went through the Academy in Quantico, just like I did. That once upon a time, we shared the same ideals.

"That's the way my mind works," he said of the hazelnut trees.

Military discipline and control.

"He was a silver-spoon kid from Connecticut with a law degree from Yale," Galloway raps out. "Gung ho on the Bureau, wanted to be led the right way and do the right thing. He starts out on a moral crusade but gets corrupted by the forces he's mingling with—drug dealers, radicals. Apparently, he had a powerful father on Wall Street."

"It's always about the father." Angelo winks grotesquely at Peter Abbott with his bad eye.

"Maybe part of it was rebellion," Galloway says, "but we didn't have undercover school and contact agents back then. These single guys had no support system, nothing to pull them back to our side. The subculture was their best friend. Stone was in his twenties, let's remember, living with the hippies and vulnerable to their influence. They told him America was wrong. Capitalism was wrong. The war in Vietnam was wrong. Marxism was right. Law enforcement meant working for the Establishment. Does that jibe with your impression of Stone at the time?" he asks Abbott.

"He was stubborn. Not a team player."

"Agent Grey worked up a profile of the bomber who made the signature device that killed Steve. Older. Impatient. Practical. Doesn't care about perfection."

Abbott: "I've read it."

Galloway nods. "There are still some people in the Bureau who think Stone got a bum deal."

"From *us*?" Abbott asks incredulously.

"That he took the fall for our failed policies. Spying on civilians did not turn out to be a popular song."

People shift uncomfortably, loyalty prickling. We give it our all, every day. Don't ask us to justify the past.

Galloway shrugs. "There was no understanding of the psychological vise you put someone in when they go deep cover. It's not easy to assimilate back."

Angelo: "At this point, what does headquarters want?"

"We want Stone."

Galloway: "Do we walk in with federal warrants and blow the operation? Or do we see where this is going? This could be bigger than Stone. We don't know. We're just getting our arms around it."

"I'll tell you one thing." Angelo is leaning forward, elbows on the table. It is interesting that he in his narco threads and I in my Oregon grunge have cornered one end of the table: two actors still in wardrobe; street players in a room of merchants. "We should install a listening device in Omar's bar. Put undercovers there around the clock. If that's where Stone hangs out, and where they buy and sell, it's likely he gets his explosives there, and Steve Crawford was following the trail."

"Done," says Abbott. "I understand Agent Grey is embedded in the cell?"

"I'm not in bed with them yet, sir."

Galloway shoots me a warning look, but Abbott only chuckles.

"Stone won't let her on the farm," Galloway explains. "His paranoia is aroused. She's got to make her bones with the organization."

"We've been kicking around a sting operation." I sense Abbott's support and decide to cash in the chips. "The BLM is doing its annual roundup of the wild horses. They cull the weak ones from the herd, put them up for adoption, and send the rest back to the wild. It's called 'a gather.' We don't like it."

"*We?*"

"Me and my homies in the movement. The BLM uses helicopters to run the horses down. *We* think it's cruel. Megan Tewksbury, aka Laurel Williams, told me right before I came down here that they're organizing to free the mustangs as soon as they're in the corrals. If I get myself arrested, it would prove my commitment. Get me access to whatever's going on at the farm."

"We've got the tech support in motion for deep cover," Donnato says. "They should be bringing Ana up a secure phone."

Peter Abbott addresses me carefully. "You will be up against a skilled undercover operative with a long-simmering grudge against the U.S. government."

"I know."

"Do you have any doubts about continuing?"

"Why would that even cross my mind?"

Abbott's expression is predatory, like that of a tiger carefully placing one paw after the other in a nest of snakes.

What does he want?

"I understand you've gone through critical-incident training."

I stand, parka flying, looking like a raving homeless person among the suits. "What are you implying, sir?"

Donnato: "Take it easy."

Abbott: "I'm wondering about your emotional stability."

"Not an issue. I've been certified for duty. I've been living with the bad guys, taking calculated risks every day, and it's paying off. I know the territory. Let me get in and I'll get this guy."

Peter Abbott doesn't lift that wise, prowling stare from my face.

"Remaining undercover, knowing who he is, will be difficult. The mission has changed," he reiterates evenly. "We are asking you to occupy close quarters with an agent that you know has gone milk-sour. It's a psychological minefield."

"I am able and committed."

He folds his clean white fingers.

"Thank you, Agent Grey. Would you mind stepping out of the room?"

"A covert operation is still the way to go," I insist. "I formally request to stay on as the undercover—"

"He realizes that," says Galloway, interrupting me.

I have noticed a good boss knows when to save you from yourself.

I gather my stuff and leave. Donnato, playing with his handcuffs, does not look up. He's on the boys' team now.

Exiting the intensity of the conference room to the quiet bull pen, I walk an aimless circle, lost in the desert. Rosalind, an administrative assistant who has worked at the Bureau for more than thirty years, gets up from her desk and pads over like a little engine, huffing and puffing with asthma.

"Hot in the kitchen?" she inquires gently.

"Like walking on coals. I think I'm out."

I set my backpack down and unscrew a jar of oatmeal cookies, inhaling the calming scent of raisins and brown sugar. I suppose the two of us make a funny pair commiserating at the coffee machine— me all wired, down a few pounds, wearing scuzzies, Rosalind wizened and round, in a black dress with cheap gold buckles, sporting processed hair. She can hardly walk on her swollen ankles, but even the Bureau wouldn't dare let her go.

"Don't let them get to you, honey. The men like to pretend they know what's going on, but it's barely controlled mayhem. You should have seen them with their tails between their legs whenever the director came out."

"J. Edgar Hoover came to Los Angeles?"

"Oh, yes," says Rosalind, fishing a vanilla wafer from a bag. "When the director was coming, you had to paint the whole office all over again."

"No kidding."

"I got sent home one time because I was wearing pants."

"You couldn't wear pants?"

"Uh-uh. Ladies could wear a pants *suit*. That was okay, but not a pair of slacks. No way. That's how it worked. That's the way things got done. Now, everything's a mess."

I feel uneasy, shifting in my boots. Already I have missed this place. I almost never feel this connected anywhere else. Rosalind's stories are gems in the repository of family history, and usually when she starts talking this way, it's the high point of the day. But in Darcy's clothes, through Darcy's ears, the Bureau sounds nothing but repressive, misogynous, sterile, and dangerous.

I wonder if Dick Stone felt the same strange dissociation when he first checked in as an undercover agent, with long hippie hair and a stud in his ear, having seen things and done things with nubile hippie chicks that would cause straight-arrow agents to fall on their knees and pray for his counterculture-corrupted soul.

It's not easy to assimilate back.

"You miss the long-timers?"

"We were young," Rosalind says. "We had fun with the agents. Well, you had to call them 'Mr.' They called us by our first names, of course, but I had a lot of respect for those young men. And they all smoked like chimneys! But they were *good family men*," she pronounces. "They were nice." She clucks her tongue and sweeps a dismissive hand. "Not like now. You can keep that Peter Abbott."

"Tell me about it. He's the one who grilled me."

"Back in the seventies, when we were into the security stuff, he was a supervisor, yes, on the beard squad. That's what we called it. The young agents who went after the draft dodgers and the hippies. You should have seen Peter Abbott when *he* first came out to the West Coast. Green as the grass and twice as bristly."

"Why bristly?"

"Acting like he's royalty. Never let us forget his dad was on a high committee in the Justice Department. *Congressman Abbott* he calls his dad, *Congressman Abbott* decides what toilet paper we get and how the Bureau wipes its behind, so you-all keep in line. When the truth is"—she lowers her voice—"*Congressman Abbott* was investigated for taking bribes."

"Anything come of it?"

Rosalind scoffs. "Too well-connected. His son comes out here and gets a free pass right to Hollywood. Well." She chuckles. "You know how they love G-men in the movies. The stars like a fella who carries a gun. And there was that show on TV about the FBI back then. The movie people wanted their favors and privileges, and they came to the new guy, and young Peter Abbott, he was so excited, he just went off on a tangent."

I laugh. "Who was it?"

"Not like an actress in particular. It was poker games with entertainment lawyers. Tennis games with the famous movie directors. He got on great with the big shots but had problems managing the gentlemen working underneath him," she recalls. "The street agents."

"Like Dick Stone?" I ask quickly. "He was on the beard squad."

Rosalind's large watery eyes show recognition. "I remember him. He was straight as an arrow until he started working on that squad. Comes back to the office all scuzzy, with a scarf around his head, and the agents, they didn't know what to do with him."

"Why?"

"He was bitter. He would sit on the floor, like the hippies used to do? Staring up at us with a cockeyed look, probably high. I believe they wanted to bring him out, but like a lot of them, he had a hard time accepting the FBI philosophy. I've seen some of those guys; they were so lost, they would cry." She clucks, remembering. "Oh Lord, he used to sit on the floor and chant 'Hari Krishna.' No wonder they sent him away."

"To a drug program?"

"Nobody knew about drug programs. No, honey, back to the street. They just turned him around and spun him out of here. Out of Los Angeles, to Santa Barbara, Berkeley—they had him on something called 'Turquoise' in the Southwest, I believe."

"Was it concerning the Weathermen?"

"Everything was a radical conspiracy. If you sneezed, it was the Weathermen."

The door to the conference room opens and the players start filing out.

"Ana?"

It is Donnato, indicating I should take a walk with him.

"I'm off it, right?"

"No. You're in. They want to amp up Operation Wildcat. Get you into Stone's face. 'Up his ass' is the way Abbott phrased it."

"Really?"

It's like hearing you've been designated the leadoff hitter.

"He agreed to the sting at the BLM corrals," Donnato says. "You got the nod. Big-time."

"I was shocked the assistant director even knew my name."

"He was very familiar with your background. I get the feeling he was waiting to meet you to seal the deal. You got the part, kiddo. You go up there and get yourself arrested. It will be a controlled operation using SWAT, the county sheriff's department, every redneck lawman in the West."

"I like it."

"Good."

"Mike?"

"Yes?"

"What else went on in there?"

"Sports talk. Dirty jokes."

"What are you not telling me?"

"Nothing. Go. They've got you on the six-forty-five p.m. flight to Portland."

"Do something for me? Take Rosalind to lunch."

"Why, is it Mother's Day or something?"

"Ask her about the beard squad and a case called Turquoise. She knows where the bodies are buried."

As we head toward the stairwell, Rooney Berwick is coming out. He wears the same black jeans and black shirt as at the off-site when he fabricated Darcy's driver's license. His boots ring off the floor and the keys and tools and stuff on his belt still clatter, but the arrogance is missing. He looks thinner and gray in the face.

"Rooney!" exclaims Rosalind from behind us. "How you doin'?"

She trundles up and hugs him like a favorite nephew, two long-timers who have been through it.

"I miss you, friend. We used to run into each other all the time when the lab was in this building," she explains. "Didn't we?"

"They keep me in the rat hole," Rooney mumbles. "Never see daylight."

The truculent techie can barely look at her.

Rosalind's eyebrows pinch. "Something wrong?"

"My mom just passed away," Rooney says, and my heart squeezes tight.

"Just?" she asks, alarmed.

"Last week. The funeral was yesterday. It was nice, but not too many people came."

I feel a pensive guilt, as if, absurdly, I should have been there.

"Why didn't you tell anyone? Now that just makes me mad," says Rosalind.

Donnato and I murmur awkward condolences. The queasy shock of it is very like the moment Rooney first disclosed his mom was terminally ill, out of the blue, in the midst of disassembled laptops and humming spectrograph machines, a hermit enthroned by the power of gizmos; how he poked down the barrel of a gold-plated assault rifle as if to impress me, as if to say he could handle anything. As if the world he had been pushing away all his life had not just collapsed in on him.

Rosalind chides him gently. "Can't you reach out, just a little? Don't you know we are family? My Lord, this young man has been here since Stone was," she adds, turning to us.

Rooney: "Who is that?"

"Dick Stone," Rosalind prompts.

"You're talking about *him*?" Rooney asks with surprise.

Donnato and I stiffen. Our interest in Stone is privileged information we do not want to spread.

"His name came up in a meeting," I say abruptly.

"I remember Dick Stone. He always liked my pugs."

Rosalind smiles kindly. "How are those pug dogs? You still raising 'em?"

"Third generation."

Let's cut off this discussion now.

"Did you have something for Operation Wildcat?" Donnato asks.

"Yeah, the phone."

Rooney opens a palm to reveal a secure phone that looks like a mini Oreo.

"There are a couple of settings." He rotates two black disks. "One direct to your case agent and one to the supervisor. It works on a scrambled signal, almost anywhere in the world."

The thing is weightless. I ooh and aah at Rooney's genius and pocket the device, telling him how we appreciate his work, especially with things being so tough with his mom. As he and Rosalind move toward the bull pen, Donnato steers me out the secure door, the very one Steve Crawford walked me in.

"You be careful," Donnato says. "Dick Stone is smart. How he survived, he probably created several false ID packages for himself. He jumps from cause to cause, like stepping-stones. He's in the Weather Underground, and then he's ELF, and now he's an animal rights activist—he pulls an identity he has off the shelf, making sure to stay two or three times removed. He's learned how to live like an outlaw. If he gets close, get out."

Inside my knapsack, Darcy's cell phone is ringing.

"Hi, Megan!" I say brightly, nodding affirmatively toward my partner. "What's up?"

Megan Tewksbury is calling from the farm to tell her friend Darcy the secret location of the action to free the wild mustangs. On the first day of the gather, protesters from across the Northwest will meet in a campground behind a grocery store, at an old stage stop in the high desert of eastern Oregon.

I promise to be there.

Closing the phone, I grin at Donnato. "I can walk on water with these people."

PART TWO

Twelve

In the high desert, where winters are cold and dry and spring winds whip across the flats, evaporating moisture from the earth, herds of wild horses roam free.

This is the big country, where you can drive for hours on empty road and never turn the wheel. The gently rolling hillsides covered with silver sage are speckled with hard chunks of snow—a painted pattern in which pronghorn antelope, rattlesnakes, quail, and pinto mustangs can easily disappear. Gray mist overhangs the rim rock to the east, silhouetting pointed junipers in a shifting white glow; to the west, the sun is bright and there are fluffy clouds.

You are traveling across an ancient lake bed of frosty green that is hundreds of square miles wide. Beyond it is another ancient lake, and another, and in between, great volcanic buttes of obsidian and cracked basalt, witness to unthinkable power. Time is also a kind of power in the big country. It suspends the human brain in wonder.

By afternoon, when the temperature has dropped to thirty-five degrees and the sporadic sun has given way to sleet, three small armies—the wranglers, the radicals, and the law—have mobilized in the struggle for the destiny of the wild horses, because genuine wonder—full-blooded and pure—is a rare and valuable commodity.

The wrangler outfit is a contractor hired by the BLM. They bring their own helicopter. The law is made up of undercover cops from the county sheriff's department and the Portland police, supervised by the FBI. The radicals are a group of maybe fifteen—mainstream true believers from rescue groups all over the state; you'd have to be, to drive almost to the freaking border of Idaho.

We, the radicals, arrive within the hour and park our vehicles at a stage stop built in 1912, now a tiny grocery store where you might get a packet of trail mix, if the snaggletoothed proprietress doesn't shoot you first. She doesn't like strangers, and she sure as hell doesn't like them using the privy, a hole in the ground out front, with a hand-lettered sign that advises, succinctly, CLOSE DOOR—KEEP OUT SNAKES.

The wind is cutting as the rescuers of lost animals gather around a picnic table adjacent to the parking lot. I scan the reddened faces squinting against splatters of rain. These are your good citizens, eminently sane. They believe in the sanctity of life. They want to be seen as compassionate. Middle-aged and mostly female (two lesbian couples), they are "guardians"—not owners—of hordes of abandoned dogs and cats, lizards and rabbits, and their phone numbers are always the ones on the oil spill emergency list. There are graying braids and nose rings, hiking boots and ponchos. You have to like a bosomy grandma wearing a cap that says *Meat-free zone*.

The dangerous element is Bill Fontana. Even in the stormy desert his lean figure—the stomp-ass boots, a camouflage parka and watch cap—radiates a concentrated black energy. He works the eclectic crew gathered around the picnic tables with a sense of his own celebrity, shaking hands and kissing cheeks. I want to say, Ladies, he is not worthy of you. But he plays to their vanity, and they adore him like a son.

"We stand for the essence of nonviolence."

Fontana speaks intimately, drinking in eye contact with each one. "This is an evolutionary moment. To make nonviolence an organizing principle. We are the people. This is the time."

I wish I could turn away. I have read so many transcripts of taped phone conversations of Fontana spreading the gospel that I know the rhetoric by heart. But I am nodding gravely, pitying the well-intentioned troops about to be led into a trap. They must know they cannot get away with this.

There are no cars on the highway. Probably none for fifty miles.

You can hear the drops of ice plinking softly on woven nylon hoods and shoulders. Behind the stage stop the proprietress keeps an aviary of chicken wire and tin. Red-and-yellow house finches hop and dive. Unsmiling, she flicks a pan of scraps into the snow.

"You found it!" whispers a familiar voice, bringing with it the scent of almond soap.

I turn to see that it is Megan, hurriedly zipping up a yam-colored parka. Flakes of frozen rain have gathered in her silver hair.

"Hi!" I squeal. "Great to see you."

She gives me a motherly hug. "I'm glad I'm not late."

"No, we're just getting started." I look around. "Where is Julius?"

"He drove to the preserve to scout out the horses."

"What about Slammer and Sara?"

"Someone has to watch the farm."

"Are you scared?" I ask, lowering my voice.

"Bill just said this is a nonviolent action."

"It's just that I'm tired of empty gestures," I say. "I want to do something that will make an impact."

Megan puts the collar of the parka up and snaps it into place. The wind blows her turquoise earrings. Her look becomes distant as she gazes toward the flatland.

"You should be careful."

"Why?"

"The FBI is here."

"Are you sure?"

Megan: "Count on it."

"Seriously?"

"They keep files on us. They come to our conventions, too. They think we don't know who they are."

A strange paralysis kicks in, like hearing two radio stations at once. Which one to listen to? I become momentarily unbalanced. This is not playing a role in a bar. I am alone, in a windblown god-awful patch of nowhere at the end of time, eye-to-eye with someone who has placed her trust in me.

"The FBI had someone spying on Julius," she says.

"I don't believe it."

"He came up to Julius at the bar at Omar's—this was months ago—

a guy nobody ever saw before, and tried to sell him drugs. Julius said he should have had a sign on his back that said 'Pig.' "

Skeptically, I say, "How could Julius know he was from the FBI?"

"The guy was an obvious asshole."

Acid burn creeps through my gut, like when you hear someone slur your religion.

"Then what happened?"

"He kept hanging around," she says incredulously. "Julius wouldn't talk to him. Nobody would. So I guess he left. Listen."

Fontana is giving orders: "We don't want a lot of cars, so you'll have to buddy up. Dress warmly and make sure you wear gloves. Eat. Rest. Meditate. Pray. We go in after dark."

I take in a draft of dry, cold air. It comes out as a sigh.

"It's all a game, isn't it?"

"No," says Megan. "It's a difficult and spiritual calling. To care about another species is the hardest thing to do."

Water drips off the tin roof of the aviary. The red-and-yellow finches peck in the snow.

Thirteen

Dick Stone has them in his sights. Hard to discern in the distance in a basin of bunchgrass. So far, he's had no luck—the brown dots he spotted through the Army-issue field glasses turned out to be cattle. But these, at the limit of his vision, move like horses.

He swerves off the highway into a gravel turnout, gets out of the truck and opens a gate in the barbed-wire fence that leads to hundreds of thousands of federally protected acres.

He loops the gate closed and drives a slow half mile past markers that warn RESEARCH AREA—NO TRESPASSING, where he cuts the engine and eases the door shut. A ground squirrel streaks by. The quiet is a muffled roar, tangible, as if he'd plugged his ears with silence. Soon the crunching of the bandit's boots on the granular volcanic dust becomes not his; nor does he care if the white wool Pendleton jacket with the colorful Navajo design draws attention from some nervous BLM patrol. It is not likely that they'd throw him against the hood of the Suburban, pat him down, and find the Colt .45 where he's holding it right now, deep inside his jacket pocket.

He trudges uphill through a valley framed by dark gray magma cliffs, some uplifted, some half-sunken in a spectacular collision ten thousand years ago. He has to watch his footing. The porous rocks are sharp. He's lost the horses in the folds of the hills, but he knows they like to shade up under the junipers, where he saw them through the field glasses. When he gains the rise, he sees their colors in the bluebunch wheatgrass a hundred yards away. He smiles at their placid grazing and begins to circle slowly upwind.

He spirals closer. His training as a sniper in the Army keeps him low. In the deep spaces of the canyon, the animals must seem to jump-cut to a larger size with every turn—from tiny toys to very large and present as he drops behind the willows and observes. The weather is changing fast. Over the butte to the west, a pulsing cloud like a black jellyfish is trailing dark ribbons of rain. The wind has shifted and the mustangs know he is there; finely muzzled heads rise and point alertly in his direction. He has come upon a band of thirty or forty—pintos, duns, and chestnuts, with half a dozen foals. Every individual is strong and perfectly formed, the essence of natural beauty.

Or maybe he is thinking about bloodshed. Dinnertimes at the farm he would lecture us assembled radicals on how the Spanish horse—the bloodline of these mustangs goes back to the legions of Rome—defined the history of the New World. How the stamina of the Spanish breed was the means by which Cortés destroyed the Aztecs, Coronado fought the Shoshone, the Shoshone conquered its neighboring tribes and then, in grand restitution, wiped out the Spanish settlers on Dead-man's Trail.

Horses, he would remind us, have made war possible on an increasingly staggering scale, just part of the continuum that led to Vietnam and beyond. And everyone knows the way those grandiose engagements always end—piles of body parts in a decimated field, the arrogance of politics, the incompetence of rank. What he withheld from us then was how he had been a victim, too, of smug and inept leadership in the FBI. Now he touches the gun inside his pocket like a talisman to calm the vengeful scenarios.

Freed of the perversities of humankind, horses are peaceful and curious. If you show patience, they will accommodate your presence. He was certain the wild herd would spook, but they just look at him and go about their business, thirty yards away. They have relation-ships. They play, they fight, and they communicate. Let's go over there, they seem to say. A spotted baby trots behind its mom. Another sits on long folded legs in the grass. A mare suddenly charges two others, neck twisted and teeth out. Without judgment, with no malice, the interactions of the horses ebb and flow as ribbons of snow begin to stream across the valley. And now a brown and white pinto stallion has trotted close enough to check the bandit out. Neck arched, ears up, its eyes and nose are pointed at him with otherworldly focus.

Pinned. He is pinned by the stallion's gaze and made to see himself alone and out of place, trespassing once again. The stallion gallops indifferently away. The bandit hugs his knees and huddles on the ground, shamefully human.

He loses sense of time.

He becomes a Buddha under a willow tree, surrounded by four-legged gods—now twenty, now ten yards away. For the first time in his life, he experiences unconditional acceptance. He knows what freedom is. Their freedom is his freedom, too. His heart softens toward the cities beyond the silent rim of the mountains, a roar he cannot remember or imagine. Out there is a world of hurt, and all balled up inside it are the bad and evil things he has done. He listens to his own breathing, close in his ears. The horses, moving through the sage, are uncannily silent. The trouble is that the absence of sound itself is elastic, and it caroms off the basalt cliffs, hitting him with a thousand stinging thoughts. One of them might be repentance.

The helicopter explodes above the ridge like thunder. The man in the Navajo jacket on the ground cries out and rolls, hands to ears, rocking like a child against the scream of annihilation. He is blasted by a turbulence of dry leaves and razor-sharp black stones and curls up to protect his eyes, and then, when it passes, he struggles to his hands and knees to survey the empty grass where the horses had been—with love and grief as profound as if he were a refugee returning to his childhood home, only to find it burning to the ground.

The horses are running. Dick Stone is running with them, gunning the pickup along a parallel dirt road that climbs through the preserve. As the ridge falls away, he can see the entire Catlow Valley and the brown and white and buckskin-colored animals, led by the pinto stallion, fanning out before the helicopter, which is like a monstrous green bottle fly with ferociously buzzing wings, biting at their flanks no matter how adroitly they crisscross the salt flats, bearing down relentlessly until their coats turn dark with foam.

The mustangs have galloped almost twenty-five miles without stopping, even the little ones. He thinks about their beating hearts and the working of their lungs. And now the black jellyfish cloud is loosing sleet, which hits the bandit in the face as he leans out through the open window to track the herd, because it is suddenly important that he not lose contact.

Out of the foothills, wranglers in bright yellow rain gear ride from their hiding places on obedient quarter horses, and the bandit, having pulled up to the last overlook before the road turns east, stands in the freezing rain and watches as they channel the mustangs through a set of camouflaged fences that lead toward the corrals. The pilot of the chopper circles low. On its signal, an air horn blasts the valley, and the bandit sees another yellow-coated cowboy standing up in the sage, holding the lead of an unsaddled dun-colored mare with a black mane and tail.

The cowboy releases her and the mare takes off eagerly, going at tremendous speed, because she has been trained to run for a grain bucket hanging at the end of the capture funnel. The tired herd sees her and follows. For several heart-stopping minutes she takes the lead. Then she flies down the chute neatly as an arrow, and the mustangs trample behind her into captivity.

The bandit lowers the fogged-up field glasses with disgust. He hates the dun mare and her handlers. He has always reserved his deepest contempt for spies, for collaborators who can be bought for a bucket of grain.

The cowboys have a name for the single animal that betrays the herd. They call it the "Judas horse."

Fourteen

I am using the Oreo cell phone that works on a scrambled signal, sitting in the Civic outside the Big River Stage Stop with the heater going, watching tiny beads of hail popping off the windshield, grateful to Rooney Berwick, deep in the warren of the lab, for fashioning this invisible lifeline to my partners in the real world. The vehicles belonging to the radicals are scattered around the rest stop. Most of us have spent the rainy afternoon in our cars. It is 5:00 p.m., still hours before dark, and the turbulent early-spring weather continues to swing between boiling black cloud and seas of pearl blue.

"What are you doing?" Donnato asks.

"Well, right now watching it hailing. So far, we've had rain, sleet, sunshine, and snow—all at the same time. How is it where you are?"

"Clear and cold. Looks like we'll have good visibility tonight."

Donnato is speaking from the sheriff department's county jail, the command center for the stakeout at the horse corrals. The department is headquartered in a flyspeck of a town twenty-five miles from the Big River Stage Stop. The town grew up around a massive lumber mill, but when it shut down, the place curled up and atrophied to empty taverns and one wind-busted main street where the last survivors are a decrepit movie house and a dilapidated Chinese restaurant.

"The strategy for tonight has changed." I'm looking at a hand-drawn map Bill Fontana has given us. "We're taking three vehicles and leaving them in a turnout at Needle Gorge, highway marker two twenty-four, just east of the corrals."

"I'll inform the SWAT team. Don't worry. Once you're in, nobody's getting out of the compound," Donnato assures me. "Be safe."

"You, too."

"Roger that."

I haul out of the Civic and for the second or third time during that long day wander into the Big River Stage Stop and poke through cans of motor oil and beef stew on the sparsely stocked shelves.

There are many interesting things to look at, such as three different color portraits of John Wayne, and a collection of old snow globes with dried-up brown insides—a gorilla, a golfer, a steamboat. In a booth at the rear I find Megan and two other activists—Lillian, a seventyish bird-watcher, and her friend Dot. They are now stripped of their thick parkas, and their mousy white hair and plain wire glasses, their thin shoulders and veined hands reveal two elderly women, defenseless as nuns. How will they keep up with us in the dark?

I wait for some acknowledgment in order to join them. They are talking about migrating birds. Spread across this surreal landscape, there are wetlands that provide sanctuary for hundreds of species. I hover at the edge of the conversation, drawn back to the banishment from the pack by my former friend Barbara Sullivan at the Los Angeles field office; boys may be stupid, but girls rip the heart out of you. Or is it that our hearts are already broken by the clumsy swipes of careless mothers? The undercutting remark, the florid slap across the face. Too jealous, too deranged, or, like my own mother, gone too early to make repairs.

When the bird-watchers report they have seen three trumpet swans sailing along by the side of the road, I jump in with *"Oh my God, how exciting!"* and am finally invited to sit down.

Now they are talking about rocks. Lillian and Dot turn out to be retired high school teachers with a lot to say—not only about birds but also about the joys of collecting minerals. Underneath her yam-colored parka, Megan is wearing a fuzzy sweater knitted with ropes of purple; her hair bursts out from tortoiseshell clips. Her eyes are bright and interested. The proprietress brings four coffees. When she is gone, Megan reaches into her knapsack and pulls out a silver flask. Dot reacts, all fluttery, but Lillian is eager and Megan matter-of-fact. I think about the empty wineglasses that littered the table at Omar's.

Megan pours a dark liquid into my cup. "Going to be cold out there tonight."

It is bourbon.

"Wow, this helps," I say gratefully. "I am so stressed."

"You'll get used to it," Lillian says. "Whatever you do, when they arrest you, don't resist."

Dot taps her teeth. "The police broke my bridge in Atlanta."

I swallow the bourbon-flavored coffee. "No, not about freeing the horses. I mean I'm stressed about my life. I'm being kicked out of my apartment in Portland. I have to find another place."

Angelo said, "Make sure they know Darcy needs a place to stay."

Lillian laughs and waves her wrinkled fingertips. "*Vasanas,*" she says dismissively.

"What does that mean?"

"It's a Sanskrit word for things of this earthly life," Lillian says. "Bad habits. Mental bondage."

"Well, excuse my French." I pout, and Lillian pats my hand.

We pull into the total darkness of the turnout at Needle Gorge. The weather has cleared and it is as if the curtains of civilization have been drawn aside to show us the stars, lush and impenetrable, as they looked 200 million years ago from this same naked plateau. Our breath forms as soon as we are out of the cars. Immediately, there is giggling. Someone has to go to the bathroom. Someone else flicks on a small red beam to check the map.

We follow the highway. I wonder what Fontana's alibi would be if a sheriff saw us walking along in the dark single file. But for Darcy, this is the most thrilling thing she has ever done. I grip the sleeve of the conspirator in front of me with exhilaration. "Your first time?" whispers the woman kindly. "Stay by me. You'll be okay."

We shuffle down a steep driveway, causing a small slide of pebbles.

Two lights are shining from posts near the entrance to the site. Between them is a gate secured by a circle of heavy chain. Fontana snips the links with a pair of bolt cutters and we're in.

No more giggling now. Ahead is the compound of corrals, lit by a single lamp over the barn. I am shivering with cold, small tremors close to the bone. Suddenly, a spotlight appears above us, a circle of white around a huge fat owl in a tree. Its markings are beautiful, the eyes glossy black. There are shushes and rasping shouts. "*Great horned owl!*" And the flashlight snaps off. Lillian and Dot. The bird-watchers. *Oh my God.*

The wide barn door is open. Inside, it smells of horse stink and hay. We creep past a system of green metal chutes, and then a box stall in which a spotted mustang mare and her foal are resting on a bed of straw. Even in the dimness, the up-close colors of their coats—their wild aliveness—makes your heart beat faster. There are muffled gasps from the group. The foal's front legs are wrapped in bloody bandages from being run by the helicopter over the coarse gravel plain. Deter-minedly, we urge one another on, not suspecting this touching nativity scene may have been set up for that very purpose.

We hurry through another open doorway and find ourselves in a maze of log railings twelve feet high, way over our heads. The lengths of the runs and the height of the fences are much greater than they looked on Fontana's sketch. You can feel a ripple of uncertainty: This is the United States government. We are small; this is big—maybe overwhelming. The lighting is poor. The far corrals blend into country darkness. Our boots sink into dry mulch that muffles sound. And then we see the horses.

The mustangs are completely silent. They circle their enclosures like fish, heads low, shoulder-to-shoulder in slow undulating patterns of chestnut and dun. A few break off and form other groups, and then they all flow together again. There is no nickering, no alarm at being captive, no rebellious kicking of heels—because the stallions and foals, I learn, have been separated from the rest. Leaderless, childless, the silence of the mares is haunting: a plaintive, voiceless female rebuke. Heard by whom?

Heard by us.

We surge forward to our assigned corrals to wait while Fontana moves down the line with the bolt cutters. It is hard to gain traction in the mulch and I feel like I am running in slow motion, but that is also because I am aware of other forces at play in the wings of darkness—armed officers speaking softly into body mikes, and invisible snipers on the barn roof. I jog past Megan, already posted at pen number four, where twenty or thirty slack-necked mares slink unconcerned toward the center. I am climbing the logs of the gate to grasp the padlock with stiff, cold fingers. I'm about ten feet up when the crack of a rifle shot echoes off the mountains.

I think it is Fontana, gone crazy, but then I realize the shot came from the darkness to the east, and Fontana is standing frozen like everyone else in the middle of the runs, having whipped around toward frantic shouts from the barn. My first thought: *Where is Donnato? Is he in the line of fire?* From my vantage point halfway up the fence, I see a black-suited SWAT officer toboggan sideways down the corrugated iron channels of the roof, then drop off the edge.

The SWAT team answers with automatic weapons and the horses spook in a thousand directions, hurtling against the rails, which are shimmying violently, as if about to blow apart. A muscular chest rams my toes and a huge equine head with bared teeth and rolling eyes sweeps over mine as I am flung off backward, hitting the ground and rolling and snapping my forehead on the foot of another post. Spitting hay and who knows what else, I get to my feet and see nothing but chaos up and down the track.

We head for the barn but are thrown back by deputies with assault rifles and in full riot gear. Two, now three and four are tackling Fontana. Some of us try to escape by straddling the railings, pinned at the top by the cops on one side and the skittish haphazard movement of the heavy-boned horses on the other. Someone is calling instructions over a bullhorn, while another numbskull has turned on the flashers of every sheriff's vehicle in the county, surrounding the compound in strobing red.

Where is Donnato?

I have to fight my own instincts and training and wrestle back into Darcy's identity, and continue to run, disoriented, like everybody else. Then Megan has me by the jacket, pulling and screaming incoherently, and we trip over each other and sprawl together in the dust and straw.

Megan is crying, "We have to get her out!"

White-haired Lillian is standing in the middle of a corral in her wilted, filth-encrusted blue parka, completely encircled by panicked animals. Her eyes are shut and she is standing absolutely still, as if some divine column of light will protect her from being trampled.

"*Get out, Lillian! Get out!*" Megan is pleading, and I find myself scaling the gate. My mind flips to an unaccountably quiet scene: After inching through a massive traffic jam on the Santa Monica freeway, I came upon the accident. Highway Patrol officers were guiding motorists in slow and silent procession around the victim—a well-dressed African-American male who was lying in the middle of the road in the fetal position. His body was intact; a briefcase lay twenty feet away. There were no crushed vehicles, no cars involved at all. How did he get there? Did he think he could run across six lanes of traffic?

"Lillian!" I shout. "Look at me! Look at my eyes. I'm coming!"

Her face is shut down. She is praying, or dead standing up. The horses are running in random circles; the patterns that kept them bonded and calm now completely shattered. That's okay. I'll focus on Lillian and the divine light will guide me, and the raging waters will part.

But inside the pen, it is as if fear has shape-shifted into raging horses, attacking chaotically like a cavalry possessed. Pinned against the railings, I wait until the surge flows in the opposite direction, then dash across the mulch to drag Lillian to safety, but she can't seem to move.

"Lillian, run. Run with me. I've got you—"

Like a sharp wind whipping back, the horses reverse direction and angle toward us. I see it in their shining dark eyes, which in my enlarged perception seem wise and close: the simple, unemotional impulse to flee. *They're going to trample us and break through the fence.* Scores of deputies have massed at the fence. And then Lillian goes limp and collapses.

I grab at the fake fur neck of the parka before she goes down, cutting a gash in her neck with the zipper, then hoist the body in two beats—one, against my knees; two, into my arms—and stand in the midst of that ring of fire, holding the old woman aloft like some awful pietà, fingers probing the flesh of her throat for a carotid pulse as the gate opens and a cowboy on a paint bursts through at full gallop. The gate is closed, locking us into a surreal rodeo, a daring ballet in which the cutting horse, outfitted in silver, plunges fearlessly through the roiling mass, its body coiled to match, movement for movement, a mirror image of each individual animal, herding the mares one at a time into a tight bunch in the eastern quadrant of the circle, and keeping them there as the long-legged wrangler, wearing a beat-to-shit suede jacket and a battered, yellowed western hat, sits perfectly still, hands low and head tipped forward, as if he isn't doing anything at all.

While the mares are held back, two paramedics enter the ring at assault speed, take Lillian from my arms, and carry her out of there in about fifteen seconds. At the same moment, the paint lets go of its position and prances backward in tiny steps until the cowboy reins it around on a dime. They're leaving me here. *What the hell?*

But before the mares can break across the ground like billiard balls, he's galloping right at me, hanging off the side of the horse like he's about to scoop a bandanna out of the dust, but it's me he's aiming for, and I am lifted off the ground in the crook of an arm of steely strength, lifted into the air, and swung into the hard leather cradle of the saddle, the cowboy riding behind me now on the bare rump of the horse, and someone has opened a narrow passage in the gate. We canter out, as if passing through the eye of the needle.

His chest is pressed against my back. I'm smelling chewing gum and sharp male sweat, and although I'm bouncing wildly, staring at a careening world through the terrifying space between the horse's ears, his suede-fringed arm remains strong and steady, and I feel the anchoring motion of his hips in rhythm with the horse. *He won't let you fall.*

We come to a halt and I manage to slip off, completely dazed. Staring up at a man on a horse—rugged-looking, mid-thirties, five ten, 140 pounds, with stick-thin legs that jeans are made for and red leather cowboy boots you know he wears every day of his life—who has just saved your life can have that effect.

"Thank you, sir." I offer my hand. "Darcy."

"Sterling McCord." He leans in the saddle to shake. "You okay?"

"Yes. Wow," I say breathlessly. "That was quite a ride."

"When are you people gonna get it? Messin' with wild animals is not a hot idea."

His rebuke is stern; more like a cop than a cowboy.

"I'm sorry. I guess you're used to it."

"I don't like to see anyone get hurt."

"I understand."

"Hope your friend's all right. You take care, now, Darcy," he says, and canters toward some other pandemonium.

Over by the barn, the whirling lights of an ambulance illuminate a knot of paramedics around the SWAT team officer on the ground; a gurney waits, riderless.

Fifteen

Mike Donnato is waiting inside an interrogation room the size of an organic lentil. He wears a windbreaker with *FBI* across the back and greets me gruffly. The two grim sheriff's deputies, who marched me over from the jail where we, the radicals, were held overnight, do not know I am undercover. The iron grip on my biceps makes that clear. Donnato instructs them to unlock the handcuffs, and we sit down and face each other across a small table as they pocket the keys and leave.

"We didn't get breakfast," I say right off. "And there are folks who need medical attention."

Donnato just rubs his reddened eyes.

"These boondocks deputies are real redneck pigs. I saw them shove an old lady and withhold water when we repeatedly asked for some. It's bullshit, Mike—"

"The officer who was shot last night died at the scene," he says heavily. "His name was Todd Mackee, a sergeant on the Portland SWAT team. Single shot to the throat."

"I'm so sorry."

"Took his head right off."

I wet my lips. "Must have been one monster bullet."

Donnato nods. "Fifty-caliber. Not your average shooter."

I resist the urge to say how relieved I was last night, in my panic at hearing the shot, to realize Donnato would be here at the command center and not with the tactical team at the barn.

"Makes you sick," he says.

"Oh God."

I'm losing my resolve. Between the primacy of the mission and the bond I've made with Lillian, Dot, Megan, and the others, I'm done. After a sleepless night crammed four to a cell and with zero food, I have a killer headache and my breath could melt steel.

"This was supposed to be a controlled operation. To lose a life—" I clamp both hands over my face. "I want to go home."

"I didn't hear that."

I raise my eyes. "Lillian had a heart attack."

"Who's Lillian?"

His ignorance inflames me.

"The lady who got trapped in the corral!" I snap. "Elderly, a bird-watcher? *You don't know about Lillian?*"

He shrugs. "I heard something about a protester being taken to the hospital."

"But you were more concerned with Officer Mackee."

Donnato's eyes grow hard. "Frankly . . . yes."

"Let me tell you about Lillian." Finger pointing again. "She's close to eighty. She had a heart-valve replacement, but she didn't tell anyone because she was afraid they wouldn't let her come."

"Good idea."

"Mike! She risked her life for the horses!"

Donnato settles into himself. "Ana," he says very carefully, "you're sounding a lot like the other side."

"I *was* on the other side, and I think the deputies responded with unnecessary force."

He waits.

"Think again."

He doesn't want to report what I'm saying.

"Mackee was one of those guys, 'proud as hell to be a cop,' " Donnato says. "The one who organizes the department trip to Kodiak Island to fly-fish for salmon, know what I mean?"

I nod, understanding the message.

"Three children, ages six through eight, and a wife of ten years who's a parole officer for juvenile offenders."

"Always the good people," I murmur, and lay my head on the table, completely dissipated. "SWAT had to respond. You're right. I don't know what's wrong with me. Exhaustion."

"Want some coffee?"

"Just shoot it in my arm."

He opens the door and speaks to the deputies, giving them the message the suspect is at that point where the thing could turn on a friendly cup of joe. He comes back in and touches my shoulder, a signal to get it together.

"I'm okay." I sit up, resuming the posture. "I'm past it."

My partner nods. *Will he ignore the lapse?*

"We located the shooting site beyond the perimeter," he continues matter-of-factly. "It was a heavy sniper rifle, an M93, something like that. You can tell from the blast-pattern plume it left in the dust. It's a sniping rifle, not for antipersonnel use, but antimatériel. They used them from fixed positions in the Vietnam War."

"Why so heavy? It must be a bitch to break down and carry."

"What the shooter had. How he was trained."

"In the Army?"

"Maybe. Army snipers shoot from a tripod. This joker shoots off a pack. There was a depression on the ground and a trail in the dirt where he dragged it behind him. Still, it was a hell of a shot. Correcting for drop and wind? A thousand yards away in the dark? This is someone with the training and resolve to sit out there and make the shot."

"Dick Stone?"

"Or," says Donnato, "someone hired by Stone. Except he didn't get his money's worth. A good sniper never leaves his brass behind. And this guy did. We recovered the bullet casing."

"That was a mistake."

"Big-time. We have the slug from the roof. All we need is the weapon it came from. A suspect is in custody. Barnaby Nuñez, Native American, thirty-eight years old, priors for DUI and domestic abuse. Picked up three miles from the corrals. Fired from working at a filling station, claimed racial discrimination, arrested for trespass and making threats against the manager. Theory is, he uses the mustang protest as a way to make things right. Former Marine, which fits."

The deputy brings coffee for the prisoner, hot and black as road tar.

When he's gone: "Did you get anything in the cell from Megan?"

"Nothing hard. I wonder if she knows what Dick Stone's really up to."

Donnato sips the coffee. "Will she flip?"

"They're in love." I blush for no apparent reason. "Here's what she told me in the lockup: 'I don't have a thing about cops. They're human beings doing their job. But when they get into our face, they have to be stopped. We have a constitutional right to express our opinions without being spied on.' She said there was 'a fed' hanging around Omar's, but that Julius was 'on to him' and he stopped showing up."

Donnato and I are silent, holding each other's eyes. The heart-heavy sorrow I felt hearing of Steve Crawford's death comes over me again.

"Dick Stone made Steve Crawford for an undercover," Donnato says quietly.

"Megan says he did. But the way she makes it sound, Steve blew it from the start by coming on too strong." Troubled, I add, "He knew better. He would not have been that sloppy."

"You're right—Steve knew what he was doing. He was like a low-flying missile when he was on to something. Remember the money he raised for Jane Doe?"

I remember looking up to find Steve Crawford bending over my desk with that look of earnest resolve. He was collecting money for a funeral. The funeral was for a little girl he'd never known, a Jane Doe, who wore teddy bear pajama pants and a T-shirt with sparkles. The remnants of a woven friendship bracelet circled the bones of her wrist.

She was badly decomposed. It took a team of forensic experts to reconstruct her age—between ten and fifteen years old. She was healthy and well fed, no drugs, strangled with a nylon rope. Steve Crawford and I were on the kidnap squad at the time. We worked with the Glendale sheriff's department and NCIC and our own cold-case files, but we never got a hit. Nobody claimed the body.

Steve Crawford did not discover Jane Doe in a cardboard box in a hospital parking lot in Glendale, but he was the one who took her into his heart. He and Tina had just had their first baby, and here was a child abandoned, in the cruelest way. The idea of her being buried as an unknown in a common crypt ate at him. "She suffered enough," he said, and took it upon himself to go from door to door, house to house, desk to desk to raise money to lay her to rest with dignity. Word spread through the media. Strangers donated more than eight thousand dollars.

Six of us from the office attended the funeral. It was pouring rain and the most beautiful thing I have ever seen. We lined up in our polished Bu-cars behind a donated hearse that held a small white casket. The Glendale police and fire departments followed in slow parade, and Jane Doe was buried under the epitaph "Here lies a child of God."

Is it the caffeine from the sour jailhouse coffee kicking in that makes me flush with restless torment? I remember Steve's look of disturbed satisfaction as he stood at the grave. Despite the clouds, he wore black wraparound sunglasses. The wind blew his blond hair, but the muscles of his face were motionless; a military stillness that said, I will stand. I will stand for this little girl. I will make it right.

Did Stone kill him? We don't know. Climbing through the forest, nothing would have given Steve a clue that things were far from right. The fern glen that exploded into a debris field, and later became a field of snow, must have been silent. Steve would have had every reason to believe he was alone, but in fact he was being set up for an ambush— exactly like FBI Special Agents Jack Coler and Ron Williams in the mid-seventies, ambushed while driving a dirt road on a South Dakota Indian reservation. The siege by Native Americans at Wounded Knee was over, the FBI humiliated by an unwinnable takeover from which they had to withdraw, but a month later the two agents on patrol were gunned down with semiautomatics, because they were symbols of the U.S. government.

"The danger is high," says Donnato. "You understand that, right? If Stone makes you, he will escalate fast."

"Like he escalated when he made Steve."

That is the nasty irony: By placing an undercover in Dick Stone's orbit, not only did we wake the beast but we armed him with righteous fury, too.

"I have to tell you, as your contact agent, that it's your choice as the undercover to decide whether or not you feel comfortable with the level of safety we can provide."

Donnato's look is deeply still and troubling. Feeling seems to overflow his eyes.

My head clears. Despite the fatigue, I find myself in a manic state of bungee-jump excitement. I want to get back—to the suspects, the drama, my role in it—to the roller-coaster ride. This is rapture, and there is no way back.

"It's a go."

"Then nail it," Donnato says. "The prisoners are being released. Make sure you go home with Dick Stone."

It is 112 degrees in the tiny interrogation room. As we haul to our feet, Donnato surprises me with a daringly swift kiss on the mouth, leaving the sweet salt taste of apprehension and longing.

The ragged activists are standing in the blustery sunlight outside the facility that houses the county sheriff's department and jail. All the prisoners have been released on bail except for Bill Fontana, who is still being held for questioning. We gather in groups, our hair matted and our clothes mud-stained, survivors trading stories.

Megan hugs me good-bye.

"This is not the end of it," she vows. "We'll be back."

"You will," I say forlornly. "I have no idea what I'll be doing. Maybe living in a crapped-up town like this."

The sandstone building that houses the jail blends into a residential area, the single part of town that does not appear to have been completely desolated by the closing of the mill. There is a brick library and a new high school, where male youth wearing baggy pants and sporting goatees linger along the fence, glued to their cell phones, like everywhere else.

"What do you mean?" Megan asks.

She doesn't have to turn around to sense that Dick Stone is standing now beside her, backlit, every thread on the shoulder of his white Navajo jacket magnified by the cold light. She reaches for his hand and their fingers entwine.

"Ready to get out of here?" he asks.

"Just a sec. What are you going to do, Darcy?"

"I don't know, Megan. I'm totally screwed. My landlord's kicking me out. The cops impounded my car because it was parked overnight at the rest stop. It'll cost a hundred and twenty-five bucks to get it back, and I don't have a job right now; plus, I've been arrested again, so *that's* on my record. And guys like Laumann get off scot-free."

"Be at peace and know that things are unfolding exactly as they should," Dick Stone says enigmatically. He ties a bandanna around his big head. His tanned skin looks vibrant, as if it belongs in the daylight of the high desert; like he's going out for pancakes, not as if he might have killed a man last night.

Wind slices our faces, bringing genuine tears.

"Really? The cops pulled my records. They saw I was arrested once before, for hacking a computer system down in L.A. They took me in for questioning and it got scary. They said if I didn't want a felony charge, I'd have to give up names."

The wind cuts like diamonds.

"Names?"

"In the movement. Don't worry. I didn't."

A pause. They believe me.

"You should have seen her last night, Julius, when she jumped into the middle of the horses to save poor Lillian. You were so determined, Darcy. I was so proud of you! You were utterly selfless," Megan says. "You have a calling for this work."

We stand in silence in the shifting air. A big, fat, hairy tumbleweed gets stuck against the fence of the high school, where two kids are lighting cigarettes.

I hope they don't set that thing on fire.

Dick Stone is watching me. I squint at his face in the billowy light but catch only the tail end of the look in his eyes, like the whisper of a closing door.

He knows.

"Could I crash with you guys? Just for a couple of days?"

"Stay as long as you like," Megan says.

"I hate to ask. This wasn't the game plan." My eyes are watering from the wind and an insane euphoria.

"She can share a room with Sara," Megan's telling Stone.

"I have skills," I offer, although not too fast. "This thing isn't over. Not until we free the horses for good."

"See?" says Megan.

Dick Stone doesn't answer. He doesn't argue, but he doesn't agree, either, just squeezes Megan's shoulder and fishes around in the big square pocket of the woolen Navajo jacket for the keys to the white truck. I pretend not to glimpse the butt of the Colt.

Patience. It's important in our line of work.

PART THREE

Sixteen

It is a common American farmhouse, with a wraparound porch supported by spindle posts and decorated with carvings of Victorian lacework—the kind of house a young man rolling off a freight train from Missouri in 1898 would have said looked just like home. For a hundred years, it has survived searing valley summers and the creeping moisture of the winter with the worn-down crankiness of an arthritic farmer's wife.

Waiting on the front steps beside Darcy DeGuzman's knapsack, I am trying to make friends with the house, now that I have come to stay, but it keeps shrugging me off with discomforting distractions: rotted floorboards, sinks rusting in the weeds, a pen with two goats and the three surviving ducks, a lidded cardboard box on the porch with mysterious scratching inside.

Around the turn of the twentieth century, Megan tells me, lots of faraway places were starting to look like home, because factory-made houses could be sent across the country on the railroads. Megan's grandfather did not have to crawl very far down the tracks to find a hog operation in the Willamette Valley remarkably like the one he'd just blown off in Jefferson City, Missouri. After a few thousand miles and a broken leg sustained in the decisive leap off the boxcar in which he had stolen a ride, this simple two-story homestead must have seemed like heaven to the boy when the farmer who owned the land pulled him from a ditch, dehydrated, two days later. At age fourteen, Megan's grandfather apprenticed himself to the farmer on the spot, in the hope—like many of us have—that one day he would get back exactly what he had left behind.

That is how Megan's family came to own the place, and why it is a sanctuary to this day. Because of the kindness of that anonymous farmer, Megan believes this land is blessed, and she will not refuse shelter to animals or humans in need. That is the history anyway. The story she tells. Knowing that she and Dick Stone have shared a secret life on this overgrown, isolated property, undisturbed all these years, suggests another reason to hold on to Grandpa's goods.

The scratching in the box is making me edgy. Carefully, I open the lid, to discover half a dozen abandoned baby rabbits. I lift one out, holding the warm, soft body in my cupped hands as we share a word-less consolation.

It's sad in this world without a mom.

A white pickup pulls into the driveway and Megan waves. I put the quivering bunny back.

"Welcome to the lost farm," she says cheerfully, carrying bags of groceries. "Whatever nobody else wants ends up here. Can you believe someone left these babies at the dump?"

"What will happen to them?"

"They're ours."

"You have a big heart, Megan."

"I never had children, so I have animals. My neighbor once asked me to watch her llamas—she left to visit her sister and came back two years later."

Two years? My bullshit detector has started to ping, but Megan is laughing. It's a joke. *Loosen up.* Megan is loose, in baggy work pants and an oversized orange linen shirt. Following her through the door, I see that since I last saw her at the BLM corrals, she has put streaks of raspberry and crimson in her ropy gray hair.

Inside the farmhouse, the hot, dead air smells like the acres of clothes in the old bomb shelter, in the subbasement at Quantico, where we chose our costumes for the Bureau's tireless mind games.

"You will be observed for signs of deceit that suggest you're not who you say you are."

Here, also, time has a smell, and the smell has accumulated in the mismatched cushions and Oriental rugs and curtains of gold lamé, and it is gripping me with vivid awareness.

I have penetrated someone's inner world.

I revel in the treachery, experiencing the same satisfaction Darcy would have felt hacking into the biotech company's computer system. Fact or fiction, I discover there is a tasty thrill in crossing the line. I am elated not to be who I say I am.

"Can I make you a cup of tea?"

"That would be lovely."

Megan goes, and I want to twirl around the room, a treasure trove of clues, although you would need a team of investigators to comb the layers of cozy kitsch—ashtrays, lamps, Depression glass, doilies, tin trays, detective magazines—everything carefully arranged and dusted.

On the wall is an authentic DeKalb barn sign—the flying corn with the wings—the same deliberate symbol of the Midwest as on Dick Stone's cap. Well, folks, we've already deciphered that one. On the wooden mantel is a collection of clocks, new and old, all of them accurate. Again, the scent and feel of time, bottled and corked—like their twenty-year outlaw run?

There is a gentle clicking sound. I look up from the broken-down sofa where I have sunk to my hips, surprised to see a stunning young woman enter through the swaying bones of bamboo.

She is the same rescuing angel I saw when I first came to the farm, yet the appearance of Sara Campbell from the same curtain through which Megan Tewksbury vanished, bearing the tea that Megan promised, seems a mocking transformation of the older woman; as if Megan, with her boozy sentiment and half-dyed dreadlocks, had been banished to the drudgery of the kitchen so this radiant being could emerge.

Not that the girl is scornful in any way. She is a barefoot geisha in blue jeans, back straight, kneeling gracefully to set the teacup down.

"Hi." She smiles uncertainly.

"I'm Darcy. We met when I brought the ducks."

"That's right. The sick one died. It was awful."

She has long, thin arms and legs, and blond hair so fine and cropped so short, it lays like a halo around her head.

She eases down, sitting cross-legged on the rug.

"Megan says you're committed."

"I am."

"So am I."

"That's good."

"We all are."

"Who is?"

"Everyone who lives here."

Sara's face has become serious. Her grave composure clutches at your heart. Barely out of her teens, her impeccable beauty, like that of the wild horses, arises from genuine innocence. Looking up, her eyes are winsome and unself-conscious, and the curve of her temple is enough to make you want to pick up a pen and draw.

"And that would be?"

"Well, it's me, Megan, Slammer, and Julius. And the animals."

Take it slowly.

"Julius—he mainly takes care of the orchard?"

"The trees are his passion. I guess he's the one who turned this place around."

"You guess?"

"I've only been living here three months."

"And Julius?"

"He and Megan have been together for a while. I'm not really sure."

"He told me he was a bandit."

Sara laughs. "Julius has a wonderful sense of play."

" 'Play'?"

"He's just messin'."

"How did you all"—I make a motion, like stirring a pot—"meet?"

Sara draws her legs up. She turns her head and lays a cheek on her knees. I can see her wistful look reflected in the large round mirror of a dressing table. Throughout the rooms, there are thrift shop Art Deco dressing tables with big round mirrors. You turn a corner and catch a shocking glimpse of yourself in the circular glass, as if the house is watching you with many eyes.

"It was Julius," she says, sighing, "who saved us from the streets."

And she's in love with Daddy?

"Slammer and I were squatting with a family under a bridge in Portland. Not your normal family—everyone was a runaway. The oldest guy, SB, was in his twenties. There were a lot of drugs, a lot of violence, but what made me want to leave was the way people turned on each other, just because SB told them to.

"His name was really Satan's Boy. It was *really* Duane, or whatever. There was this one girl who was mentally retarded—we used to call her Bubbles—and one day SB accused her of lying to him. . . . You know what?" She stops. "That's negative energy, and I'm here now."

"Did something bad happen to Bubbles?"

Her face closes up and she presses her lips against her knee, then sinks her teeth into her own skin and chews on it in order to keep from seeing it again, the bad thing that happened to Bubbles.

"You don't have to do that." I gently touch her hair. "It's okay."

She stops and turns her face away. The sun raises a soft orange corona along the ridge of her bare shoulders. She is wearing two fraying tank tops, one over the other, and a heavy silver pendant of three interlocking triangles.

"Megan has the same necklace," I observe.

She sniffles. "It's a valknot."

"Nordic, right?"

"There was a king in the seventh century." She turns her head and lifts wet, translucent eyes. "King Odin. It represents his powers—to *bind* or to *open* our minds. It means 'knot of the chosen.' "

"Cool. Can I get one?"

"Only if you've taken the vows to follow the Allfather," she says cautiously.

"Is Julius the Allfather?"

She nods.

"And the vows?"

"I can't talk about that."

I grin. "Well, I guess we're all chosen. For something. Like you guys winding up here together." I make the stirring motion again. "Slammer, huh? What's his story?"

"Survival."

"Got it. Did you two run away together?"

She laughs a little and wipes her eyes. "Are you kidding? We're from totally different backgrounds. Where my parents live, he couldn't get past the gate."

"Your parents must be looking for you."

She shrugs. "They gave up on me in high school. They are not in my life. In the squat, Slammer and I made a pact to stick together, so when Julius showed up and said he could live on the farm, Slammer said if I couldn't go, he wouldn't go, either."

Dick Stone cruises the underbelly of Portland, recruiting street kids—young and vulnerable and not easily traced.

I sip the tea. It tastes like twigs.

"I left home, too. Moved to Portland from Los Angeles."

Sara is bemused. "I can't see *you* on the street," she says, which I find vaguely insulting. "Don't ever go to Pioneer Square at night. You can't imagine how those kids are living." Her eyes fill again. "It's so sad."

I give her a moment and ask, "Where are you from?"

"Dirt," she says, floating to her feet as Megan comes back through the curtain.

"Let's get you settled."

The three of us climb the dark-wood staircase to the attic room the girl and I will share. The wallpaper is fragile and old-fashioned, sweetheart roses, original to the house. I pick out the daily life of this jerry-rigged clan from the smells that have risen up the staircase on strata of hot air: cat food, musty rugs, herbal shampoo, sage incense, and weed.

"Where is Julius?"

"Out on his tractor," Megan replies. "He's always on his tractor." And I hear it through the window on the landing before I can see Dick Stone through the panes of glass, a small figure in a straw hat on a red machine, going up and down the rows with unwavering resolve.

At the turning of the stair, directly on the wall in front of us, is yet another timepiece, an antique wall clock in a simple wooden case, hands as thin as pencil lines, trembling past the hour. The steady drone of the tractor goes back and forth, a rhythm of comfort and plenty, in harmony with the swaying of the pendulum of the clock and the roses on the wall, and the scent of baking piecrust blooming up the stairs—promising to fill you up, whatever your emptiness may be.

Seventeen

Herbert Laumann's sick baby is up two or three times in the night, so they take her into their bed. She is finally asleep, a soft, warm weight on her father's chest, when he is forced by the alarm to face the dawn. From the quality of light peeping underneath the Roman shades, he knows the sky will be clear. No rain.

Ambition, that indefatigable gear, gets the priority of the day turning in Herbert Laumann's sleep-deprived brain. The priority is water. As deputy state director, the continuing drought in the eastern part of the state is first thing on his mind these days. It means he'll keep on hearing complaints—from ranchers as well as his own district managers—because nothing has changed out here in the West in the past two hundred years. It is still the cattlemen versus the farmers in the fight for public lands and water, only now you've got the radical element mixed in.

Guys like Laumann are in the middle, trying to balance the politics of multiple use; doing the eight-to-five civil servant bit because it's better to be wearing a shirt and tie and commute and have the weekends on the boat with your family than be driving a rig through alfalfa and timothy grass like your father did 24/7, cracked red hands blown up like balloons, the inhaler always in the bib pocket.

Being allergic to your life's work is a tragedy.

Still in bed, he reaches for cigarettes and gets one lit without singeing his baby's hair or waking up his still-fat and irritable wife. He does not have to worry about waking Alex. On the cusp of being a teenager, the boy could sleep until noon.

The first nicotine rush of the morning is like God's own inhale before He blew life into the creatures of the earth. Laumann savors a divine pause. A lot of people would run from this FAN thing, afraid of becoming a target for extremists just for doing the job you were hired to do. There are lunatics everywhere; you have to stand up to them.

Laumann replays his triumph at the animal rights convention. It pumps him up, gets him going: how he ignored the intimidation of four hundred people booing and hissing and got up on that stage; how he put that punk away with the courage of a father defending his children, just as every day he goes into his office and defends our precious public lands. Those accusations of him allegedly buying horses and selling them—to a *slaughterhouse*? Bumbled paperwork! Never happened! A deplorable and false personal attack, he insisted to the crowd. Then, a brilliant diversion: He invited the whole rowdy bunch to go out to the corrals and *see* how the horses are treated. *Understand* the BLM is the good guy, doing the right thing. At the end? He got applause! And the punk, Fontana? Thoroughly deballed.

"Don't blow smoke on Rosalie!" complains his wife without opening her eyes.

"You take her," he replies.

Not even halfway out of his arms and the kid is screaming. The wife unbuttons her nightgown.

Laumann pulls a plaid wool shirt over his pajamas and goes down the stairs, which smell of the new navy blue runner. He likes the feel, like walking barefoot on a carpet of lichen. Already he has lit a second cigarette, hit the coffee machine, the weather station on a small TV, and picked up the newspaper, running his eye over the headlines. He has to focus on these things before the other thing, the uneasiness, kicks in.

He forces his gaze from the garden window. A cup of Irish vanilla, and he is at the computer, fully charged. He'll send an e-mail to his district managers and drum up support for building that reservoir out near Steens Mountain, where the drought is impacting the rangeland.

FAN will make noise about it. *Screw them.* These amateur thugs do not have what he has: the big picture.

Laumann's wife is running downstairs with the baby wrapped in a blanket. The baby's face is pomegranate red and she is making rasping coughs.

"Croup," she says. She is a nurse; she knows.

"Get her in the shower."

"I did. We have to go to the emergency room."

"What about Alex?"

"Drop me and come back for him. Remember to take his tennis bag—he's got a tournament."

Laumann stops typing mid-sentence, reaches for his car keys, lopes up the navy blue stairs, pulls on pants, runs downstairs, runs upstairs again for the car keys he left on the bed, checks on Alex, beautiful and asleep, runs downstairs, to find his wife already out, the back door banging behind her.

They've been through this twice before, and each time the panic is the same. That is the real uneasiness. Damn it to hell. Rosalie's tiny lungs. Damn, it almost makes him cry. Which impurities of the modern world are making her sick? What weakness did his father pass along? He stumbles through the early-morning air, icy cold, like mountain water, and thinks irrationally, *I must provide.*

The Explorer pulls out of the driveway and accelerates fast.

There is a pause, ten seconds of negative time, long enough for the dust to settle, and then a hard percussive shot and one side of the Laumann house volcanoes out, spewing lumber and new carpeting with orange fire-tongued breath, raining down the unspeakable.

Eighteen

The screen door in the kitchen opens hard, banging against the wall.

"Attack of the vegetables!" Slammer shouts, lunging through with the energy of an entire basketball team. *"Destroy all humans!"*

He is carrying crates of fresh-picked produce, wearing a denim jacket with the sleeves cut off to show a colorful swirl of tattoos on both arms, as if he dipped them up to the elbows in Easter egg dye.

Sara takes the weight of one of the crates, heady with damp earth fragrance, and looks past his shoulder to the organic garden, where the sun has deepened the morning shadows. She stays a foot against the screen door, gazing at the beds of violet-tipped lavender. Her breath forms in the cold country air.

"What?" Slammer asks.

"Reminds me of home."

"Your parents must live in a pile of goat shit."

She smiles ironically. He stamps his filthy boots. Draping an arm over my shoulders, he whispers, "The feds are here."

"Really? Where?"

"Look."

Peering through the kitchen window, we can see the utility truck. A repairman is up in a cherry picker.

Slammer had a good look when he went into the garden.

"The feds wouldn't be that stupid," I say.

"They're on to us. The BLM dude's house got vaporized, dog."

"Yeah, but why would they care about us?"

He grins. "We blow shit up."

Me, innocent: "Did we blow up Laumann's house?"

The bomb was detonated by a cell phone. Same as the device that killed Steve. Herbert Laumann and his wife and baby escaped by minutes. Twelve-year-old Alex, asleep in bed, sustained third-degree burns. He is expected to survive. Angelo considers Bill Fontana and Dick Stone both suspects in the bombing. Fontana is in custody. The motive would be murderous rage. No question the hero of the movement was humiliated when the deputy state director invaded the stage.

"*I* didn't do that bomb," Slammer says warily.

"Was it FAN?"

"We are FAN," Sara says, wanting my attention. "But so are a lot of people."

I have noticed sibling rivalry never ends, even when you're not related.

"Allfather says they're tapping our phones," she jabbers on. "I hear clicking all the time when I'm talking, don't you?"

Yes, and that's why we're up in the cherry picker for the second time this week. Why can't they get it right?

"Sometimes I say, 'Hey, Fed? Are you listening?' "

I chuckle, but my throat is dry. "Make sure you only talk about embarrassing personal stuff."

Slammer, teasing: "Not Sara. Sara's a little prude."

Sara's cheeks turn pink. "You suck."

He gives an evil grin and snaps a carrot between his teeth. Completely the opposite of ethereal Sara, who could float away on the steam drifting out of the kitchen, Slammer (aka Jim Allen Colby) is always banging and stomping, eager to destroy whatever's standing still, usually with a dim-witted expression of glee.

The prominent ears sit equidistant between a fringe of light hair and a long chin, directly in line with the fair eyebrows and narrow eyes that appear to have been passed down through generations of con artists and thieves. His nose is flat and his lips are full (actresses would pay a lot of money for those plump lips), but on Slammer, they seem childlike, on the verge of lying—or, if that doesn't work, blubbering.

Megan describes Slammer as "a feral animal" when Dick Stone recruited him from under the bridges of Portland. The boy, if you believe him, is a warrior without a soul. His mission is to "expose cowards." Incorrigible since he was kicked out of day care for attacking other children, he set fire to his father's house and ran away from a detention center at age fourteen, pissing all over a lumber town up in the state of Washington, for a half-starved squatter's life with a street family of violent youth—exactly the kind of hot-blooded seventeen-year-old you want in your army.

And he is still uncontainable, shooting off guns, setting pesky little fires, stealing from the drugstore when they take him into town, flying down the sidewalk on a skateboard with his neck chains and do-rag and baggies that are halfway down his ass, a black-garbed neo-pirate, jumping the curb and flipping the bird to drivers too stupid to stop.

Sara goes back to kneading whole-wheat dough. It is 10:30 in the morning and we are starting dinner. It takes a while when you bake your own bread and extract your own almond milk. For some families, I guess, food is a pleasant ritual; on the lost farm, it is another form of slavery.

Everything is strictly vegan, and to Dick Stone's specifications. The first night, I cut up sweet potatoes to be roasted in the oven, but Megan made me take them out, still sizzling with hot oil, and make the wedges smaller, because that's the way Allfather likes them. The scorched fingertips were part of the initiation.

Yesterday, we had to hand-rake every twig and piece of bird dropping from the orchard floor, which must be kept "smooth as a pool table," according to Stone, because when the nuts drop, you don't want chaff in the harvester. That's fine, except hazelnuts don't drop until September, and it's barely June. Abruptly, he told Slammer he did not appreciate his "work ethic," and made us all run twenty laps around the trees in the afternoon heat.

Sara, not in any kind of shape, was struggling hard. Her legs were slow and rubbery and her face was hot pink.

In undercover school, they would have asked, "What is the lesson learned?"

"Sara's getting heatstroke," I told Stone on the pass. "She's had enough."

He put out his foot and tripped me.

The earth under my knees and in my mouth was soft. I got up and kept on running, so he could not see the look on my face. That was a killer moment, the hardest so far. *To put aside your core values in order to accomplish the mission.* I had to spit it out. I had to think about justice for Steve Crawford's family. About the day the sky will be filled with helicopters, and Dick Stone will be in prison the rest of his life.

I stare at the zucchinis with distrust. They are fat as blimps. I will need a computer model to figure out how to dice them into the tiny squares that Megan demands. I sharpen the ancient blackened carbon steel knife for the umpteenth time.

"What's *up* with Megan?" Slammer is asking. "Why is she in the basement all the time?"

Megan has been working on her quilt, stretched on a frame that takes up almost the entire room. Since the action at the BLM corrals, which she calls "a total disaster," she has abandoned the kitchen to the children, and we have heard raised voices behind the closed door of the master bedroom.

"She's sad." Sara picks up the dough and slams it. "She thinks it's our fault the cop died at the corrals."

"That's so weak? The pigs were waiting in ambush. Fuck them. They brought it on themselves."

Slammer's sitting on a kitchen chair, knees splayed, flicking bits of dough on the floor.

"Stop that!" I snap.

I am not going to make it if I have to chop zucchini and babysit a couple of spoiled, ignorant, hormone-deranged teenagers for the next six months, waiting for something that might not ever happen.

Angelo Gomez warned about this very moment: "You're driving yourself deeper," he said of one of his own undercover assignments that lasted thirteen months. "Losing your identity and becoming part of the criminal element. I looked bad, smelled bad. I had a big beard all filled with food and crap. I lived a lie. I was a lie. I wore this big gold cross, and that's what saved me. I'd lean against the bar so the cross would press against my chest, and something inside would keep me going."

"Look," says Sara. "The pig's still there."

The lineman's truck has moved down the road, but he is still up in the cherry picker, a splotch of blue overalls below the branches of a pine tree, face hidden in the green. He seems disembodied—a faceless man in a generic uniform, the top of his body gone.

The smell of burned brake lining seems to rise from the pots on the stove. I cannot look again, because I know it will be the face of the police detective that I shot, suspended between heaven and hell. Like a clumsy drumroll, my heart skips a beat and hits race pace in three seconds. The ghost outside the window, ordinary as a telephone repairman, splits my mind.

Who owns me?

"The cross would press against my chest," Angelo said. "And I'd remember, There's something else in life besides what I'm doing."

A crimson trail is crawling down the sink.

I've sliced my finger and it won't stop bleeding.

Dick Stone lumbers into the kitchen, boots unlaced after the morning's work.

"I found this."

He shows us Darcy DeGuzman's cell. He's gone through my stuff.

"Thanks." I reach for it.

He swallows the phone in one big hand. "No personal cell phones allowed."

"Nobody told me."

Slammer and Sara have become alert. Suddenly, the boy is busy helping form the whole-wheat loaves.

"No wallets." Stone is holding the one he has confiscated from my pack. "No watches, either."

I remove my watch and smile feebly. "My time is your time."

He drops my things into the bib of his overalls. Tension crawls into the kitchen and hisses.

Dick Stone waits, eyeing us.

Megan is downstairs, unable to intervene.

He raises an arm and presents a neon orange daypack.

"Who wants to test this out?"

"Me!" Slammer shouts.

The bandit considers. "I want Darcy to do it," he says, and you can see the hurt cross Slammer's face.

"Okay with me if Slammer really wants to." I am pressing a paper towel around the finger cut.

Stone, quietly: "I said Darcy."

Under a tree away from the house, Stone orders Slammer to help me put the backpack on. It weighs maybe fifteen pounds.

"What does it do?"

"Blows shit up," Slammer replies. "You pull that cord."

"I don't think so."

I try to wriggle out, but he's latched the buckles.

"No big deal. Just a little pop and red stuff sprays all over the place."

"Another blood bomb? Like the one at the school?"

"New prototype," Stone says briskly. "Ten times more powerful. For the Big One."

He adjusts something sticking out of the pack.

"What's the Big One? Hey, what are you doing?"

He has flipped open my cell phone and is scrolling through the numbers.

"Where is area code five six one?" he calls, backing away.

"West Palm Beach, Florida."

"Nervous, Darcy?"

"Not at all. Are you?"

"My heart is going pitty-pat." He reads a number. "Whose is this?"

"My dad's."

"Pull the cord!" Slammer yells.

Sara's beside him, arms crossed over her chest.

"Should I hit redial and find out?" Dick Stone asks. "You tell me."

Is this another head game? He was undercover. Does he know how the phony phone numbers work? Did the FBI use the same technique in the seventies?

"Go ahead and hit redial. Say hi to my dad."

The relays worked at the off-site, but they haven't been tested since. Why does Stone hesitate, staring at the phone?

Slammer: "Pull the cord, dingdong!"

Now I see. Stone has rigged the cell so it will detonate the bomb inside the backpack—just like at Herbert Laumann's house. Just like with Steve. A seven-digit key code on an FBI phone is about to make another undercover go up like a roasted guinea pig.

What a turn-on for him.

"You are such a chicken shit," Slammer yells, and rushes me, roaring like a linebacker. I run, but he makes the tackle. We both go down and roll as Dick Stone warns, "I'm hitting redial," and Slammer gropes for the cord and pulls.

The sharp report of a firecracker. The world goes silent. Burning vapor stings my legs, and in an instant we are both covered in slime, staggering in the center of a perfect twelve-foot circle of blood.

Dick Stone whoops with delight. "It works! The Big One, man!"

Sara is bent over, laughing at our crimson horror-mask faces. "Look at you!"

Stone lumbers toward me, giggling, the phone outstretched.

"Sorry, darlin'. Dad's not home."

This sounds extremely funny to Sara and Stone.

I put the phone to my ear.

"This is George DeGuzman. I can't get to the phone right now—"

The voice is familiar: George DeGuzman, Darcy's dad, as played by SAC Robert Galloway.

Backstopping.

A screen door between the truth and me.

My fingers are trembling and slippery. It is hard to keep a grip. The phone wants to leap out of my hand.

Megan appears on the front steps, breathless from the run up the basement stairs at the sound of the explosion. She stares at the ludicrous scene, like a postmodern take on hell, Slammer and I swathed in bloody stigmata, blinded souls in a Day-Glo ring of red.

"Are you all out of your minds?" she says.

Sara and Stone are helpless, holding on to each other, wiping tears of manic laughter.

"We're having some fun," he manages to reply.

Nineteen

"He's on to us."

"Calm down."

"He found the cell phone. Went through the numbers, like he knew exactly what he was looking for—a leak. A mistake."

"Were there? Mistakes?"

"No, but Mike, he took my wallet and watch. Removed all contact with the outside world. He's watching me."

"Of course he's watching you. He's protecting the cult. Besides, he's a raging paranoid. Reality check: You're talking to me, so he has failed. Where is he now?"

"Flailing."

"Sailing?"

I have no patience. "He is *flailing*—pulling a rotor to clear the vegetation between the trees."

Dick Stone has not discovered the tiny Oreo phone, hidden in the barn under a heavy tack box. I volunteer to feed the animals at first light because it is the only time to be alone. I put on sweats and clogs and hurry across the yard, past the rabbit pen (their numbers dwindling—another one stolen or escaped) before the others wake. The worn barn boards ring with a note of optimism. Here is grain. Here a warm muzzle. The clang of the bucket, the needy cry. In the quiet, the dualities that shout inside my head like opposing political commentators settle down to nothing but the hollow thump of hindquarters on wood, the chesty cough, the uneventful silence in between.

At this same hour in a gated community of postmodern homes in Simi Valley, California, family life is stirring. A grueling commute to Westwood lies ahead for Mike Donnato, who takes my reports while getting dressed and his three sons off to school.

I go on to tell Donnato about the punishment in the orchard—being tripped up when I defended Sara, and the bullying with the loaded backpack.

"He was testing a blood bomb—more powerful—for what he calls 'the Big One.' "

Donnato considers. "Dick Stone is sounding like another David Koresh."

"Please God, no!"

Koresh, who believed he was the incarnation of Jesus Christ, was the leader of the Branch Davidians, a religious group that went down in flames during a suicidal standoff in Waco, Texas. It was another government debacle, as tragic and deluded as the FBI's confrontation with Native Americans at Pine Ridge, South Dakota, where Jack Coler and Ron Williams were killed. In Waco, seven hundred agents and law-enforcement personnel, including Delta Force, attacked with Bradley fighting vehicles and tanks, recklessly shooting tear gas into the compound and causing an inferno. Koresh and some eighty of his followers killed themselves or were burned to death, including children.

Here on the lost farm, birds are singing their hearts out and wind ruffles the big-leaf maples. In the distance, cars begin their noisy claim to the country roads, and deep in the valley, a chain saw. Closer, there is the scrape of hooves on the old planks, and the faint ringing of chains in the cross ties. As I gaze through the wide doorway of the barn at the placid Victorian farmhouse, half-sunk in coronas of lavender, my stomach churns. The Branch Davidians believed their spread was a sanctuary, too.

"What's the mood?"

"Megan is depressed, Stone is high. The kids are staying out of the line of fire."

"What's going on with Megan and Stone?"

"She wanted to return these beautiful horses to freedom, and it all turned to shit."

"Sounds like an opening."

"She's a lot more practical. He's all Action Jackson, flies off the handle."

"If there's a wedge between them, drive it."

"Roger that."

"Hold on a minute—"

I overhear Donnato speaking sharply to his wife, Rochelle, and wish I hadn't. It's the kind of talk that other people shouldn't hear—the phone tap that blows the cover. If I were married to him, we would sound like that sometimes, too, which kind of kills the fantasy. On the other hand, would I rather be in an air-conditioned bedroom, arguing with a good-looking man in his underwear, or standing in a pile of horse manure?

I turn for solace to Sirocco, a pretty mustang mare with buckskin coloring and a white blanket with black spots on her rear. Three months ago Megan rescued her from a racetrack where she had been a companion horse to Thoroughbreds. She had fallen on the track and broken her hip. She was pregnant at the time and lost the baby. Now she is unrideable, suited only for a pet or the slaughterhouse.

Sirocco is patient with amateurs like me and doesn't kick while I hide out in her stall. From here, I have good sight lines through the barn doors. Across the road, the tops of the hazelnut trees are still in darkness, but as the sun rises, golden light begins to play across the orchard floor, each rut and groove struck visible, as if a ghostly herd had left a thousand hoofprints filled with shadow. The crows are making a racket, pierced by the engine of Stone's tractor starting up with an aggressive whine.

"Now is not the time," Donnato tells his wife. "Can't you take the kids to school?" Then to me: "Hi, I'm back."

"What's the matter, pal?"

"Pressure."

"How's her dad?"

"Not good."

I can hear his tension, but it is nothing compared to the sound of the tractor, like a raging alarm through my nervous system. I am pacing, keeping a lookout through the open doors in both directions. Stone, wearing the battered straw hat, keeps on going back and forth.

I don't like it. I don't believe it. Why would Stone give it all up to plod the same rectangle day after day? Why, after those mint-issue Los Angeles mornings, when everything is possible, would you cut yourself off from success? Twenty-five years old, freshly shaven, wearing a starched white shirt and tie, he had to have felt like a hero about to be made—the Smith & Wesson in the shoulder holster, draping his coat on the seat back, Mr. Cool, hanging the handcuffs over the brake pedal in case he had to make a quick move out of the Bu-car.

Why did Dick Stone, "eager to be led in the right direction," renounce it all and quit, so bitter he went over to the other side? Catching sight of the rig, precisely arcing in the turning space beyond the trees, I am certain of one thing: A cop does not surrender his weapon. Not ever.

"Mike? Are you there?"

Donnato and Rochelle are still squabbling. "All right, I'll take them. Do they have their lunches?"

Sirocco's head is hanging lax, eyes shut. I brush her back. Dust rises. My eyes are on the furrows made by the bristles, the way the buckskin hairs line up glossy and flat; I'm concentrating my impatience on this small but solvable task. Faintly, a screen door slams. Inside the house, they are awake and moving.

"Damn it, Mike! I am in a covert situation here."

Sirocco wakes up and shimmies her neck like a dog with fleas. She stamps and backs up quickly, squashing me against the corner of the stall. Over her spotted rump, the shape of Dick Stone is looming against the light.

"Who are you talking to?"

I flip the Oreo phone shut and enclose it in the palm of my hand.

"Sirocco," I say, petting her. "Right, girl?"

Dick Stone's face is sweaty and his breath comes hard. Pieces of straw and a fine spray of dirt he must have kicked up marching through the barn at the sound of my voice are floating in the backlight. I can't believe I was not alert to the fact that the drone of the tractor had cut off. It is quiet now all right.

"You scared her," I say.

Drawing the brush along Sirocco's spine the way Megan showed me, maintaining contact with my hands on her coat, I slip around to the other side, keeping her body between us, and slide the phone into my underpants and, with one quick thrust, up into that place where the sun don't shine—well, not usually.

Stone, mocking: "I scared *her*?"

"Coming up suddenly like that."

Sirocco's ears flick and she swings her hindquarters.

Dick Stone levels a dead-on stare into my eyes. Alone and close, his male scent is strong, like my grandfather's, like the old-fashioned Vitalis that Poppy used to put in his hair.

"Where'd you grow up, Darcy?"

I squeeze my thighs in order not to drop the phone.

"Southern California."

"Where?"

"The Valley."

"Are you with someone?"

"I wouldn't be here if I was."

"Ever been married?"

"Nope."

"No exes? No boyfriends?" He appraises me. "I can't believe that."

My mouth is dry as the straw dust suspended in the air. "Yes, boyfriends. But I left them in L.A."

"Don't you have anyone in the world?" he presses. "Besides your dad, who lives in Florida?"

I pay attention to the distrust spreading through my body, core to fingertips.

Go on the attack. Get right back in their face.

"Why are you so interested in my dad? You want to send him a Father's Day gift?"

"Up to you."

What does that mean, Up to you?

"Where is *your* father living?" I counter. "I'd like to send *him* a card."

Dick Stone's left eyelid twitches. "I haven't thought about my father in forty years. I can't remember the sound of his voice."

"Tell me."

He snorts derisively. "About my *father*?"

You are pushing it. Get him out of here.

"You know what I did with all that?" Stone continues bitterly. "Wrapped it up in plastic, looped it around with tape, tied it up with rope real good, and shipped it the hell out of here."

He turns, expecting me to follow, but I have picked up a broom.

"I've got to finish."

If I move, I'll give birth to a communications device.

Dick Stone walks out of the barn. But then, in the wide square of daylight, he turns.

"Why'd you come here, Darcy?"

"To kick the government's ass," I say while holding my breath. "I came for action, not sweeping up horse shit."

"Uh-huh. Well you just muck out the stalls and feed the rabbits, and we'll see about action."

"We lost another rabbit—"

Shut up and let him go.

"I saw this morning," I continue perversely. "I can't figure how they're getting out."

"Nobody locks the cage," says Stone.

Twenty

I am awakened by gunfire. Crossing the rough floorboards of the attic room I share with Sara, I snap the roller shade. The tattered paper rises lazily, enough to let in a warm current of air perfumed with blackberries that hits me like the delighted slap of a baby on both of Mommy's cheeks. My brain lights up like a scoreboard. The sharp cracks coming from a distance are definitively shots. Who is killing whom in this pastoral psycho ward?

After feeding the animals that morning, I lay down again and fell into a doze. Now everyone is gone, I discover on this gorgeous summer morning as I hop around the house, pulling on shorts and sandals. Stone and Megan may have gone over to the grange, I remember; if so, they've taken Slammer to help load the hay. Sara's bed is empty.

Dick Stone has bad habits. If he's not out on the tractor, he's generally asleep. He has a lot of ailments. Megan keeps a slew of Chinese herbal remedies for his back, knees, and spleen. In the murky hours of the afternoon, after his morning nap, he will hobble downstairs and someone will be waiting to try to talk him out of his usual lunch of sweet rolls and cheap champagne.

But Stone is not in the disheveled bedroom, or the orchard, and the crackling shots have started up again.

I follow the sound, going out the kitchen door, past the rank old goats, the rabbits and ducks, into the barn to retrieve the Oreo phone, then out the back, running through high grass bordered by rampant blackberries. There is a vineyard of dead vines with unkempt half-assed spurs, and stakes in the ground that mark an abandoned garden. *Watch out for the hose and rusty wires.* Dick Stone keeps his orchard groomed; but behind the house, where nobody can see, everything runs wild.

Breaking into open field, I sprint past a marsh with a silver oval of groundwater in which you can just make out the vertical stance of a great white heron. Megan says that in her grandfather's day the acreage was used for wheat. She has given it back to migrating birds. I've found a trail through the cottonwoods and speed-dial Donnato in Los Angeles, wanting him to know I am heading into an uncertain situation. The sky is clear and the clouds are white and racing—there should be good reception, but the screen says, *No Service.* Even Rooney Berwick isn't perfect.

There's a streambed and I stumble through it, thrashing up the other side. I cannot say I am a woods person; always seem to pick the route with the most thorns. But now I've hit a maze of dirt roads and the going is easier and the shots are nearer. Tall cottonwoods have given way to a wasteland of scrub manzanita, crossed by an overhead grid of high electric wires. I'm in some kind of power station. The air changes. Fetid. Septic. Flies are buzzing an overflowing garbage can of trash—beer bottles and a recently disposed-of diaper.

Coming around a curve, I see a new half-ton Silverado, obsidian black, parked at the edge of the clearing. Beside it are a beach chair and a picnic cooler, and an old-fashioned portable radio playing country music, which you can't really hear over the exploding rounds. Straight ahead, his back to me, a white man of medium build is firing at silhouette targets on wire pulleys a hundred yards away.

The sleeves of his T-shirt are rolled up, James Dean–style, exposing gleaming muscles, and damn if he doesn't have a pack of cigarettes tucked in the fold. Out near the tree line, below the targets, are some sorry shot-up benches and piles of broken glass and rusted debris accumulated over the years, where the locals have been having a grand time blasting the hell out of innocent objects, like a refrigerator. Amazingly, a posted sign declares we're in a bird sanctuary.

I'm starting to get mad. Maybe it's the diaper.

"Hold your fire, please. Would you mind *holding fire?* Do you know this is a wildlife sanctuary?"

The man lowers the weapon and turns, squinting into the blinding sun.

"I ain't botherin' the birds."

"You could, though," I shout. "You could shoot one by accident. I just saw a bald eagle." *Okay, a heron.* "You realize you can go to jail for killing an American bald eagle?"

The rifleman says, "I think I know a target from a bird."

One hand shading his eyes, the man is peering at me with slow astonishment, as if I'd landed on his picnic table and swooped the hot dog off his plate.

"This land is protected! There are all kinds of life-forms here that shouldn't be destroyed. That's why we have laws, and why *the signs are posted!*"

I am delivering the rap with a passion that does not come from playing the undercover role, but from a deeper shift in my awareness. Remembering how it feels to run my fingers over the sore spots on Sirocco's back, I think maybe caring for another species *is* the most important thing that we can do. This is a new idea. Is it dangerous? Enlightened? Does it mean I am slipping over to the other side?

The Oreo phone is vibrating—Donnato returning the call. I guess there is intermittent service here, but suddenly I don't need it.

The man cradles the rifle so the barrel points up. It is a .308, common to every weekend shooter. He comes closer, until I notice the pointy toes of the worn cowboy boots in a peculiar shade of red, crunching over a carpet of spent casings, and the bandy legs in jeans.

His sunburned face has broken into a wide, sassy grin. "I sure hope you're not gonna call the police."

"I'm thinking about it."

"Truly. I would never shoot a protected animal."

"I already know how you feel about wild horses."

It is the wrangler from the BLM corrals.

He digs into his ears and removes two soft plugs. "What is that you're saying, ma'am?"

I am staring at him sternly, one hand on a hip. "Why are you following me?"

"No problem, ma'am. I'll go."

He may be using an ordinary hunting rifle, but nobody except an FBI agent calls anyone "ma'am." The bastards have put a tail on me.

"We've met, remember? My name is Darcy."

He wears a Nomex flight glove on his left hand and extends the right, the rest of his lean body shyly arching backward in an irritatingly boyish way.

"Sterling McCord, ma'am. Pleased to meet you again."

"What are you doing out here?"

"Just gave a shooting lesson. Ever fire a gun?" He smiles wickedly. There's a gap on the side of his mouth where a tooth is missing. "I bet you'd like it."

"Come on, Sterling, if that's really your name. I saw you at the BLM corrals, and now you're here, a mile from where I happen to be living on a hazelnut farm, which is not my usual territory, but you know all that, don't you?"

Sterling shakes his head.

"Sorry to bust your bubble, Darcy, but I had no idea I would have the pleasure of meeting you again. I'm just following the work, that's all. Doing some cowboyin'."

"For who?"

"Oh, a fella named Dave Owens, owns a little ranch just up the road."

"Uh-huh. What kind of work are you doing for Dave?"

"All kinds. Just drove a trailer full of cattle down from Idaho. Dave has cutting horses; I work them with the cows. You know cutting horses? Well, they're big money these days. Big show prizes. Dave's a good boss, but he's never there. He's in the insurance business, down in San Francisco."

"And this is your idea of 'cowboyin'?"

McCord cocks his head away. "Truthfully, I don't want to be a hand anymore. I want to be a horse trainer."

"Sounds like a cover to me."

"Cover for what?" Puzzled, he opens the lid of the cooler, offers a Corona. "Refreshment?"

"Guns and alcohol don't mix."

"I'm done. Sun's hot."

"All right."

"Thank you," he says mockingly. "Score one for my side."

I accept a cold beer and reject a packet of fried pork rinds. My eye, drawn to the red boots *(Are they ostentatious or not?)* falls to the gleaming litter of spent casings on the ground. Lying in the carpet of brass, two or three of an unusual caliber stand out. Most commonplace rifles, like McCord's, use .30-caliber bullets, but the shell I'm looking at is .50-caliber—harder to find because they are mostly used by Army snipers to knock out tanks.

And to kill cops.

Somebody out here has been taking shooting practice with the same unusual-size bullet that killed Sergeant Mackee.

While Sterling McCord pulls in the targets, I scoop two .50-caliber casings into the pocket of my shorts.

Silhouette targets are unusual, too, as most marksmen use bull's-eyes. And this guy is consistently scoring body shots, which shows a fair level of skill.

"Where'd you learn to shoot like that?"

"U.S. Army, Delta Force."

The openness of the answer is not what I expected.

"Delta Force? Isn't that an elite"—I want to say *unit*—"thing? How do you get to do something like that?"

"You have to be invited" is all McCord says.

You have to have ten years' service, be smart, have sniper-level skills with a rifle, and endure an eighteen-day selection course of physical deprivation and mental hardship that makes undercover school look like a sunny day in Tahiti.

"Is being in Delta Force like the movies? Secret missions, all that jive?"

"I don't know about that. Delta Force was good to me, but right now, I'm going back to the only thing that makes sense, which is horses."

I watch him clean the weapon. He is meticulous, patiently running a bore brush and guide rod from the back of the barrel toward the front. That's how the pros do it.

"You ask about cowboyin'?" he says, concentrating on the gun. "I'll tell you what it is. It's livin' in some itty-bitty trailer on the back of someone's property out near the dump, being treated like dirt, getting into a fight with the boss because he's some rich guy who doesn't know dog doo about cutting horses, and then moving on after six months. But I figure whatever low-rent job they throw at me, I'll do it if it makes me a better horseman."

"I'm taking care of a horse."

"Is that right?"

"Just learning how. I live on the hazelnut farm. Do you know Megan Tewksbury and Julius Emerson Phelps?"

He loads the cooler into the truck.

"No, but I heard the names from that other little girl lives over there."

"Sara?"

He is latching up the doors of the Silverado.

"That's right. She's the one I was teaching how to shoot."

"How do you know Sara?"

"Seen her around town. Told her my sorry story, just like I told you." He shrugs. "And she says she wants to learn about guns."

"She say why?"

"I never asked."

"We're . . . political, you know."

"Not my business. So maybe we'll meet up again. Stranger things have happened."

I hesitate. "Did I say thank you, Sterling?"

"For what, Darcy?"

"Saving my life."

"Back at the corrals? Nah, you were fine. Horses don't generally *want* to kill you, if they can avoid it."

McCord's got the door open and one boot up on the running board.

He waits. Again, the patience as one wrist in a tight copper bracelet rubs at the back of his sweat-stained neck. His hair is spiky and dirty blond; his eyes, like the bracelet, are rimmed with copper, green at the centers.

"Can I give you a ride?" he asks as someone shouts, *"Sterling! Wait!"*

Sara Campbell, in a pair of cheeky cutoffs and a scant top, charges around the curve in the road, running in her awkward knee-knocking gait. Her face is flushed persimmon. She falters.

"Sara!" he calls. "What's wrong?"

"Oh my God!" she sobs.

We both run toward her. I'm thinking, *Dehydration!* And, with a jealous edge, *Something's going on between these two.*

She is panting. "I was hoping you'd still be here."

"What's the matter, hon?"

"On my way back, I saw a baby horse. It's in the bushes—hurt really bad—and there's sickening blood just pouring everywhere."

"Blood *where*?"

She screws up her face. "Coming out of his eyes."

"Get in the truck," says McCord.

Twenty-one

The terrain rises and the vegetation becomes sparse as we roll out of the power station toward the mountains. Looking back from higher ground, you can see the cat's cradle of high-tension wires and transformers enclosed by manzanita, like an alien marker on a planet made of sand; only in America could there exist a sanctuary both for birds and bullets.

Wheeling the vehicle with the palm of one hand, McCord swerves off-road to the riverbed where Sara saw the foal, east of where I crossed the wooded stream. The bulky black machine raises veils of dust as it lurches over the sandstone grist of an ancient floodplain, no doubt fertile as a jungle a million years ago.

"What does it mean if a horse bleeds from the eyes?"

"Snakebite," says McCord. "The venom is an anticoagulant. They bleed out from everywhere."

"Can they die?"

"Yes, ma'am."

"Down there!" cries Sara.

McCord brings the truck to the edge of a ridge. We scramble out, into the kind of baking heat you feel with all the skin on your body all at once. A sun-dark lizard skitters at our feet. Below, a stand of cottonwoods marks the trail the river took, but since the drought, it has not passed this way in years. Birds with different voices are hidden everywhere; some sweet, some warning.

"Look! Underneath the branches."

A slender tree with a network of smooth willowy branches, bending to the ground like an old woman where the water used to flow, seems to gesture toward the body of a white baby horse lying on its side. All four legs kick out in a spasm that breaks my heart.

Coils of heat bake the sweat off my bare shoulders. The foal, where it lies, is fully exposed to the sun.

"Let's see what we got," says McCord. "*Quietly*. The wind's comin' that way. Don't want him to smell us and get aroused."

He motions that we get down into a squat and crab-leg it slowly toward the animal, stopping every ten feet to test the wind. Finally we are close enough to see it clearly in the lee of the branches. Its muzzle is swollen twice the normal size and bright red blood has covered its face, attracting glittering swarms of greenflies.

McCord reaches toward the chalky, almost translucent coat. It is not pure white; you can see dark clouds of pigment underneath, like a stormy desert sky. He runs his fingers along the neck, below a two-inch strip of bristly silver mane, and down the long and fragile legs, rosy with sores. In response, the baby tries to lift its head. Its face is long and delicately etched. The eyes are crying tears of blood. Pink-rimmed, with thick white lashes, they are opaque spheres of shiny blackened indigo.

"Shh now, just lie still."

Sara, whispering: "Was he just born?"

McCord is checking the scrawny ribs. "He's one month old and just about starved."

"Is he wild?"

"Probably got loose from a ranch. Looks to be part Arab. The mom either took off somewhere or she's dead. Anyone have a cell phone?"

Sara and I stare at each other, helpless and ashamed.

"We're not allowed to have cell phones on the farm," she says.

"Why's that? So you can't talk to your boyfriends?"

"We just can't."

I look at the ground and say nothing. My fingers clutch the Oreo phone in my pocket.

"Will this little guy live?"

"Depends if the toxin's already in the bloodstream. We got to call the vet."

I am about to curl up and die with guilt. I cannot make the call. To pull out the tiny phone now would be to expose myself.

You cannot blow a half-million-dollar operation on one stray horse.

"Don't get near his face. It's sore and we don't want him to move or raise his head. Damn. Everybody in the world has a damn cell phone. I left mine at the damn house."

"Why don't you get in the damn truck and get help?"

McCord holds his answer. He climbs up the embankment with long strides.

The girl is standing with her arms and feet all crossed up. She looks anxiously toward the truck. "Is he just gonna leave us here?"

I'm running my hand down the thin, pale throat of the foal, feeling the shuddering nerves.

"Touch him. He's soft."

"I don't want to. It's disgusting."

"Scary, huh?"

"Not at all," says Miss Nothing Affects Me. "I just don't enjoy watching something die, okay?"

"Then why were you taking shooting lessons?"

"Shooting lessons?" she says, as if she'd forgotten. "I don't know. He was coming on to me at the ice-cream store, so I said to myself, 'Okay, this is different.' He's cute, but kind of old."

McCord skids back down the hill on his heels, carrying a bottle of water and an old shirt.

"Keep him quiet. Sponge him down to cool him off. The rattler's most likely still around, so watch where you step."

"*Shit,*" says Sara, jerking her feet.

"What's wrong with his eyes?" Flies are walking on the darkened pupils.

"Oh," says McCord matter-of-factly. "This little baby is blind."

My stomach lurches. "Are you sure?"

McCord replies, "Yeah," and passes a hand before the dark violet eyes of the horse, which do not blink. "Could be why he was abandoned. I'm going for the vet."

McCord turns, but Sara grabs his arm.

"Just shoot him."

The world goes silent, except for the clicking of crows and the dry maraca rattle of insects in the grass.

"Shoot him," she insists.

McCord is astounded. "He's not my horse to shoot."

"He's nobody's horse. *Scary,* isn't it?" she taunts, mocking me. "Why not? You have guns in the truck."

McCord and I find each other's eyes, if only to affirm that we're the grown-ups here, not about to be manipulated by an overly indulged runaway brat. What, exactly, does she wish to kill? And what does she know about the acrid smell of the aftermath?

"Taking a life is serious business," says McCord, and then I am certain of what I have suspected: that he's been the places I've been.

"The horse is going to be *blind* the rest of its life," says Sara with disdain. "What's the point?"

The look between us deepens, not over the suffering of the child or the animal, but something much more tender and sad. McCord and I both know that way out here in the wash there are no landmarks beyond a yellow fire hydrant and a concrete bunker with some pipes in a mesh cage. This is where your heart is exposed, or where it's buried.

He does not wait, but climbs the ridge.

"Sara!" I am giving orders now. "Get in the truck and go with Sterling."

McCord looks down from the top of the embankment.

"Sara? Come on now. Come with me."

And he holds out his hand patiently until she finally scrambles up. He pulls her over the top and the truck disappears.

Space unrolls in every direction. I take a breath full of sage. I sit beside the foal and sponge the blood off its face. *Please don't be in pain. Please forgive me.*

The bees hum like a plucked string. I sit beneath a dead oak, against a mud bank where the broken root system is exposed. There are holes and burrows in the mud and it is stained with dried-out algae, like the cross section of a melted civilization. The smell of deadness is rank. The sky is white and far away, the sun a burning locus. Here at the bottom of the riverbed, the lives of the foal and I are as inconsequential as the flash of a mirror in a very great plain.

Hundreds of miles to the north, across a harsh volcanic basin, wild mustangs forage freely, fight, and play—until they are betrayed by the Judas horse for a bucket of grain. I remember how the captured mares would circle the corral, lost in silence, all the subtle scent and body messages with their babies and the stallions snapped.

Beneath my hands, the tiny horse is laboring to breathe. I stay with him, dabbling water with the blood-soaked cloth, as if I could accompany his sightless soul into the greater darkness. I feel a deep and wordless kinship, as if we are bound by some transparent force of kindness. *I will not abandon you.*

Am I the Judas horse, cynical and beaten? Or the innocent foal?

After a very long time, the amber lights of the veterinarian's truck show above the ridge.

Twenty-two

July. Intruders are everywhere.

False dandelion invades the perfectly swept orchard floor, no matter how often Stone drives the flail, or makes us rake by hand. We are halfway through the development of the hazelnuts, and tiny larvae of the leaf-roller moth have appeared on the new clusters. Bad news. The larvae cause nut abortions, not a pretty sight. In the still heat of the afternoon, I am up on a ladder setting insect traps, using the work as a cover to check in with Donnato.

I have discovered that poking around the topmost branches of the hazelnuts is an excellent way to conduct a covert conversation. For one thing, it's great up there. You see things differently, like opening a secret hatch to a world of sky. Rooftops and mountains become your ground—and unlike hiding out in Sirocco's stall, if Dick Stone ventures into the orchard, you would be the first to know.

"The fifty-caliber casings you found are a match to the slug that killed Sergeant Mackee," Donnato is saying from L.A. "The shooter is the same as the one at the BLM corrals."

"What about the Native American we took into custody?"

"He had a pretty good alibi. At the time of the shooting, he was in a local emergency room being treated for ulcers. Now we need the weapon."

"The sniper rifle that matches the casings," I agree, watching a white butterfly skimming perfectly through the leaves.

"Stone has it somewhere. Make a search," he tells me, "room by room."

"Got it," I say without enthusiasm.

"You should be ecstatic."

"About the casings? Yeah, it's cool."

"What's up?"

"Just be straight, okay?"

"Always, buddy, you know that."

"Do you have an agent tailing me? Because I can't function that way, and frankly, I resent the hell out of it."

"A *federal* agent?"

"Yes."

"I don't have a clue what you're talking about."

"The cowboy? Come on. Good-looking, mid-thirties? He shows up at the corrals, working on the gather? Then he appears again, a mile from the farm, hitting targets like a pro?"

"At the same shooting range? You're kidding. What kind of gun?"

"Don't get excited. It was a hunting rifle, a .308."

Your handler doesn't tell you everything. While you're alone and isolated undercover, the Bureau will be working things from the other end, putting operatives in place you don't know about. They'll say it's for your safety, but it can make you paranoid fast.

"If you don't like this guy, check him out," Donnato says.

"I don't like him," I reply.

"Search his vehicle, for a start."

"That would be difficult," I say. "He's riding a horse."

Because there, in the heaviest torpor of the day, when stubborn fever becalms the air and the stringed vibration of the bees hits an even riper pitch, Sterling McCord is riding slowly down the sun-soaked lane on a bay, leading the white foal on a halter rope.

It's the bay mare who rescued me, loaded up with the same silver-encrusted western saddle, but this time walking leisurely at loose rein with head low, flicking her ears at the flies. McCord's posture is identical to when they were at full gallop, head tipped forward and shoulders relaxed, as if he is half-asleep.

He is wearing the high red-tooled boots and spurs, jeans, a clean white shirt, and the Stetson with the vintage cowboy crease. As the lazy clomping of horseshoes passes below me, I can see the tight copper bracelet on one strong wrist, a braided leather one on the other, and I have a clean downward angle of vision on the squarish hands with wide finger pads resting on the horn of the saddle—manly and competent hands you would entrust to complete the mission.

Whatever the mission might be.

I stay silent until he passes. Does he know without looking that I am here—the way Dick Stone knew when I first arrived?

"There's something about this guy," I tell Donnato. "He's not who he appears to be."

"What name does he use?"

"Sterling McCord."

"We'll check him out."

I cannot tell if my partner of twelve years is telling the truth.

That is what I mean by paranoid.

Megan and Sara have gathered around the horseman in the shaded driveway.

"Look at that sweet thing," Megan says, crooning over the foal. "You're our new baby."

McCord tips his hat. "Good afternoon, ladies."

His eyes remain hidden in the shadow of the brim, but his skin seems to have acquired a darker tan, with deeper leathery lines, and the blond sideburns have grown long and rough. It occurs to me that in his outdoor life, he, too, is a creature of transforming elements, same as the eroding granite outcrop; unlike city folks, he wouldn't try to put the brakes on aging, and he wears it well. He's dropped the reins and the horse dozes beneath him. I like this touch: a knife in a leather sheath buckled to his thigh.

The foal has gained weight. Its sculpted head is up and alert, the bristly mane long enough to flop over, and the small pinkish hooves strike the dirt inquisitively. But the dark violet eyes are empty as mirrors.

"Does he have a name?" Megan asks.

"Geronimo."

"You are cute as the dickens!" she tells the foal, and actually kisses it on the nose.

"Sara," McCord calls from the saddle, "look at your boy."

"He's not mine."

She is wearing skintight jeans that hit below her slack hipbones, and a gingham top somewhere between a bra and a bib.

The foal's dark muzzle has shrunk to normal size, small enough to fit in the palm of my hand, which it explores with eager lips.

"Sorry, big guy." I laugh. "I don't have anything for you."

"He wants to suck," Megan explains plaintively.

McCord's attention is still on Sara. "What do you think?"

"He looks all right."

"He *is* all right," McCord replies, cheery.

Megan: "Will he ever get his sight back?"

"Afraid not, Miss Tewksbury. The vet says it's difficult to determine exactly the cause of the blindness, but the corneas are permanently scarred."

"Poor sweetheart."

"He'll do fine with the right care. You'd have to keep his environment consistent, in a corral where he always knows where's his water and feed. But his other senses will become more accurate, and he'll be able to get around, maybe as a companion animal to another horse."

"Like Sirocco?" Megan gazes up at McCord with the expectant look of a wife who really wants that washing machine.

"That's what I was thinking. How long since she lost her baby?"

"She had that accident on the track and came to us . . . maybe three months ago?"

"Then she could still lactate."

"Really? Nurse Geronimo?"

"It's possible."

He slides off his horse.

"So, Sara, do you like him?" he asks.

She shrugs. "He's cute."

"Like to keep him?"

"Keep him?"

"Look after him awhile, you and Sirocco, help him along. He needs a lot of TLC, and Dave Owens's barn is full."

Sara blushes. Her shoulders collapse with doubt. "Me?"

"You're the one who found him. In my book, that gives you claim." McCord offers the rope.

Lifelong skepticism does not allow me to believe that Sterling McCord has traveled down the road this dusty summer afternoon simply to give Sara Campbell exactly what she needs, but as he patiently holds the lead out to her, whatever dark possibilities I conjure just don't seem to hold. Whether McCord is an FBI agent on my tail or a cowboy doing a job, he is offering the girl what has been missing from her life.

Something to love.

Sara reaches out and her fingers close around the rope. The blind foal's head comes up to her chest and his spindly legs match hers. She tentatively strokes his neck and fingers the fluff hanging off his chin.

"Let's take him to Sirocco," Megan says hopefully. "See if she'll nurse."

We walk in procession toward the barn—McCord leading his horse, Sara and the herky-jerky foal, Megan and I—passing the white cat, the ducks, and the wire cage, now empty.

Someone has stolen all the rabbits.

"We're having a party," Megan tells McCord. "A midsummer festival. Please come. I'd like to buy you a drink for taking care of Geronimo."

"Not necessary but much appreciated. Especially if this lovely young lady's gonna be there."

He is talking about Sara.

Sirocco is standing placidly in the pasture when Megan leads the foal inside. She unsnaps the lead rope and withdraws, latching the gate. They approach and sniff each other. Sirocco dodges away. The baby chases her, and she wheels in the dust. He follows, absolutely desperate, but she won't let him near, making little nips and kicks. Abruptly, when she's ready, she just stops, and after a moment, he finds the teats.

Megan, leaning on the fence, quietly thumbs the tears from her eyes.

The gun that killed Sergeant Mackee is a single-shot bolt-action sniper rifle about fifty inches long, weighing between fourteen and eighteen pounds. Not the kind of thing you can hide in a sugar bowl.

Every day, with quiet urgency, I search another part of the house. Every night, lying in bed, I perform a mental inventory of the rooms, noting anything missing or out of place. I visualize the porch. Grasses have grown tall around the rusted sink. Thick stands of lavender and wild daisies remain unbroken around the crawl space underneath the steps, and the basement windows show an untouched glaze of dust, meaning nobody's been creeping around down there, hiding weapons. The narrow windows at ground level look in on Dick Stone's work-shop, which is always locked, and I have never rubbed the dirt away to spy inside. Stone is likely checking his own inventory every day.

The front hall is a staging area of floating possessions—jackets, umbrellas, junk mail, Slammer's skateboard—but there is also a closet jammed with vacuum cleaner parts, tennis rackets, rain gear, and brooms, at the back of which is a latched door. Hurried inspection with a flashlight reveals the door and latch have been thickly painted over. Probably leads to a crawl space beneath the stairs.

The kitchen, to the left of the entryway, is a public space that would be hard to use for hiding contraband. The living room is a challenge. There are so many collections of tiny things, it is a perplexing game of Memory to place every piece of Depression glassware and each china cat. I have moved them just to see if Megan will move them back. She does.

In the living room, the TV is always playing, even in the daytime semi-darkness. At night, we assemble on the caved-in couch grooved with body imprints, like any other cobbled-together American family, placing our heels on the coffee table precisely in the spaces between the old wine bottles and bowls of dried-up guacamole, watching cop shows or a movie from Dick Stone's collection of tapes. He has become obsessed with *Apocalypse Now*.

Also, he has begun to get in shape.

Stone is jogging ten miles in the mornings, a major change, which gets my attention. Offenders have rituals. They will alter their looks, get high, call Mom, or rob a store before they're ready to go out and execute a major crime.

Like the Big One.

Along with a dedicated running schedule, he has been screening this movie regularly—once or twice a week—all of us saying the dialogue out loud like a gospel choir. Stone is as fussy about his tapes as Megan is about the candy dishes—he always keeps *Apocalypse Now* on the fourth bookshelf, at eye level, between *The Deer Hunter* and *Taxi Driver*.

One day, I noticed his favorite cassette was missing. It stayed missing for seventy-two hours; then it was back in the same place. Had he lent it? Is he playing with my head?

The sewing room is a drafty screened-in porch with tilting bamboo shades and bolts of discount cloth infested with earwigs. I call it the "Room of Unfinished Dreams." An old Singer sewing machine is the island in the storm, black lace panties caught in its teeth, as Sara comes in here to sew her samples of lingerie—original designs that she claims she'll sell one day to big department stores. There's a dressing table with a big round mirror, drawers stuffed with Megan's bags of yarn. The white cat likes the rattan love seat in the morning sun.

Lying in bed at night, I float inside my head like a dreamer to the upper limits of the sewing room, recollecting that the dropped ceiling tile showed no signs of removal (for illicit storage in the space above); then my inner eye travels up the stairs, past the German wall clock, to Stone and Megan's bedroom, and the mondo mess of pills and herbal remedies in the master bath—including the heavy-duty antipsychotics Mellaril and Haldol, and benzodiazepines for anxiety, Ativan and Librium. It would be excellent to trace the doctor who wrote the prescriptions, but they are all generic, from Mexico. Megan, who did a stint as an aide in a psychiatric facility, has apparently been playing amateur shrink with Dick Stone's brain.

Every day, I inspect Slammer's room, the outbuildings, and of course the attic, and in every night's review so far, this aging Victorian dame of a farmhouse has convinced me that she has herself in order— nothing wanton, nothing to hide.

The only place I have yet to search is Dick Stone's locked workshop.

I was in there only once, on the pretext of going down to the basement to get laundry detergent.

Megan had been working on her quilt. A Christian station played on the radio. Megan likes that because it reminds her of her childhood. She was the eldest of five, growing up in an austere minister's home in snowy northern Michigan. All the other siblings took up charitable work. One of her sisters was killed on a mission to Africa, but Megan doesn't say how.

The large frame that holds the quilt barely leaves enough space for a couple of hanging bicycles and metal shelves with household supplies—canned food and bleach. In an L-shaped room beyond, they have installed an industrial stove for the seasonal chore of making hazelnut brittle.

It was damp in the basement and Megan was wearing a plum red shawl over an Indian blouse with fringes at the hem, a peaceful look on her face as she sewed patches on the quilt. I noticed a glass and half-empty bottle of wine on the floor. The door to Stone's shop was open, yellow light spilling out. It was almost romantic to imagine them on winter nights, pursuing their rustic hobbies side by side.

I filled the canister from a bin of laundry detergent, then wandered over to the woodworking shop, where Stone was applying lacquer to a cross section of tree trunk perched on a pair of sawhorses.

"What are you making?"

"A table."

"What kind of wood is that?"

"Douglas fir."

"It looks like marble."

Quickly, I advanced through the doorway, sucking in the details like an alien invader: *Table saw. Drill press. High window at ground level. Built-in cabinets, home-improvement clutter.*

"Thirty coats of varnish. That's how I get it to look like marble."

Jars, tiny drawers of screws and nails; pliers, drills, drill bits, chisels. A pair of steel storage cabinets with a padlock.

"The grain is beautiful. How do you know where to cut it?"

"You have to read the wood." He dragged a blackened fingertip across the polished slab. "See that darkness? That's when the tree began to die."

I saw a black cloud, like a squirt of ink, spreading V-like through the amber rings of growth.

"That's death. You're looking at it," Dick Stone said.

He keeps the guns in the locked cabinets.

At that moment, in the workshop fragrant with cedar dust and hard work, he could almost pass for exactly what he seemed: a hazelnut farmer with eager, skilled hands, awed by the inevitability of nature.

But then I saw the videocassette of *Apocalypse Now* on the workbench. I was certain I had just seen it, moments before, upstairs.

"You must really like that video to have two copies."

Dick Stone said briefly, "It's the greatest movie ever made."

I cannot get into the workshop again until one rare morning when they've all gone into town and Dick Stone has left for a run. I wait fifteen minutes after he's gone, and then hustle down the basement steps, clutching the set of lock picks delivered earlier by an FBI agent posing as a U.S. postal worker. In undercover school at Quantico, we ran time tests for defeating dead bolts; Stone's workout has handed me at least an hour.

It takes only five minutes to blow Operation Wildcat sky-high.

Twenty-three

Inserting a tension wrench into the keyhole of the cylinder and then alternating several picks, I finally find the one with the right angle to lift each pin. The plug rotates and the lock opens.

The door to Dick Stone's woodshop swings wide. I hesitate, as if someone is waiting in ambush. Sterling McCord, maybe. He has a way of appearing when you least expect him. But there is nothing. Dead air. I pull out a penlight and aim it at the floor.

As the light passes the legs of the sawhorse that holds the fir table, a wastebasket flips, and brown mice scatter. The scent of orange peel rises from the garbage. I right the wastebasket. My heart is racing and I have to pee. The smell of resin and lacquer in the enclosed space is dizzying.

I seriously hope there are no more mice.

The cone of light walks up the tall steel cabinet and stops at the padlock that secures the handles. This one is a common tumbler lock, using wafers instead of pins, and can be picked the same way. I'm getting good at this. The tumbler clicks and the hasp slides open.

Alone at the bottom of the quiet house, I insert the penlight between my teeth and open the cabinet doors, anxious to reveal Stone's secret arsenal—expecting to find the sniper rifle, automatic weapons, Tovex explosives.

Instead, I am looking at a four-split television monitor.

In each corner of the screen is a different view of the empty house: living room, kitchen, sewing room, stairs.

It is an arsenal all right: a sophisticated wireless surveillance system, including a high-sensitivity receiver, whip antenna, and down converter.

Before I can begin to think of a way to cover up this horrendous breach of Stone's security system, I notice the cassette of *Apocalypse Now* is resting on the upper shelf of the cabinet. I know he loves the movie, but why hide it in here?

The moment I pick it up, the quadrants on the TV monitor flip to four *different* views—driveway, bathroom, attic, *inside the cabinet*—and there is Special Agent Ana Grey, staring into the camera like a bonehead tourist. As I move the cassette, my image on the split screen moves accordingly.

Stone has hidden a tiny camera in the spine of *Apocalypse Now*. He kept the camera aimed from the shelf in the living room, but he must have switched it for the real videotape when I noticed there were two. He has the whole place under constant surveillance. I can see from the monitor there is even a covert camera inside the German wall clock, keeping watch on who's going up the stairs. And who's been searching the house.

The apocalypse is looking at me now, through the pinhole of a live camera, less than an eighth of an inch in diameter.

My nose, on the screen, is as big as the snout of a moose.

That night at 1:00 a.m., a flashlight shines in my face.

"Get up," says Stone.

I am already up, speed-dialing a thousand explanations. I have avoided him all day.

"You broke into my shop."

"What are you talking about?"

I swing out of bed, but he pushes me down, his hand squarely on my chest.

"You broke into my workroom and my personal cabinets."

"Why would I do that? It's the dumbest thing in the world."

"It's all on tape, Darcy."

I say nothing.

Neither affirm nor deny.

"Yeah." He nods, reading my face. "That's right. You're toast."

I notice Sara is not in her bed. He has me alone. He has set the stage for—what?

"All right!" I shout, and surprise him by lunging for the wall switch, defiantly flicking on the light, making him squint.

"I did break into your shop, and I'll tell you why I—"

"Is that so?"

He sits beside me and the mattress sinks. Again, that scent of male, and the threat of two hundred pounds of leaned-out muscle and bone. He's wearing a loose rayon shirt and jeans, long, hairy toes blackened with sawdust gripping the shower thongs that pass for slippers. He must have just come from the basement, checking his daily surveillance tapes.

"Everything around this place is a huge big secret," I rant on. "I've been here *weeks,* and you still don't trust me? Now I find out you're spying on *us*? Your own people, who live in your house?"

"It's for everyone's protection."

"What if those tapes wind up on the Internet? Or maybe this whole operation is some kind of a setup."

"Setup for what?"

"Maybe you're working for the cops."

"Why would I?"

"To destroy the movement from the inside. They pull that shit, you know."

Dick Stone rubs his forehead, shiny from the warmth of the night.

"No need to freak, little sister. I came up here just to say 'Right on.' "

What is that in his amber eyes—besides middle-aged fatigue, glazed by the lateness of the hour? Something I haven't seen before:

Amusement?

He lays a heavy arm across my shoulders.

"Darcy, I would have done the same damn thing. Looked through Daddy's drawers when the folks weren't home. You know, I did that once when I was a kid, and guess what I found? In my father's nightstand? A heap of condoms and a huge fucking kitchen knife he kept right by the bed. That was a shocker."

"Which? The condoms or the knife?"

"The knife, man. What was he thinking?" Stone shakes his head.

"Protecting the family, just like you."

"We lived in suburban Connecticut."

"Gotta watch out for those serial stockbrokers."

Dick Stone snorts with laughter. "You're not far wrong. He was a competitive old bastard."

"You're not mad about the cabinets? I see a lock, I can't help thinking there must be something righteous inside, worth protecting."

He nods. "I dig it. You've got skills, girl."

"Used to be a pretty good thief. Got busted for stealing data, served my time, but a regular padlock—that's just too tempting."

Dick Stone's face is now so close, I can see the tiny bristles on his cheeks.

"One question. Where did you hide the tools? You can't just pick a lock."

"Have you been going through my stuff?"

"Regularly."

"That's why I kept moving them."

I reach under the bed, pull out a small bundle that was duct-taped to the frame, and toss it over.

This open display stops him. Could anyone actually be so guileless?

I've pasted on a casual smile but I think I've stopped breathing. For several long seconds I watch Dick Stone waver, like a high school coach who discovers his best starting pitcher smoking weed in the locker.

Screw it. He likes the kid.

"Darcy," he says slowly, "you're okay. You're the same as me. All you want is to have some fun. You like to start little fires, don't you?"

I rest for a moment in enormous relief. He hasn't made a move on me, hasn't doubted my story. And there is truth in what he says—sitting butt-to-butt on the edge of the bed, seemingly at ease in the heart of the night like father and daughter, or supervisor and agent, we recognize something inside the other that is the same.

A paradox is unfolding. The longer I stay under, the larger Dick

Stone becomes. Rather than working his way into ordinariness through everyday contact, he grows more vivid, and my own sense of self-cohesion fades. The boundaries between Darcy and Ana seem inconsequential, not worth defending, as we are swept toward the Big One by some inner momentum of Stone's that the meticulous procedures of the Bureau are powerless to stop. Donnato's voice on the Oreo phone and my former life in Los Angeles dwindle and disappear like radio signals moving out of range.

The first time I drove through the Marine base at Quantico as a new agent, there was that orgasmic surge of ecstasy: *This is what I've always wanted!* Now, out of this cozy intimacy with Stone, the same words echo, but with a newly ominous tone: *This is what I wanted, going undercover, isn't it?* To forget the past and my mistakes and the larger-than-life figures who dominated, even as the realization creeps at the edge of my mind that I have replaced one despot with another.

There is no retribution here. Dick Stone believes what he has said— that he and I are somehow the same—and now that he is done saying it, he simply gets up and leaves.

And the Darcy part of me experiences a rush of feeling for the old bandit that Ana, still the FBI agent, could never admit:

Affection.

Twenty-four

The panic in Donnato's voice brings Ana Grey back instantly.

"You breached Stone's security system?"

"I was looking for the sniper rifle."

"What'd he do?"

"He laughed."

"What the hell does that mean?"

"He likes me, or he's nuts."

"Or he's made you and is playing for time."

My stomach flips. "I have no way of knowing, do I?"

Neither of us speaks. I am up in the hazelnut trees again, fussing with the traps for moths, and not liking the symbolism one bit.

"This is not a disaster," Donnato muses, as if to assure himself. "We can piggyback on his wireless signal. Hear everything going on inside the house."

"If he made me, he wouldn't let you do that," I remind him.

"Tell me this—where does he go every morning?"

"He started running and lost fourteen pounds. I told you, it's a new ritual. I think he's preparing for the Big One."

"Does he always go by the front door?"

When I first came to the lost farm, the agent in the cherry picker who was dressed like a repairman, aside from wiretap devices, installed cameras on the telephone poles. Command center in Portland can see everything that comes and goes.

"Because we don't always get a visual until he's a quarter mile away from the house," Donnato says. "How does he get out? Suddenly he pops on-screen, heading north. We don't know how he gets there or where he's going. Find out."

At 7:45 a.m. the next day, Stone, wearing a fluorescent yellow Grateful Dead T-shirt, running trunks, and a belt holding a water bottle, heads out through the kitchen door. No big mystery about that. I watch from the second-floor window—careful to stay beyond the range of the camera installed in the German clock—as he jogs twice around the soft track of the orchard, then veers into the wooded parcel behind the house.

I'm out the kitchen door, across the overgrown garden, and on the trail, keeping a hundred yards between us. As we move through the woods, I can see his shirt flashing up ahead. Then I lose him, but he has to stay on the trail or run through scrub. When we come out at the cottonwood trees, I duck below the wash. Now he's in open territory, looking like any other fitness runner, tuned in to his iPod, dark stains on the T-shirt, churning muscular calves. The music keeps him focused—eyes ahead, not even thinking of watching the rear—so I stretch out and match his pace as we come up to the muddy tracks of the wildlife sanctuary.

Against the sky, the matrix of power wires becomes more defined as we draw close. To my right is the plain where the blind foal was found. As Stone keeps on moving through the maze of manzanita, an epiphany of logic breaks over me like a cold shower: He's heading for the shooting range where I found the .50-caliber shell.

This is where he practices shooting his weapons. Including the sniper rifle that killed Sergeant Mackee.

I am getting excited now. I wish to call Donnato, but I know there is no cell phone service here. The hard-furrowed roads are hazardous for turned ankles, and Stone is slowing down. No shots echo—it's too early for your ordinary amateur shooter. I take a spur trail and circle around to where I suspect he's going, accelerating to beat him and duck into a concealed position behind the Dumpsters overflowing with trash and flies.

He stops in the center of the firing range, heaving and throwing drops of sweat. He swigs water and spits it out while turning around in a 360, checking the perimeter.

Where does he hide the guns? A chest buried somewhere? A cave in the wash?

Now he slides a black-and-silver phone from the belt holding the water bottle and glances up at the sky, moving until there are no power lines above him. The phone is way too big to be a cell. I can make out the profile of an antenna, like a little finger pointing up. He is using a satellite phone to get past our wiretaps.

You can only use a satellite phone outside, with a clear view to the sky. That is why he comes to the shooting range.

"Gemini? It's Taurus. What have you got? You're the expert. You're the one with access to intel, the off-site, the whole deal. Don't leave me hanging out here with my pants down, buddy."

He waits. I wait. My breath comes fast.

"You said you could get past the SAC. I'm counting on it."

The cold shower of logic becomes a deluge of ice. It is unmistakable. Dick Stone is talking to someone inside the Bureau.

On an untraceable satellite phone.

Twenty-five

Once again, I am a passenger in the dark, being driven along unknown roads to an uncertain destination—just like in undercover school. As in undercover school, I have made the strategic decision to imbibe an illegal substance, meaning I am as stoned as the rest of them on some awesome weed.

That night, before I could alert Donnato to the discovery of the satellite phone, we learned through a posting on the FAN Web site that Lillian, the sweet old bird-watcher rescued from the mustang corral, was dead.

Dinner was quesadillas, and Megan was quiet.

"What happened?" Sara said. "I thought she was okay."

"She'd just had a heart-valve replacement and it got infected."

"Too bad," said Stone with a mouth full of cheese.

"It was a direct result of the action," Megan snapped. Her face looked slack, darkness beneath the eyes. "She was traumatized, and then she's taken to a bad hospital in a piss-poor excuse for a town."

Slammer was jamming green apple halves and carrots into an industrial juicer.

"Do you have to do that?" Sara asked.

"Fiber, man."

The juicer must have been outfitted with a jet engine.

Megan told Stone she was leaving for two days.

"Why?"

"Lillian's memorial service."

The juicer howled.

"Where?"

"San Jose."

"Turn that thing off," Stone shouted. "Fuck your fucking fiber."

The motor ticked to a stop. Slammer had extracted a quarter cup of amber-colored juice.

Megan put her head in her hand. I laid my arm around her shoulders.

"Megan's upset. She saw the whole thing at the corral."

"Never should have happened," declared Stone.

"The lady was too old to go on something like that," Sara added.

"It wasn't her being old." Megan raised her burning eyes. "It's *us* who were arrogant. We were breaking the law when—"

"What's the law anyway?" asked Stone. "Whatever the government decides. Arbitrary bullshit."

"I'll be back late Sunday," Megan said tiredly.

"You're not going. It's a trap. The feds will be there."

Megan stood. "That's crazy!" She had gone shrill. "I am so sick of your paranoid fantasies. The world is fucked and we can't save it. We've been living in fantasyland all these years, without one normal day. Without peace of any kind. Without family."

"We could have had a family."

"All I ever wanted was a baby."

"You could have had a baby."

"No! I couldn't! We were always on the run."

"Hush up now!" Stone said menacingly.

"I won't! This is my house."

"You want me to leave? Because I'll leave," said Stone.

"Thank you," Megan said. "After you have ruined my life." And she walked out of the room.

We waited in silence until Sara and I got up to collect the dishes. Stone told us to sit down.

We sank back into our seats.

"This is a tragic situation that did not have to happen," Stone repeated in a hurt voice. "Nobody would have had to get messed up with wild horses if it hadn't been for Herbert Laumann. He is the oppressor. He is the United States government. Megan has a right to be angry. A lady is dead who didn't have to be."

He was good. Low-key and light on the rhetoric. You could feel him gathering up the fractured energy left in the room, wrapping it ever so piteously around himself.

Hours later, Megan was gone and Stone roused the household—Sara, Slammer, and me.

"We're gonna have some fun," he promised. "Gonzo political action."

Now, miles away from the lost farm, we are squeezed into the white truck, and Dick Stone is singing Otis Redding: "They call me Mr. Pitiful. That's how I got my fame—"

He keeps switching songs, genres, decades. Inside his head must be some crazy mix of rhythm and blues and screaming black-leather motorcycle metal. In a fraction of a second that goes on for eternity, he can hear Blue Oyster Cult expanding like the day of reckoning since 1975.

"Music is consciousness; it never dies," Stone proclaims. "Music exists forever, somewhere in the universe."

"If it never dies," Slammer apes, "where was it born?"

"In a thirty-twoer laced with windowpane." Dick Stone grins.

Rewind.

We are forty minutes outside Portland. Real time. It is way past the midnight hour, and this, in the grand saga of injustice and revenge, is what Dick Stone has been given: two kids passing a joint as if they are on a lark, the boy running his mouth about his wicked life, the poor little rich girl without a clue; and the pretender, the eager stranger with wild dark hair and shifty eyes, slouching in the seat beside him.

But he is pleased with the discipline of his rock 'n' roll commando unit. Under his leadership, they have put together a goody bag of plastic squeeze bottles you would use for catsup, now filled with hydrofluoric acid; cans of red, white, and blue spray paint; a video camera; and Molotov cocktails made with the bandit's signature Corona beer bottles.

Still the original, still the best.

For no discernible reason, he jerks the joint from Slammer's mouth and flicks it out the window.

"What the fuck?" The boy laughs uneasily.

The bandit punishes him with silence.

Sara is all of a sudden in a fit of giggles, rolling on her back in the rear seat, long, thin arms and legs kicking out at funny angles.

"You're a little butterfly." Dick Stone looks in the rearview mirror. "Just like Megan, back in the day."

It was Megan, he tells us, who shared that thirty-twoer of psychedelic malt liquor in the Civic Auditorium down in San Jose, when BOC was at the height of their satanic debauchery; the concert from which he never came back. Like the apparition of young, idealistic Megan (aka Laurel Williams, the environmental scientist at Berkeley), Sara, he intones, is a butterfly who alights on your hand, revealing magic yellow granules of powder on its wings. Why would such a vision be given to you?

Meanwhile, the new one, Darcy, keeps to herself, staring at the suburban night. Dick Stone smiles at some reverie and rolls his window down, dropping an arm out of the truck, letting the cigarillo hang, wasting good Dominican smoke as a rush of air tears hot embers off the tip, leaving a trail of extinguishing sparks. It satisfies him, like pages burning in time.

"Hey now," says the boy, "what's *that* asshole doing?"

Slammer jumps up and hits the horn and a van in front of us swerves to a stop. The driver of the van throws the door open, shouting in Farsi.

Stone turns his head very slowly toward the boy. His graying stubble looks Halloween raspberry in the cold red intersection light.

"Don't . . . do . . . that." He accelerates, but not too fast.

"I really feel like slapping someone right now." Slammer pounds a fist hungrily. "I really feel like getting into a fight."

Dick Stone ignores him.

"That's what I mean!" Slammer agrees, as if the old dude had said anything. "There's two chicks in the car, know what I'm saying?"

"I have no idea what you're saying."

"We should hit 'em." The boy is pointing and alert. "McDonald's, man."

The drive-thru is bright as an alien spaceship. There is a line of cars. The bandit asks, "Why?"

"Babylon profits by killing animals," Slammer chirps. "Why not?"

The bandit sighs. "It's a cliché."

I guffaw. He cocks an appreciative eye. He loves Darcy for being a little rebel, and right now, stoned as the rest of them, Darcy loves him.

Sara sits upright in the backseat. "McDonald's is too corporate. Too big."

Slammer scowls. "You're a freak."

Kindergarten.

The bandit makes a U-turn and heads out of town.

"Sara has a point," he instructs, and pulls out a well-worn piece of rhetoric: "Evil needs a face."

The road becomes a country lane, no lights. The houses are spread farther apart. Only by slowing down and scanning the fences caught in the hard white headlights do we notice a small metal sign that says THE WILKINS. Stone turns down a road that bisects a pasture and leads to a newly constructed four-bedroom home with a spindle-post porch—just the kind of hypocritical western touch that ticks the bandit off.

He pulls off the road, beneath a stand of juniper trees, and cuts the lights.

"*That's* the target."

"Who are the Wilkins?"

"Our friend BLM Deputy State Director Herbert Laumann's in-laws. The government whore is mooching off the grandparents now."

Because someone destroyed his house and his kid is still in the hospital.

My stomach tilts with the sickening recognition that old obsessions die hard.

Slammer whispers, like he's seen a prophetic city: "Babylon."

Beneath the dashboard the prudent bandit has mounted a sophisticated scanner that picks up encrypted radio signals used by law-enforcement agencies. He fiddles, listens to the static. Nothing threatening on the airwaves.

The bandit holds up the bag of tricks. "Who wants it?"

Slammer: "Me!"

Perversely, Stone hands the bag to Sara instead, watching the disappointment grow once again in Slammer's face. But then, another whiplash turn of mood, and he offers the boy a Colt .45 pistol.

Like the scenario in undercover school, reality shifts to a perilous key. A screaming siren wakes me from this loopy daze. The kid is armed.

Slammer handles the gun. "What am I supposed to do?"

"Figure it out, genius." Stone gives me the video camera and unlocks the doors. "You have three minutes. Go."

We scamper down the driveway, past a couple of bicycles and a redwood tree house with swings, along a path to the backyard. A raccoon darts from the shadows. The yard is open, no cover. We hunker against the garage wall.

Sara, indignant: "Why'd he give *you* the gun?"

"Because you're a pussy."

You can see the weed shining through Sara's huge eyes. "He wants you to shoot Laumann?"

"Let's do it." Slammer pushes unsteadily off the wall.

I grab his arm. "No! They have an alarm system," I say, pointing to random telephone wires.

But Slammer is hyped. "Two more minutes! All we've got!"

Absurdly, he gets on his belly and combat-crawls across the lawn. Seems like a plan, so I follow. Sara's behind us, dragging the bag of tricks. This is good. We're leaving loads of evidence—footprints, fibers off our clothes. Then the lights go on and figures appear in the downstairs windows.

"Freeze!" Slammer hisses.

We are too far away to make the people out.

"Get the video!"

Lying down in the sharp, wet Bermuda grass, zooming in on Herbert Laumann's family through the camera lens, we discover a mother, father, and baby girl. The baby is sleeping on the mother's shoulder. She walks up and down as the father yawns, rubbing his temples with two flat palms. They are all wearing nightclothes. The mother has a towel over her shoulder, on which the infant's cheek is resting, blue-eyed slits staring into babyland.

Slammer says, "Babylon nation, prepare to die."

The mother sits slowly at a table, balancing carefully to keep the baby still, as the father talks. His ordinary white bureaucratic all-American face—the face of evil—looks collapsed with exhaustion. He reaches out to touch the baby's head—a cupped hand, a blessing.

"Are you really going to do it?" Sara whispers, mesmerized by the family on the tiny video screen, like a snow globe showing a scene of mystery and magic. In its light, a tiny floating square of light in acres of pitch-black farmland, the youngsters without a home and the spy with a soul of ash are watching transfixed, through a secret window, the simple arithmetic of two loving parents and a child. You would think they had never seen such a thing.

Prone, Slammer tries to sight the gun on wobbling elbows. He should take a lesson from Sterling McCord. The gun quivers.

"Wait!" I say, allegedly watching through the camera. "You don't have a shot."

"*I have it,*" he grunts, but he lays the gun down to wipe his sweating palms on the wet grass.

I am a millisecond from disarming him.

He picks up the weapon but doesn't shoot. The gun is shaking wildly. Comically. This is not surprising. In real wars, there are troops on the battlefield who refuse to fire, because they can't. Unlike the movies, it doesn't come naturally, killing another human being.

"Three minutes are way up," I say gently. "We're out of here."

Slammer slumps down to the grass and sobs. Helpless, deep, undifferentiated sobs. I lift the gun away.

Sara strokes his bristly head, then kneels and awkwardly puts her arms around his shoulders, laying her cheek on his back.

"Allfather will be mad," she whispers.

"He can fuck himself," Slammer replies.

I erase the videotape.

Twenty-six

The following day, Slammer walks into the kitchen, to find Dick Stone sitting at the sloping counter with the broken tiles, reading the daily fish report—how many chinook salmon and steelhead have passed through the bypass systems of the lower Columbia River dams—and holding the Colt .45.

The gun is aimed at the doorway. At the next person to walk through the doorway, who would be Slammer, back from the grocery store.

The devil boy stops in his tracks.

"What up?"

"You tell me."

The gun is pointed at Slammer's belly.

"*What?*" Slammer shrugs and grins foolishly, as if missing the joke. "Can I at least put the groceries down?"

Slammer notices his voice has grown small. Besides the black hole of the barrel, Dick Stone is showing him the Look. Slammer, Sara, and I have talked about the Look. You can't see his eyes when he does it: narrows them to a pair of emotionless chinks that the angry part of him seems to be just gazing through, like the faceless column of light that pulses behind the crack in the TV cabinet where the doors don't shut. You have no idea what's on. When Stone hunkers in like that, the worst part is the excruciating silent anticipation, because you know he's slowly taking in your worthless mistakes and calculating the punishment. "The tax," he likes to say.

Slammer lowers the grocery bags, shoulders aching, as if he'd been holding sacks of rocks.

"What'd I do?"

Slammer is drowning in panic. He is seventeen years old, a long way from last night's tears, but the memory of terror is right there.

"Just tell me what I did wrong, okay? So we can talk about it maybe."

The terror comes from Slammer's incarceration in the Mississippi Training School, the type of state-run correctional institution for juveniles where they strip you naked and throw you in a freezing cell, hogtie you, and withhold medical care. Slammer had a toothache so bad and so unattended, the abscess ate into his jaw. He was put there in sixth grade for being chronically late to his regular school. This was because his birth mother was an alcoholic and slept all day. When he was released, he hitchhiked west to live with his father. The Mississippi Training School is currently under federal investigation.

"You did not complete the mission," Stone replies, "you ungrateful little shit." Now his eyes seem pinched and tired.

"I am grateful. You got me off the streets, man." He bounces around the kitchen, flinging his arms.

"I gave you a job, to kill Herbert Laumann," Stone says philosophically. "You failed."

"Hey, I'm still up for the Big One."

Slammer thinks he is showing loyalty by endorsing the bandit's mysterious plan—"the Big One" that will "bring down the house." Now he takes up another of the bandit's themes.

"I didn't do it because the *FBI* is watching us, dude. They're tapping our phones, following us around—"

"Someone surely is. But the larger point I'm trying to get at," Stone says, "is that people around here do what I tell them to."

Discipline.

"Of course. That's a given." Slammer smiles with fine white teeth. The sight of his smile is beautiful and rare, like an eagle in flight. "You're the Allfather."

"I gave you a gun," he says. "I gave you my trust. You abused it."

"They weren't home!" Slammer protests, thick lips blubbering. "I would've done it—but they weren't home!"

"Come with me. I am the tax collector," Stone says.

"Hey, what about the ice cream?"

"Put the ice cream away."

Slammer may be wildly thinking of attack or escape, but in the end, he goes quietly. The bandit did not even have to show the gun.

It is dark when Sara and I get back from picking Megan up from the airport after Lillian's memorial service. We took along a new black-and-white kitten we'd adopted in order to cheer Megan up. I am driving. I take my eyes from the road for an instant—to smile at Sara's pretty profile as she teases the little guy with a tassel on her bag—when she looks up and shrieks, *"Oh my God!"* and I slam the brakes.

The tires kick up gravel and the pickup fishtails to a stop. In the white glare of the headlights we see Slammer's head sticking out of a hole in the ground, in which Dick Stone is burying him up to the neck.

Slammer's garish face is red and contorted and stained with tears. At eye level with the chassis of the truck, he has been screaming for us to stop.

We rush out of the car like fiends let loose, washed out almost to transparency by the hot light, all three of us shouting and reaching through ribbons of iridescent dust to stop it, stop him.

"What's wrong with you?" Megan bellows at Stone as I grab for the shovel.

"He's a traitor."

We wrestle for the handle, and he's strong, flailing wildly, like someone beating at the bars that imprison them.

"I gave him a gun. He didn't do the job."

"What job?" Megan cries, pulling futilely on his shirt. "What job? What job?"

"The boy has turned on me," says Stone. "The FBI is all around us. What is he? A cocksucking little wimp ass piece of shit."

"Talk to me, Julius," I gasp, watching Sara emerging from the dark with a heavy pitchfork. "What do you want?"

Stone's voice has dropped to a mocking growl. "Tell them about the atrocities. Tell them about the lies."

"Help me," Slammer sobs, twisting futilely in his grave.

Sara tries to dig the hard-packed dirt.

Megan is still tugging on Stone's shirt, sliding her arms around him from behind. "It's safe," she croons. "We're here on the farm and we're safe. Let's calm down."

Stone's is the grating voice of madness, coming from a hollow gourd: "Direct action is nothing to take lightly. Government lackeys have to die."

My hands still grip the shovel. "Government lackeys like Herbert Laumann?"

"I want Laumann to die like a pig. Cut his throat, cut it like a pig's—"

"He can't hear you," Megan gasps, wild-eyed.

Stone's manic desperation short-circuits my ability to think. I have to fix it, take it in, do what it takes to relieve his confusion and pain, as I always did with my grandfather, Poppy.

"All right, all right. You want Herbert Laumann dead. You're mad at Slammer because he didn't kill him. It's not his fault. Leave the kid alone. He can't do it, but I can. I'll do it for you, Allfather. I will shoot the guy, okay? I'll shoot him fifty-two times, until he's dead, really dead, okay? Give it to me! I can do it."

He jerks the shovel away from me and raises it to strike, throwing Megan back.

"Darcy, watch out!"

"You're a liar, too!" Stone tells me.

"I will. I promise! I know what it's like. I once killed a man."

Panting, we eye each other in the screaming headlights.

"And I'll tell you something else!" I'm pointing the finger, dancing with a kind of hysteria. "You think Slammer betrayed your trust? You are not the only one, pal. I know what that's like, too. When someone you are stupid enough to fall in love with turns on you and completely undermines you and destroys your life and there's no way back and you have to kill him."

Even through the blinding paranoid rage, he can see the truth of what I've done. What Darcy's done. Stone lets the shovel drop.

"Come on, baby," Megan whispers. "I have you, safe and sound. Come on now. You're with me," and she guides him through the shadows.

Sara and I dig Slammer out. Encrusted in damp earth for long, torturous hours, he has fouled himself.

We help him to his feet.

Sara is crying. Slammer's arms are around us both, leaning heavily on our shoulders. As he walks, he sheds loose rocks and torn roots, a man so debased, he is made of dirt.

"We can't stay here," Sara whispers, but then she hears the kitten crying from where it is hiding under the truck, and thinks of the orchard of hazelnut trees, and the rescued ducks and goats, and Sirocco and the white foal, Geronimo, all living peacefully on the farm. She can't understand the contradictions.

"God—I'm so sorry—I couldn't see you until the last minute." My voice is genuinely shaking. "What was he doing?"

"He said it was a test. Of fire and ice."

A light is on upstairs. We move toward the house.

Twenty-seven

A trial of fire and ice. That's the way you might describe my grandfather's visit, when he flew out from California to attend my swearing-in as a new agent from the FBI Academy. Steve Crawford and I were in the same graduating class, of course, and had naïvely planned to announce to our families that we were getting married, anticipating that our excitement, on top of graduation, would make it one hell of a bang-up weekend celebration for all.

My grandfather was booked into the Days Inn at the very same mall where I would play out Darcy's first contact with the counterfeiters when I returned more than ten years later for undercover school. Back when Poppy stayed there, the motel was newly built and did not smell of urine under the stairs, and behind the property there was just the Dairy Queen, where I would devour that memorable double cheeseburger—not a full-blown shopping strip with a multiplex and gym.

I spotted Poppy from the pool area, striding along the upper deck of the motel. You could tell he was in law enforcement by his sporty disregard of the surroundings (I'm here; get out of my way), an authority he always carried, licensed or not in that particular locality, as if the special nature of his calling extended worldwide supremacy to Everett Morgan Grey. Never mind the only felons were shrieking boys, cannonballing into the pool with huge atomizing splashes; my grandfather's eyes were fixed on the door of his room with intention to prevail. He wore a white Panama hat, a brown suit, and a sport shirt open at the neck, exposing a freckled chest. His ham hand swung my mother's old lacquered suitcase as lightly as if it still held dresses for my dolls.

The boys charged off the edge of the pool, gleaming bellies white as those of frogs. I did not jump up and wave at my grandfather. I did not want to leave that lawn chair, ever. It wasn't just the considerable fear of telling him about Steve, which, by extension would be a statement that I'd actually had sex with a man and was continuing to do so. Even though I had barely left the grounds of the Academy, I realized there in those hothouse corridors, I had finally seized on a clear identity, and in that clarity was liberation. I was free to fall in love, to make mistakes, be harangued and harassed, but they never shut me down. Just the sight of my grandfather threatened my new pride in being Ana; I knew he would turn my achievements into competition with him. Already I was looking back on new agent training as a bright moment of independence, in whose light I was able to shine because I had been on the other side of the country, away from Poppy.

There was a kamikaze scream and tepid water rained on my sandals. You did not just enter Poppy's world. You surrendered to it. I forced myself out of the chair and headed for the pool gate.

"No running," I told the boys.

I knocked. The curtain peeled back and there was the man who had raised me, not giving anything to the steamy morning light but a glimpse of grizzled cheekbone and a shank of nose, squinting between the brown folds of fabric like the beat cop he had been forty years ago, cagey as ever.

But then the door opened wide and the sun found his quick blue eyes.

"Annie!" He grinned and crooked an elbow around my neck, pulling me close. His leathery skin smelled of barbershop spice.

"How are you?" I asked.

"Goddamn airlines" was his reply.

. The door swung shut. He had not turned on the lights, and the suit-case sat unopened on a shiny quilted bedspread the color of ripe cherries. It occurred to me I had never been in a hotel room with my grandfather.

"Want some ice?"

"What for? It's cold as a witch's tit in here."

"Poppy. Don't. That kind of talk exploits women," I announced crisply.

"I don't know what you're talking about."

It didn't matter; I liked the sound of my brave new voice. I had endured. I was almost an FBI agent. I could make pronouncements now.

"You sure you don't want something from the soda machine?"

"What's the hurry? Take a load off."

I plunked down on the bed. The frame wobbled like Jell-O, dipping me up and down as Poppy unpacked the old suitcase that had belonged to my mother, Gwen. It matched a makeup case she used to own, "a train case," they called it, with unfolding trays that would rise up and present their treasures as you opened the lid. She died of liver cancer when I was fourteen. My father was an immigrant from El Salvador, a man I barely knew. I remember my mom as a passive and defeated person, but she must have had moxie to fall in love with a brown-skinned man in the 1960s. It would be years before I understood the circumstances under which my father, Miguel Sanchez, disappeared.

At a moment like this, you crave completion—parents, aunts and uncles and cousins, noisy and embarrassing, to shower you with affirmation and envy. Steve had a ton of family coming down from West Virginia; it was unsettling to be in that ice-cold motel room with Poppy, alone.

"So," I asked him, "any words of wisdom as I go out into the big bad world?"

He considered. "My father always told me, 'Wear a rubber.' "

"Nice."

"What's the matter?" he teased. "Does that exploit women, too?"

Just outside the window was a poisonous-looking tree with ugly hanging clusters of lavender blossoms and long green pods—something that belonged in a swamp, something out of a southern horror story, whose evil perfume had the power to put you in a stupor.

Maybe that was it.

"That advice sure comes in handy with my new little artist friend from Venice," he mused, not wanting to let it go.

"You have an artist friend?"

"*Very* friendly," Poppy insisted. "But she dropped me because she wanted a younger guy. Can you believe that?"

Poppy laid a hand towel on the sink and carefully set out the double-edged razor that screwed open, a shoehorn, and the black leather brush that strapped into the palm of his hand, with which he curry-combed his immaculate white crewcut.

I watched sulkily.

A few weeks before, at midnight, the supervisors had rounded up the new agents and led us to a room lit only by candles. We stood in a silent circle, sweating it out. They pulled that stuff all the time: *We know, and you don't.* A supervisor wearing black stepped to the center of the circle and ceremoniously drew a dagger from his belt. A second supervisor was handing out sealed envelopes. There was an ominous pause. Now what? Kill your partner? As the dagger passed from hand to hand, we were allowed to open our envelopes—and cheers and shouts filled the room. It had been the Bureau's memorable way of letting us know our first field assignments.

"I've been assigned to Los Angeles," I told Poppy finally.

He did not acknowledge the joy of having me close to home. "Do whatever it takes to get on the bank robbery squad," he advised. "Hottest spot in town."

"I know." I took a very deep breath. "The only problem is, my boyfriend has been assigned to Miami, so we don't know what to do."

"You have a boyfriend?"

I broke into a great big smile. "Yes, his name is Steve."

"Do I have to meet this cracker?"

I had not yet understood that the more I wanted love from Poppy, the more he would withhold it.

"Steve is not a cracker. He's very intelligent."

"What about common sense?"

"He has that, too."

As a lieutenant with the Long Beach police department, Poppy had liaisoned with the Bureau on hundreds of bank heists. Now he was hanging his full-dress lieutenant's uniform on the rod that passed for a closet.

"Is that what you're going to wear to the graduation?"

I couldn't help it. I was touched.

"Damn right. Show those FBI bastards where you come from," he said.

When we arrived on campus, he was curious about everything.

"Why do they have a bust of *Jefferson*? When did you say these buildings were built?"

He took pictures of the brick corridors. He took a shot of the grass where our groundhog lived. He stood a long time by the wall commemorating FBI service martyrs. He read every one of their plaques.

"Those are the real heroes," he whispered reverentially, too awed to encroach upon their dignity with a photo flash.

The Academy had shed its austerity to become a college campus on visiting day, where awkwardness and pride prevailed. We who wore the uniform (same old tactical pants and polo shirts) beamed at one another in fraternal spirit. Traffic in the hallways puddled and slowed. You could no longer charge around the corners, there were too many soft-bellied moms and dads wearing bad clothes. *Civilians.* I felt a sloppy love for all of them—these were my people now, whose freedom I would soon swear to give my life to protect.

Out of the dark, frigid motel room, out now in the mix, I was able to recover the sense of myself that had been growing steadily those past fourteen weeks, and here it was: I had been inducted into the elite. The brothers and sisters with whom I had shared the crucible were at that moment closer than blood. We had secret ceremonies and hidden powers those innocent visitors crowding the steamy glass atrium for coffee and cookies knew nothing about. All of them— including Poppy—were outside the cult. I was glad of it. I forgave them for it. And I was filled with happiness.

"Here he is!" I exclaimed as Steve Crawford, ramrod straight and youthfully muscled beneath the tight polo shirt, emerged from the crowd. I introduced him as "my boyfriend," which sounded soft and girlish and out of sync in that military environment.

Steve and I smiled at each other encouragingly. I had tried to prep him, but my convoluted descriptions of Poppy's hot-and-cold behavior only made him totally uptight, afraid to step on a land mine. As a result, Steve drew up tall and presented as a locked-jaw FBI newbie—exactly the kind of condescending fed who rolled over Poppy on the job.

I noticed I had stopped breathing when they shook hands.

"My folks don't get here until tomorrow. Let me treat you to dinner, Lieutenant Grey," Steve offered.

"My treat. You two are the star graduates," my grandfather added resentfully, eyeing us back and forth.

It was early evening when we pulled into Fredericksburg, the sun a fireball behind the hickory trees. We crossed a bridge where flame-tinged water dragged over shallows of black stones.

I had been to town only once, for somebody's birthday, even though it was just twenty minutes from the Academy. We had so much studying, we rarely left. The Board Room, a cafeteria by day, became a full-on bar at night, in order to minimize the need for outside contact.

The tidy Colonial churches and side-gabled homes in the historic district of Fredericksburg were enchanting—until you got out of the car and staggered through the lifeless heat. All the quaint little stores were closed. Poppy, Steve, and I moved at half speed, but not fast enough to avoid a plaque at the site of a famous five-and-dime store, where, back in the sixties, a young African-American woman had been the first to sit at a white's-only lunch counter.

My stomach was hurting even before Poppy went into a tirade about "good-for-nothing blacks." I prayed none of the midwestern tourists, materializing slowly out of the spongy air, could hear his words.

But Steve did.

"If you don't mind, sir, I don't appreciate that kind of talk. I have a cousin married to an African-American doctor, and he's a terrific guy."

"I used to be like you," my grandfather replied, "until I was a patrol officer in the worst neighborhood in Los Angeles."

"We don't want to hear it, Poppy," I said.

I was only in my twenties, not far removed from a childhood that had been dominated by his self-important anger. It buffered him from fears and losses too astringent for his macho taste—instead, the acid curled inside my gut. I had become so entwined in his emotions as a child that my role in life had been fixed as the vessel for holding the things that he despised and cast away.

There, on that brick sidewalk in Fredericksburg, Virginia, secretly brushing hands with the first young man for whom I'd had real feelings, I hated my grandfather. I hated to be stuck in this world with him. I felt ridiculous. At the Academy, I was myself, big and three-dimensional and real; now I was stuck on this historic street in someone else's history, three figures in a sweltering diorama, a shoe-box Colonial miniature like you make in school.

Steve raised an eyebrow and gave a grim shrug. Poppy seemed unaware. He was looking in the window of the Scottish Center, where stuffed cats were wearing kilts. *Nothing affects him,* I thought bitterly. When I looked again, he had wandered down the street to some god-awful military store. Headless torsos were dressed in U.S. Army uniforms. There was a *Life* magazine from 1945 featuring Audie L. Murphy.

"See this guy? *He* did his part."

Implying that we didn't?

"Audie Murphy was the most decorated soldier in the U.S. forces," Steve agreed, mustering respect.

Poppy turned away, somehow offended.

I looked at my watch. It was barely 5:30. Time had slowed in the impassive heat.

"I think the restaurant is open now."

On the advice of a middle-aged Academy librarian, who seemed, in her silk bow-tie blouses and wool skirts, closest to Poppy's aesthetic, we had chosen La Petite Auberge. Inside, it was cool and dark, the air-conditioning a sensual pleasure. There were silver candle lamps with fluted glass shades, white latticework walls, and oil paintings of dogwood trees. Half a dozen well-heeled couples had come in for the early specials. They all knew the waiters; it was, after all, a living small town. Now we were like them—three people seated at a table in a nice French restaurant, none of whom can fathom why they are together.

Steve and I ordered Cokes, which came with lime and lots of ice in a narrow bar glass that contained the sweet carbonation perfectly. The dinner rolls were soft and fluffy white. Things were looking up. Steve's thigh, hard inside the perfectly creased dress slacks, edged reassuringly close to mine.

Poppy decided the following day would be an excellent time to visit Manassas National Battlefield Park, forty miles away.

I protested. "Tomorrow is graduation."

"Not until three-thirty in the afternoon, according to the schedule."

"I have to get ready."

"How long does it take you to get ready?"

"I want to take the morning off, and pack, and take a shower and—"

"I came all the way out to the other side of the country to find Joseph Grey."

"Is he a relative?" Steve asked genially.

"A dead one. Poppy thinks he has a great-great-uncle who fought for the Union and died in the first battle of Manassas. So he wants to go there." I rolled my eyes.

"Can't you find old Joseph on a computer?" Steve suggested.

"A computer is not the same as being present on a field of honor. What is wrong with you?"

"Sorry, sir."

"No need to be sorry," I murmured as a waiter in a white dinner jacket offered the appetizers.

I took a glistening bite of a farm-fresh tomato with onions and tarragon.

"How about we drive up to Baltimore and see the Orioles instead?"

"No, ma'am," Poppy replied. "We are on a mission."

I groped Steve's hand under the table. It was damp.

"Sir, you should know that Ana and I are serious."

"Serious what?" He scraped the bottom of his bowl of mushroom soup.

"We care for each other and we want to get married."

Poppy shocked me by simply asking, "When?"

It threw us both off. "Well," said Steve, coloring red, "we don't know exactly when. We just haven't set a date. One day, I'll wake up and I'll turn to Ana and say, 'Let's get married.'"

"So in the meanwhile, you're shacking up, is that what you're saying?"

"No, sir—"

"We're planning to get married in the chapel at the Academy," I interjected quickly.

"Aren't you the one who said that soon-to-be Special Agent Crawford has been assigned to Miami and you'll be in L.A.?"

"Yes, but—"

"I'm just a dumb cop, so explain to me. Exactly which bed is it where Special Agent Crawford turns to my granddaughter and says, 'Let's get married'? Because I can't figure anything but a Motel 6 in the middle of Texas."

"One of us will be reassigned."

"And that'll be who?"

"We don't know who," I said.

"It'll be you, that's who," said Poppy. "When it comes down to it, he'll be like any man; he'll say, 'My job is more important. *You're only the wife.*'"

"So what?" Steve said angrily. "If we love each other."

"You'd ask me to give up my career?"

"Not give it up."

"But—what?"

"We'll work it out," said Steve.

"How?"

He didn't answer. He didn't know.

My mouth had set in that shut-down way. Steve was watching with distaste. He'd never seen that expression on my face. It made me look like Poppy.

And I had never seen the cold, self-centered steel in his character.

"You're over twenty-one," my grandfather said. "You can do as you damn well please."

The morning of graduation, I picked Poppy up at the Days Inn (he was waiting outside—camera in hand, wearing Bermuda shorts, high socks, an FBI T-shirt and FBI cap) and we headed north. It was 10:00 a.m. and already we were drowning in the muggy, listless air.

Avoiding a revisit of last night's dinner—how we ate quickly and skipped dessert, how it was endured in tense silence except for an argument about which exit Steve's family should take from the airport—Poppy posed one of his "educational" questions: "What is Bull Run?"

"It refers to an Indian chief whose tribe was massacred by U.S. troops and who tried to run away. They thought he was a coward, but history proves he was outnumbered."

Poppy was incensed. He liked to run these quizzes to demonstrate my stupidity, but there was a limit.

"Bull *Run* is a *stream!*" he shouted. "The rebels were hiding in the woods along the banks of *Bull Run* and the Yankees were trapped. They couldn't get across and they couldn't go back. There were no goddamn *Indians* in sight. Goddamn it, Annie, don't they teach anything in school?"

"I guess I was thinking of Sitting Bull."

"I'll tell you what's bull."

I smiled with evil satisfaction for having provoked him. *Manassas* had a haunting sound, like a sultry breeze sweeping high dry grass. I knew it was the first major battle of the Civil War, a catastrophic fiasco, which is why I was struggling to maintain respect as we inched through choking traffic at Manassas Mall.

It was ugly.

"Imagine what lies beneath all this crap," I said.

"What?"

"Bodies. History."

"The battle was fought over *here*." He stabbed impatiently at a map. "Not at the mall. What's the matter with you? Turn right after the overpass. *Battle View Parkway,* that has to be it."

The rental car was overheating, so I turned right. Battle View Parkway had no view of the battleground. It was an access route to an industrial development that ended in a cul-de-sac.

"Well that just tears it."

Poppy folded his arms, as if perversely satisfied by yet another example of the failure of the world to see it his way.

"What I don't understand is the disrespect." He shook his head. "Using the sacrifice of our war heroes to name a street that goes nowhere."

It occurred to me that I had never heard my grandfather admit that he was wrong.

We came upon a split-rail fence that bordered a grassy hillock. The driveway rose and passed a spreading locust. Beneath its canopy, on the near horizon, were framed the crisp black silhouettes of half a dozen cannons. Instantly, my restlessness was stilled. My grandfather removed his FBI cap. The gravity of war seemed to toll the stagnant air, just as it had, hour by hour, the past 130 years. A taste came to the tongue—iron bitterness, like blood.

The car doors slammed and we stood in silence, looking over the rolling countryside, which had once been marked by tree lines, groves, a small white house—each a key location as the advantage of battle whipped from one side to the other like a thrashing snake. Now it was all open fields, and a tractor slowly worked the hay. Small groups of visitors paused here and there. The day was glaring, hazy. An American flag was drooping—limp as the flags that stultifying afternoon, July 21, 1861, when the grass was as high as the chests of seventeen-year-old boys, who fired on their own troops because they couldn't tell the color of the standards they were carrying.

But that sort of thing was just a stitch in the whole mad carnality of it all, a hideously misjudged engagement, in which nearly five thousand naïve volunteers from both sides were killed or wounded. The red-soaked earth that day was strewn with body parts. In the makeshift hospitals, stacks of arms and legs and hands and feet were described as looking like piles of shucked corn.

The slaughter ended only when the Union retreated in terror, a disintegrating mob stampede. The politicians in Washington, D.C.—the Peter Abbotts of the past century—had promised "a great and glorious Union victory" in a week.

We paid ten dollars for a computer search for Joseph Grey or Gray, who could not be found. Poppy was in a swoon, taken with every detail he could swallow of the massive hand-to-hand encounter. Heroes abounded.

By then I was impatient with his petty chatter and eager to get back to the base and take an ice-cold shower. It was time.

"You never said what you think of Steve."

"I didn't like his eyes."

"You don't like his eyes."

"They're small."

"I see."

"They've got that hooded, criminal look."

I turned toward his stringent profile. "Can I ask you something, Poppy? Are you and I on the same planet?"

"You're not going to marry that cracker."

"You can't stop us."

"I wish I were that all-powerful," he said ruefully.

But he was. And I didn't marry Steve. I met his parents only briefly, after the ceremony. There were polite excuses for us not to get together—too many relatives, not enough time. We never made our announcement. He went to Miami. I went to Los Angeles. We wrote letters. We phoned. In six weeks, it faded to nothing. It never had a chance. Stillborn.

"We have to leave in fifteen minutes," I told my grandfather, and left him in the gift shop.

Outside, the sounds were vivid—the call of birds and children's voices shouting *"Eee-ha!"* as they scrambled over the barrels of the cannons. Fat black gnats flew in my ears and up my nose. And there was the slow, mysterious grinding of cicadas, like a mechanical toy winding and unwinding. Winding and unwinding, like an old lady rocking on a porch.

In the white house in the center of the green battlefield, there had, in fact, lived a lady named Mrs. Judith Carter Henry. Her pretty china dishes were preserved in the museum. Eighty-five years old, a widow, she refused to leave the safety of her bed, even when Union sharp-shooters took over the house. The Confederates fired back with howitzers and Mrs. Henry was mortally wounded. Some say she took more than twenty hits. Sources vary.

By then I knew enough about the movement of the battle to see it play out vividly in the still, hot fields. I thought of Poppy, traveling all over the map, California to Colonial Virginia, in search of a hero to heal his wounded heart. Would I ever be that hero in his eyes?

In a few hours, I would become a federal agent of the United States government, bound to carry the shield of core values upon which I, good soldier, was about to swear. Us and them. Black and white. Law and order. It was the defining moment. I was about to become Special Agent Ana Grey, for good. I wonder now, *Would Darcy have let Steve Crawford go?*

A tractor slowly rolled the hay. The fields fell off toward the north, toward the glittering haze of Washington, D.C., from whose alabaster domes I would receive my orders.

I heard the cicadas singing. Their musical clicks went up and down. Far away, in the white house, Mrs. Henry was rocking.

This had been her property. It had been a farm.

Twenty-eight

Special Supervisory Agents Angelo Gomez and Mike Donnato are waiting at a rest stop on the I-5 when I pull up in Darcy DeGuzman's Civic. My cover is an appointment with a local dentist at a phony number manned by an FBI agent in L.A.

"Guys? This was bad."

"That's why we're here."

Donnato indicates a picnic area behind the brick restrooms, not visible from the freeway.

"Let's go around back."

They have dressed down for Oregon—polo shirts and jeans—but I've been up here long enough to make them for out-of-staters, by their clean shoes and precision haircuts. We swing our legs over the seats as they set their supersize coffee cups on the weathered redwood table.

"Dick Stone just about buried the kid alive!" I am still incredulous. "And he sets it up, the bastard, so I almost run over the kid's head."

"Was Megan part of this?"

"No, she was in the car with us. Sara and I were just bringing her back from the airport. Mom leaves, and Stone runs amok. She was panicked. Even she couldn't calm him down. I'm feeling completely degraded by this guy. No matter how much backup and surveillance you provide, I still have to live in that house and play by his rules, and he keeps changing them."

Donnato: "No control."

"Over what Dick Stone is going to do? You can't predict his crazy shit."

"Okay, hold it." Angelo leans forward on the picnic table, Mr. Stability and Reason. "Remember the scenarios in undercover school, where they kept on changing the framework, so you didn't know if it was day or night, or what was real and who was on your side?"

"Yes, the counterfeiters turned into drug dealers, shot a couple of their own—very convincingly—and held a gun to my head."

"What'd you do?"

"I did the cocaine. Just like I smoked the weed when we were out having some fun with a Colt .45 at Herbert Laumann's in-laws' house."

"You survived and Laumann survived," Angelo says. "That was the *lesson learned*."

"Living inside the criminal mind . . ." adds Donnato. "The best we can do is stay with it, and you did."

I exhale deeply and fluff through my hair with both hands, trying to release the tension in my scalp.

"Right."

"Try to put a finger on it. Why is this different from training?" Angelo asks.

I think about it. "Because this wasn't me, a paid U.S. government agent, who was put in harm's way. This was a seventeen-year-old *boy*, who's already suffered unbelievable abuse in some awful state-run institution, and on the streets, and now he's been traumatized to the point where he might never come back, because we screwed up."

Angelo looks puzzled. "How did we screw up?"

"We should have had a covert team sweep the house for electronic surveillance devices before I even moved in." I look at Donnato. "Am I right?"

"Peter Abbott vetoed the expense," he says quietly.

"What is in his head?" I exclaim.

"That's a management issue," Angelo cautions.

"When I get off this case, I'm writing a complaint about—"

"You sound bitter." Angelo's observing me with that cockeyed look.

"I *am* bitter. Peter Abbott swoops in from headquarters like some kind of god, doesn't know the first thing about life on the ground, in the real world, and, as far as I'm concerned, has already made some ill-informed decisions. You have to ask yourself what Abbott's doing commanding this operation. He's about to retire and become a political honcho."

Angelo's got his cop face on and fingers laced with deceptive calm on top of the table.

"Are your feelings about Peter Abbott making it difficult to continue in the undercover role?"

Donnato shoots a look toward Angelo. His eyes tell me: *Warning.* I got that.

"I don't *have* feelings for Peter Abbott, I just want the latitude to do my job. Look, Angelo, I want to nail Dick Stone. After what he did to Slammer, more than ever."

"Because you're sounding awfully bitter," Angelo repeats.

I glance at Donnato. "Just blowing off steam."

"Talk about it with the shrink," he says.

"Do I have to?"

"You've been under almost three months."

He is talking about a psychological evaluation with a therapist when you've been undercover a certain amount of time. It's required. No way out. Just like critical-incident training. I'm looking forward to it about as much as a body scrub with a vegetable grater.

"I am committed to the operation, and I'm fine," I say. "But I'll tell you what I am worried about. The satellite phone. Stone is talking to someone inside the Bureau, and we have no way to trace it."

The moment the words are out, the world begins to waver with vertigo and distrust. *Have I said too much?* What if the spook inside is Angelo? Or could it be Donnato? No, not possible. I wish I had said nothing about satellite phones, that I'd waited until I had more information. Or gone straight to Galloway. Can I trust him, either? How alone can you be?

"No way to trace it," Angelo agrees, "unless we involve NSA, and that's a whole other thing."

He stands and tosses his coffee cup into the trash.

"We should at least put it on a three oh two to headquarters," Donnato suggests.

But I object. "What if someone at headquarters is involved?"

"Okay, let's not go further with this until we have something solid," Angelo says. "Ana's intel is noted."

Is this a reasonable conversation, or are they covering up?

I focus on the reality of what I can actually see, at the rest stop, here and now. Nobody else is around except a couple of red squirrels, squawking on a swaying branch. The noonday forest radiates a lazy, sun-filled, pine-scented heat. Beyond the parking lot, the highway is a searing blur of semi-trailers and logging trucks rattling along at eighty.

They could shoot me in the rest room and be back in L.A. for dinner.

Donnato: "We haven't addressed the problem. Ana has breeched Dick Stone's security system. He has pinhole cameras hidden everywhere—in videocassettes, in pencil sharpeners, in the clocks. What if he's made her, and he's just waiting?"

"Nah," counters Angelo. "If he suspected she was FBI, he'd have blown her to bits like Steve Crawford."

"Always a comfort." My partner sighs.

Angelo shrugs. "You want me to lie?"

Okay, stop. Collect your mind. These are your buddies.

My head clears. "Why don't we arrest Stone now?"

"We don't have the whole picture. Especially if he's talking to someone else. We get much more if we wait."

"It's hard to read this guy," Donnato agrees. "Stone's been running his game so long, he's lying when he says hello. We'd pull you out if we thought you were in danger. You do know that?"

"It's not my personal safety. It's about blowing the operation."

It is a fear I have been carrying, not of physical danger, but worse—the fear of total humiliation. That you have ruined the operation—*you*, single-handedly responsible for destroying everything everyone has worked for, like dropping the fly ball on the third out of the last game of the World Series.

Angelo pauses in his pacing, standing against a backdrop of pines. Sunlight pours on his slick wavy hair and tiny gnats pinwheel the shimmering air.

"There are contingencies. If Dick Stone gets too close to you."

He sits back at the table and we follow.

"Does Stone still have that schmuck Herbert Laumann in his sights?"

"Yes, he does. To get Stone off the kid, I promised I would murder Mr. Laumann. I hope that's okay."

Donnato raises an eyebrow. Angelo frowns.

"What is his state of mind?"

"*Laumann's* state of mind?" echoes Donnato, as if it were obvious. "Scared to death. Terrified for his family. He's had enough of being a rock star. He wants out of the spotlight."

Angelo: "Then let's take him out."

I am sitting on top of the picnic table, listening with admiration and relief as Angelo and Donnato plot Laumann's murder. I scold myself for mistrustful thoughts. These two are pros.

"You're saying we should take Herbert Laumann out of the picture?"

"If we don't," Angelo says, "Stone will have it done."

"Headquarters will have to authorize the hit. Something this sophisticated would go to the director and the attorney general. It could take weeks."

Angelo is dismissive. "Someone at headquarters will have to bite the bullet."

"I know what they'll say." For some reason Donnato won't let it go. " 'What is L.A. trying to pull off now? It's another argument to stay in longer. What's the Big One? What the hell does that mean? What are you creating just to keep the operation going?' Peter Abbott will have to weigh in, and that's a crapshoot."

"I don't give a good goddamn," Angelo snaps. "What the hell do I care? This will prove her loyalty beyond a doubt. Ana? Are you with us?"

"No screwups," I say. "No budgetary crap."

Angelo waves a hand and the sapphire ring glints pink.

"Done it a million times. The Hollywood studios are good at this;

they love to help us out. They can do it so it looks like the guy is dead and we fed him to the sharks. You walk up, shoot the victim at close range. He's got squibs inside his clothing, it's a big bloody mess, he dies an agonizing death, and we relocate him and his family in the witness protection program. No worries, and Dick Stone thinks you're the greatest thing since sliced cheese."

"Believe me," says Donnato, warming to it, "Laumann will go—happily. But we have to put a fence around the family. They need to be protected twenty-four/seven."

My mouth has become dry as the pine needles. The hot bleached sky seems to swirl.

"Are you sure you're okay with this?" Angelo asks, reading me perfectly. "I mean, we all know what you've been through."

The shooting incident.

"I think I have a fairly good handle on reality, Angelo. This is acting. The bullet is a blank."

But my thinking mind goes vacant as my senses seem to cut off one by one—except for the slight scent of burning brake lining, and a high-pitched chatter, like headphones at full volume pressed against my ears.

Angelo consults his watch. His voice sounds faint. "We can catch the three forty-five to L.A. if we leave right now."

As they head back toward the car, Donnato says something about scheduling the psychological evaluation.

"*You're* going to fake a killing, and *I'm* the one who needs to see a shrink?" I say, managing a grin through the deafening clamor of the two red squirrels, jumping branch to branch.

Twenty-nine

Cars are parked way up the road. It is the midsummer festival at Willamette Hazelnut Farm. Megan is sticking close to Stone, who presents himself tonight in a neatly pressed western shirt, the red suspenders, and a crisp straw farmer's hat—your happy host to the alternative lifestyle, urging people to gather in the large bubble shed, where a borrowed sound system plays a cheerful band out of Austin, Texas. Stone told me they had poured the concrete floor just for dances, which sounded pretty goofy, but with the silver blow-up panels animated by moving shadows and the doors thrown open, warm yellow light tumbles across the gravel road, illuminating the American flag, and you can believe in country music.

It is an eclectic blowout—a mix of neighboring farmers, "kindreds" from the pagan community, straitlaced hazelnut distributors from Portland, and random tourists from the local B and Bs, all happily passing the traditional Asatrú libation, great huge horns of beer.

Slammer is standing on the roof of the farmhouse with the local boys, totally hammered on rum. That has pretty much been his MO since the burial attempt, despite empty threats to beat the crap out of Allfather, which came in a whispered confab with Sara. They were huddled like frightened children at the foot of the stairs as Slammer struggled out of his filth-encrusted clothes. Sara quickly balled them into her arms, as if to shrink an unthinkable humiliation down to the size of a load of laundry.

"You can't let him do that to you."

"That's him, dog."

"We should get out of here. We should call the cops."

"Are you serious? You want to go home?"

"No, but . . . He scares me." Sara flushed pink and began to hiccup with tears.

"Poor little princess."

"Guys!" I stepped between them. "Don't get on each other."

Sara had dropped the clothes and was staring at me defiantly.

"Slammer, you have every right to call the police," I said. "Is that what you want to do?"

Slammer's eyes went vacant. "Actually," he said, "I'm kind of hungry."

After that, you could hear pickups burning rubber at two o'clock in the morning and raucous male shouting as Slammer came and went with the locals. Nothing changed on the farm. Maybe Stone had made his point. Maybe he was waiting to make another.

I see Sterling McCord has arrived and is talking to Sara, who doesn't want to stand still and listen. He's been on her case about Geronimo—how it would do her good to care, really care, for an animal, get up at dawn and muck the dung, not just mouth off about it—but she's laughing, tossing it off, flirting instead. Incapable, is more like it. Meanwhile, McCord has the loosest pelvis on the planet. He's standing tilted back on his heels, as if in the saddle at a trot. He's wearing a silver conch belt and his usual washed-out jeans, a midnight blue shirt open at the chest.

I have noticed that you can't go wrong on wardrobe if you're a cowboy.

The sorting equipment and red tractor have been moved outside, so there is room for line dancing. The song is something about "old Amos." I draw back from the doorway and the shining, eager faces go past the American flag and into the colder shadows. Sara and McCord are free to get it on—but me, I'm on the job. *Undercover work—this is how it gets to you.* The loneliness digs down like fast-growing roots and cracks your resolve. This is exactly when you are supposed to call your contact agent. Dose of reality. Remember who you are. It is 9:36 p.m. and Donnato is most likely home with his family.

Candles are still burning in jars on a half-cleared table near the orchard, illuminating a forest of smudgy fingerprints on abandoned wineglasses. An older couple is camped out at one end, picking at brownie crumbs in an aluminum pan. I move past, fishing out the last Heineken from the frigid waters of the cooler.

"Looks like Noah's ark," Sterling says from behind.

I turn toward the lighted shed and smile.

"They've got all the animals, right?"

"And they're all gonna be saved. Any more beers?"

I give him the Heineken and pull out a Coors.

"I could use a set-down," he suggests. "How about yourself?"

At the other end of the table, in the half dark, an enormous white man is holding forth to a slight man of color—the first black face I've seen in Oregon. As we sit, I recognize the voice: like a sixteen-wheeler groaning uphill in second. That's when I realize the fuzzy shape in the diffuse light is Mr. Terminate.

"John! It's Darcy! From Omar's bar."

The other couple take a good look at John and decide to get out of there, leaving us with the dour biker, massive thighs dwarfing a folding chair, clutching a bottle of Jack Daniel's. He has left the black top hat at home, revealing long, thin tresses trailing off a half-bald dome.

"What are you doing here?" I ask.

"Crashin' the party."

"Who's your friend?"

"Toby Himes," says the black man, extending his hand.

In the rural crowd, Toby Himes is a standout, neatly dressed in pressed slacks and a windbreaker. He keeps his hands inside his pockets while surveying the scene. He sports a tweed snap-brim cap and a white goatee, and takes his time, not intimidated. At first, I make him for another cop.

Because it takes a minute to dial it in. The biker and the black man, having a drink in the dark? This isn't random. They know each other.

And Mr. Terminate is not eating ashtrays, or washing his hands in someone's pitcher of suds.

He is calm, like Vesuvius on a good day.

This is so inconsistent with John's attitude toward the darker nation that the hair goes up on the back of my neck and I hook a leg over the bench, curious to find out why.

I introduce McCord as the wrangler who saved me from the wild horses, tell them the story of the arrests at the BLM corrals and try to draw them in.

"Should we all go out and save the wild horses?"

"I'll tell you about horses," wheezes Mr. Terminate, and begins a tale that has nothing to do with horses. "Up in Colorado, some of the fellas came into a load of computer stuff."

"Just dropped from the sky, did it?" Toby Himes laughs and takes a sip of beer. "I know how *that* is."

"You know bull crap. Excuse my French, but this is top secret shit, vital pieces of our national defense system."

"A vital piece of our defense network is missing?" McCord says. "John, you know, that really helps me sleep at night."

"How'd they steal it?" I ask.

Mr. Terminate shakes his head and pours a little Jack into a plastic cup.

"That I cannot say. But I do know *this*."

He points a pinkie with an inch-long curved fingernail, a built-in spoon for snorting coke.

"Those computers were sold to the Indians for *a shitload of silver and turquoise*."

We are openmouthed. Toby Himes giggles.

"And then," whispers Mr. Terminate dramatically, "*they buried it*."

Pause.

"Who buried it?"

"That I cannot say."

But he furrows his eyebrows menacingly, as if telling a ghost story, which he probably is.

Toby Himes: "Get the story straight. The bikers buried it, or the Indians buried it?"

Mr. Terminate looks confused. "The way I heard it from Julius is the Indians buried it. After they stole it back."

"The Indians stole it back?"

"The Indians damn right stole it back. Now, the fellas *I know*—"

"You mean Hell's Angels?"

"That's a dated concept, darlin'. We are businessmen." Another sip of Jack. "*The fellas I know,* that knew where the turquoise was buried, when it was buried on the reservation, happened to be in prison at the time. But before they got murdered, they got word to the outside."

Another dramatic pause.

"So," ventures McCord after this baffling recitation, "did your boys ever find the turquoise?"

Mr. Terminate chuckles. "Rest assured it is buried in a very safe place. You think I'm fibbing? You ask Julius. He's the one got custody of it now."

"We're asking you."

"They say it's buried beside a pipe."

"A peace pipe!" echoes McCord with a straight face.

"All's I know, there's a marker, and it's yellow. And a cage of wild beasts guarding it. But don't go running out there."

"Don't worry. We won't."

"*Because the turquoise is guarded by an ancient Umpqua Indian curse!*"

"Thanks for the warning, John."

When Toby Himes is ready to leave, I claim that nature calls and follow him up the road and get the tag number on his 1995 Dodge pickup. I figure if his talking to Mr. Terminate is nothing, it's nothing. If it's something, then it is.

Sterling McCord is waiting with two fresh beers, as I somehow knew he would be. We go a couple of rows back into the orchard and sit on the clean-swept dirt and lean our backs against a tree. We can hear the music clearly. The crescent shed still rocks with talk and laughter.

"What do you think?" he asks.

"About the turquoise?"

"Uh-huh."

"I think John was making it up as he went along."

"I heard the same story," McCord tells me, "from an old-timer, works in town at the Seed N' Feed. The curse, the same darn thing."

Against the current of two beers, the nearness of a tightly knit male body, and a summer night crazy with lavender, a nebulous connection forces itself to focus. Rosalind, administrative assistant and keeper of the family flame down in Los Angeles, told me Dick Stone worked undercover on a case called Turquoise. And now he allegedly has possession of so-called buried treasure. Is it real, or does *turquoise* have a double meaning? Some other layer of deception Stone has embroidered over the past, like the flying corn on his cap?

"There was a yellow fire hydrant out in the wash. Where we ran across the foal. Maybe that's the marker."

McCord nods, chugging beer. "I saw it."

"You did not."

"I might look like a dog-eared fool, but occasionally I do pay attention."

He takes his time to grin real slow. I wish he didn't have that brown spot on his gum where the tooth is missing.

"But why should I share the treasure with you?" he asks.

"Because you like me." I notice that sparkly feeling creeping up from where it hides, damned if I'm on the job. "Let's be honest. You liked me from the very first time you were rude to me."

"When was that?"

"When you saved my life. You said, 'Hey. You shouldn't be messing with wild animals.' Hell of a thing to say to a lady in distress."

"That wasn't rude, ma'am. That's a fact."

"What's a fact?"

"I am never rude to beautiful ladies. Let's go find the turquoise."

The luxe interior of the Silverado softens the wallop of rocks and crevices along the access road leading out of the power station. The first time we drove it in the noonday sun, with Sara, panicked, between us, clouds of dust rose in our wake, and they may be rising still, but in this blackness it is impossible to see anything except what is pinned by the headlights.

McCord eases the truck off the road and cuts the engine. This time I am shivering as we stand at the edge, and not just from cold. Behind us, the power station, illuminated by security lights, looks like a futuristic prison. McCord, holding a flashlight, leads down the embankment, following something—an instinct or a trail—searching for the riverbed where we found the foal, but nothing looks familiar in the half-light. No old-woman tree. No ancient streambed with banks of dying roots. But alive inside of me, that complex delta twists and turns with desire, as if all the tiny sparks in this dark landscape had been melted together to form a glittering molten river of light, aching for the release of the sea.

Across the low terrain we can hear the distant party on the farm, like voices from a speaker in an old wrecked car. A lone wind thrums through my earrings as a drowsy voice argues the *lessons learned: Never sleep with a suspect.* But McCord isn't a suspect. Is he?

"Where was it?" he asks.

I remember that as I sat by the foal and cooled its body with a rag, a small concrete bunker rose from the wheatlike grass. When McCord's flashlight sweeps across it, I direct him that way. Climbing through an oak grove and then coarse shrubs with leathery leaves, we discover the bunker and a wire cage built over it.

"There're your wild animals guarding the treasure," McCord says dryly, running the beam over a gate valve with screw wheels enclosed in the cage.

"What is it?"

"Flood control."

We stand there like two idiots, staring in silence at the work of some engineering drone twenty years ago.

"Nice," I say.

"Thought you'd like it."

"Give me dried hoofprints and the smell of old manure any day."

McCord laughs. At least he has a sense of humor about himself. I can feel the giggles rise like bubbles. . . . Maybe that's how it will begin.

"One thing about wranglers," he says. "We take you to the best places."

"Really? I thought you were interested in Sara."

"Sara's hot but way too young."

"That's what she said about you. The opposite. In reverse."

I snicker self-consciously. Awkward, too, he kicks at the wire cage covering the pump. It moves. It is not secured by the rusted lock, only looks that way.

Wordlessly, we catch our fingers in the wire mesh and pull. It comes off easily and we set it aside.

"Someone's been messing with this, for sure."

We squat closer. The flashlight reveals a hole in the iron plate that is fitted around the pipe assembly. A hole for lifting.

McCord checks with me. "Are you ready?"

"Go for it."

He hooks a finger in the hole, but it is hard to lift. No hinge—it just sits in the square opening.

"Need a crowbar. Got one in the truck."

"I'm not staying here alone."

"No problem." McCord finds a heavy stick. "I'll lift, you get the stick under there and pry."

"Ready."

"Wait a minute!"

"*What?*" I whisper with alarm.

"Watch out for that Indian ghost," he hisses. "If he comes charging out of here, I'm gone."

"Don't make me laugh!"

"This is serious stuff. Indian lore. Buried treasure."

"Just lift."

"You know the old Indian chant—"

"*Just do it before I pee my pants!*"

McCord hooks his finger firmly, sets his back, and lifts. I push the stick underneath the edge and we slide the plate to one side of the hole and shine the light inside.

I scream like a madwoman. "Close it! Close it quick!"

Inside the culvert, four feet down, is a nest of rattlesnakes.

"Just stand still."

"Oh my God, Sterling—"

"Don't move. They're cold. They're resting. This is not their time of day."

Resting? The slow, slithering mass is pit-of-the-stomach hell. Mc-Cord keeps his flashlight on the entwined bodies—big ones, inches thick, with long rattles and darting wedgelike heads.

"These guys are old," McCord observes, "and full of venom. If one of these daddies bit that little horse, it's amazing that he lived."

"They're waking up—"

Like the Indian curse.

Their eyes glint. The rattling, faint at first, is quickly becoming deafening, like medicine men hallucinating wild dreams.

"Put the cover on," I plead.

McCord whistles and bends closer. I grab his belt, terrified he's going to fall in.

"Look at this!"

I cannot look any longer at the glistening knot of reptiles.

"What is it? Is it the turquoise?"

"I don't see no turquoise," McCord drawls, "but there's a hell of a lot of guns."

Now I do look, and carefully. The rattlesnakes are crawling over a pile of semi-automatic weapons and boxes of grenades.

McCord ticks them off: "You got your Heckler & Koch MP5s, a Berreta Model 12, a couple of Ingrams, and your basic Makarov handguns, extremely popular in the Arab world. It's a global terrorist barn dance down there."

And a .50-caliber McMillan M87, heavy sniping rifle, made in the USA.

Just like the rifle that killed Sergeant Mackee.

Careful. What would Darcy say?

"All this stuff is worth money."

McCord shoots me a look too quick to read in the dark. "Seen enough?"

"Wait!"

Scattered across the cache of firearms, like offerings in a tomb, are the skeletons of tiny animals.

"What are those?"

"Looks like rabbit bones," says McCord.

"The baby rabbits," I whisper. "Stolen from the farm. Do you think someone's been feeding them to the snakes?"

"They sure didn't hippity-hop down there on their own," says McCord.

We drag the lid over the seething pit.

Thirty

Some very unlucky FBI agents (I hope it was the dopey duo from Portland who brought the ducks) dig through the rattlesnakes guarding the cache and replace the .50-caliber M87 sniper rifle with an identical model, sealing everything back the way it was. Forensics determines the gun found in the pit is, in fact, the same one that fired the round that killed Sergeant Mackee. Dick Stone's fingerprints are all over it.

As a result, a horrendous argument breaks out in the conference room in Los Angeles.

"We have the cop killer," Galloway says right away. "Case closed."

"Dick Stone is more than a killer." Angelo has loosened the Rolex and is spinning it around his wrist. "He's an anarchist who hates the FBI."

Donnato: "That's why we bust him and get Ana out."

"What are we in there for?" Angelo yells. *"FAN!"*

"Stone is moments away from making her. If he hasn't already."

Angelo: "We don't want to blow the operation on a lousy murder charge."

Donnato gets up from the table to confront him. "Killing an officer gets Stone the death penalty."

Angelo shrugs. "Stone being dead is not the mission."

"What is the mission? Remind us."

"Stone giving up his contacts."

"He'll talk when he's in prison."

"A former FBI guy? How does that work?"

"He gets protective custody."

"Peter Abbott wants the big picture," Angelo says impatiently.

"Peter Abbott sits at a desk in Washington while Ana Grey is at risk. He's exactly the guy we should be worried about." Donnato is incredulous. "Whose side are you on?"

"You're asking me that? You are really asking me that? Think twice about walking to your car alone, buddy."

Donnato: "Is that a threat?"

"I see we are taking our testosterone pills this morning," says Galloway by way of warning.

They back off, but only to regroup.

"Anybody remember a case in the seventies called Turquoise? Ana flagged it from a conversation with Rosalind, who subsequently provided me with confirmation and pulled the abstract. We connected the Weathermen to a string of armored car robberies taking place in Arizona. Dick Stone went in as the undercover. Ana says there's talk of some kind of buried turquoise up in Oregon. She's wondering if there's a connection with Stone and the old Turquoise case."

"In reality?" Angelo says. "Or in his head?"

Galloway: "Pull up the complete files and court transcripts." He mouths the dead cigar. "Let's review. Angelo's feeling is that whatever is taking place in the here and now, Dick Stone isn't pulling this off alone. The cache of weapons indicates international connections. He's up there on the food chain but answering to a higher power."

"The higher power is someone in the Bureau," Donnato says, barely keeping a lid on it. "Given the Toby Himes revelation, we'd better look closely at who's in charge and why."

They don't tell me until later, but as a result of running his license plate at the midsummer festival, Toby Himes has become a "person of interest" to Operation Wildcat. More, the star quarterback. He lives in Stevenson, a tiny river town on the Washington side of the Columbia River Gorge, where he is employed as the town engineer. If he had come from there the night of the midsummer festival, it would have been almost a three-hour drive to see Mr. Terminate at Dick Stone's farm. The black man and the biker didn't meet to discuss hazelnuts.

Even more compelling: Toby Himes, the recipient of a Purple Heart, served in Vietnam in the same unit as Peter Abbott. Himes's specialty was ordnance. Like Stone, he was trained to blow things up. A trap placed on Toby's phone shows calls made to Peter Abbott's private number.

Three names on the table and they all connect: Dick Stone, domestic terrorist, former FBI; Toby Himes, former military with training in explosives; Peter Abbott, deputy director of the Federal Bureau of Investigation, on the fast track to a political career.

The Abbott link is way too hot for an SAC in a field office to handle alone. But Galloway knows if he is going to follow this trail, it will have to be solo. And extremely treacherous. His equanimity in that meeting is a façade.

"What about our request for the hit on Herbert Laumann?"

"Not a word."

"We knew it would take weeks," Angelo grumbles. "Some low guy at headquarters has to write a document and get it to the attorney general, then back to the director, and back on down. What's your problem, Mike?"

Donnato: "At this point, we have to ask: Do you trust the chain of command? Why does Toby Himes, a known associate of terrorists, have the private number of the number-two man in the FBI?"

Galloway tries again.

"Let's stay on track. One scenario is for Ana to hang in there until Stone shows his cards—who he's working for, and to what end. Until he slips up."

Donnato: "Stone ain't gonna slip."

"Operations are fluid," Angelo argues reasonably. "We started out looking for one thing; now we've got two focuses: Stone and FAN."

Donnato: "They're the same."

With the good side of his face, Angelo agrees. "Stone is running a cell of FAN. We have an operative in deep cover; this thing is going where we want it to go. At this point, it's real simple: Watch the boat."

"While we're watching, he buries Ana Grey up to the neck like that kid."

"What does Ana want?" Galloway asks.

"She wants to stay in," Donnato replies. "She wants to be a hero."

Galloway considers his cigar.

"Does she know what it means to be a hero? A hero is a picture in somebody's office."

There is a prolonged silence.

Finally, it's Galloway, his voice reluctant and low, who says it: "Do we have a problem in-house?"

From the look on the faces of his two trusted agents, veterans whose combined service records add up to almost forty years, Galloway can no longer ignore the elephant in the room.

"Approach Peter Abbott like you would any other bad guy. This stays with us. For her own security, keep Ana out of the loop."

They nod.

Around a conference table in Los Angeles, in complete secrecy and at great personal risk, three men who put loyalty above all else agree to launch a clandestine investigation to determine whether the deputy director of the FBI is aiding and abetting a group of domestic terrorists.

Thirty-one

"Get out of my way."

Stone rummages through the kitchen drawers and then moves to the front closet as Megan follows him from room to room.

"Julius—what are you doing?"

"You should know."

"I have no idea!"

From the safety of the landing on the staircase, beneath the eye of the pinhole camera inside the German clock, the black-and-white kitten cries, one paw curled. Sitting there and stroking him, I try to fathom Dick Stone's state of mind. He seems possessed, as if powerful aromas are assaulting him from every side. As he pushes Megan aside, his body seems to be aflame with irritation.

"The whole superstructure of this country is collapsing," he says, charging upstairs. "There's downward pressure on everything."

"Including me," she replies, exasperated, as they pass.

I take the kitten in my lap and watch from a child's point of view as the arguing parents thunder by. Stone's boots raise dust on the runner tacked along the treads—which I remember checking out, piece by piece, for false compartments beneath the stair. That was before the discovery of the arms cache—before I knew that Daddy stole the bunnies that were rescued from starvation at the dump, in order to feed the rattlesnakes that were guarding Daddy's guns.

"It's everywhere," Stone is lecturing. "Even for people who are medium well-off. Nobody can make it anymore."

"Could the apocalypse wait until Saturday? I'll drive you wherever you want to go after the market."

"You?" He laughs as they disappear inside the bedroom.

"Oh, stop being silly," clucks Megan, but a few minutes later she is heading back downstairs with a purpose.

I find her in the dining room, digging through the sideboard until she has what she is looking for—two bankbooks I have already examined. Neither shows a balance of more than fifteen hundred dollars.

"Phew!" She uses them to fan herself dramatically. "Last time he was in a mood like this, he took out three hundred dollars with no memory of what happened to it."

"He doesn't remember? Really?"

She slips the bankbooks in her pocket.

"We have 'happy Julius days,' 'depressed Julius days,' and 'just plain crazy.' "

"How can you stand it? I thought when you left for Lillian's funeral, you might not come back."

"We fight, but that's the way it is. We've been together a long time, Darcy."

"That's what women say whose husbands beat them up."

Mistake!

Megan's eyes narrow, defending her man.

"Julius has never laid a hand on me. Or any woman."

Stuttering, I say, "I didn't mean to say Allfather was like that."

"It has gotten worse." She considers me with an insinuating stare. "Actually, a lot worse since you arrived."

Sticking an agent under his nose, as we might have learned from the Steve Crawford tragedy, only succeeds in aggravating the paranoia of a person like Dick Stone. His behavior has become irrational, and Megan is close to stating the truth: Once again, the FBI is responsible for letting the genie out of the bottle.

"I used to be able to talk him down. But what he did to Slammer . . ." Her voice breaks. "He was gone. He couldn't hear me. I couldn't physically stop him."

We hear Stone stomping around upstairs.

"Where is he going?"

"To see his friend Toby," she replies fretfully. "All of a sudden he's got to see Toby, the most important thing in the world. The single day I have to go to Portland, and it's a long drive in the opposite direction."

"Why don't I go along and keep an eye on him, Megan?"

Her eyes rise to the old beamed ceiling and her lips pinch.

"I wish I could get him to stay on his meds, but he refuses. Stubborn man."

She looks at her watch.

"What time do you have to be in Portland?" I ask helpfully.

Megan hesitates. It is clear she'll never make it to the market to sell her hazelnut brittle unless somebody volunteers to babysit Stone.

"Go with him," she says, "but if he's still like this, promise me you will not let him drive."

Clouds of fog lie in the valleys, and the hills are saturated black. It stays that way, everlasting twilight. Nothing moves beside the houses and fences that blur the edge of our vision except the suddenly peaceful bandit, who seems to be flying past at eighty miles an hour, as if without benefit of a vehicle, like one of those maharishis known to levitate cross-legged over the mountains of India.

No way was he going to let me drive. He is the center. He is on the flight deck. He checks the green dials pulsing at the changes in the atmosphere—changes I imagine that he needs to know. Green dial faces are loyal. Amber ones are false. The amber ones do not worry him because he knows the truck is secure. As we crossed the misty yard, he called to me to make sure the engine hoses were clamped tight and there were no explosives hidden under the seat.

Now he is just steering the truck, maybe wondering what in hell made him so touchy when, in fact, he has everything! They tried disinformation, but he knew the game. They sent a provocateur, whom he skillfully disabled. His euphoria is rising. He feels like Jesus Christ—in a good way.

"Careful," I say for the second or third time. "Who is this guy Toby Himes? I saw him at the festival."

"Old pal of mine. He's selling a boat. Check it out." He pats his stomach. "Lost four more pounds."

"Good for you."

Then Dick Stone decides to drive for a while in the opposite lane.

"Let's get there alive, if you don't mind."

He laughs until he can't stop laughing, swerving back across the road.

No soldier at a reckless gallop, no jet pilot screaming upside down, no Navy Seal in dead of night, mad junkie, murdering, thrill-seeking sadistic monster; no hero under fire or Purple Heart, adrenaline-locked-eighteen-year-old-joyful-virgin-fucker; no one-eyed god, no God-drunk raven razoring the most primitive chartreuse skies of perpetual black rain was ever as purely out-of-body high as Dick Stone is now.

And he is like this recently, a lot.

The two-lane blacktop rounds a curve and we are afforded an inspirational view of mountains meeting mountains, whispering to the horizon beyond the wide green water of the Columbia River. There are a preposterous number of waterfalls in the mountains along this road, and we are passing yet another, a needle-thin cascade that falls maybe two hundred feet, raising clouds of mist that blanket stands of wildflowers—white anemones, Dick Stone has said.

"Beautiful."

"That's the spirit of Bob Marley, right there."

"Bob Marley? Are you a fan of reggae music?" I ask just to say something.

"Major fan. He had it right about Babylon nation."

"What is Babylon nation? When Slammer was going on about it, I figured he was just stoned."

"Babylon is the Vampire. The inability of the white race to live in the natural world without destroying it. Babylon System is America, the whore of nations, gorged on luxury and fornication—but remember, that's before Armageddon."

"Gotcha."

"See these waterfalls? A gargantuan river of melted ice comes raging down from Canada, fifty miles an hour, a thousand feet deep, gouging through those cliffs." Stone is in a kind of rapture. "You want to talk *cataclysmic*?"

"All because of the white man."

He disregards my wit. "It's coming."

"What is?"

"The Big One."

"Another cataclysm?"

"Of major proportion."

"What is the Big One, Julius?"

"The end of arrogance and superiority."

"That could mean the Yankees. Come on, give me something to work with."

"Funny girl."

"What's going on, Julius? Are we—the people at the farm—are we involved in something a lot more violent than I think?"

He smiles slyly. "I wouldn't want to freak you out."

"I can guess."

"What?"

"You're going to blow something up with a blood bomb."

Somehow, this flatters him. He settles back in the seat. "A long time ago, before I switched careers to filbert farming, I firebombed a power tower."

"Really? Cool! Where was this?"

"Ski resort."

"Why? You didn't like waiting on the lift?"

Stone chuckles. Today he is allowing me to tease him. It's like scratching a pit bull behind the ears.

"The neat part was that all we had to bring the thing down were a couple buckets of fuel, a kitchen timer, and an igniter they use for model rockets. You should have seen that thing keel over—power lines, trees, man, that was a tangle—tipping, tipping . . . *tipping* . . . into twelve feet of pure virgin snow."

"Because?"

"Somebody was pissed off about endangered cats. I can't remember what kind."

Caution. No, it's okay. Darcy, the activist, would know.

"Were they lynx?"

He looks pleased. "That's right."

Ecoterrorism. Vail, Colorado. A wave of unsolved fire bombings the Bureau has been chasing since the early nineties.

"That was impressive. Nobody ever took credit."

He slaps my thigh in a friendly way. "Now you know."

I can get anything I want from him now. What a feeling! It's exciting. Tremendous! This is the good thing about penetrating without an informant: Nobody can snitch off you; nobody can compromise you. If we had tried to flip Megan, I'd never be where I am at this moment, confident and relaxed, riding up front with Stone. It's as if you've stepped through the danger and you're actually being sheltered by the source. The *real* source, which is Stone's mind, a mandala of private symbols and pulsing hurts, in which the figure of Darcy DeGuzman has come to stand as a trusted ally. I see why guys like Angelo are addicted. It's the greatest high in the world, to carry the shield you swore upon, to be representing the good people of this country, and the innocent, to be their emissary, to have the ability to talk with somebody who actually wants to harm you—talking to that person's heart.

"This was in your badass revolutionary days."

He raises an eyebrow. "Who said they're over?"

I can barely control the eagerness. Everything seems so close. So possible.

"Does Toby have something to do with all this? You seem hell-bent on seeing him today."

"He found the kind of boat I need."

"For the Big One? Tell me."

Now he is teasing. "Mmm, I'm not sure you're ready to know."

"Why not?"

Another trial of fire and ice?

"You promised to do something for me."

"Off Herbert Laumann? I said I'd do it and I will."

He assents in a fatherly way. That's all for now.

"Be at peace and know that everything is unfolding as it should."

"Swell. I'm in nirvana. When is lunch?"

When do we get approval from FBIHQ for the hit? What will it take to get the accountants off the dime? Because that's the way it always is—the criminal side of the house versus the bean counters, leaving undercovers stranded on a seductively beautiful road like this one, guessing which fork leads to paradise, and which one to perdition.

We are edging along the Lewis and Clark Trail. In pictures you always see the explorers pointing, and with good reason. Imagine if you had discovered this plentitude of lumber and the riches of the salmon run. Not anymore, as Dick Stone vehemently points out, since a chain of hydroelectric dams has displaced the chinook's ancient pathways to the sea.

"Look at those monstrosities, totally fucked the river. They are everything that's wrong with big business and the U.S. government."

"Without 'em, we wouldn't have electric lights."

"Fascist pigs," Stone growls. "Monuments to ego."

I stare at the dams going by—colossal concrete bunkers crested by powerhouse electric grids—remembering the surveillance photo of Megan, aka Laurel, confronting Congressman Abbott somewhere along this river, and that Dick Stone would have been there, too, but there is no credible way to bring it up. Below the spillways, where tons of water empty downstream from the dams, colorful windsurfers flick about the anthracite surface of the water, scraps in the bottom of a chasm.

"What did you do before you blew up that tower?"

"I was in the FBI."

I just about eject through the roof of the truck.

"And I was in the CIA," I say calmly.

"Don't believe me."

"You're just playing." Pause. "Am I right?"

At that moment, two sheriff's cars pass at normal speed. What is this? A signal?

This can't be happening. He can't be telling me this now.

Dick Stone replies amiably, "What'd you think? Can you see me wearing a suit, in the FBI?"

"Suits with guns?"

He laughs. "Guys in suits, with no sex life, who fight alien life-forms."

"Yeah." I grin. "That's you."

But Stone is deliberating something. "Do you remember the Weather Underground?"

"That was a little before my time, but yeah, they were anarchists who were against the Vietnam War."

" 'Bring the war home,' " Stone says grimly. "That was the slogan."

"They set off bombs, right?"

"Three of them blew themselves up trying to build a bomb in a town house in Greenwich Village."

"I vaguely remember."

Memorized the files.

"What about the Weather Underground?" I prompt. "Were you part of it?"

"Me?" He dismisses the thought. "Hoover's gangsters really fucked those people. Destroyed their lives. Hard times comin', no matter which side you were on," he says. "Sad. Really sad."

The truck window is down and a river wind is washing Dick Stone's commanding profile clean, blowing his long blond hair back over the built muscles of his neck, so a tuft of white in the honey-colored sideburns is revealed. In the deep lines of the forehead, and the clenched brows trying to grip whatever vision keeps eluding him at the far side of the journey, I see a middle-aged man asking if his life has been a fake.

Then he attempts to discard it, the past thirty years of it, with a rapid shake of the head, but a long silence follows as the road climbs the dark pine highlands, and we exit, loop up and back toward a spectacular gleaming bridge that leads to the Washington side of the river, as if leaving one fairy-tale kingdom of spells and lies for another.

From the bridge, a hundred feet above the Columbia River, the vault of space the water carved is enormous, enough to contain the talk of all this history and more; it's as if you could lift off the railing and lie in the hammock of the wind, out of time, like the hawks.

But as we cross the bridge, I feel the threads of my connection to the Bureau tug and unravel. Dick Stone's aborted confession hints at more than what management has been telling me. I know this because of the transparency of the way we are together in the car. I know because he's dropped the craziness he cultivates with Megan, as if he's aching to find someone with whom he can come clean. For the moment, Dick Stone trusts me enough to take a brief ride on the violent currents of the past—entwined and gone, and constantly renewed, like the twisted air.

"What the fuck is that?"

We have crossed into the state of Washington, passing sunny fields of yellow mustard. Ahead we can see flashing lights and backed-up vehicles surrounding a traffic accident. I spot unmarked vans and the same cars from the sheriff's department that passed us an hour ago, and wonder if it's a trap.

Stone's paranoia is infectious. Have the orders come through from Washington? Is a SWAT team waiting to rush the car?

Not now. Not yet.

"Let's avoid this, go left," I vamp, and we turn sharply, ending up on a long private drive that leads to a contemporary lodge of huge logs and flower-covered walkways, something out of a Swedish Western. We double back, avoiding the accident by a couple of miles, and take the first fork east.

Not to perdition, or to paradise.

To a river town called Stevenson.

Where Dick Stone's pal Toby Himes wants to sell a boat.

Thirty-two

We enter the town by crossing an old railroad bridge, which runs into a nostalgic street of local businesses—your time-honored pharmacy and coffee shop, picture gallery and independent bookstore—and stop for gas across the street from the Dough Folk bakery.

Dick Stone sends me inside to get crullers. "Best in the world," he says.

I wait while a pair of elderly sisters, both wearing overcoats and high socks in the summer heat, order biscuits and gravy to go. Across the street, Dick Stone is putting gas into the white truck. Engaged in this most American moment, he seems to be an ordinary, slightly grizzled outdoorsman who takes his freedoms for granted.

The sun is shining and someone has driven by towing six canoes.

The white truck pulls to the curb and waits.

A hot breeze scented with cinnamon-sugar follows me as I hurry out the screen door of the bakery. Clutching a box of fresh fried crullers, I walk around the truck and slide into the front seat.

"Aren't these great?" Stone wolfs one.

He smiles with pleasure at the old-fashioned taste of crisp dough and powdered sugar. We pass an inlet where a kayaker drifts in ripples of blue. Mountain buttercups are blooming in the new grass all along the road to Toby Himes's house—an orderly house in a spick-and-span town.

Northwest tidy, you might say, like the ubiquitous trimmed mustaches and khaki shorts: a clapboard cottage painted buttermilk with pumpkin trim, a concrete slab for a porch where a golden chow sleeps beside a pot of geraniums. There are two cobalt blue metal chairs, the Dodge pickup in the driveway, along with a small powerboat on a trailer hitch, and a muddy ten-speed bike, unsecured, near a vegetable patch.

Toby Himes opens the door and the men embrace, Toby patting Stone on the back with thin, nervous fingers and calling him "Doctor." He seems to match the clean and fluffy dog, and the neat yard. He is even more tailored than at the midsummer festival: a tall black man with glasses, white hair, and a neat white goatee, wearing a pressed shirt, slacks, and moccasins.

Not your image of a wacked-out Vietnam vet.

Toby Himes, who has an engineering job with the town of Stevenson, is still the only person of color I have seen. He must be Dick Stone's age, but he is willowy and thin, whereas Stone has bulked out. The courtly manners and soft accent feel like the Old South, but in these austere bachelor chambers, there is no trace of a likewise genteel woman. One room is entirely bare except for free weights and Chinese drawings depicting the poses of kung fu.

Stone has made himself at home in a recliner with a glass of orange juice. A golf tournament is playing on TV. Toby is reluctant to take his eyes from the screen. During the commercial he asks Stone what he's been up to.

"Messing with people's minds again?"

Stone grunts, satisfied. "We had some fun. Tell Toby how we got right into the face of evil at the BLM."

I describe the midnight raid on Herbert Laumann's family as Stone's buddy listens politely, big brown eyes alert behind the glasses.

"This dude Laumann is a bureaucrat," Toby concludes. "He's got no say whatsoever over the wild horses—that's policy out of Washington, D.C. He can't do anything about it, so why are you busting his chops?"

"Laumann is a symbol," Stone replies testily. "Symbols are important in political work."

"To hell with politics!" Toby smiles and waves a spidery hand. "Right, Darcy? Tell me, what do you think of boats?"

I used to live in Marina del Rey, California, with a view of three thousand sailboats.

"Never thought much about them."

Toby slaps his knees conclusively. "Doctor? What do you say we initiate this young lady in the pleasures of cruising our beautiful river?"

Death by drowning. In those rapids, all it would take would be a nudge over the side.

"No thanks, Toby. I get seasick. It's embarrassing."

Dick Stone stretches out his legs and leans back in the reclining chair. "The boat looks fine."

" 'Fine'?" Toby clowns, popping his eyes. "How can you tell?"

"Saw it in the driveway. It's fine."

Toby shakes his head. "Julius, my friend, you are full of surprises."

"Always."

I'm looking around, sniffing the air. It is a comfy masculine nest, with a worn leather couch in front of a river-stone fireplace, kindling neatly stacked in a brass pot, driftwood and candles arranged on the mantel. A homosexual liaison between these two is not out of the question. A maple bookshelf holds magazines in plastic holders: *Western Gunsmithing* and *Guns & Ammo.*

"Quite a collection."

"I don't like guns," Toby jokes. "I *love* them."

"Well then, you're the one to tell me—what kind of a gun would you use to shoot somebody?"

"Why would you ask that?"

"Because I'm going to kill that guy, Herbert Laumann. I said I'd do it for Julius."

Toby: "He's one convincing dude."

"She can use my Colt .45."

To Toby: "Is that a good choice?"

"It'll do the job. Just make sure you're close."

"Contact shot." Stone nods, eyes closed.

"Well then, no problem."

"How do you know so much about guns?"

Toby grins charmingly. "I'm an old soldier. A tired old soldier." He sits slowly on the leather couch. "Hear those old bones crack?"

Dick Stone gets up and goes into the kitchen.

Toby leans forward and confides: "He doesn't like me to talk about Vietnam. He flips *out,* like he's back in the jungle with us, which he never was. Julius has a way of appropriating other people's stories."

"What do you mean by 'us'?"

"Me and his little brother, Colin. The boy died over there."

"Julius has a brother who died in Vietnam?"

Toby nods. "There's a park back east, named for his brother and his battalion."

I fumble, trying to assess what this means. Stone must have joined the FBI at the same time Colin enlisted. Both young men were patriots—too young to imagine such a thing as death by idealism, or the bitter, vengeful burden for the one who survives.

I need air.

"Nice view of the river." I crane toward the windows. "Mind if I go down and look?"

"You go on. I'm gonna see what our friend is up to in the kitchen."

I smile nicely and pull on the back door a couple of times until it becomes unstuck. Outside, the breath of the river is humid and fresh. My shoulder blades are tight as screws. Despite the coziness, there is a stale repression in Toby's cottage. I look back at the pumpkin trim and perfectly pruned impatiens. What *is* going on in the kitchen? A gravel walk leads to a garage. There's a stylish lantern mounted above a side entrance, indicating use. I open the door and wander in.

The sharp smell of cordite grabs me like an old friend. I am back in the basement shooting range at Quantico; in the gun vault at the L.A. field office. Toby's shop is basically a Peg-Board and a bench, but at a glance, it has everything the recreational gun owner might need, including the wardrobe, all the clothes neatly hung: camo jacket, wind vest, rain togs, and polished black patrol boots.

There's a rack of common hunting rifles—7-mm ones and .308s, like the one Sterling McCord was using on the shooting range. The bench is organized for reloading cartridges—bright red cans of rifle powder, a mounted powder measure, a fancy single-stage press, and sets of dies, punches, lifters, wad guide, drop tube, the whole extravaganza for making your own bullets. The dies are organized according to size. A quick glance reveals .30- to .40-caliber ones, neatly stacked. God bless Toby's obsessive-compulsion: at the bottom of the pile, exactly where it belongs—except it does not belong—is a die for making .50-caliber bullets.

A highly unusual size for your average hunter.

The same-size bullet that killed Sergeant Mackee.

The same-size bullet that matches Dick Stone's rifle.

Toby appears at the door.

"I see you found my love."

He offers me a glass of iced tea.

"I didn't mean to pry. It just looked so interesting in here."

Toby picks up a shotgun and handles it well. "I hope you weren't touching anything."

"Of course not."

"Accidents do happen with firearms."

His big brown eyes are soft and slightly insane.

"I'm getting some weird vibes, know what I mean? Like you're prancing around in here, trying to pretend to be something you're not."

"I'm not pretending anything."

"You're not some prissy white girl," he says. "What are you?"

"Half Salvadoran. Got a problem with that?"

"Yes, I do. My problem is this: What's a homegirl doing way up here, no brown faces in the whole damn state?"

I hold his look.

"I could ask the same question."

"I got a job with the town," says Toby Himes.

"And I'm on a visit with Julius."

"You gonna shoot someone, just for kicks? Just because Julius says?"

"For the movement. For the sake of animals."

"If you're the Man," he says, "I'll kill you."

The chow is barking. Outside, there is commotion and the sound of voices and heavy boots on the gravel walk.

"Whenever."

"You tell me."

Mr. Terminate crashes open the screen door of the ammo shed and marches through, along with another squinty two-hundred pounder with a full beard and red-checked shirt I call Mountain Man.

"... You can use it underwater," Mountain Man is saying.

"Why in hell would anyone care? Hey, Toby."

"Afternoon."

"Hi, John." Mr. Terminate ignores me.

"It's stable," Mountain Man insists. "Safe to transport."

"Seriously, you don't want to be around that shit."

"Me? I don't want to get anywhere near that shit."

"Julius knows you can't get that shit. The only place you could get that shit is the armory out on the base."

This is it. This is the Big One: They're talking about meth. They're running a methamphetamine operation out of a military base.

I am beginning to get excited, when Toby Himes breaks in.

"I guarantee what the Doctor has in mind is strictly MOS."

And then, as we say in the Bureau, the hair goes up on the back of my neck, and I know what I know. In the language of bomb experts, MOS stands for military occupational specialties.

The Army Corps of Engineers, whose job it is to locate land mines.

Mr. Terminate, Mountain Man, Toby Himes, and Stone are not working some ordinary drug deal.

They are talking about military-grade explosives.

Thirty-three

Donnato is waiting at the usual rest area off the interstate at the time of another of my alleged appointments with the dentist.

"If the suspects were talking about explosives you can only get from military occupation specialists, it means they're dealing in very powerful, restricted material. What the bomb techs call 'high explosives'—dynamite, plastics, TNT, ammonium nitrate—stuff that can shatter things and move things around, like rocks and trees, which is how they use it in the Army, clearing landing zones."

I have brought a cooler this time, and we sit at the same picnic table around back—just a couple of tourists eating tuna sandwiches.

"But those kinds of explosives don't fit the signature."

"No."

"The devices that blew up Laumann's house and killed Steve weren't military-grade."

"Correct. Now we're thinking your friends at Toby's were talking about a special order. For a special mission."

"I don't like it."

"Neither does headquarters. Toby is obviously the link. He's the reloader who made the bullet that killed Sergeant Mackee. He's the munitions expert getting ready for the Big One. We've installed a listening device at his house and put the other individuals under surveillance. Agents are visiting explosives manufacturers in the region, asking for cooperation in reporting anything gone missing."

"How do the bad guys get restricted matériel?"

"Steal it from the base and collect it over time."

I nod. "That sounds like Stone. I wouldn't be surprised if he's been planning the Big One since he split the Bureau."

"I really wish you'd been wearing a wire when he handed you that jive. I'd give anything to hear his version of events."

"Here's what I think: We drove him crazy."

Donnato believes I'm joking and cracks another potato chip.

"We didn't know our ass from our elbow, and the country was in a revolution. Dick Stone is a casualty of war."

"I'm glad you're *not* wearing a wire."

"Is it treason to tell the truth?"

An immaculate RV has pulled up, and a portly gentleman wearing a bow tie has disembarked, along with two magnificently groomed Cardigan Welsh corgis, who hop down the ladder like a pair of princes. Show dogs, rehearsing their stuff. The trio trots ludicrously around our table, the dogs keeping stride with their master's swaying gut.

As they pass, Donnato switches to upbeat gossip.

"Kyle Vernon's son is moving back from Virginia."

My mood perks up, hearing of old buddies on the bank robbery squad.

"Didn't his son just graduate from UVA?"

Donnato nods. "He's moving to California. Looks like he sold a script to the movies about a black kid whose dad is a black FBI agent. . . ."

We sit for a while at the weathered picnic table under the shimmering boughs of pine, while the dogs rebelliously bark at squirrels, and Donnato does his job of bringing me out of the dream I've inhabited on the farm, back to my grounding in the Bureau family.

"Your friend Barbara Sullivan is pregnant again. They did the test. It's another girl."

"That's great. Will she quit?"

"It's doubtful she'll come back from maternity leave. You two ever talk?"

I shake my head. This will be our final passing. Barbara Sullivan will retire just as I reenter the Bureau, and we will let each other go.

The RV pulls away. I get up from the table, but Mike Donnato stays where he is. He is looking at his fingers, which are peeling the bark off another twig. I notice there's a pile of naked twigs on the ground between his feet.

"What's the matter?"

"We have a situation, Ana."

I sit back down.

"I had lunch with Rosalind."

"Oh, really? Where'd you go?"

"Factor's Deli." He squints in the wash of sunlight. "Do you have to know what we ordered, too?"

"I know what you ordered. A grilled chicken sandwich."

Donnato goes on, beleaguered. "Rosalind had good information. Dick Stone had a brother who died in Vietnam."

"I know. I'm a few steps ahead of you, bud."

"What you don't know is that Toby Himes and Peter Abbott served together in Vietnam. We were going to tell you."

No need to answer that.

"Rosalind said Dick Stone's brother served on the same squad as Himes and Abbott. All three of them. Only two made it back."

"Does Peter Abbott know that Toby Himes is a person of interest to Operation Wildcat?"

Donnato hedges. "He reads the reports young Jason Ripley sends out."

"Why didn't Peter Abbott tell us about the link between himself and Himes and Dick Stone's brother? Why'd we have to find it out from a secretary?"

"Believe me, Galloway is asking the same questions."

Donnato finally reveals their suspicions. They put a trap on the deputy director's phones and discovered Toby Himes has been calling Abbott on his private number. This is so explosive that neither of us moves. My partner remains seated at the table, elbows on knees, in profile. The sun glints off the top of his wavy hair and the short curve of his forehead.

"Stone's a former agent; I know his game. But Abbott scares me. What's he up to, and on what level?"

"I promise we'll find out. Let us face the task before us. I'm here to tell you that headquarters has authorized the hit on Herbert Laumann."

"How can I go through with it after what you've just said?" I lower my voice. "That the boss could be involved in a conspiracy?"

"You'll have full backup. I'll be there, Ana. I'll be running the show."

But deep uncertainty has hit me in the gut. Not just about them but about myself, too. My ability to pull the trigger. Already I am feeling queasy. I kick at a mound of sawdust at the base of a tree stump, chewed up by bugs. It takes a moment to refocus.

"Laumann. Okay."

"You specified a Colt .45?"

"Stone's gun, right."

"Jason got this for you."

Donnato fishes inside his pocket. A family with three little kids comes screaming toward the restrooms.

"How good a shot are you?" he asks, his voice clear despite their earsplitting shrieks. "Because the first bullet in the chamber will be live."

He holds out his hand. I hold out mine. Our palms touch in slow motion, and the magazine for a Colt .45 is transferred. I slip it smoothly into my pocket.

Jason provided a magazine filled with blanks. When Dick Stone gives me his gun, I will switch magazines. But the gun will have already been loaded, one live bullet already ejected into the chamber, requiring my first shot to be precisely accurate. When I approach Herbert Laumann—on whatever darkened street, or maybe in the middle of the day—I must hit him squarely in the bulletproof vest.

The parking lot in the rest area seems filled with smoking vehicles, each exuding a black cloud of burned brake lining. The noise of the engines is raw. The tuna fish was bad; it's making me sick. The sun is hot; it's making me weak. My mind unhooks and ruminates on the detective I shot. The world fragments and he is everywhere. My heart pounds. The magazine of blanks in my pocket is heavy as the weight of original sin. Donnato is throwing the garbage away. I'm back in the spinning car, bloody and gruesome, looking at the detective's unseeing eyes. The blind foal is nursing. Sirocco's tail whips the flies and the pasture vibrates with bees. The cicadas are singing on the battlefield.

When young boys came home from the Civil War and lay at night in the safety of their featherbeds, their pulses would still race unaccountably. It was a condition doctors recognized, even way back then, as "soldier's heart."

No bad judgment.

No mistakes.

No cowgirl stuff.

Thirty-four

On his last day on earth as BLM deputy state director, before a radical animal rights activist named Darcy DeGuzman murders him in front of his own house, Herbert Laumann is still fighting the fight—not just the massive traffic over Portland's Broadway Bridge but also call after call through the headset as the droning voice of his assistant bombards his brain with end-of-day problems at the office. Idling on the bridge at rush hour, trucks and buses blocking the river view, he must be wondering if the FBI, an agency he believes in, is leading him into an even worse predicament.

Can he trust anyone? He must be insane. *Yes, that's fine. Walk up and shoot me, whatever fits your bill.* But he has no right to question. He has failed to protect his family. He is a hollow man in the wrong skin—his son's skin—that has become a searing penance, night and day. It was the promise of world-class medical treatment for Alex that sealed the deal with the all-too-understanding FBI men. But they still won't say which burn center he will be admitted to, in which part of the country. Or what type of new job Laumann will be given.

They keep promising a painless death and peaceful afterlife.

Maybe secretly he wishes the bullets would be real.

We, the assassins, follow.

Dick Stone, down to fighting weight and back on his meds, is a force of nature, like those glacial rivers roaring down from Canada. I never saw until today how the fragments come together—the loyalty that made him an FBI agent, and the demonic intelligence that opens the soul's unwilling gate to murder.

Stone has never been more lucid. Even his skin looks baby soft and shaven. His hair is clean and straight; the summer sun has made it more blond than gray. He is back to the agreeable persona of the lawyer of the people, a northwest professional in a denim shirt and tie, moving confidently through the city.

"Nervous?" he asks.

"Terrified."

He makes me recite it again. We drive up. We wait. At 8:00 p.m., Laumann comes out of the house and walks down the driveway. He plays tennis at the club on Thursday nights. His court time is always 8:30. We put on the ski masks. I get out of the car. Stone keeps the engine running. I walk up to the target. I make my speech and empty the gun into his chest.

"Less than a minute," Stone promises.

"I'm still nervous."

"You can't miss at point-blank range."

And I've been practicing. Not just shooting Stone's pistol up at the range but figuring out how to switch the magazines—the blanks that Jason provided, for the live ones in the gun—in two swift moves.

"I've been thinking about his wife and kids."

"Don't. Focus on the target. You've done it before, or so you say," Stone comments.

"That was emotional. This is cold."

"You're paying the tax, as promised," he says flatly. "The tax on Slammer's foolishness."

"Okay, and then?"

"After you do this, the tax will be repaid."

"And the family will be okay?"

"Everyone in the family will be okay."

I pop a mint. No bad tastes, no bad associations. I'm not going to be suckered into the past.

As we follow him across the bridge, through the prism of stacked-up car windows, I get a glimpse of the victim's neck. Just like any other commuter's neck.

"You have to put the good round into him. You have to shoot him squarely in the vest. The adrenaline will be pumping," Donnato warned.

"I'll be prepared."

"Get close. Knock him flat. He knows what's coming, although I didn't go into detail about the first shot."

"Right!" I laughed a high and desperate cackle that was sounding more and more like Stone's. "Who in their right mind would agree to be a walking target?"

Donnato: "A man with a guilty conscience."

Waiting makes the tension in my chest unbearable. We sit in the truck, watching the dashboard clock. Dick Stone is running his game, and we are running ours. There are agents in the in-laws' house and in the house next door. Those females with the empty strollers are under-covers.

I study the Wilkins' house, the tacky hacienda that we raided in the dark, marking the curve in the bushes where I'll make the switch. I fix it in my mind. For reassurance, I think about Donnato calling the shots from the stakeout. Stone is calmly smoking a cigar. He's been on stakeout, too.

At 8:06 p.m. Laumann appears at the front door. A light goes on above it, signaling all is ready. He is carrying a tennis racket and wearing white. *This is going to make a big mess.* Stone and I pull on our woolen masks. He hands me the Colt .45 and I unlock the car door.

With a thousand hidden eyes upon me, I have never felt so alone. I walk half a dozen steps and start up the driveway, everything still and glittering and clear. My heart is hammering—more than hammering: It's closing off my mind. I pass the crucial point in front of the bushes. I turn to block Stone's view and switch the magazines, slipping the live one into the pocket of my black cargo pants, while all the time my legs keep marching forward, and Laumann in his whites keeps coming toward me in the precise evening light, floating, as if he is already dead.

His eyes meet mine. Behind the glasses, there is nothing but terror. *They had to shove him out the door.* Both of us have been pushed together by our respective sides—the bride in black and the groom in white—to meet in middle of this surreal driveway, a doomed blood wedding.

"ANIMAL KILLER!"

My voice comes from some distant gravel pit. I raise the gun with both hands, plant my knees, sight, and fire.

The first shot throws him backward. He's down. I run up close. The shot was good; he is unhurt, squinting his eyes and twitching and stuttering, *"No, no, no, no!"* as I stand over him and fire. *Two, three, four, five.* The squibs inside his clothes go off, red fountains against the white.

Dick Stone's blood bomb is a wee-wee compared to this.

I am busting back toward the getaway car, but here comes Stone, running hard, passing me in the opposite direction.

"What the hell?"

"Get in!"

I continue toward the car. Stone is in the driveway. *He's going to finish him off!* But on cue, there are screams and people running. Now Stone is back, the car door slams, and we're gone.

I'm shouting, "What the *hell*? What was *that*?"

He coolly steers around the corner. "A good shooter never leaves his brass. You can only make that mistake once."

Stone opens the fingers of his right hand to reveal the five bullet casings that were ejected from the pistol.

An ambulance driven by FBI agents has pulled up and loaded the blood-soaked deputy state director onto a gurney. At the same time, agents are storming the back door, getting the family out. There will be TV news stories, an obituary, and a funeral, but by then the Laumann family will be safely relocated in the witness protection program, where they will live undercover for the rest of their lives.

Everything goes like clockwork.

PART FOUR

Thirty-five

Four pug puppies will always cause a hullabaloo, even in West Hollywood. When Rooney Berwick takes his babies walking, some tourist will always shout, "How cute are *they*? I have a pug, too!"

What are you supposed to say to that?

Across from the cobalt blue shell of the Pacific Design Center is a neighborhood park with a small open field that provides a clear patch of sky—not an easy spot to find in the heart of L.A. So if you saw a loner—late fifties, wearing a black T-shirt, pants with a lot of pockets, and thick-soled combat boots—camped out in the middle of the field, pouring water into a collapsible bowl for four panting pugs, that would be Rooney Berwick, getting ready for a call on the satellite phone to his old buddy Dick Stone.

Dead cases are kept in a room-size automated drum in the federal building on Wilshire Boulevard. For two days Mike Donnato moves files around a track, like the clothes at your dry cleaner's, grabbing at whatever fragments might remain of a case in the seventies code-named "Turquoise."

It was a failed operation, in which the Bureau targeted a series of armored car robberies thought to be linked to radical students at the University of Arizona who were allegedly part of the Weather Underground. Dick Stone was the rookie uc—short hair and creases in his jeans—who infiltrated the campus coffeehouse. Strangely, none of the radicals, who nicknamed him "the Fed," wished to share their plans for the revolution.

The Bureau went high-tech, bringing in another young buck from Los Angeles, a whiz-kid technician named Rooney Berwick (the photo ID shows him thin-faced and detached, a hundred pounds lighter), who installed listening devices on the armored cars. Three weeks later, arrests were made of two drivers with unchecked criminal records, who had conspired to stage "robberies" with the local bad guys.

The Weather Underground had nothing to do with it.

Intrigued, Donnato runs the full sweep on Rooney: personnel reports, bank accounts, phone records, traffic tickets, pharmacy prescriptions. A picture emerges of a highly intelligent, socially isolated individual, who lives with his mother in the same Hollywood apartment complex in which he grew up, apparently addicted to painkillers, which he has been getting from five different doctors.

Donnato looks at Rooney's recent cases. His latest assignment was to turn sand into gold. (*If I could do that, I wouldn't be in this rat hole,* I can hear Rooney say.) The target was a ring of thieves in Brazil, with ties to U.S. organized crime, that was selling counterfeit nuggets. The Bureau's undercovers would pose as manufacturers of counterfeit gold. Rooney's mandate was to make fake nuggets as good as the thieves'.

Under pressure, Rooney was working the graveyard shift. On a scarred desk in the faceless JR Trading Company, in the midst of the displaced Hispanic nation, he set out rows of shiny rocks, ranging in quality from the real stuff to the Brazilian counterfeits. He knew they were melting authentic gold and mixing it with water and sand—but how much of each? His notes say he sectioned a Brazilian nugget and examined the slices under the microscope at fifty times normal magnification.

Skimming the phone log attached to the lab records, Donnato sees that a call came in on Rooney's private line that morning at 5:48 a.m.

From an area code in Oregon.

Rooney had probably been counting gold globules when he decided to take a break and work on one of his subversive little projects that

turned up later—a digitalized photo of himself shaking hands with
President Bill Clinton. It was another phony, but at least it was *his*
phony, which is why, when the phone rang, he was in a bad mood about
being interrupted and answered with annoyance, which he would
immediately regret.

All calls to the off-site are recorded in the archives. You just have to
lean on the right person.

"City morgue, George Romero speaking."

"Hey there, champ."

It was the voice of Dick Stone.

Rooney reacted with silence. Stone: "Is this phone secure?"

"Not entirely." Rooney was testy. "But it's six in the morning.
Nobody's here. Just me and the skeletons in the closet. It's been a
while. Where are you?"

"I'm a farmer. Do you believe that?"

Rooney chuckled. "The number-one cash crop in California?"

"Nothing illegal, my friend. I grow filbert trees. I'm an arborist."

"Sounds fancy. Making a living?"

"Occasionally. But that's beside the point."

"Not for those of us in perpetual slavery."

"How is Ruby doing?"

"It's nice of you to think of Mom."

"How could I forget the Ambrose Dairy and your mom at the window making soft-serve cones? Dipped in chocolate? Oh my Lord."

Mrs. Ruby Berwick had been a jolly fixture at the famous drive-
thru Ambrose Dairy, one of those iconic Los Angeles landmarks with
a twelve-foot milk bottle perched on top, where you could get icy bottles of cream and homemade cottage cheese without leaving the car.

"How many times was I over at your mom's apartment, eating Pol-
ish, playing with the pugs?"

"You haven't heard the news. Mom passed on not too long ago."

"I'm really sorry to hear that, pal."

"I miss her every day. She never hurt a soul."

"What was it?"

"Cancer of the esophagus. Skip it if you can. My brain-dead supervisor keeps saying shit like, 'It's for the best.' People are ignorant. Makes you want to put your fist through a wall."

There was inaudible scratching and scuffling. Rooney's voice emerged:

". . . The Bureau's going through changes, but they're still after your ass."

"How do you know?" asked Stone.

"Saw your name on some lists."

"What kind of lists?"

"I don't play politics; you know that. That's me, flying below the radar. But you still have supporters in this organization, myself foremost among them, who have always felt you got one raw deal. They trashed your reputation, went around saying you'd gone over—based on what?" He was getting worked up. "They never had proof; they were using you as a scapegoat for their dumb-ass mistakes. Justice was not served by the Justice Department."

"Don't stress. The intelligence you have provided over the years about my former friends has been very useful."

"That's something.

Stone, upbeat: "Still have the pugs?"

Rooney might have glanced at the photo poster above the ID machine.

"Brand-new litter. Three girls and a boy. Mom would get a kick out of 'em. They were her 'grand-dogs.' "

Both men were breathing audibly into the phone, cautious, psyching each other out.

"Is that a rooster I hear up on the old farm? Cancel that," Rooney said quickly. "Don't say what you don't need to say."

"I am feeling a little paranoid these days. Got a sixth sense about the Bureau."

"They're heeeeere!" Rooney could be unbelievably juvenile.

"Up close and personal," Stone agreed. "Can you do me a favor and check it out?"

"Anytime I can say fuck you to management, I am there."

"See what they've got going in the Northwest. There's something else. Soon I'll be digging up the turquoise. It's time to move on. You're entitled to your share."

Rooney choked up. "You got out, but still, after all these years, you remembered?"

"You trusted me, so I'm keeping my word. Some things are simple. What are your plans?"

"Plans?" Rooney's voice deflated. "I have nobody left. What would I do?"

"Anything you want, buddy."

Uncertain: "I guess I'd have to take the dogs."

"You could buy a whole kennel."

"I wish Mom were here."

"She would want you to be happy."

"How do we do this?"

"I'll be in touch."

There are no records of them talking again. Once they started using the satellite phone, Rooney would take it to the park. It was probably there that he blew the whistle.

Thirty-six

"This is a waste of time. I don't need to be here."

"How are you feeling? What's your mood?"

"Right now? I'm buzzed, thinking of a million things, like how long we are going to be sitting in this motel. When my partner is coming to get me. How long I can hide out in Portland. How to keep all the balls in the air."

"You're good at it? Keeping balls in the air?"

"Have I dropped any lately that you know about?"

"The FBI doesn't tell me the details of their cases."

"That would be messy."

"I'm a psychiatrist; I'm hired as an independent contractor. My concern here is only about you—your mental health, how you're handling the pressures and demands they put you under."

"This is a standard evaluation, right? Like they do for all our undercovers?"

"Tell me what's been going on."

"I've been in deep cover, in an extreme situation, for about three months. I'm living on a Podunk farm with a bunch of violent anarchists who could pop at any minute."

"Stressful?"

"Kind of."

"How do you handle the stress?"

"By having chest pains, what do you think?"

"When was that?"

"About a week ago. I was watching TV."

"No unusual exertion? No change in medication? Just watching TV?"

"Yes. I've been doing a lot of that lately."

"Would this TV watching be normal for someone working undercover?"

"Umm. Yes and no. Depends."

"Do you like TV?"

"Yeah, I love it. I'm addicted to stupid, mind-numbing crap."

"I'm wondering if you use it as a way to deal with stress."

"I don't watch the shows. I only watch the news."

"You watch the news."

"There's really only one story I'm interested in."

"Which is what?"

"It's a local story. There's a guy named Herbert Laumann, from the Bureau of Land Management, who was killed recently."

"Yes, he was gunned down in his driveway by some animal rights fanatics. I'm afraid there are a lot of them up here."

"You saw it?"

"It was all over the papers."

"I did that!"

"You did it?"

"I shot the dude. The whole thing was staged. But it looked real, didn't it? It was perfect. He and his family are in the witness protection program now. Isn't that cool?"

"This is when you started having chest pains?"

"After it was over."

"So you're watching the news stories about the so-called murder."

"Obsessively. I have it on tape. All the national coverage, everything from the local stations, and a close-up of the animal rights movement they did on 20/20. My story was the lead."

"You sound proud."

"It wasn't easy to pull it off."

"I'm sure. So you're watching the tapes, over and over. Are alcohol or drugs involved?"

"A little weed. A little beer. That's how we do it on the farm."

"Okay, you're getting high and watching how this man died. The one you supposedly killed."

"In the line of duty."

"I understand. You say the operation went well?"

"Very well."

"And your superiors are pleased?"

"Yes, because now I'm really tight with the bad guys."

"I've got a note here that your communication with the FBI has lagged."

"Who said that?"

"Do *you* think you've been communicating with your office less than usual? Are you feeling withdrawn from the Bureau?"

"No, it's just a hassle. I have to get up early and hide out in the barn, or up in the trees. Right now, there's not that much to say."

"The important thing, in your view, is that you've been initiated into this group—kind of like being a 'made man' in the Mafia. And the tapes of the news stories—they're fascinating to you."

"Because I did such a . . . a really good job."

"Here. You're feeling some emotion."

"I'm sorry."

"What's going on right now, Ana? Take your time."

"I don't know why I should be upset. I did a really good job. Does it say in there— Do you know my history?"

"What do you mean?"

"Does it say that I once shot a police detective at point-blank range?"

"Yes, I know."

"Okay. That's all."

"Do you think about that incident a lot, Ana?"

"All the time."

"Can you describe your thoughts?"

"Like a track playing in the background."

"Do specific images and ideas intrude into your daily activities?"

"Yes."

"How often?"

"All the time."

"How's your mood lately?"

"Sad."

"Ever since this second shooting?"

"No, because I'm bored! The case is going nowhere; there's nothing to do. We're waiting for the harvest—we grow hazelnuts—and for the leader of the group to make another move, but all he does is read the fish reports."

"He's a fisherman?"

"No, he reads the fish counts in the paper. Out loud, every morning. How many salmon went through the fishways at the Bonneville Dam. It's nuts."

"Well, they're spawning. Some people think it's a big deal."

"Like I care."

"Are you more irritable lately?"

"Obviously. More like numbed out."

"Remind me—how long ago did you go through critical incident training at the FBI?"

"A couple of months after the shooting incident. It's standard before they let you back to work."

"Did you receive a diagnosis at that time of PTSD?"

"Post-traumatic stress disorder? Yeah, we all had it; that's why we were there."

"I'm curious—"

"You're curious about a lot of things."

"Did you have follow-up with a psychologist? PTSD usually takes more than a few sessions to improve. But it can improve. Dramatically."

"Well, a woman doctor in Los Angeles evaluated me—I forget her name, but she's the one who approved me for duty."

"I'm not sure that she did."

"I'm confused."

"Let me try to clear up the confusion. You fit every criterion for a diagnosis of PTSD. You've had life-threatening trauma, resulting in intense fear and horror. Your current symptoms include mental replay of the trauma, numbing, avoidance, intrusive thoughts. . . . And all of this has been going on since your evaluation, months ago. Frankly, I can't see why they put you on this case."

"I fit the profile."

"Hundreds of other young female FBI agents fit the profile, too. Let me explain. I'm retired from private practice, Ana. I own an office building in downtown Portland and property in Seattle. I have a very nice life and I don't need the money. I'm an old lefty, and I don't give a damn if I'm fired by the FBI or if they screw with my tax returns, or whatever. You're smiling."

"We don't do that, but go ahead."

"I do this to keep my hand in, and because I want to be of service. So I can be objective, and say, objectively, that there's been an egregious error."

"You think they know about the PTSD?"

"Any examining doctor would have recommended that you not serve undercover."

"The SAC and the assistant director approved me."

"Then somewhere along the line, the doctor was overruled."

"Are you saying they put me on this case on purpose? Hoping I would crack?"

"I'm strongly suggesting that there has been an error—error, not malice—because I would like to believe that no ethical commander would intentionally send a disabled soldier back into battle."

"Unless he wanted you to fail."

"That has not been my experience of the Bureau."

"Do you know Peter Abbott?"

"The son of the congressman from Oregon?"

"Yes, well, now Peter Abbott is a deputy director of the FBI. My boss believes he is trying to undermine this case. Or at least bend it his way. We don't know why. It all started out so crystal clear, but now I couldn't tell you who is running their game on whom. This is exactly where you're *not* supposed to be, and it's pissing me off."

"You're an excellent foot soldier, Ana, and you have extraordinary qualities of persistence and dedication, but you're still coping with long-term effects of the shooting incident. It's like telling someone with pneumonia, 'Go swim the Atlantic.' I'm going to recommend that you're removed from this case."

"No! You can't do that! I'm fine. I'll take back everything I said!"

"I am deeply concerned about your safety. What would you like me to do?"

"I need to talk to my contact agent, Mike Donnato. He's the only one I trust."

"What do you mean, the only one you can trust?"

"I wasn't feeling crazy before I came here, but I'm sure feeling crazy now. Do all your patients say that? Doctor? That was a joke. Look, I have to go. My partner is meeting me downstairs. I'll talk to him, and then—can I call you?"

"Please."

"As I said, it will probably be from a hazelnut tree."

"I've had stranger phone conferences. Are you okay to wait alone?"

"Yes."

"Let me hear from you."

The dusky street smells of falafel and pigeons. The city has a faraway look as seen through a fishbowl. Disoriented by the flash-bang of cars and urban walkers, I realize my perceptions are confused. I am trying to understand what the psychiatrist said, but it is hard to think clearly. I am waiting for Donnato. When he arrives, it will make some kind of sense.

"Get in the car," Mr. Terminate says.

The biker's wrenchlike fingers close around my arm. A gun presses my ribs. We are in an alley and I don't know how we got there, but with the full force of his body, he twists my shoulder and pops me like a cork into the open door of the car, where Mountain Man is waiting behind the wheel.

Thirty-seven

When we arrive at the farm, the thermometer on the barn reads 110 degrees—candy-apple red and about to burst. Unlike the dry heat of Los Angeles, a sultry fever rises from the earth, with a smell like roasting barley and manure. It hangs there, baking you to a stupor. The coolest spot in the valley is the hazelnut orchard. When Mr. Terminate and Mountain Man deliver me from Portland, Dick Stone is sitting on a beach chair set in its oasis of shade.

Old-timers say the first nut drops on the first of September. Those late-summer days, each of us on the farm seemed suspended in a kind of waiting. Sara and I would climb the ladders in 106-degree heat to count the dried-up moths in the traps, then spend the rest of the day reading fashion magazines. Nobody cooked anymore. The vegetables were sold, allegedly to help pay for the Big One. Despite the abundance of the garden, we were living on pancakes.

Slammer was so creepily polite to Megan and Stone, I thought one day he'd go berserk and kill them with an ax. But Mom and Dad kept him busy, preparing for the harvest. Inside the steamy shed, Slammer and Stone labored over the homemade nut sorter, a ludicrous contraption of green scrap metal, gas motors and exhaust pipes, rusty conveyor belts, and plywood hammered together with no apparent logic. I was really looking forward to what happened when they turned it on.

In the heat, brushfires kept breaking out among the troops.

"He's lying," I heard Slammer whispering to Sara. "He's flat-out lying when he says the Big One's coming. It's just to keep us here."

"How do you know?"

"Because that's him. He's a liar. Don't defend him, 'ho."

"I'm not defending him, and don't you dare call me that. It's like nobody cares what I'm going through. Nobody cares if I walk out the door into the middle of the freeway."

"If nobody gives a shit, why don't you do it?"

Megan and I weren't getting along, either. To prepare for brittle making, she had me disassemble and clean every part of the industrial stove in the sweltering basement. She kept hauling out giant spoons and candy thermometers, and I dreaded the hellish days and nights when we would have to keep pots of scalding sugar syrup boiling around the clock.

Indications are the harvest will be good, and standing in the full-blown orchard, I can't help feeling pride in our fake little farming family. Stone's prudent trimming has created thick new growth. Underneath the leafy canopy is an Alice-in-Wonderland world of cool shadows and secret whisperings. The cries of blue jays pierce the murky gloom, and the smooth orchard floor is chilly as marble.

"You wanted to talk to me?"

Stone avoids my eyes. Instead, he rises, turns his back, and wanders toward a tree, fingering the sprouts at the end of a twig. I wait in silence while he inspects the new green buds.

"How much do you know about the sex life of filberts?" he asks at last.

"Got to be more interesting than mine."

"It's one of the stranger perversities of nature. Filberts require cross-pollination from two different plants. Their sexual fulfillment depends on the wind."

"I can identify."

"That's why we cultivate both the Ennis and the Butler variety." He indicates two trees, which look the same. "The Ennis is the germinator and the Butler is the pollinator."

"Let me guess: male and female."

"Yes, but which is which?"

I squeeze a little green bean hanging off a shoot.

"Male. The flower is called a catkin."

This is the value of high school biology.

Stone nods in a distracted way, the weary science teacher.

"Despite the lateness of the season, some of the female flowers are still rudimentary. This is the ovary." He rolls a bud between his fingers and then crushes it beneath a thumbnail. "It hasn't developed and it never will."

"I see that."

"I know who you are," says Stone.

Very slowly, he turns his face. The seething rage echoes the time at the traffic light when the rock 'n' roll commandos were on our way to off Herbert Laumann the first time. Stone's half-bearded cheeks glazed in the red stop light. Three measured words to Slammer when he honked at the Iranians in the van. *"Don't . . . do . . . that."* And Slammer didn't.

The hot breath of summer puffs against my clammy forehead. My palm goes involuntarily there, like a woman about to faint. Crows are barking in the far branches.

"Which of us is more pathetic?" The pain in his eyes is like a hot flash of metal.

"What do you mean?"

"You were duped by the Bureau, just like me. Skip the humiliating dance, Ana."

"Why do you call me that?"

"I like you, Ana. Don't blow it by being stupid." He sinks back into the beach chair, rubbing his meaty cheeks like Don Corleone.

"You've been initiated into this group—kind of like being a 'made man' in the Mafia," the psychiatrist said.

"I'd play it the same way," he says, "so you don't have to. I have an excellent source. As you no doubt learned way back, there are different kinds of sources. There are longtime sources and open sources, both on the Bureau's payroll, and 'pocket sources'—personal connections who won't take money because they think cooperating with the FBI is the American thing to do. . . . But this old friend of mine, he's impeccable. He is an *inside* source. Someone who's been ripped off by the Bureau culture and is only too happy to fuck someone else in return.

"This impeccable source of mine, he tells me an agent named Mike Donnato is working the national security side of the house. He describes how Special Agent Ana Grey was outfitted with the cover of Darcy DeGuzman in order to penetrate FAN. We're the terrorist cell and I'm the big bad guru." He touches his chest softly. "I told you. I'm not the one who made me paranoid."

He hasn't killed me yet, so maybe there still is a way.

An image comes to mind from a documentary movie, in which a mountain climber falls through the snow into a bottomless crevasse and clings to an ice shelf 150 feet down. No way can he climb up. His only choice is to descend into the unknown—go deeper into the vertical shaft and hope to find a way out.

Keep making decisions. Even if they're wrong.

Go deeper.

"You're right. I am an agent. And you're a former agent who dropped out in the seventies."

"They're still after me." Stone allows a smug smile.

"Yes, they are."

"More than thirty years later. The incompetence is really something. No wonder we're losing the war on terror."

"This impeccable inside source you describe. We thought there was a leak, but that it came from higher up."

"Uh-uh. Bottom-feeder. Rooney Berwick is the name."

But you won't live to tell.

"What tipped you off to me?"

Dick Stone fishes around in the pocket of his shorts and shows me the five shell casings he picked up in Laumann's driveway.

"Never leave your brass at the shooting scene. I made that mistake with the cop on the roof. Otherwise, I'm a pretty good sniper, because I'm a tight-ass finicky bastard. I always use the same brand—Remington. But there was only one Remington on the ground, the live round I loaded into the gun. The other four are Winchester. See?"

The tiny etching on each copper jacket says WIN-45.

"You switched the magazine for blanks, didn't you, darlin'? Very slick, but the Bureau screwed up. The dummy bullets should have been Remington."

Jason Ripley secured the blanks.

"A rookie," I say bitterly. "He wasn't thinking."

"What do you expect?" Stone claps my shoulder sympathetically. "They're not all as good as you and me."

"I wasn't that good, apparently."

"You were doing fine. Until I talked to Berwick. The arrows started lining up."

"Frankly, Dick, it's a relief. I couldn't have kept it going."

"Enlighten me, Ana Grey. What were they thinking?" He removes the Colt from a holster under a loose guayabera shirt and holds it in both hands. "They already sent one of their clowns."

Indignation flares and I don't try to stop it.

"If you're talking about the agent you murdered with a bomb, he had a name—Steve Crawford. He left a wife and children, and he was a friend of mine."

"You think he was a together guy? He came across to me as a real asshole."

"That was his cover," I say angrily.

"Nope, sorry, that was *him*. He's supposed to be dealing methamphetamine, but he's wearing a Harvard University ring, for Christ's sake. And nice-looking boots."

Stone is busy unscrewing the top of a water bottle, then soaks a red bandanna inside. He ties it tightly over his head, gangsta-style. Water drips along the pink flush in his neck.

"Your buddy Steve was pushing too hard. He comes in way too fast and fancy. You're thinking, Man, what is this? You know what was the tell? He's cheap. He acts like a high roller, but he doesn't tip well, like a person on an expense account trying to shave a little. Working people know that barmaids have to make a living. That was paltry."

"So you lure him into the woods and blow him up?"

"Why do that? Why off an agent and send the whole world up here? He blew *himself* up. He hears a rumor I've got a buried fortune in stolen turquoise and silver, and he decides, I'm going to do something about this kingpin. I'm going to take the turquoise. Because I'm the government, and the government can do anything. He out-and-out threatens me, just like any crooked scumbag cop. He says, 'I'm going to take the goods off you. I'm gonna steal it because it's stolen anyway. If you don't cooperate, I'll have you arrested.' So I told him where it was."

Then it collapses, like a sand castle undercut by waves. "That's not the guy I knew."

"I'm amazed you didn't see through the act."

"Did you tell him what the turquoise is? Don't say Indian jewelry."

Dick Stone smiles. "I like symbols. I like the great western myths—like preserving the freedom of the wild mustangs—it stirs people's loyalty. There's an open secret—one I've cultivated for years, like the orchard—that I have the means to finance operations. Otherwise, nobody would pay attention.

"No, it's for real. Back in the day, I was working a deal we had going in Arizona, called Turquoise. Case closed, bad guys in jail, and Berwick the techie and I find ourselves alone in a garage, disabling the crap he'd installed on this armored car, and sweet Jesus, there is a bag with a hundred and fifty thousand dollars in the bottom of the trunk. It was nowhere on our inventory. Nobody knew it existed. The Bureau was acting like I was an orphan child they'd disowned, so screw it. We took the cash. Berwick was scared, so I kept his share for him. Then some dudes from the Paiute Nation got ripped off of a load of semi-precious gems, and thus a legend was born.

"Don't lose sleep over your buddy. He was just another insignificant, corrupt little Bureau shit, who only made my life that much harder. And then there was you."

He shakes his head, then pulls out a joint and lights it, carefully extinguishing the match against the sole of his sandal. Despite the coolness beneath the trees, heat is shooting through my body.

"Ana, I cannot express to you the depth of my disappointment and sorrow. I would never have said it to him, your friend, the father of two—'Prove your loyalty and I will share my treasure.'" His eyes bulge as he holds the smoke. "But I would have said it to you."

"I can help you out."

"How is that?" asks Stone.

"I feel you, brother."

Stone doubles up laughing, spewing fragrant smoke.

"You're kidding, right?"

I'm speed-talking, careening into street jive.

"No, dig it, look. You come into the FBI all bright-eyed and bushy-tailed, a well-educated attorney, a patriot like your brother, who made the sacrifice in Vietnam, and all you want is to follow the rules and do your duty, and look how you were treated. Sent undercover with no protection, no support. So here's me. Female, biracial, and it's the same tune. They throw me into this situation here and walk away. My supervisor is a jerk. He doesn't care about my safety; he's just worried about his career. I'm the way he's going to advance, no matter how the case turns out with Dick Stone."

Stone exhales a cone of smoke. "So I'm preaching to the choir?"

"I can't argue with the evidence. The bullet casings? Berwick on the inside? What's my choice? What would you do? You'd do the smart thing, too. You'd flip. It's a no-brainer. I'll come over and help you out."

Stone extinguishes the joint. His tone is magnanimous.

"You can flip all you want. You can flop around like a goddamned salmon. But one day, I will take your life. In spite of the fact you're good. Or maybe because you're good. It completes a certain cycle of nature. You like science? I like science, too. No worries, Ana. It won't be a surprise."

"They know where I am and they'll come and get me."

"Yes, they will, but not before the Big One. After that, darlin', it won't matter much to either one of us."

A task force of Bu-cars and tech vans moves in formation across the Harbor Freeway in downtown Los Angeles. Lanes of traffic give way to the flotilla of black vehicles as it passes the Staples Center and the painted eyes of the twelve-story violinist on the famous mural, which are following the caravan with subtle surprise.

Curving down an exit and underneath the freeway, maintaining the speed limit, it moves with the precision of a fleet of Hornet warplanes. Entering the Central American nation, it slows for pushcarts selling ices and throngs of women and children shopping the *mercados* and botanicas in the early-morning particulate dust. The security gates roll back and the lead sedan, in which SAC Robert Galloway is riding, enters the secure lot of the JR Trading Co.

The sweep is a total surprise. The task force invades the ancient hallways, charging past the cubicles of the defunct unemployment office, where bewildered agents sit before computer screens, to the innermost heart of covert operations—the secret laboratory—securing doors and exits in less than four minutes.

Nobody is going home today.

Stone walks me out of the orchard. Like Slammer to his burial, I go willingly. He doesn't have to show the gun.

We probably look like hippie father and daughter, or master and acolyte, strolling past the dusty blackberry bushes laden with ripe fruit and bees. It probably looks like everything's okay in the heartland of the USA. In the center of a small ring, willowy young Sara is reluctantly learning to lunge Geronimo. Sterling McCord is teaching her how to exercise him, standing close behind her, spooning almost, with that uninhibited pelvis, as he reaches around to guide her hands on a long lead rope and whip. Just a whisper on the hindquarters, and the little white horse starts up a trot.

Like figures on a music box, the cowboy and Sara revolve in tiny steps together, guiding the foal with the lead and the whip in sprightly circles around the ring.

I cannot hide the bitter envy. "Isn't it pretty?"

Little Geronimo gets frisky and kicks up his heels, hitting a hind leg against the rail. A *smack* rings out and the wood vibrates. Sterling halts the lesson.

Everyone who works at the off-site is herded into the central lab. Restrooms are searched. The roof is secured. Galloway addresses the crowd.

"There has been a breach of security at this facility. A suspect is being apprehended. Our purpose right now is to evaluate the viability of this workplace. You will be required to take a polygraph. We are counting on your patience and understanding in getting everyone through this as quickly as possible."

When Mike Donnato discovered the tape of the phone conversation with Stone, and realized that Rooney Berwick had failed to report for work the past three days, the off-site was put under lockdown, and L.A. County sheriff's deputies dispatched to his residence.

The Villa de Andalusia on Harper Avenue in West Hollywood is one of those garden courtyard apartments built in the 1920s. It would seem romantic if you were a nineteen-year-old would-be actress just off the bus, until you met your neighbors—a bleached-blond lesbian bartender and Rooney Berwick.

The bartender has a soulful, heart-shaped face, is covered below the neck with body tattoos, and is also nine months pregnant. She illegally sublets apartment 1A, Mrs. Berwick's old place, while Rooney lives over the garage. Neither one of them would loan you a cup of sugar.

Nobody is answering in the garage apartment, so the deputies pound on 1A. The tattooed bartender comes out snarling and refuses to unlock the metal security door.

"Ruby Berwick?"

"Not in a million years."

"Do you know where she is, ma'am?"

"She doesn't live here."

"What about her son, Rooney Berwick?"

"He says he works for the FBI, but that's too weird for words."

"When was the last time you saw him?"

"I don't have a fucking clue."

The deputy thanks her and walks past a fountain holding pools of scummy water to join his partner on the landing outside the cheaply built garage apartment. The door is locked. A bundle of mail is stuck in the slot, yellowed by the sun. Forced entry is required.

A couple of jabs with a crowbar splinters the thin veneer of the door, and then the entire lock assembly gives way with a groan. There seems to be weight on the other side, like sandbags, preventing them from opening it. Old people drop while answering the bell. . . . Sick people collapse before getting help. . . . But as they push against the door, a tearing sound like bandages from skin alerts the officers to the disturbing fact that it has been sealed with duct tape from the inside.

When they enter the grubby studio apartment, the deputies notice the temperature is elevated to over ninety degrees. All the windows are shut and there's an ominous smell. Propped on a chair where nobody could miss it is a three-foot drawing of a skull on poster board, with handwritten words that say **DANGER! CARBON DIOXIDE!** RUBY "MOM" BERWICK, REST IN PEACE.

A Superman comic book from 1965 is taped open to a page on which the Man of Steel is spiraling into space, fist raised. "He knows what he must do!" the caption reads. An empty vial of Percocet and cans of beer have been discarded on the floor.

The bathroom door is locked, and again taped from inside. Once they gain entry, the deputies see the amber plastic doors that enclose the shower-tub have also been sealed, along with the bathroom window. Clearly, the intention was to create an airless chamber. But what of the two mysterious blue plastic milk cartons stamped AMBROSE, with a clock and a partially burned candle set on top?

Inside the tub is the fully clothed body of a decomposing white man, about 190 pounds, long white hair, lying in a fetal position on its side. Near the feet are the bodies of four pug dogs in similar states of decomposition. Fluid has collected in the bottom of the tub.

These five beings died together from lack of oxygen—but how? Sealing a chamber and burning a candle doesn't suck the air out of a room. After the origin of the milk cartons has been identified as the Ambrose Dairy, where, it is learned, the deceased's mother worked for thirty years, the coroner will rule that death resulted from environmental hypoxia caused by exogenous carbon dioxide exposure: dry ice.

Rooney Berwick had returned to the landmark drive-in dairy and purchased two blocks of dry ice (frozen CO_2), commonly used to handle milk products. As a tech, he knew carbon dioxide vapor would drift toward the ground, and therefore he placed the blocks of dry ice inside the tub. Then he got high, laid back, and watched the clock as the blocks smoked and shrank, disappearing into an invisible toxic gas.

Eventually, deprived of oxygen, his heart would stop. The props he used from the Ambrose Dairy to effect his death expressed, with subconscious elegance, the attachment and rage he felt for his mother. At the last, he might have been quite comfortable lying down with his dogs, entombed by loneliness that had finally become a rock-hard cocoon.

But the genius part of Rooney's suicide was not the methodology. The genius part was to be found on the computer, left in screen-saver mode on Mrs. Berwick's Formica and chrome dining table, no doubt where little Rooney used to eat his mom's kielbasa and cabbage.

Staring at the deputies is the FAN home page with a brand-new link—"In Memoriam—Ruby Berwick, Beloved Mother, and Rooney Berwick, Son"—which takes the visitor to pages and pages of classified documents on Operation Wildcat, stolen by the deceased and put on the Internet for all the world to see.

Even more brilliant was to post the ID picture Rooney took that day at the off-site: "Darcy DeGuzman, aka FBI Special Agent Ana Grey."

He burned the Bureau but good.

Galloway's response was unhesitating: *"Get Ana out now."*

Thirty-eight

In Quantico, Virginia, the hostage rescue team is put on standby. Out at Andrews Air Force Base, a CF-5 is loaded up with helicopters and light armored vehicles to be on scene within twelve hours.

Local FBI SWAT teams from Salt Lake, Seattle, and Los Angeles are called up as a west regional asset. Donnato, Galloway, and Angelo are on a commercial flight, and Peter Abbott on a jet from D.C. to Portland, where, in the Operation Wildcat command center, agents monitoring Dick Stone's surveillance system are carefully watching the movements of those in the house, waiting to see if Special Agent Ana Grey has holed up in the sewing room—the Room of Unfinished Dreams—signaling an emergency.

Within hours, warrants for the search and seizure of unregistered automatic weapons have been signed by a local magistrate, giving probable cause to investigate Dick Stone, living at Willamette Hazelnut Farm under the false identity of Julius Emerson Phelps, for firearms violations.

If you are serving a warrant for guns, you want to isolate the suspects from the location and their access to those guns. At the Branch Davidian standoff in Waco, the ATF did not intercept the key players while they were away from the compound, which led to catastrophe. The Bureau would not want to repeat that mistake; on the other hand, in hours of watching the surveillance cameras, it becomes clear not only that nobody is about to leave the farm for a trip to Wal-Mart but that two other hulking players have arrived—Mr. Terminate and Mountain Man—which indicates that while Stone is preparing for his Big One, the Bureau had best get ready for its.

Under cover of darkness, a perimeter is established around the farm. Snipers are out there gathering intel, reporting on movement, describing the buildings and their entry and exit points. Beyond the perimeter, in vans equipped with monitors that show the same surveillance images as at the command center, SWAT team leaders huddle over drawings of the interior Ana Grey had made for Donnato, revising the scenario for a controlled dynamic entry—contingency planning that had been in place since the very day she walked in and activated when it became clear that she had disappeared somewhere between the psychiatrist's office and the pickup by her handler in Portland. By first light, the snipers have found their final positions of cover and concealment, and an SOG helicopter is readied for takeoff in a distant field.

The scene in the kitchen could not be more domestic. Every box of cereal in the pantry has been taken out and lined up on the counter, and Megan and I are mixing lurid rainbows of flakes and chips and marshmallow bits like kids at a sundae bar. It's either Armageddon or a sleepover. Stone has been studying the fish report in the newspaper, as usual.

" 'Yesterday five hundred and twelve chinook salmon moved through the fish ladders in an hour,' " he reads. "That's the highest count all summer. Having fun undercover, Ana Grey?"

I give him a grimace. I spent a sleepless night on the couch guarded by Mr. Terminate, who stayed awake doing coke, an AK-47 across his knees. But this morning, he and Mountain Man were gone.

"I'm glad we've all come clean," Stone says. "So we can trade war stories. I remember one time undercover on the beach in northern California with a dozen naked hippies, all tripping on acid, entwined in a mound like a bunch of seals, like something dumped out of the sea. And here we are, right back to it." He fingers the Colt in the holster. "Just like the old days, minus the pussy—no offense."

"I was *there*, darlin'," Megan deadpans.

Stone laughs as Sara comes downstairs wearing flannel drawstring pants and a lingerie top without a bra, still all soft focus from sleep.

"Where's Slammer? Did he already eat?"

Dick Stone informs her that Slammer has left.

"Left where?"

"Left the farm. He's gone. Just took off. Said he couldn't take it here anymore. Because I'm a prick, evidently."

"*What?*" Sara is disbelieving. "He wouldn't just split like that. Without telling me? Darcy, did you see him go?"

I shake my head. "First I've heard of it."

Sara flushes pink. "What did you do to him?"

"Nothing. Left of his own free will."

Megan: "He walked out wearing his backpack. Check his room; you'll see it's gone."

"I don't believe you. What is going on?"

"Well," says Megan, "for one thing, Darcy here is a fed."

"A what?"

"She's a cop. A spy. It's a brand-new day, Sara," Stone announces. Sara's look goes blank and her delicate face shuts down. *Unreachable.*

"I'm with the FBI and I've been working undercover to infiltrate FAN. This is what it *really* looks like when your cover has been blown," I say, waving a spoon toward the collection of fluorescent cereal boxes with cartoon characters flying spaceships and riding tricycles.

The gesture takes in the superior look on Dick Stone's face, Megan's "I knew it all along" coolness, the hazelnut trees, lost animals, and, just beyond the cottonwood trees, hopefully, a hostage rescue team assembled from three states.

Her eyelids flutter.

"Did my parents send you?"

Ignoring Dick Stone's chuckle, I say, "No, Sara, I was sent by the U.S. government to destroy a terrorist cell. These people have broken the law and they are going to jail. When the time comes, do what I tell you, and you will be safe with me."

The chuckle again. He's enjoying this.

"What about Slammer?"

Stone touches her wrist. "Don't let it break your heart."

"He wouldn't leave me. We're *friends*."

"He'll show up again. You know how he is."

The girl still can't make sense of it. "Slammer just left—on foot?"

"John and his buddy gave him a ride."

"Where to?"

"The bus station."

My gut tightens. The fact that Stone has disclosed Slammer left with the goons is ominous. Maybe Slammer became too rebellious, too much of an obstacle, like me. "The bus station" could mean the Dumpster at the shooting range. Alerted by the sound of heavy tires on gravel, we watch as McCord's Silverado turns into the driveway. Sara runs toward the door.

"Where do you think you're going?"

"Sterling's here. He's got the wraps for Geronimo's leg."

"What happened to Geronimo?"

"He banged his leg against the rail yesterday. It's all swollen."

"Go," says Megan with a tired wave. "Take care of the baby." Her eyes have reddened and pooled.

Stone allows Sara to leave.

Stone fills a small enameled pot with water. He turns the knob on the stove until the electronic igniter clicks. He waits for the flame. With smooth, familiar movements, he pops the scarred white cabinet open, removes a paper box, and holds it against his belly while choosing a packet of red bush tea. He slaps the door shut.

The tension at the kitchen table is like waiting for a hurricane. We are losing the sun and palm trees are blowing inside out; traffic lights swing wildly on their cables. The storm shutters are up and the house is sealed, but within the hour we will be beset by knocking winds like a thousand screaming inmates.

Stone sits down and stares into his cup. A sightless maroon surface stares back at him.

"I'd talk about the philosophical aspects of these people I was living with," he says, "but all the FBI cared about was 'Where are the fugitives? If they're not planning to blow something up, we're not interested.' There was no intelligence gathering. My supervisor wasn't listening. 'Where are the fugitives? Where are the fugitives?'

"They were trapped inside their own box. It was Hoover's dirty little war and the Weathermen were the guerrillas. They knew the land. They had allies. It's amazing how many well-to-do, educated people helped them out."

"That's how pissed off everyone was about Vietnam," Megan says.

"Then I go back to the office and get shit from the straight agents. So now I'm bitter toward the Bureau. Now it's really them and us. Except I don't fit in anywhere. Hoover's saying hippies are filthy and depraved, but that's the only place people like me are comfortable. The only folks who'll shelter us. I would cry. I'd sit in my apartment in Venice and get high and eat nothing but candy for the sugar rush, and cry.

"And they knew it. The Bureau knew I was going wack but they did just the opposite—sent me back in. 'This guy is good. He's done it. He got himself accepted. Let's send him back.' Which really fucked me up. I shifted up to Santa Barbara, lived in a tepee in a public park. Looked like a radical, hair down to here. Smoked dope, engaged in group sex. I knew Vietnam vets who threw their medals away. We tripped out together, cried for our brothers. I remember lying in a park on the grass and letting my tears go into the ground, like they were mixing with every casualty that ever was. The country was blowing apart. Our government was killing millions of civilians in Vietnam. The war drove everyone out of their minds.

"This is not how I was raised. My family had *decorum.* My father was a deacon of the church. But I'm still carrying the flag, tattered as it is, so I go up to Berkeley and do my thing. Agitate. Penetrate. Lie to the college kids who smoked my dope and were my friends. Sleep with chicks, big ones, ugly ones, lesbians—'Put a flag over her face and do it for Old Glory,' the Bureau used to say. 'Get information and move on.' Things were so volatile that before I took the assignment, I went back home to say good-bye to my parents, because I thought I might get killed on the job. I couldn't tell them what I was doing, but I wanted them to know it was for the right reasons.

"But, yeah. The right reason. Agents I came up with, my own buddies, we would raid a suspected Weather collective in an apartment building in east Los Angeles and hang people outside the windows upside down by their ankles. I did that. True. We'd rob their houses, intimidate their families, spread false rumors about them at work, because our government said that was the way to win hearts and minds, remember?

"Here I am, living on campus, stoned out of my mind, getting down with the folks while trying to hold on to my Bureau identity—*really holding on*—believing we had right on our side and this scum had to be caught and put in jail because they were criminals, because they were blowing up the Capitol Building and the Queens Courthouse and Gulf Oil. See, darlin'? Anarchy is nothing new. But then the Bureau fucked with Megan, *and I told them not to*—and I couldn't hold it together any longer. This thing split inside me. The job itself was blowing me apart."

"What did they do to her?"

"They spread disinformation. I was a Communist and a slut," Megan says. "They got me fired from my job at Berkeley."

Stone takes her hand.

"She was a hot, sexy, rebellious professor, and I was a student radical supposedly taking her class. A little old for the part, although I was a lot skinnier—and I had this cornball alias, 'Aquarius Bob'—but she liked me anyway. They arrested her at a demonstration on phony, cooked-up charges, I signed her out of jail, and we never looked back. Both our careers were over, so what the fuck? The Bureau went ballistic. They sent guys to my old apartment in Venice, and all they found was an empty wreck. Clothes on the floor, nothing washed, nothing put back in drawers, fast food and candy wrappers—as time went by, the layers just piled up. They let it drop, ever so subtly to everyone in L.A., that I'd flipped out and gone over to the other side, when for all they knew, I could have been living on the beach in Hawaii. They totally trashed me."

"He was a beautiful young man." Megan is suddenly self-conscious, eyes downcast. "He was motivated by ideals, even though they were different from mine. But that's why I fell in love with him. He was a lanky, serious guy who kind of stumbled over the rhetoric. For all his conservative outlook, there was something edgy and unsafe about Julius, more dangerous than the most radical hippies."

"Because I was playing both sides. It's a high. Right, Ana?"

"We were young, ready to take on the world. I didn't know he was an agent until he showed up at jail. He looked completely different. He'd cut his hair and put on a suit. He brought me these horrible clothes! Where did you get those clothes? I looked like a school-teacher, but it got us to Canada."

I smile sadly. "I knew this was a love story."

But there is bitterness, too. "What did we have?" Megan asks. "Nothing but sex. I mean, literally, nothing. But at the time, it was the only thing that seemed to matter: Making love was the ultimate political act. As if two people in bed could change the world. Then it got cold and winter came and we were sick all the time, living as fugitives until the movement started to eat its own tail."

"You wanted out."

"Where could we go with no résumés and no work histories that matched our ages, except the abandoned family farm that nobody wanted? We pulled out the old u-pick peach orchard and planted hazelnuts. He went back to school and learned tree farming and became a pillar of the community, and by then, well, there was no chance of children, but that's okay, because we had our rescue animals."

"When I went home that final time," says Stone, "and said good-bye to my parents, I wanted them to know I wasn't taking a top secret assignment to cause them more hurt, but of course it did, because they never saw either one of their sons again, after my brother was killed. Some days I can put a good face on it. To their dying hour, they could hold my brother up as a hero. He was a hero, but I'll always be a criminal. If Ana Grey and friends have anything to say about it."

"I have nothing to say."

They all were criminals. In the late seventies, Acting Director L. Patrick Grey III and two other highly ranked FBI officials were indicted for violating the constitutional rights of relatives of the Weatherman fugitives.

"I'll tell you what's worse," Stone goes on. "I tried to go public. I talked to Jimmy Breslin—"

"Stop it now," Megan says. "Enough."

But Stone is on a hectic roll.

"He wanted proof. Where was the proof? I'll tell you. In forty-seven drawers of files on deep-cover operatives that the Bureau destroyed. See, that was a violation of *me*. Of my history. My sacrifice. My rights as a human being. And hers. I knew everything they did to Megan Tewksbury, play by play. I went to my supervisor, another sidewinder, Peter Abbott, and I said, 'This woman is entitled to free speech. She is not a national security threat, nor is she a whore. Leave her alone.' I was in love with her and that's why he wouldn't stop. Just to test me. Mess with my head."

"That's not the only reason," Megan says crossly. "You forget. I was speaking out against the power companies that were destroying the West, one of which was owned by the Abbott family."

I remember the surveillance photo Peter Abbott displayed at the conference table in Los Angeles. Megan, wrapped in an American flag, was shouting nose-to-nose with his congressman father at the building site of a dam along the Columbia Gorge.

Nice sideburns, Dad.

"They were given a free pass to own the Northwest electric grid by destroying the natural rivers. People in the movement knew it. *Knew* it was totally corrupt. They used every obscene trick in the book to persecute us, and eventually, sickeningly, we gave up and ran."

Stone's voice is rising. "I warned him when he was my supervisor: If he didn't lay off you, I'd bring him down. The yachts, the mansions, the whole damn empire—"

Megan is scornful. "Yachts? Now you're talking nonsense."

And Stone's eyes take on a vacant look, meaning that he's shifting gears. Even his voice is throaty when he says, "I've got the goods on Abbott."

I ask, "What goods?"

"Illegal contracts."

"How?"

"Pay attention. I said I had an impeccable source on the inside."

"Rooney Berwick? He works in the lab."

"He's a computer wonk, a master hacker. It's a game to him: *Beat the assholes.* It took us years."

"This impeccable intel—where is it?"

"Buried. For now."

"You always go too far," Megan scolds. "You get stuck on these obsessions, and what good does it do?"

Stone is conspiratorial. "Megan Tewksbury wasn't her real name. It was Laurel Williams."

Megan begins to cry. "Oh my God. I haven't heard that said out loud in thirty years."

There is a sick lump in my throat. Dick Stone takes off his glasses and rubs his small damp eyes. After a while he says, "It's time."

Megan looks over from the sink, where she has splashed her flaming cheeks.

"Are you still with me?" he asks her with a heart-wrenching look of disembodied loneliness.

Megan reaches for a dish towel and dries her hands. She rests in that gesture of finality, fingers kneading the cloth.

The white cat stalks along the windowsill, neatly avoiding the plants. Stone sits with his eyes out of focus and shoulders slumped, a mountain of weightiness. I look back and forth between them. The limpid light from the window washes over us with incongruous peace.

When I was in college, I once stayed up all night, driving the Pacific Coast Highway with a wealthy girlfriend who owned an MG convertible. We forced ourselves to stay awake because neither of us had ever actually seen the dawn. We wanted to mark the very instant the darkness crossed that line in the sky into day.

I learned that night there is no marker, no precise delineation for change, but as the sun rose over the red tile roofs of Santa Barbara, I witnessed for the first time how the world slowly blushes open, the way it has just now, in this long moment of disengagement—without words and without a look—as Megan and Stone have begun their good-byes to a long shared life on the run.

When the service of the warrant and the assault begin, Sara and McCord are still in the barn.

"This is an ice boot." He secures the neoprene wrap around Geronimo's leg. "You keep it in the freezer, then it goes on the swelling."

Sara kneels beside him in the straw. "How come you know every-thing?"

"Because I care. I make it my business. Just like I care about you and your welfare."

"You do?"

"You're a good kid. Just in with the wrong folks."

She glances furtively toward the house. "Something's going on."

"All right."

"I don't understand it. This morning, Slammer disappeared with-out telling me where he was going."

Sirocco is pawing and pulling violently on the cross ties. The baby's ears are up. Alerted, McCord glances through the open barn doors.

"Get out, *now*," he says and hauls Sara to her feet.

They reach the yard as the surveillance helicopter breaks over the trees. McCord has only time to grab an aluminum suitcase from the Silverado before pushing Sara through the back door and into the kitchen, where all of us are craning to look through the windows.

"Who is it?"

"FBI," McCord tells Stone.

"Bitch!" he shouts, and backhands me across the face. I reel against the sink as red drops from a split lip find the drain.

McCord: "What's that about?"

"She's a fed," Sara announces breathlessly.

Pressing my hand to my mouth, I see Sterling McCord make an adjustment. He straightens his back and regards me in a different way, as if an entire sequence has locked into place for him.

"In that case, we use her as a bargaining chip. They'll attempt to negotiate."

"I know exactly what they'll do," growls Stone.

Sara goes spacey and begins to wander off, but Megan pulls her back. "Stay away from the windows."

McCord: "You two go down to the basement."

"What about you?" Sara cries.

"We're going to talk to the feds," replies McCord.

"Like fuck we are," says Stone. "And who the fuck are you?"

McCord shows his palms in deference. "Your house, your call. But can we agree to get the women out of the line of fire?"

"Except Ana Grey."

McCord, bemused: "Is that your real name?"

I nod yes.

The helicopter swoops low and deafeningly loud, most likely checking our positions with infrared devices. They've already got a pretty good picture from listening in on Stone's surveillance system. When the chopper fades, an amplified voice from somewhere out there begins calling us out.

"This is Deputy Director Peter Abbott with the FBI. We have a warrant to search the premises. Please come out with your hands up."

None of us in the kitchen moves. Stone is leaning against the counter, head down, staring at his bare crossed ankles.

"They sent the brass," he says sarcastically.

"Megan Tewksbury? Laurel Williams?"

Megan startles, as if hit with a cattle prod. "What the hell?"

"I believe you're innocent. I know you've been coerced. This is a dead end. Don't put your life in danger."

Her eyes go wild. "Why me?"

"They're trying to drive a wedge," I say.

"If I go out there, they'll shoot me."

"No, they won't," says McCord. "They want you out of here. One less potential casualty."

"Megan, Laurel, step outside the door."

Megan is red-faced, confused as a girl. "What should I do?"

Stone says, "Go on."

"Without you?"

"All I've ever done is bring you down. They'll cut you a deal. Sara, too."

Sara has begun to quiver.

McCord says, "Go ahead. You'll be safe, little girl."

Megan extends her hand and Sara takes it.

"You stay here," Stone tells me, unholstering his gun.

Megan and Sara, holding hands, walk awkwardly to the front door. Megan glances back at us, then opens it a slice. Somewhere out there is the supreme warrior-bureaucrat, the man who took away her freedom, offering it back.

"What do you want?" Megan shouts.

"I promise you safe passage. We don't want you to get hurt. Tell Dick Stone to let you go."

"I am my own person!" Megan declares melodramatically. "I am free to go or stay. I have someone else with me. A girl. Sara."

"Good. Where is Agent Grey? Is she hurt?"

"She's in the kitchen. She's fine."

"You and Sara come out now. Everything will be okay."

We cannot see what Megan sees through the crack of the door, but I doubt it is the guns that frighten her. Or the aftermath of surrender, too unimaginable to grasp. She hesitates on the threshold between two men, two lives, and maybe it's the distance that decides it—not more than fifty yards from the porch to the road, but a still, wavering sunlit space of almost four decades too charged with passion to be dismissed in a banal gesture. Megan slams the door and locks it. Dragging Sara, she hurtles back through the dining room to the kitchen and stands before Dick Stone, who opens his arms and takes her in.

With a sigh, the refrigerator shuts down.

Stone tries the stove. No electric click. The faucets spew air.

"They cut the water and power." He picks up the receiver. "But not the phone."

When night falls we will be trapped in darkness, while they will follow every move with night-vision. They have the jump, and he knows it. All that firepower, but all they have to do is wait—days, months—who cares? Why provoke a siege? When dehydration and the stink of our own filth have fully driven us insane, they can simply pluck us out of here.

Megan and Sara are down in the basement with the cats, while Stone, McCord, and I sit around a table littered with cereal bowls and used cups as the kitchen warms to medium rare in the midday sun. Already we look like renegades, haggard and rank. Sometime after noon, an armored robotic vehicle crawls across the yard and delivers a throw phone to the front steps.

"All we're asking is to talk," says a new voice on the bullhorn. *"Please open the door and take the phone. We guarantee your safety."*

Through a swollen lip, I offer to open the door and retrieve the phone.

"You know what this will become," says Stone. "A slow, protracted crisis-negotiator scenario."

"What's the alternative?"

In answer, McCord slaps the battered aluminum suitcase down on the table.

"They send in counterterrorist assault teams trained for close combat," he says. "They move fast and use extreme violence. They know it's just you and me. For them, it's a walk in the park."

McCord unsnaps the suitcase and opens the lid. Stone and I both gasp. The case is custom-fitted with a collection of handmade weapons I have never seen before except in kung-fu movies: double-bladed knives, with one curved blade and one straight; throwing stars like giant jacks with lethal barbs, meant to blind an enemy in pursuit; miniature razor-sharp scythes.

Stone has his arms crossed and is chuckling again.

"Special Ops?"

"Delta Force. Now I do it for money."

It is my turn to reel, unable to make sense of it. "You're a mercenary?"

"We don't particularly like that word. I am a soldier for hire by a private military company. Outsourcing, ma'am. We run every war that's taking place in the world right now."

"Were you in Pakistan? I've seen those there," muses Stone, pointing to a machete with a rawhide-laced grip.

"Peshawar."

"I was, too. Many years ago."

"We must have people in common."

"Are you two going to start exchanging recipes now?" I say sardonically.

"What's your problem, Ana Grey?" Stone loves to taunt me with the name.

I stare hard at McCord. "I don't like being lied to is all."

Stone guffaws and the so-called cowboy hides a smile. I am furious with the pretender, and the attraction that I felt for him, but why should it matter? He is just another player in this depressing endgame.

"You're a hired killer!"

"First of all, I never fight for Communists," McCord explains pleasantly. "Second, it's not like being a hired gun in the Old West. Some guys are trigger-happy, but they don't last. The long-timers know how to protect the client's interests without the use of force. There's always the fine art of negotiation. But I wasn't lying to you, ma'am."

"How is *that*?"

"I believe I did say that I am a professional wrangler. I was raised with cutting horses in Kerrville, Texas. And that's the truth."

"Meaning what?"

He shrugs. "Nothing to hide is all."

"You can hide in plain sight," I snap.

"This is the FBI. Please take the phone into the house. It is very important that we contact former agent Dick Stone."

Stone has been sitting calmly, hands on knees.

"I've decided to talk to them. I have only one demand. If they give me what I want, this will resolve. If they don't, this will be the worst day in the history of the FBI."

That's what David Koresh said before the siege at Waco. And he was right.

"You," orders Stone. "Miss Secret Agent. Get on the phone."

McCord: "What do you want me to do?"

"Hang tight. There will be compensation."

Without a flicker, McCord says, "Good enough," and snaps the suitcase shut.

Stone stays close as I call 911 on the house phone and ask to be connected to the sheriff's department.

"This is Special Agent Ana Grey with the FBI. I'm inside the farmhouse."

"How many with you? Is anyone hurt?"

"We demand to talk to the lead negotiator." I hold Stone's

shrunken red eyes and repeat his message word for word: "No lackey Bureau assholes. I will open the door and pick up the phone. That's all."

We go to the front of the house. Using my body as a shield, Stone crooks a forearm tightly around my throat while holding the Colt .45 to my head. I try to stay loose, a compliant dance with his. I reach for the knob and open the door. Outside, the wide world shouts. A quick scan reveals no snipers; they are hidden on higher ground. Afternoon heat hits our faces as we bend together, and my hands reach out to pick up the phone.

We retreat and slam the door.

No shots are fired.

Then he brings Megan and Sara up from the basement and orders me to help them prepare for evacuation.

We pull everything out of the front closet, dragging the vacuum cleaner and its attachments, and all the attachments from the previous vacuum cleaners, too, the unstrung tennis rackets and stiff yellow rain suits, and toss them out of the way. Megan insists on sweeping the floor, painstakingly digging a mouse corpse out of the corner.

All that's left is the naked closet—wire hooks and pegs, a single lightbulb on an old chain fixture—and the painted-over inner door: the one I discovered while searching for the gun that killed Mackee.

Megan runs upstairs and returns with several backpacks already loaded for an emergency getaway.

Sara is trembling. "I don't want to go."

The two anguished women stare at each other and embrace.

"We can't leave the animals," Megan says, sobbing along with her. "Geronimo is just a baby."

"We don't have to!" Sara cries. "We don't have to go! We can make it a condition. They have to take care of the animals, and then we'll surrender."

Megan and Sara are clinging to each other, keening like widows.

I crawl inside the closet. The painted seal is already breeched. The inner door has recently been chiseled open.

McCord is suddenly crouched behind me. "What is it?"

"It's a tunnel. Stone's secret escape route."

How he avoided the cameras. How he spirited Slammer and the goons away.

I push on the hobbit-size door. Doom. It is doom to look through such an opening into absolute darkness. Nobody should do it. Nobody should have to look. A draft of cold, unworldly air unwinds through the overheated closet, as if the house had been waiting to release its death rattle.

"Listen to me, Ana," McCord whispers urgently, close to my ear. "We're both on the same side."

I turn to him, annoyed. "Are you a merc? Or what?"

"I am a contract soldier for a private military company based in London. We don't just fight wars"—he sneaks a backward look through the door—"we protect private interests. We find people. Like Sara Campbell."

"Sara?"

"The girl has run away a dozen times. I was hired by her parents to find her and bring her home."

"She says she comes from 'dirt.' "

"Well, it's pretty rich manure. Her dad is president of an oil company. We provide protection for American executives in Saudi Arabia; that's how he got to me."

"Does she know?"

He shakes his head. "I've been easing in gently. Working from the edges."

"When you showed up at the BLM corrals and at the shooting range—you weren't following me; you were tracking Sara."

"I thought she'd show up at the protest." He smiles. "But it was no hardship running into you."

"That's why you gave her the foal."

"Workin' on trust. She's bolted before. She's tried suicide. The parents and the shrink all said to go slow."

I glance back through the open closet door. The hallway is empty.

"Sterling," I whisper. "We can take Dick Stone down. You have his trust. Your weapons are *right there* in the kitchen."

"Not my job."

"Then I'll do it."

"Can't let you." He restrains my arm. "I was hired to protect the girl. If things go south, she'll be put in harm's way."

"Are you crazy? This place will blow any minute. If Stone is dead, the game ends and nobody else gets hurt."

"I won't risk it."

"You are a royal pain."

"Just so you know, when it comes down, I *will* get Sara out."

"All right," I hiss. "The sewing room is the designated safe room. The rescue team will deploy through the screened-in porch."

We crab-crawl backward out the closet door.

Stone is shouting into the secure phone, "Nothing changes with you people. *Listen to what I say.* I want it printed in every newspaper. I want it read on TV. My true manifesto! The truth of what the American people need to know about the fascist abuses of the FBI. I have it all right here."

Megan and Sara enter the kitchen, tear-stained, clutching the dusty emergency backpacks. McCord is plucking weapons from the suitcase of horrors.

Megan says, "Are we out of here?" as Sara shouts, "Oh no!"

Through the window we can see the small white horse has wandered from the barn. He is thirty yards from the house, tearing the leaves off tomato plants.

"Screw me. We left the damn stall door open," says McCord.

"What about Sirocco?"

"She's still tied."

Megan is transfixed by the stranded foal. "The baby." She drops the backpack.

"Leave him be," warns McCord. "He's fine where he is."

Dick Stone slams down the phone. "Lying bastards."

With a high, piercing whistle, the window implodes, and flash-bangs pop all around. The acrid choke of tear gas sends us crawling from the room.

I push Sara into McCord's arms. She is stunned, resisting.

I'm screaming, *"The safe room!"* but they can't hear me, and I can't see through swollen eyes.

More shrill canisters. More lightning bangs.

McCord has overpowered the girl and is dragging her toward the Room of Unfinished Dreams as a huge explosion throws everyone in the house to the floor.

Someone says in a faraway voice like a tinny old recording, "The barn's on fire!"

Where is Stone? Where is Stone?

The floor is hot. I grope forward, trusting that McCord and Sara have made it to the sewing room, where SWAT will breech the windows and the twisted bamboo blinds at hostage-rescue speed.

Where is Stone?

Peering through the smoke I find the wretched shapes of two older, slower people feeling their way through the fractured debris of the front hall. Behind them is the closet and the tunnel of escape. Ahead, through gaping holes where the front door used to be, helixes of orange flame are exploding from the outbuildings. The white foal is zigzagging blindly through the yard in terror.

Megan is struggling to get out. She has to save the foal. Stone pins her arms and drags her backward. She kicks at him. They fall over the heap of junk from the closet, sprawling on top of each other. She fights free and crawls toward the open hole, turning her head to shout something at Stone. Her hair has begun to smolder. A curtain of heavy charcoal smoke falls between us. Scraps of incinerated paper fly on whirls of heat like fiery demons. Stone is up, hopscotching across the gently burning floorboards, bellowing at Megan, who is just out of reach. The faraway old-fashioned voice says, "The baby," and she stumbles through the shattered opening into the fresh air, Dick Stone close behind.

My guess is there was never going to be negotiation. And this wasn't another mistake like Waco. The mission was to massacre every living being on the farm. The tactical commanders took orders from Deputy Director Peter Abbott, who was willing to risk scrutiny to be certain the terrorists—and everything they knew—were eliminated.

Snipers are trained to cultivate patience. They are told, "You have one opportunity. Make it count." A team of two elite shooters with tripod-mounted AR-10s had the front door sighted up the past five hours, their breath moderated like one wave after another in a tide that never breaks, still as the leaves, infinitely enduring. When Dick Stone reels into the luminous circles of their scopes scuttling with Megan in the shattered doorway, they take the shot, a calm, straight-forward release of two high-powered bullets. At the same instant, Megan pops up in front of Stone and inadvertently becomes the target. The two bullets simultaneously penetrate her left cerebral hemisphere.

Just like that. The heavy guns, familiar as big brothers, kick hard into the curve of their shoulders, but the shooters are braced to absorb the shock, unlike Megan's skull, which instantly fractures in radiating spiderweb patterns, likely the only sting she feels, as the brain has no pain receptors, along with awareness of some sort of impact that might have registered a second or two before she loses consciousness, the bright library of a lifetime gone.

Stone ducks back into the house, from which we stare at Megan's body, lying prone in the blasted doorway, appearing to be smoking like the fallen timbers swollen with heat that are crumbling around us, a century of farm life hissing away in vapors. Dick Stone's mouth howls in anguish like the silent cavernous winds of hell; a meaty arm hooks my neck and does not let go as we stagger away, conjoined like primordial brutes as a savage twister of coal black smoke drives us away from daylight.

Thirty-nine

We drive to a turnout where a chain hangs across a dirt road. When we emerged from the tunnel, we ran across a hundred yards of open wash beyond the perimeter, clouds of ink black smoke roiling behind us. We kept on going—a call on the satellite phone to an associate of Mr. Terminate—and then a grandma biker chick right out of Omaha, a wrinkled witch a hundred years old, met us and took us to a safe house in a trailer park, where we were given a stolen car. We drive for ninety minutes into the national park. Only when we passed a green sign for the parking lot for the Hard Edge Trail do I realize that our destination is the place where Steve Crawford died.

Stone gets out and unhooks the chain, gets back in and drives the sedan over it. Branches sweep the windshield as we ascend a rutted fire road. The Northwest fir is as impenetrable as the Virginia woodland surrounding Quantico; voracious organisms choking one another out for the sun.

At times the car is almost engulfed by closely growing colonnades of young Douglas fir, and I am gripped with a claustrophobic unease, as sickening as having crawled through that tunnel. Spring rains cut deep gullies in the moist terrain and now our heads hit the inside roof of the car as we launch out of our seats. Ten miles an hour seems way too fast.

"Watch out!"

"Got it," Stone mutters, slowing to a stop before a huge tree felled across the road.

We stare at an impassable tangle of branches and fine sprays of dark green needles spewing out in all the wrong directions. Nothing looks more like a forbidding mistake than a huge horizontal tree lying across your path.

"We're not that far," Dick Stone says, arming himself with the Colt, a Commando submachine gun, three hundred rounds of ammunition, and a collapsible snow shovel.

We climb around the tree and follow the road on foot. During the drive, we gained altitude, and the mountain air is pure and chill.

"I've been in some odd situations, Dick, but this is one of the strangest. Ever zoom out of yourself? All the way out, so you're looking down from somewhere else?"

"Not sober."

"What are we doing in the woods? I don't even like the woods. There're ticks and poison oak."

The road is wide enough to walk side by side, but sometimes one of us will walk ahead, over gullies cut by cascading rocks, sometimes along the lip of the road. We continue that way, flowing around each other, as Stone twirls the shovel lightly over one shoulder.

"Why are you and I always digging another man's trenches?" I muse.

"Some of us are soldiers. Born that way."

We are walking single file where the road washes out. At the bottom of a huge rounded boulder split by a tree, Stone takes a turn onto the well-kept Hard Edge Trail. A Forest Service sign points back to the parking lot at 5.7 miles.

We continue up, retracing Steve Crawford's steps.

We crest a ravine and look down at the creek where the hiker found the remains. I recognize the rock formations from the postblast photos.

"Good God!" says Stone. "What are you two doing here?"

Toby Himes and Mr. Terminate are sitting on a fallen log. Toby, always appropriately dressed for whatever occasion, wears an impeccable hiker's outfit—clean boots, wind-resistant pants, lightweight black quilted vest, orange hunter's cap. Mr. Terminate, wearing a T-shirt with a faded message that has to do with sucking, is smoking a cigarette, the AK-47 cradled in his arms. His presence is so improbable that it instantly reframes reality.

Before, the forest was treacherous.

Now, it is incendiary.

"Figured you wouldn't leave town without saying good-bye."

"Course not," says Stone, climbing down the slope. "I owe you, big."

"No problem, it was a lot of laughs," says Mr. Terminate. "I see you still got your shadow."

"Hi, John," I say, just so he can ignore me one last time.

Stone bums a cigarette and puts one foot up on the log.

"Megan is dead."

"Really? Oh *shit*! Oh *man*!"

Toby's eyes grow round in surprise. "Deepest condolences, my friend. What happened?"

"They mowed her down. About how many bullets would you say she took, Ana Grey?"

"I don't know, Dick."

"When I was on the Los Angeles bank robbery squad, we ambushed a gang of bandits in an alley. The guy driving the getaway car—it was a convertible—took a hundred thirty-two hits. He was hamburger. Those were the good old days, am I right? I'll make them suffer a thousand times worse. A hundred thousand. I should have followed the very first rule: *Never negotiate with terrorists*. It's the Bureau I'm talkin' about."

"We know exactly what you're talkin' about." Toby lays trembling fingers on his friend's arm.

"But, no," says Stone, squeezing his face up. "I talked to them, and she walks into an assassination."

I stare at the thick bed of mulch under my feet. I am thinking how many papery layers of brown oak leaves have been laid down over how many centuries and with what patience, and about the beetles gnawing dumbly through the fertile dregs.

"Make no mistake," says Mr. Terminate, his growl downshifting to first. "She was a good lady."

Stone smokes some more.

"Anything I can do?" the biker asks.

"I have some thoughts."

Mr. Terminate nods. A switchblade appears like the tongue of a snake from his hand.

"Then we split the turquoise. Three ways."

Stone sighs. "There is no turquoise. It's just a rumor, John. A story I made up to mess with their minds."

"I knew it." Toby slaps his own leg.

Mr. Terminate is not convinced. "Why are you carrying a shovel?"

"To cover up . . . whatever." He jerks his head toward me. *Whatever's left.*

Mr. Terminate considers. He gets up from the log. *Yeah, okay.* He walks toward me, the knife held low.

"It's cash," I say.

"Come again?"

"Dick calls it 'the turquoise,' but that's a cover, so he can cheat his best friends. He stole a hundred and fifty thousand dollars from the FBI, and it's buried right there."

Mr. Terminate squints at Stone. "You wouldn't cheat me."

"Oh for Christ's sake!" cries Stone, fed up and totally frustrated. *"This is the turquoise!"* And he pulls the PalmPilot from his pocket. In the sage forest light, the plastic cover sparkles like sea green semiprecious gems.

"O-kay," says Mr. Terminate slowly.

Toby blinks. "It's blue."

"You dumb fucks. This is my manifesto. This is the truth. This will sink the FBI. Names, records, and documents going back to the seventies, when they fucked Megan and they fucked me, and who was in charge of the undercover operation? My own boss. Peter Abbott. I've got his signature on memos that approved the whole damn bag of dirty tricks. But that's nothing. That's just the warm-up. I've got the drop on his fucking corrupt father, too."

Mr. Terminate has planted his feet like a gunslinger.

"I stood by you. All these years, I delivered the goods."

"I'll get you the money," Dick Stone says impatiently. "After we take care of business."

Mr. Terminate isn't stupid. "You didn't have to bring her all this way to do the deed."

"I came to collect some papers I've got stashed. Buried in a metal box. I'll show you."

"Papers?"

"Travel documents."

"*Cash!* He's lying to you, John. He's a psycho liar."

"I'll bet it's over here," says cocky Mr. Terminate as he heads for a boulder veined with rose quartz. The rock is standing in a growth of chokecherry. The distinctive glassy pink markings make it look as if it had been rolled there to mark the spot. And he's right. A trip wire— thin as a spider's web—glints in the underbrush. It is the same kind of setup Steve Crawford must have walked into when he was looking to rip off a stolen fortune.

Stone yells, "Don't!" as Mr. Terminate lumbers toward it.

The shock wave of the explosion pummels my body, arms windmilling backward, then slams me up short against a granite outcrop, loose earth like burning sparks raining in my hair. The force of it crunches my left shoulder at a bad angle against the rock and I feel that sickening snap, when you know something has dislodged somewhere important.

As I stumble forward, a big inhale of chemical smoke causes me to choke and cry. Mr. Terminate's disarticulated body parts have been launched in a radius fifty feet wide. Coming to rest within my view is a facial fragment containing a partial set of bloody teeth, and a hand still wearing the silver rings. Above the blasted ridge of rock, a rhododendron bush has silently caught fire. Everything is silent because my eardrums have gone numb.

A tall, thin figure stumbles across the orange backdrop of burning trees and kneels beside Dick Stone, who was knocked down flat on his back.

"Doc!" I'm hearing as if underwater. "It's Toby, brother."

Thick wine-dark blood has pooled beneath Stone's body. Toby kneels and cradles his head.

"He's got a skull fracture. Small hole you can just stick your finger through." Toby wipes brain matter on his jeans.

"For God's sake, don't touch it!"

Dick Stone's face is pale and shocky, but he's still breathing. He opens dull and searching eyes.

"Get me up."

The fire is dancing across the highest canopy of branches. Black smoke boils and intense heat presses against our skin. In moments we will be trapped inside an inferno.

Stone's lips say, "Water."

Toby has a bottle in the pocket of his vest. Carefully supporting Stone's wounded head, he maneuvers on his knees to wet his mouth.

"What are you up to now, you crazy coot? Is this the famous Big One?"

"It's happening," Dick Stone murmurs. "The salmon are running."

I'm trying to lift Stone's shoulder over mine. "Let's get out of here."

The choice is get him up or let him burn to death. We lift, but then Stone's heavy legs give out and he ends up sitting. His bloody head lolls forward. My heart contracts with dread.

Toby shakes him. "Stay awake. Help us out."

Dick Stone relaxes back toward the ground. A mischievous smile plays around his lips. To the last, I don't know what he's playing.

"Dying's no big deal," he says quite clearly. "People who get upset about it haven't lived their lives the way they wanted to."

"Medics!" Toby yells. "Code blue! Abort!"

He looks around, but nothing happens.

"Where are you?" he shouts.

I think that he's gone nuts, flashing back to a burning jungle in Vietnam, but then SWAT advances from the forest like surreal toy soldiers in Nomex battle gear, with automatic weapons drawn.

Stone is whispering and motioning for me to hear. I bend close to his bloodless lips. He gropes for my shirt. Although our faces are almost touching, Stone's roaming eyes cannot find me.

"He has taken advantage of all I stand for." Dick Stone must have realized with his dying thought that beneath the tidy hiking gear, Toby Himes is wearing a bulletproof vest. And a wire.

"But you . . ." His voice trails off. He presses something into my hand. It is the PalmPilot. "Take this."

Angelo and Donnato, festooned with earphones, ID tags, and gun belts, wearing bright blue FBI windbreakers, emerge from the blur, shouting questions.

I find that I am holding Dick Stone's hand, and I place it gently on his chest while slipping the device into my pocket. There is nothing more to be learned from the half-open eyes of the dead.

I get to my feet. A malevolent presence fills the sky. The sun looks distorted through an atmosphere of brown, an orange-red alien disk. Black smoke billows toward the north, but ash is falling like the frozen drops of hail that tapped against our parkas on a turbulent day last spring as we waited in the lee of a volcanic plain to save the last free wild horses in the West.

"Who the hell is Toby Himes?"

Donnato takes my elbow, but I jerk away.

"Who is he? Is he an agent? *He's* wired, *he's* wearing a vest, and I'm playing it out. I'm for real. I'm *involved* with these people, and he's—"

"I hear you."

Which is difficult, because I'm blubbering and trying to keep my mouth clamped shut at the same time.

"It's been tough on him, too."

"Tough on *him*?"

Donnato maneuvers so he's blocking my view; his face is all I see. "Toby Himes is a source."

"A *source*?"

"He is Peter Abbott's pocket source."

"The deputy director of the FBI has a *pocket source*? He's been off the street for years."

"Toby Himes has been Peter Abbott's unpaid informant, pretty much since they came back from Vietnam. We've known they were talking. We thought Abbott might be involved in a conspiracy. We ran an investigation under Galloway's command. Abbott finally gave it up that Mr. Himes has been providing him with intel on criminal activity in the Northwest for years. Himes is nowhere on the books because he refuses to take money or be acknowledged. He's an unsung hero. Doing the right thing for his country. When he told us Stone had recently acquired half a dozen cast boosters, we knew it was on."

"What are you talking about?"

"High-energy explosives. They provide the initiation you need to ignite a major amount of Tovex. Do serious damage. We knew Stone was onto the Big One."

Angelo approaches, having grabbed Toby Himes.

"A Highway Patrol officer picked up the APB on Jim Allen Colby, also known as Slammer, getting off a Greyhound bus in Cascade Locks. What does that mean, Mr. Himes?"

Toby replies, "That's the Bonneville Dam."

We should be running for the helicopters, but instead we are drawn to watch in respect as the paramedics strap Dick Stone's heavy body onto a gurney.

Toby Himes's face is tight. "Why did you wait and let him die?"

"We thought he might say something important. You did right," Angelo assures him.

"It speaks to what we do to ourselves," says the former Marine, and he walks away.

Sadness is rising. I swallow hard. An empty space is opening up, much like the empty space around my grandfather. Disappointment, mostly, in what might have been.

As for Darcy DeGuzman, without Dick Stone, she is lost.

Good-bye, soldier, Darcy thinks, and dies there, too.

Slammer gets off the fourth bus of the day at the Bonneville Lock and Dam, a National Historic Landmark. What a complete and total pain in the butt—but still, he is happy to have been chosen, back in the good graces. The old dude better appreciate this, hours and hours of waiting in stinky old bus stations in nowhere towns, and it's late in the day and it's cold and he's starving.

Slinging the backpack, he crosses the parking lot toward the visitors area and picks up a brochure, as instructed. This thing is huge. It spans the river a mile wide, connecting the states of Washington and Oregon. The powerhouses are kind of scary, huge networks of high-tension wires and transforming stations that produce electricity from turbines deep inside the dam—enough to power the entire city of Portland, it says.

He opens the map and locates the Fish Viewing Building.

Two huge luxury tour buses have pulled up to the entrance, and quicker than you'd imagine, hordes of white-haired old folk have disembarked in a parade of walkers and wheelchairs, limping through the glass doors. Slammer holds the door politely for a chalk-faced living corpse attached to an oxygen tank, then heads for the elevators, totally freaked by the guy at the desk—an old fart from the Army Corps of Engineers wearing a black eye patch, who is staring directly at him with one lucid eye.

But it's a great day for the fish. The Visitor Center is filled with tourists. The benches in front of the underwater window are crowded with kids and strollers, in a claustrophobic room that smells of old radiators and cafeteria lunch. Slammer stares through the glass at the silver forms flying by as they climb the fish ladders that get them over the dam—hundreds per hour. Some old lady is standing in a booth, clicking each one off by hand. People are staring at her like she's another exhibit.

Okay, he's seen enough. He can't wait to drop the dye. Man, it would be cool to see it happen from this window as the water slowly fills with red like a slasher movie. Better than blood and harmless to the fish, Julius promised. He checks his watch. Allfather said to pull the cord at precisely 4:15. It is 4:10 now.

Slammer takes the elevator to the top level, where you can walk outside and have a view of the whole river, and get close to the salty smell of the fish ladders, which are basically steps flowing with water. You think of a dam like something out of a children's book, all neat and sparkly, but when he looks around, he decides the place looks more like a prison. There are high barbed-wire fences to keep people away from the banks of the river. If you somehow fell in, you'd be swept into the rotor blades of giant turbine engines. The skies are gray and the water dark. He trudges up to the top of the weirs, out onto a catwalk where a toddler is squatting and pointing to the water.

He fingers the rope dangling from the backpack. Remembering the small explosion of gunpowder bound to occur when he pulls the switch, he moves away from the family.

"Don't let the little dude fall in," he advises.

"Slammer. Stop."

Still smiling, he answers to his name, and there's the chick from the farm coming toward him. She looks all different. She's got on a baseball cap and a vest that says FBI, and she's walking funny, tilted over to one side.

My left shoulder is bandaged up underneath the blastproof vest, but the pain is breathtaking.

"What are you doing?" Slammer asks.

"Don't move. Do not pull that cord."

"How'd you get here?"

Military helicopters fill the skies. On the shore, a fleet of cop cars and ambulances is lining up along the road.

I keep a distance.

"Slammer, please don't move. Do you know what's in that backpack?"

"Nothing is going to happen. It's just dye, to stop them from destroying the salmon runs."

"That pack contains explosives. Not just a blood bomb. Something a lot more powerful."

"Why?" the boy asks, confused.

There is a ripple of anxiety in the crowd that moments ago had been peacefully watching the fish jump through the roaring water. SWAT teams in combat gear are quickly moving families away, while moon men in bomb suits and helmets with built-in microphones direct a score of firemen ready with hoses. The woman with the toddler picks him up and carries him away, staring at Slammer with hate.

"Julius wanted to blow up the dam. To get revenge on the U.S. government, and because he was a sick individual. A lot of innocent people could get hurt—"

Alarmed, he says: "Where is Allfather?"

"He's dead. There was a fire at the farm. Everyone is dead except for Sara. She's okay; you can see her as soon as we resolve this. Right now, it's very important for you to listen to me. Do not move. The bomb squad will remove the backpack."

Slammer laughs. "No way he'd do something like that. Besides, one little bomb can't blow up all these tons of concrete. He wouldn't send me here just to blow myself up? For a couple of fish?"

"We're not going to let anything bad happen to you."

"You're trying to trick me."

"I'm trying to save your life. I did that once before, when he buried you alive, remember?"

"You're a liar!" Slammer screams. "You sold us out! You're a fed! You're a liar! You deserve to die!"

"I do care, Slammer. That's why I'm standing here. These guys could take you out in a heartbeat."

Slammer glances above him; the snipers are set up on the roof.

"You're a good person. You know how I know? Because you didn't kill Herbert Laumann when you had the chance. There is good in you, Slammer. It shines. You've had a real hard time of it. People haven't let you be good. But I know you are. I wouldn't be risking my life if I didn't think *your* life was very important. More important than the fish. Come on, dude."

"Stay back," he says.

"No. I'm coming to help you." I take a step closer.

"Why should I believe you ever again? You think I'm that incredibly stupid?"

I stop just short of tackling distance. Slammer's eyes are glassy and big, and he's chewing indecisively on those childlike lips. We face each other in a standoff as the human crowd recedes like a tide, leaving the windswept concrete walkways quiet except for the peeping song of the ospreys patrolling low over the water.

"I trust that you're not going to do this, Slammer, because you're smart enough to know you've been set up by Allfather. He's the one who was lying to you."

"It's another test," he decides. "Of fire and ice."

And then he jerks the cord.

In one stupefying moment, I grope for a lifetime of reconciliations. A series of *pop-pop-pop* explosions blows me backward and knocks Slammer to his knees as red dye fumes and spurts in all directions. While it continues to spray like a fireworks sparkler gone wild, he wrestles the backpack off and throws the whole thing into the fish ladders, and the water turns blood red.

Just like Stone's test run.

And that's the extent of it.

Slammer can't stop laughing for joy, even as a pile of agents brings him down.

"I believe in Allfather!" He keeps on snickering. "I belieeeeve, oh yesss!"

Stunned, the bruised shoulder searing with pain, I wipe at the splattered dye on my face. The wind off the river is icy. The helicopters keep circling. Radios crackle, and SWAT reinforcements overwhelm the top level.

My hair is whipping across my eyes. From the catwalk is a panoramic view of the river. Below, fish continue to flop over the weirs, the big clock of nature ticking placidly along, but now I am listening to a different buzz in a higher key. All the craft on the water have been diverted, except for one that has torpedoed through: a small powerboat heading in a perfectly straight line toward the dam.

I grab a pair of binoculars from one of the SWAT guys.

It is the boat I saw at Toby Himes's. The wheel is tied down. Otherwise, the boat is empty.

Except for large plastic barrels that contain military-grade explosives.

Mountain Man must have sent it on the final voyage. Slammer and the red dye were a diversion. The real attack bears down on us now on an automated suicide mission at eighty miles an hour, loaded with enough high explosives to blow a crater in this concrete monolith, where hundreds of agents, police, and tourists have massed—powerful enough to cause the river to overflow its banks, flood towns, destroy farmland, shut down the Northwest power grid. It is what terrorism experts call "a secondary explosion," the dual purpose being to inflict the greatest human casualties on responding personnel.

"INCOMING!" I scream. "THE BOAT IS ARMED."

Orders are relayed and everything starts moving backward. Ambulances screech off the road. Police units back out of the parking lot. Fire trucks and panicked tourists push toward the woods. Only the military helicopters swing forward in unison, flying low over the water, gunners leaning out the doors, firing .50-caliber automatic weapons at the boat, intercepting its kamikaze mission a scant two hundred yards before the target. The choppers jam it, up and away, as an orange ball of fire explodes out of the water. The boom echoes off the riverbanks, and every living creature along the Columbia River Gorge quakes.

The catwalk shakes under the confident steps of Peter Abbott. The SWAT gear he wears looks more like a costume now, his bearing that of a civilian, with a civilian's priorities of personal gain and comfort, not justice; no longer one of us. Tall and balding, glasses blank as coins, he fairly bounces with authority.

"Give me the data."

"What are you talking about?"

"Toby Himes reported that he saw Dick Stone hand it to you."

"Good old Toby."

"Don't fuck with me."

"What happened at the farm?"

"It's gone," says Abbott impatiently. "Everything burned to the ground."

"The barn and the orchard?"

"Orders were to destroy everything."

"They were your orders. You assassinated an unarmed woman."

"She was not the primary target. But she was a terrorist."

"And you burned the trees. Why did you burn the trees?"

"Calm down. You are not in control of yourself."

"Did you kill the little horse, too? Did you mow him down, just for the hell of it?"

"Give me the data, and let's go inside."

"I don't know what you're talking about."

"I'm talking about the device that Stone gave you."

"Why? What did Dick Stone have that brings you here, way out on a limb? We know he had an inside source. So? Ah well, you're right. You never could tell what was real with him anyway. But what about you, sir? Which side are you on? Was Toby Himes relaying information on criminal activity in the Northwest . . . or was he your lackey to get to Stone?"

"Toby Himes is a loyal patriot," Abbott replies swiftly. "And you are done, Agent Grey. Your picture was posted on the Internet by Stone's accomplice." He describes Rooney Berwick's personal Big One. The suicide. The photo ID of Darcy DeGuzman. "Your identity has been exposed. Your career as an agent is over. Let's go out like a hero."

We are standing alone on the narrow walkway that spans the fish ladders. Water rushes in shallow channels under our feet. What are my options? The rampant power of the river is far beyond the concrete decks and barbed-wire gates.

"If I give you the data, what are you going to do for me?"

Abbott rubs his nose disdainfully.

"You've been down in the muck too long. This is not a negotiation."

"Everything is negotiable."

"You can walk off this ramp whole."

"No censure? You won't make me look bad?"

He shifts on his feet. What a girlie question. "No censure."

"All right, fine."

I show him the device in my hand. "Here's the data," I say, and rocket the thing in a fine sparkling arc, high over the fences and deep into the wild green-white current of the river, where it is sucked into the giant turbines.

Abbott laughs and a stray wisp of setting sun lights his face.

"You look relieved," I say.

"Oh, I am. And you are under arrest."

Inside the control room of the dam, long, curving banks of computers trigger the gates of the navigation locks and release the spillways. You can sense the rumble and hear the huge weight of water as it spumes out of the downstream side. The techs have been evacuated except for one nervous shirtsleeved supervisor behind the main desk. Two baby sheriff's detectives allegedly guarding the rogue FBI agent are perched at workstations, nosing through other people's personal stuff. The cold air smacks of the bloody ice of a fish market. We've been contained here for hours.

SAC Robert Galloway nearly blows the door off its hinges as he bursts inside, ordering everyone else out.

"What the hell are you thinking?"

I cradle my left arm in its sling. "I could ask the same of you."

"You flat-out defy the deputy director."

"He set me up and you know it."

Galloway staggers slightly backward, as if stunned by the accusation. "You better slow down."

"Abbott had me pegged from the beginning. He had read my file before that first meeting in L.A. He knew I had been diagnosed with PTSD, but he overrode the doctor's recommendation, because he wanted me on this case."

Agitated, my boss sits on the edge of a rolling chair. "You tend to think a lot of yourself, Ana, but many agents could have done this job."

"I happened to suit his needs. Abbott had a personal interest in reining in Dick Stone, going back to when his family was involved in building the powerhouse for the Bonneville Dam. The one we're sitting in right now. Remember that photo of Megan wrapped in the American flag? This is the project she tried to kill. Abbott put an end to that by adding her to the 'dirty hippies' list. Dick Stone imploded and they went underground."

"And what about you?"

"I'm getting to me. Stone took thirty years to implement the Big One, his ultimate revenge on Peter Abbott and the federal government that abandoned him. If anything makes him a terrorist, that's it: the patient planning, the fixed beliefs. He used his influence with the vulnerable Rooney Berwick to uncover illegal deals with the Abbott family. Stone always said that symbols are important, and destroying the dam was a good one. What is it except a massive monument, literally, to power?"

Galloway has been sitting forward, hands on the armrest. His body has become still, but his worried eyes take everything in.

"And you?"

"Me? Well, I was the perfect dunce for Peter Abbott. Good enough to get Stone, and then totally disposable. He wasn't worried about family dirt coming out, because that could be manipulated. You could blame it on the source. The undercover was unstable. Disturbed. Am I sounding a lot like Dick Stone? And if the deputy director was very lucky, I might go over the edge and identify with the suspect, and die in a tragic shoot-out."

"That's a stretch, Ana."

"I could easily have been the first one out that door, Robert."

Galloway's expression goes from cautious listening to pissed as hell. "This is terrific."

He gets up so abruptly, the chair scoots backward. The hostile Brooklyn accent hits like a bludgeon.

"We did everything possible not to let this happen. Despite training and supervision, you allow yourself to get in too deep, and let a nutcase, someone out for nothing but sick personal revenge, destroy your career."

"Are you talking about Abbott or Stone?"

"Lady, you are cruising. You defied the deputy director during a tactical operation."

"I made the determination he had something to hide."

"So you toss crucial evidence into a river. In a case of domestic terrorism."

"I didn't want him to have it."

"How stupid can you be?"

"I guess that's obvious."

"This is big-time stupid. I am here to tell you that Peter Abbott is charging you with treason. Destroying evidence in a terrorism investigation is a treasonable act."

Lights blink. Computers tick along, mockingly doing their job. *There is hydropower to output! Fish to manage! But you are trapped inside a concrete bunker ten feet thick and you will never see daylight!*

The future will be this: imprisonment in a stale progression of lawsuits and appeals, maybe even jail time, until my vitality is sapped.

Just go on being Ana Grey.

I notice Galloway has been watching me during this brief meditation, jacket open, fists on hips, totally perplexed.

"I have something to tell you, too," I say. "About Steve Crawford."

"What about Steve?"

"He wasn't who we thought he was. Going in, you couldn't have asked for a more loyal friend, a more good-hearted person, but when nobody was looking, he got hungry."

"Is that so?"

"That's right. The most talented agent to come through L.A., isn't that what you said? The golden son? Steve knew that Stone had a valuable stash and figured to steal it, but the thing blew up in his face. He wasn't killed by an act of terrorism. It was greed."

I watch Galloway's face as the shadow of uncertainty deepens.

"Or, you could say, it was due to the stresses and strains of under-cover work. He was a casualty of war. Like a lot of us." I take a ragged breath. "I'm just as devastated as you are. I loved the guy."

Galloway's hands fall to his sides.

"I choose not to believe it."

"Lucky you."

Donnato escorts me out of the powerhouse and into a black sedan. He maneuvers through the remaining rescue vehicles and news vans and hits the darkening road. The locks on the doors go down.

"Did they really burn down the farm?"

"Yes."

"Did they kill Geronimo?"

"Who is Geronimo?"

"The blind baby foal, goddamn it—"

"I think he's fine."

"You *think*? Don't lie to me."

"I have never lied to you."

"All right."

"Are you okay?"

"I want that horse to go to a good home."

"Don't get teary. Jesus, what's the matter?"

"Promise me. It's the last thing I'll ever ask of you."

"I'll do my best."

"I have the data."

"No you don't. You threw it in the river."

"That was Darcy's cell phone. She didn't need it anymore."

In the dashboard light I see Donnato's face squinching up.

"Don't be telling me this."

I reach inside the sling where I have secreted the PalmPilot from the clumsy searches of baby deputies and the sharp eyes of my SAC.

"Dick Stone gave me his testament."

"What's on there?"

"The manifesto. What he wanted to be printed in the newspapers. What he said the American people need to remember."

Scrolling past planting schedules and shopping lists, I discover a file called "Career of Evil."

"This is it! Memos dated 1972 to 1974, signed by Peter Abbott, authorizing illegal phone taps against 'suspected student radicals.' "

"Keep looking."

The screen is filled with numbers.

"Fish statistics. Great."

And then a map. "A map of Bonneville Dam. Hey, wow. It's a schematic."

Donnato looks over. "Detailed?"

"The building plans for the dam. What Stone must have used to plot the bomb attack. There were several contractors." I'm punching buttons, enlarging the type on the plans. "Hamilton, Meizner, Adams-Vanguard—"

"Adams-Vanguard is one of Abbott senior's shell companies."

"So Peter's father, the congressman, was lining his pockets with a multimillion-dollar contract."

"I'll bet if we had another twenty-four hours, we could come up with a link between the builders of the powerhouse project and contributions to young Peter Abbott's political career," adds Donnato. "But we don't have twenty-four hours."

I hold it out to him. "You do."

"It's collateral," Donnato says. "It was Stone's collateral; now it's yours."

"He wanted to cash it in. He wanted Abbott to roll on the floor like a pill bug."

I press the device into Donnato's hand and find that mine is trembling.

"Get him," I whisper.

"Roger that."

I realize that I am becoming incoherent.

"Where is Galloway sending me? Why would he burn me? I'm a hero. Aren't I?"

"Shhh. You're valued. Believe me, at the highest level."

"I don't know what to believe."

"If you knew everything, you wouldn't do the job. These aren't the days of Dick Stone. The tentacles were working—all those people behind the scenes, helping to protect you until the case came together. The supporting elements of the undercover are like your crystal ball—we see your future and help you dodge it."

He kicks it up to eighty on the country road.

"What is my future?"

I watch a big green freeway sign for Portland snap backward into the dark.

"Aren't we going to the county jail?"

Donnato does not reply.

"But I'm in custody."

Donnato's voice is breaking. "You just have to trust me."

We drive in silence through the poignant end of day. The little road is sweet, the way it flows between the silver river and vertical slopes of scree, where multiple waterfalls sport like nymphs. It is the same drive I made with Stone when he began to tell his story of betrayal by his own people; we are simply going in the other direction. Stone wasn't asking for trust or belief. He wasn't asking for anything when he told it. But Donnato's tone is full of pleading.

A rusted shell of a gas station and a neon sign half-buried in leaves that says MOTEL put you in mind of 1940s detective stories, where scheming lovers escape to a motor court out in the boonies with a million bucks in cash—only to discover the final, bitter twist.

There is always a double cross.

How far would the Bureau go?

In the car, my teeth are chattering with cold. We turn down a short road and past a restaurant. The restaurant is closed, but as we swing around, I see it is adjacent to a private airfield. If you sat on the patio, you could watch the planes. They look thin and flimsy, like scraps of paper.

The tower is lighted. A small jet waits on the tarmac, engines running. The door is open and the stairs are down.

"It's best if you leave the country," Donnato says.

I reel out of the car. The air is freezing and my shoulder is stiff. The sky has dropped to deep and final lavender.

"It's waiting for you," he says. "Go on."

"Go on? To where?"

"I have no need to know."

"You have no need? You can't just dump me here."

"Ana, this is the hardest thing I've ever had to do."

"What's *hard*? Knowing nothing? Leaving everything? The Bureau," I whisper, almost ashamed. "The Bureau is my family."

He grips my arms. "I wouldn't have been able to bring you here without cooperation on the highest level. From Galloway," he adds, relenting. "Do you understand?"

"Come with me," I say desperately. "You once said you loved me."

"I love you completely."

"I love you, too." I hold on to him. "I've never been so scared in my life."

"You'll be flying into a private airport where there will be no customs. No questions asked."

"How is that possible?"

"Sara Campbell's parents sent a private plane to pick her up. The mercenary, Sterling McCord, is bound to deliver her back into their hands. He was kind enough to say he would help get you out of the country."

I pull away and look into his eyes.

"Mike, he wasn't just being kind."

Donnato says, "I know."

"What are you doing, baby?"

I search his face. The face I've loved and relied on every day of my life in the Bureau.

And then there is no hope for it. We kiss, just once, but so much so that when we stop and I open my eyes, everything—the airfield, the plane, the silhouettes of trees so full of life—looks washed with blue, as if the retina screens in the backs of my eyes have gone out of whack and I can no longer reliably describe the world.

My partner says, "You have to go."

We grip each other until he releases me and walks to the Bu-car and does not look back.

I move numbly toward the plane. Sterling McCord is waiting at the stairway. A uniformed steward hesitates in the lighted door.

"You have a real good friend. He always will be."

I have no answer but the ache in my heart.

"Sara's inside. We better take off before she does. Would you like a hand?" he asks, and offers his.

"Where are we going?"

"You'll know when we get there," he says, and guides me up the metal steps.

I follow, like a blind horse being led out of the flames.

ACKNOWLEDGMENTS

I am grateful to the dedicated professionals in the Los Angeles Field Office of the FBI who shared their expertise with frankness and generosity: Special Agent George Carr, SWAT; Special Agent Kevin G. Miles, bomb technician; Supervisory Special Agent Bruce Stephens, retired; Special Agent in Charge Randy Parsons, retired; and especially Special Agent Larry Wilson, retired, whose experience as an undercover helped inspire this book.

At the FBI Academy in Quantico, I was educated in the rigors of undercover school by Stephen R. Band, Ph.D.; Carl Jensen III, Ph.D.; and Arthur E. Westveer, violent crime specialist. The interviews were facilitated with the much appreciated support of Philip L. Edney, public affairs specialist at FBIHQ.

This book grew out of a research trip to Oregon undertaken with my stalwart husband, Douglas Brayfield, and daughter, Emma, whose care for and knowledge of horses informs every page. Special thanks to Halle Mandel and Rick Sadle for their warm hospitality in Portland; to our guide, Crofton Diack; to Norm Sharpe and Frank Klejmont, formerly of the Portland police department; Captain Donna Henderson; Patrick Barry of the U.S. Army Corps of Engineers; and at the FBI's Portland Division, Public Affairs Specialist Beth Anne Steele.

I owe an enormous debt to the accommodating folks at the Bureau of Land Management, Burns District, who allowed us to observe the mustangs in the wild, a life-changing experience. Thomas H. Dyer, Mark L. Armstrong, Ramona Bishop, and Tom Seley all work tirelessly on behalf of the horses.

Thank you to hazelnut farmers Harry and Carol Logerstad; horse trainer Richard Goff; music expert Piero Scaruffi; Barry Fisher, Crime Laboratory Director, Los Angeles County Sheriff's department; pathologist Lisa Sheinin, M.D.; author and FBI historian Richard Gid Powers; equine veterinarian David Cox, DVM; and Michael Grunberg of Sandline International, who were all kind enough to answer dozens of inquiries.

An author is sustained through three years of writing not only by the compassion of strangers, but by the good humor of family and friends, publishers and agents. I am thankful to my son, Benjamin, for his spirited counsel; my parents and my brother, Ronald, for their faith; to Michelle Abrams, Susan Baskin, Carrie Frazier, Lauren Grant, Joy Horowitz, Evan Levinson, Janice Lieberman, Linda Orkin, and Julie Waxman for being such good pals; Angela Rinaldi for wisdom in all things; to everyone in the first-rate Knopf organization, headed by the incomparable Sonny Mehta; and to the terrific assistant editor, Diana Coglianese. On the agent side, thank you once again to the beloved Molly Friedrich; Bruce Vinokour and the team at CAA; and the two outstanding individuals to whom this book is dedicated: FBI Special Supervisory Agent Pam Graham, for her integrity and friendship, and David Freeman, who gave the greatest gift one writer can give another, which is to find the soul of a troubled manuscript and light the way home.